THE ONLY WAY

Catching her fingers, Deke brought them to his mouth, kissed them gently, sadly, then released her. "Go home, Anna."

"Go home . . . because you don't want me here? Or because I might get in the way if you decide to pick up that gun and do something insanely stupid?"

His mouth quirked at one corner, an odd little half smile that didn't touch his eyes. "Baby, you don't know anything about me, and if your luck holds, you'll never learn."

On the crime beat, she'd been persistent in the extreme, and she was no less so now. It was the only way to get answers.

Give up, give in, back down . . . get nothing.

BOOK YOUR PLACE ON OUR WEBSITE AND MAKE THE READING CONNECTION!

We've created a customized website just for our very special readers, where you can get the inside scoop on everything that's going on with Zebra, Pinnacle and Kensington books.

When you come online, you'll have the exciting opportunity to:

- View covers of upcoming books
- Read sample chapters
- Learn about our future publishing schedule (listed by publication month *and author*)
- Find out when your favorite authors will be visiting a city near you
- Search for and order backlist books from our online catalog
- Check out author bios and background information
- Send e-mail to your favorite authors
- Meet the Kensington staff online
- Join us in weekly chats with authors, readers and other guests
- Get writing guidelines
- AND MUCH MORE!

Visit our website at
http://www.kensingtonbooks.com

S.K. McCLAFFERTY

NOTHING TO LOSE

ZEBRA BOOKS
Kensington Publishing Corp.
www.kensingtonbooks.com

ZEBRA BOOKS are published by

Kensington Publishing Corp.
850 Third Avenue
New York, NY 10022

All Kensington titles, imprints, and distributed lines are available at special quantity discounts for bulk purchases for sales promotion, premiums, fund-raising, educational, or institutional use.

Special book excerpts or customized printings can also be created to fit specific needs. For details, write or phone the office of the Kensington Special Sales Manager: Attn. Special Sales Department. Kensington Publishing Corp., 850 Third Avenue, New York, NY 10022. Phone: 1-800-221-2647.

Zebra and the Z logo Reg. U.S. Pat. & TM Off.

First Printing: August 2006
10 9 8 7 6 5 4 3 2 1

Printed in the United States of America

For Rochelle.
Welcome to the clan.

Chapter One

Nazareth, New Mexico

It was after midnight, and a chilly mist hovered a few feet above the ground where Lucas Swift-Water lay, the kind of night when sight was limited to a few scant yards and sound didn't carry. Moonless and black. The Ridge-Walker preferred nights like this one, when no one ventured out of doors and there was no one to see.

No one but a crazy old man with a rifle.

Bad things had started happening during the last dark moon, when the Ridge-Walker first appeared. Obee, his sheepdog, had gone missing three weeks ago, shortly before the spring lambs started disappearing. Lucas had found the faithful old dog days later, apparently killed by coyotes. The body had been too far gone to tell.

Next, an owl had taken his favorite rooster, landing on the porch rail for a few seconds with its prey still clutched in its talons. Lucas, standing in the cabin's open doorway, had looked in the owl's round eyes and seen death and destruction. The owl, he knew, had come to warn him.

Lucas listened. Something really bad was coming. Something evil. And he had to be ready.

The very next evening, and every evening since, he'd waited for dark to descend, then he took up his rifle and he watched and he waited. Eventually, his patience had been rewarded. Stealthily, on random nights, when the cloud cover or the absence of the moon made the chance of detection slim, the shadowy form would appear. It moved slowly, carefully, with only a pinpoint beam to light the way, keeping close to the ridge summit, near the heavy stand of ponderosa pine, uncaring, or unaware that it was watched from below.

Could be the Ridge-Walker was aware but felt he was no threat, Lucas thought. Or maybe the shadowed figure was a *chindi,* a spirit bent on revenge, and gave him no thought at all beyond the mischief it perpetrated. A *chindi* emerged from the dying's fingertips as the final breath left the body and could take on the form of many things—animal, bird, man. It was reason enough to resist calling the authorities.

Who would believe him?

Who would listen if he insisted that an owl had come to warn him that evil stalked the ridge high above his cabin? Sheriff Harlan Rudy? Lucas's breath hissed through his teeth at the thought. Lucas and Rudy went way back, and their dealings hadn't always been cordial.

If Lucas mentioned his suspicion that the Ridge-Walker was actually a ghost, no one would take him seriously. Not Harlan, certainly—not even Deke, Lucas's nephew.

Deke was a good man, but he was troubled, and he'd lived in the white man's world too long. A blind man could have seen that. He'd come home from Arizona a few months before, and it didn't take Lucas long to figure out that he didn't know much about the man his nephew had become. Their contact had been limited to a few brief visits since Deke left town fresh out of high school. Lucas had gone to see him a time or two, to visit. He'd been in the audience the day he'd graduated from college, and again from the police academy. He'd sent a gift when informed about his marriage to Melissa Mayview, a trauma nurse at a Tucson hospital. Melissa seemed like a real nice girl, but the marriage didn't last five years. Lucas didn't know what happened, and when Deke came home, he didn't ask. He respected that Deke was a man now and he would tell him what he needed to know when he felt he needed to know it. At the time, it was enough that he was back in Nazareth in one piece.

Being a cop was a dangerous job.

Lucas remembered offering his hand when his nephew pulled in the drive and got out of his car. Deke took it, hesitating for a second before stepping close and clapping an arm around Lucas's shoulders. *"Shi-Da,"* he'd said, using the Navajo term for uncle.

"Welcome home, nephew. It's good to have you back." He stood back, taking in the changes—the long hair, the small gold hoop earrings, the pair of elaborate tattoos that encircled both arms at the biceps and trailed down one arm. "You never mentioned what it is you do at the TPD, but I'm guessin' you aren't a beat cop."

"A long way from it," he'd said, and that haunted look had come into his dark eyes. The same look that had come over Deke's mother, Maddy, years ago when she thought nobody could see.

Then, the moment passed. That had been months ago, and Lucas had no more of an idea what had happened with Deke in Tucson than he'd had that first day. He only knew that his nephew had a letter of commendation in a drawer, shoved back and forgotten as if it didn't mean a thing, and the only thing he would say was that his career was over and he didn't want to talk about it. Since then, his mood seemed to plunge. He drank too much, and the look in his dark eyes worried Lucas.

Lucas put the thoughts of his baby sister's eldest child and only son away, watching the Ridge-Walker disappear into the pines. The spirit in human form did not come again that night. Lucas waited out the darkness, and when the first golden streaks appeared above the trees, he took the rifle and walked to the ridge to scout the area. A few footprints, the impression of a heel in the mud—a white man's walk, heel down first—and a few inches from it a long, curved feather. It glistened blue black in the dawn's light, the tail feather from the rooster the owl had taken. As Lucas bent to retrieve it, something slammed into his left shoulder, knocking him to his knees. A half second later, he heard the report of the rifle, echoing off the tall pines. His shoulder felt like it was on fire, the pain running down his arm to his fingertips, but he managed to reach the timberline and stay there until he was certain the shooter had fled.

The farmhouse on Echo Canyon Road was a pale skeleton in the predawn darkness. Local kids had used the windows for pitching practice, and only a few unbroken panes of glass remained. The front door was boarded up with plank, an attempt to keep people out when no one with an ounce of superstition would venture across the threshold. Deke stood gazing up at the second story, the window on the left, and for a second he thought he saw his own face reflected there, years younger, with cheeks that were more round than hollow.

The thought was a pebble dropped down a dark, empty well, and it took an eternity for him to realize that it would never touch solid ground. He was empty—as empty as the house looming up before him, abandoned for twelve long years.

Pushing the comparisons aside, he went slowly up the walk. Thready grass spikes jutted through the cracks in the sidewalk. Several of the plank steps had given way to rot. The door had a hasp and lock, so he stepped in through one of the broken windows.

Cobwebs glistened white in the doorways. Dust lay thick on everything, and the smell of must and neglect was thick in his nostrils. Somewhere in the back of his mind, childish laughter echoed, a ghostly overlay, past on present. The delighted squeal of a little girl playing with her puppy, hurried footsteps on the stairs. From the direction of the kitchen, he could have sworn he heard the faint metallic rattle of pots and pans, the trickle of running water, all of it as haunting as it was bittersweet. His throat ached, but his eyes remained dry as the high desert air.

The stairwell led upward into blackness. He chose the hallway beside, his footfalls creaking until he stopped in the kitchen. Slipping the Colt Python .357 magnum from the waistband of his jeans, he laid it on the same wooden table he'd eaten breakfast at as a kid. Taking the pint of whiskey from his shirt pocket, he ran a finger over the D he'd managed to carve into the table's top before his adopted father, Matthew, had caught him and cuffed him hard. With a soft snort, Deke broke the seal and tipped the bottle up for a long swallow, other, darker fragments creeping in.

The waiting silence of the house when he entered that night. The sickening realization that something terrible had happened . . . the bodies on the floor of the kitchen and the taint of blood in the air. Then, Harlan Rudy's voice, "I know how hard this must be, but son, you've got to level with me. Did you have anything to do with this?" Harlan had been Matthew's deputy, his right-hand man, and Deke had hated him even then. He'd hated everything and everyone connected with Matthew Call, except for Maddy, his mother, and his little sister, who adored her daddy.

At the time, Deke had shaken off Harlan's questions, breaking away and setting out on his own to look for his mother before Harlan could stop him. Her survival was a long shot, and he'd known it even then. She never would have left Matthew and their daughter of her own accord, especially if she'd thought they were in trouble. Matthew Call had been a first-class prick, but he was her husband and she loved him, and to Maddy, love had been everything.

Feverishly, he'd bounded up the stairs. His heart raced now with the emotional impact of the memory. The second floor, the attic, even the dark hole that was the basement. He'd found nothing. Aside from the bodies of Matthew and his half sister, the house had been empty. Not a single trace of Maddy had ever been found, not a drop of blood that could be attributed to her—she had simply . . . vanished.

Deke took a long swallow from the bottle, then drank again, a vain attempt to drown the swirl of dark emotion threatening to flood his chest cavity. He couldn't remember the last time he'd eaten. The liquor should have hit him hard on an empty stomach, but he couldn't seem to feel it. He didn't feel anything but a vast, throbbing numbness where his vitals should have been.

The long-ago tragedy receded into the back of his mind, replaced by a scene that was a lot more recent. . . .

He saw himself standing in the doorway of the small house he'd bought shortly after he and Melissa married. It had been the first time he'd been home in almost two months, and he only had a few hours to make up for all the time he spent away from her. He sure as hell didn't want to fight. A dozen red roses lay scattered on the pale carpet near his feet, and his wife of almost five years was tearing his clothing from the closets and drawers, throwing everything into a suitcase. "Wait, wait, wait. Missy, wait! Baby, please, you've got to talk to me," he heard himself say. "Just tell me what's wrong, and I'll make it okay."

She whirled on him, her soft mouth twisted in a snarl. "You want to know what's wrong," she said. "You're what's wrong, Deke. Jesus Christ! Look at you!" Her glance swept him, scathing. The tattoos, the piercings, the ragged denim. "You aren't the man I married. In fact, I don't even recognize you anymore."

"Baby, it's window dressing," he insisted. "That's all. It enables me to do my job. It doesn't mean anything." But he'd known as the words came out of his mouth that he was lying. Melissa knew it too.

"You haven't been home in two months, and I can't take it anymore. I lie awake, picturing you lying in an alley somewhere . . ." She shook her head.

"All I need is a little more time. I can't quit now. I'm too damn close to taking the whole thing down—" He'd caught her by the shoulders, brought her body close to his, and as he did she hit him with everything she had, a sharp blow that he knew he deserved. It turned his head aside, and the handprint she left on his cheek burned like fire. "Go back to the streets, Deke! I'm sure your little whore's waiting for you. . . ."

Melissa's voice faded, one more wreck he'd left behind.

She'd traded up sometime later. Found herself a nice, safe insurance executive who pulled a straight nine-to-five. Ski weekends in Telluride or antiquing in Albuquerque.

Not that Deke blamed her. Melissa had always been smart, and she was so much better off. In a way, he'd been better off too. With no one waiting for him, with no safe, normal life to return to, he'd sunk into his life on the streets, working his way up on the inside of *El Propios Del Diablo,* The Devil's Own, gaining more trust, more responsibility, more information. . . . Reaching out, he traced a finger over the trigger guard of the .357, caressing the cold steel as tenderly as he would have caressed a lover.

But that was over too. The click of a switchblade had brought it all crashing down around him, and when the dust settled, he was barely clinging to life. Too ornery to die, he'd recovered and walked away from everything. Now, he'd finally come full circle.

What had begun here in this house on a warm spring night a dozen years ago could end here this morning and nobody, aside from Lucas, would even give a damn.

His life was a shambles.

What was the point of just existing for one more day? Tan fingers curled around the piece. *Shit, man. What are you waitin' for?* As Deke's grip tightened around the pistol's grip, he saw a blur of movement in his peripheral vision.

Glancing up, half-expecting to see his mother's wraith standing in the doorway, he went still. It wasn't

Maddy, but it was a woman—young, beautiful, and very much alive. Outside, the light was changing, the sky a soft gray instead of black. The dawn filtering in the kitchen window washed over her long, dark hair and golden tan. Her dark eyes were wary and gave nothing away, but Deke could tell from the rapid rise and fall of those gorgeous breasts that she wasn't easy with finding him here. She glanced at the open bottle, the hand still resting possessively on the revolver. Lips that were luscious and softly red parted slightly. "You surprised me. I didn't expect to find anyone here," she said.

"I didn't expect to be interrupted."

"I got that," she said. "A party for one, complete with refreshments. You come out here to pink rats? That's what the locals call it right, Deke? Pink? Pretty word for a bizarre and ugly pastime."

Deke laughed, a low ripple of sound that surprised him. He didn't think he'd had it left in him. "Rats. Now that's funny." He cocked his head, giving her a sidelong glance. "Just who the hell are you, and how do you know my name?"

"There isn't a single person in this county who doesn't know Deke Call on sight," she said, her mouth curving. "Whether you know it or not, you're more than a little famous. Big-city cop who quits midcareer for no apparent reason. Everybody loves a mystery. Including me."

There were secrets behind that smile. Intrigued, Deke's focus changed, and he forgot his reason for coming out here. It felt surprisingly good to let her air of sensuality wash over him, warm, inviting. For just a second, he allowed himself to imagine that a heat had kindled in those heavily lashed, dark eyes. "That answers half my question. You got a name, pretty lady? Or should I just call you Baby?"

"It's Anna." She came slowly into the room, careful where she stepped, watching him all the while. A full flash of even, white teeth, Salma Hayek in a tight white tank top and low-rise jeans. She took the whiskey from his hand and brought the bottle to her lips, her gaze locked with his. A small sip and she handed it back. "Top shelf. You have expensive taste."

He raised a hand and chafed its knuckles against a two-day growth. "A man only lives once, Anna. I've seen you before?"

A lift of a fine arched brow. "I help out at Coyote Moon. Carlotta's a friend of my father's."

"I know Carlotta, all right," Deke said softly. "She's been a fixture in Nazareth since I was a kid. So, what are you doin' out here? This place has been posted for years. No trespassin'. There's a sign on the tree out front."

"That didn't stop *you,* now did it?"

It was Deke's turn to smile. "You've got a point there. But it's a whole lot more dangerous for a pretty lady to be wanderin' around an old wreck like this than it is for a man like me. You aren't even within screamin' distance of the nearest house."

"Who says I'm alone?" she said, her voice seductive.

As if on cue there was a scrape of a boot outside and a curse as the screen door was pushed wider. A man in jeans, a denim jacket, and Western hat stopped in the doorway to the kitchen, his eyes narrowing as he caught sight of Deke and Anna standing inches from one another.

Back in the day, Matthew Call had been so popular with county residents that Harlan's only chance of fur-

thering his ambitions and making the natural step up to
sheriff lay in leaving the county and going elsewhere.
Then the unthinkable happened, and Harlan's fortunes
took a sharp U-turn. Matthew was murdered, and Harlan became acting sheriff. The following November, he
ran uncontested, and he'd held the office ever since.

Harlan was as hard as he was weathered, and his
cold blue eyes never seemed to lose their look of quiet
suspicion. "Deacon Call. What on earth you doin' out
here?"

"Pinkin' rats," Deke replied. "Big ones. How 'bout
you?"

He didn't care for Deke's tone, that much was clear.
"Givin' you notice," he said, moving to where Anna
stood. "This place was sold at the sheriff's sale last
week. Barely brought in enough to cover the back taxes
owed to the county. The couple who bought it'll be
takin' it over tomorrow. They got a work crew comin' to
start renovations. Miss Sandoval wanted to see it before
they start changin' things. She's researching the town,
and this place in particular. As a matter of fact, she's
gonna write a book about the murders."

Deke didn't respond to the piece of news about the
house. It had changed hands several times over the
years, but nobody seemed to stay more than a year or
two and until now they hadn't made many changes. The
place looked pretty much the same as it had that night.
"You could pick a safer subject." The murders stirred
passions on both sides—the folks who thought Juan
Martinez was guilty and those who felt he was rail-
roaded. "Some of the people around here haven't gotten
past it. Could be you're askin' for trouble."

"Some of the people around here," Anna asked, "or
you?"

Deke shrugged, unwilling to answer. "Don't say I didn't warn you."

She turned to the sheriff without replying. "I really should be getting back. I promised Carlotta I'd help her open—she'll be wondering where I've gotten to." She met Deke's gaze one last time, and he knew that little was lost on the lady. "Good luck with those rats, Mr. Call."

"Son," Harlan said, "whatever your business is out here, I suggest you conclude it and go on home." Then the sheriff took her arm and guided her to the front entrance, brushing the cobwebs aside to let her pass.

Deke picked up his revolver and shoved it into the waistband of his jeans at the small of his back. The darkness had lifted temporarily. Fishing his harmonica out of his front pocket, he leaned against the sink and began to play.

Twenty minutes later, Anna closed the Jeep truck's passenger door and made her way up the staircase to the apartment she rented from Carlotta. The help at Coyote Moon would begin preparations for the breakfast crowd in half an hour, but that was time enough for Anna. She locked the door behind her and walked to the windows overlooking the street. The sun was partially visible above the distant mountain range, a ruby sphere that turned the roofs of houses and businesses a rosy pink. Harlan Rudy was *the* man around here, and he hadn't gotten where he was by being stupid or gullible. She'd been very aware that she was playing with fire where he was concerned, and she hadn't drawn an easy breath until she entered the apartment. Yet she'd succeeded in getting what she wanted.

So far so good. He'd bought the story that she was planning to write about the Call mass murder, and he'd been more than willing to take her to the crime scene. He'd given her the details with the matter-of-fact precision of a man who'd spent thirty-odd years in law enforcement, and Anna had listened, recognizing when he omitted something because she knew the story from every angle by heart. His behavior had been surprising. Small-town sheriff with bragging rights on the biggest case this county had ever seen—only Harlan Rudy didn't brag.

Anna sighed, strangely dissatisfied despite the morning going just as planned. That dissatisfaction had Deke Call's name written all over it. She hadn't expected to walk into the farmhouse kitchen and find him standing there . . . the heir to the tragedy that had taken place there. She'd seen photos of him, but nothing more recent than the few taken after the murders and published in the papers. He'd been handsome then, but young at seventeen. At nearly thirty, he barely resembled the angry young man who'd lost his entire family to an insane act. Hard-muscled and brooding, he had all the earmarks of an outlaw biker—even though she knew better—and he was as sexy as he was intimidating.

The chambray shirt he'd been wearing had the sleeves torn from it, and the ink on his arms was one of the first things she'd noticed. Double strands of barbed wire circled his left arm just above the biceps; eagle feathers and bright blue beads hung from inked leather thongs dangling down his arm. In the space between the barbed wire was the word *Chaca* in an Old-English-style lettering. *Indian warrior.* On his right arm, a climbing vine wound around the flesh from shoulder to wrist. Lush and thorn ridden, three scarlet roses bloomed among the thorns. On each rose, a name had been etched in stark black ink. Maddy, Delia, and Angel. The thorns near the blooms dug into the skin, and a single drop of blood dripped from each prick. *Maddy, his mother. His sister, Delia.*

And for one tantalizing second she'd wondered, who was Angel?

He hadn't expected anyone to intrude upon what must have been an intensely private moment, and she'd gotten the impression that he'd resented her presence. He'd been on the brink of doing something drastic and ugly, something that no one was meant to witness. During the drive back to town, she'd struggled with doubt. It was almost too big a coincidence, finding him there, and she wondered if it was fate's way of warning her to abandon her plans, to let it go.

The look in his dark eyes as he caressed the gun on the table—as if it were the only way out. He was about as low as a man could get, and there was a chance that what she was about to do would push him over the edge. Strangely, as she'd walked from the house, the heartfelt strains of a harmonica echoed through rooms clogged with dust and crowded with memories. Anna recognized the song, and Neil Young's "Heart of Gold" had never sounded so poignant, so incredibly sad.

An hour later, she was still thinking about him, and she wasn't happy about that. Getting sucked into Deke Call's world was not on her agenda. But he was going to haunt her. She could feel it.

Standing in the window above the street, fingering the small, gold, heart-shaped locket she always wore, she wondered how she would live with herself if the news came that he had gone through with it.

Then she caught sight of a familiar figure, leaning

against a porch post across the street. His dark head was bent, his hands cupped around the cigarette he was lighting. He shook out the match and dropped it on the pavement, raising his head to face the morning light. Deke Call, looking rough and unshaven, but nonetheless very much alive.

Chapter Two

Deke got the news about Lucas thirdhand, from Kathy, the pretty little waitress at Café Matamoros. She plopped down an omelet loaded with green chiles and cheese and refilled his coffee cup. Kathy was a better source of information than the *Nazareth Times,* the privately owned rag that disguised itself as a legitimate newspaper.

"Mornin', good-lookin'."

Deke looped an arm around her waist—at least as far as he could reach. He went one-eighty-five without his boots on, and Kathy outweighed him by a good sixty pounds. "I think that's supposed to be my line. Listen, darlin' . . . when you gonna dump Benny and move in with me?"

"When pigs fly, honey," she said, plopping down a handful of prepackaged creamers beside his cup. "Even with a bum ticker, poor old Benny's a better risk than you. When you gonna clean up your act, Deke? Find some nice girl? Settle down and get you a few dark-eyed ankle-biters?"

"Been down that road, Kath. Damned if it ain't a dead-end."

"Not always," Kathy said. She shot a warm glance at the trucker holding down one of the stools at the lunch counter. He was fifty-plus and had a paunch impressive enough to all but hide his big silver belt buckle, a thinning crew cut, ruddy complexion—and she looked at him like he was Tom Cruise. Deke was relieved when she changed the subject. "So how's Lucas?"

"On'ry as ever." Deke took a sip of his coffee, then cut into the omelet. The heat from that first bite cleared out the residue remaining from last night's bender. Despite his pounding head, he began to feel human again. "His rheumatism was botherin' him last time I was out that way, but he wouldn't go to the clinic. He's makin' some kind of homemade shit out of cayenne and Vaseline."

Kathy shrugged off the notion of the old man's stubbornness. "Maybe Doc'll give him somethin' for it while he's over there this mornin'."

"Lucas at the clinic?" Deke snorted. "What? Somebody carry 'im in?"

Kathy's expression cleared. "Oh my God. You really don' know. Somebody put a bullet in him early this morning. He drove in here covered in blood 'bout an hour ago."

Deke didn't wait to hear more. He threw down a bill and left his breakfast barely touched and cooling on the table.

Sarah Webster's clinic was on the corner of Pony Street and Waco Avenue, but some genius with a can of spray paint and too much time on his hands had altered the spelling to read "Wacko Avenue." The building was an old storefront, converted by the doctor herself shortly after she came to town six months ago. Like so many of the new arrivals, she'd come from somewhere else, and she'd been so beguiled by the beauty of the high country that she decided to stay.

Tilly Radic glanced up from her computer screen when he walked in. Tilly had been the fat girl in high school who couldn't get a date. She was twenty-nine, and as far as Deke knew, that much hadn't changed. She lived at home with her mother and her three stray cats, which probably accounted for the excess of attitude. "Take a seat in triage, and the nurse will see you in a few minutes," she said, pretending she didn't recognize him.

Deke ignored her, heading for the bowels of the building and the curtained exam rooms. "Excuse me, Deke Call. Just where do you think you're going?"

"To see Lucas."

Sarah Webster was exiting one of the alcoves when she caught sight of Deke. "It's okay, Tilly. I'll handle it."

A last frowning glance in his direction and the receptionist returned to her desk. The physician turned back to Deke.

"How is he?" Deke asked.

"Doing okay, considering he's got a gunshot wound to the left shoulder. Looks like a .22 slug to me, but the sheriff will determine that for sure when I turn it over to him. He's had some bleeding, but he should be fine in a day or two. I extracted the bullet and cleaned the wound, and I'll give him some antibiotics, just in case."

"Kathy said he drove himself in?"

Sarah shook her head. "Honestly. I don't think I have ever met anyone more stubborn than your uncle. He took a seat in the waiting room like it was no more than a hangnail. He's tough, I'll give him that." She closed the chart she was holding, tucking it under her arm. "Curtain two. You can go in. I just have to write his orders, give him a couple of scripts, and he can go, but no strenuous activities for a while, and no driving until I see him again next week."

"Thanks, Doc."

"Don't mention it," she said. "Just do me a favor and try to keep him out of trouble."

Lucas was sitting on the exam table when Deke walked in. "Mornin'," he said simply. "You ain't lookin' so good."

"Thanks," Deke replied, not about to give Lucas the details. Lucas had enough to worry about without the added concern of a nephew who'd hit bottom so fucking hard he'd bounced. "It was a rough night, and findin' out secondhand that you'd been shot didn't make for a great morning, either. You mind tellin' me what happened out there?"

Lucas shrugged, and a pinprick of bright crimson appeared on the white bandage covering the wound. He winced. "Oops. Gotta remember not to do that."

"That might be a good idea," Deke agreed, pinning Lucas with a look that clearly said he wanted information.

"Somebody turkey huntin', I guess," Lucas said. "Up on the ridge above my place. Must've been an accident." Though something in his dark eyes said otherwise.

"Doc Webster said it was a small-caliber rifle. If they were huntin' turkey, don't you think they'd use a shotgun?"

"Who knows? People do crazy things. Anyway, just because they're in the pines lookin' for birds don't mean they know what they're doin'. Any fool can buy a license. I was just in the wrong place at the right time, that's all."

"Is that the line you gave Sarah for the report she's sendin' to Harlan's office?"

"It's the only one I got." Lucas's dark face remained closed, his expression impassive. Only his eyes gave his wariness away, and Deke wondered what he was hiding and why. "I saw the nurse scribblin' something, but if you want details, you'd better go to the source. My readin' glasses are in my truck, so there's no tellin' what was written down." He reached for his shirt, but it was torn and bloody, so he left it for the nurse to dispose of. He got down off the exam bed, retrieving his jacket, moving carefully. "Gotta get home. See you 'round, nephew."

"Hold up," Deke said, falling into place beside him. "Doc says you ain't allowed to drive. Besides, I wanna go up on that ridge and have a look around."

"You can look," Lucas said, "but you won't find nothin'."

Lucas laid the bait and Deke bit. "Why's that?"

"*Chindi* don't leave evidence unless they want to."

Deke threw him a skeptical glance, but he could tell he was serious. "*Chindi?* You think you were shot by a malevolent spirit?"

"I don't just think," Lucas said, "I know. Bad things have been happenin', and they coincide with the Ridge-Walker's appearance. He haunts the ridge above my place on random nights, a shadow figure."

"Ridge-Walker," Deke said. "You tell the doc that you hit your head when you fell?"

"Have some respect," Lucas said. "Just 'cause you don't believe it don't mean it ain't real." He inclined his head in Deke's direction. "Some folks been livin' in the white-eyes world too long. Those feathers on your arm have deep spiritual meaning. Could be you need to think about that."

They stopped by the desk on the way out, and Lucas got the paperwork Sarah had prepared for him. Instructions for caring for the wound, when to make an appointment, and symptoms that would require immediate attention. Lucas chucked them into the glove box as soon as he got in the truck. Deke just shook his head. Arguing was a waste of time and effort, and he couldn't say he wouldn't have done the same thing in similar circumstances.

Lucas's place sat at one end of a wide valley—Mirror Lake at the other. The ranch consisted of forty-eight acres of pastureland that extended as far as the crest of the pine-covered eastern ridge. Curly-horned Churro sheep dotted the grassland on the right side of the drive and stood in the middle of the rutted, dusty road.

"Somethin's been at that fence again," Lucas said, opening the passenger door of the pickup and stepping out. He started for the toolshed at the side of the house, and Deke whistled sharply to get his attention. Lucas jerked around, a frown on his face. "Now what?"

"Where the hell do you think you're goin'?"

"To the toolshed. You ain't listenin'? Fence needs fixin'," he said. "*Dine be iina,* nephew. If I lose the sheep I got left, how'm I gonna live?"

Sheep is Life . . . it was tightly tied into Navajo tradition . . . and Lucas's way was a curious mixture of past and present, innovation and tradition. "I'll see to it," Deke said. "You wanna do somethin', then make some coffee. I sure as hell could use some."

He found a shovel and bar in the shed at the side of the house and got to work.

Lucas brought the coffee. He handed Deke a cup and

took a sip. "Pretty fair coffee, if I do say so myself," Lucas said with a sigh.

"*Shi-Da,*" Deke said. "Why don't you level with me about what's goin' on out here? I count fifteen lambs in the night pen, and I know you had double that two weeks ago. Somebody stealin' your stock?"

Lucas closed down, clammed up. "Among other things. Like I said—"

"*Chindi.* Yeah, I got that."

"Think what you want. Things ain't been right since that owl took my rooster. Sure was a big mother. Sat right on that porch rail with the rooster in his claws and looked at me. After that the Ridge-Walker came. Walks that ridge, deep in the night. I was out last night, waitin' for him, watchin' with my rifle scope. Thought maybe I could get a good look at him. When daylight came, I went up there to look for sign. Here's what I found." He reached into the pocket of his jean jacket and produced a leather pouch, which he held out.

Deke took the pouch and opened the drawstring, dumping the contents into his palm. "A feather?"

"Not just any feather," Lucas replied. "A rooster's tail feather. But not any rooster. My rooster. The one the owl killed."

Deke knew where this was leading, but he waited him out anyway.

"The Ridge-Walker's a *chindi,* an earthbound spirit," the older man reminded him. "They can assume the form of a man or animal. An owl, even. When I was up there, finding the feather was when it happened. Bang—just like that."

Lucas finished his coffee, dumping the dregs on the ground. "And that's what I know. You gonna stay to dinner? Beef stew and corn dodgers . . . and if you're really lucky and I feel up to it, I might whip up some peach cobbler."

Deke cut him a glance. "I thought you were supposed to be takin' it easy."

A smile played around the corners of Lucas's mouth. "Dinty Moore and Sara Lee. The corn dodgers are left-over from last night. We can nuke 'em. Makes 'em good as fresh baked, almost."

Deke snorted. "Well, Jesus. When you put it that way, how can I resist?"

Lucas went into the house. By the time Deke finished the fence, it was late afternoon. He put the sheep back in and, with the spring breeze cooling the sweat on his face and neck, took a walk across the valley and onto the ridge. Careful where he stepped, he walked the tree-line, easily picking up the narrow strip of grass beaten down at the roots. A path, made by Lucas's Ridge-Walker. A single bootprint was clearly visible on the soft loam where the path veered off into the trees. He searched for the better part of an hour, but there was no trace of the discarded brass from the spent shell of a .22-caliber rifle. The shooter must have retrieved it to keep from leaving evidence behind . . . and the only thing Deke was 100 percent certain of was that the shooting was no accident.

The weather had been clear and fine for nearly a week. With a slight breeze going and the sun a bright yellow-white in the afternoon sky, Wheeler Dobbs sur-veyed the rear view of his little piece of heaven from the comfort of a mesh hammock, strung in the western corner of the pergola outside the back door of his travel trailer. He'd finished his latest masterpiece the night before, and tourist traffic was moving through his slightly out-of-the-way gallery at a trickle. If sales didn't pick up soon, he was going to have to think about getting a real job. The thought pained him. He was passionate about his art, but passion didn't always pay the bills.

The Repo Man had paid him a visit at four-thirty sharp that morning, hooked up to his new Silverado king cab, and rattled off down the drive, and all he could do was to run to the door in his jockey shorts and throw the prick a one-fingered salute. If he didn't come up with a serious infusion of cash soon, he could lose this place, and his usual resources seemed to be drying up.

A thin cloud of dust rose above the place where the lane met the blacktop road, and thoughts of his missing truck were obliterated before the possibility of a sale. Wheeler rolled out of the hammock as the old black van with a logo of a coyote howling at a full white moon painted on the side parked out front. It wasn't exactly an SUV full of rich tourists, but it was the next best thing.

Anna was tall and leggy, with a killer booty and a smile to make the Mona Lisa envious. For just a second, he allowed himself a half-blown, totally implausible fantasy. Then it was back to reality. Back to business. Anna was inaccessible, totally uninterested, tuned into something other than a less-than-successful artist and small-time entrepreneur with a shitload of baggage and a rugged Kirk Douglas jaw.

Somehow, knowing he didn't have a snowball's chance didn't stop him from enjoying the view. Curvy, sexy, secretive, she might have been a small-screen starlet on the run or an undercover spy instead of the angel who'd recently appeared on Carlotta McFadden's doorstep.

"Hey, gorgeous. You come all the way out here to see me? I'm flattered."

Anna ignored the bullshit. "Hey yourself. How's business?"

"Shit," he said, his voice laced with disgust. "If it slows down any more, it'll be moving backward. Money's tight, the tension's high, and I could do with a night on the town. What'dya say, sweetness? You want to take me out? Your treat?"

"I like you, Wheeler," Anna said with a smile. "Why ruin it by introducing me to all of your bad habits?"

Wheeler shook his head. "You're too young and way too beautiful to be so jaded."

Anna just smiled. The man was full of it, and she wasn't naive enough to buy into any of it. He was flaky and undependable, a bad risk even if she'd been looking to hook up with someone. She wasn't. Sex was the last entry on her list of priorities. She had too much on her mind for that, and a man in the mix would only complicate an already complicated situation. Not that Wheeler wasn't interesting. Aside from his metal sculptures, he had set up a small but thriving microbrewery in the back of his gallery, specializing in oddball designer beer. "Is the order ready? There's been a big run on your product this week. Carlotta would like to double the usual order. Can you fill something that large?"

"No problem," he said, flashing a killer smile. "As a matter of fact, I have a couple of new flavors to throw in, if you think Carlotta will go for it. Peppermint, and Old World Oregano—a trial basis, as always, and if they do well, we'll settle up next time."

"I'll ask her, and if she's willing, I'll make another run to pick up the inventory."

"Good enough. Back in a bit." He disappeared into

the gallery, then through a second door in back, into the brewery. Anna had already taken the grand tour—the brewery resembled a mad scientist's lab, with beakers, vats, and wall to wall stainless steel—so she opted to check out the gallery instead.

Wheeler's collection was anything but humble, though most of the pieces were too abstract for Anna's taste. The raw power and soaring elegance of a flock of primitive metal birds suspended high overhead was striking, but it was the wooden carving of an old Indian woman grinding corn in a shallow bowl that caught and held her interest.

The sculpture was simple, honest, soulful, and at the same time haunting. Across the room in a glass display case was another piece from the same sculptor. A Navajo man with an upraised hand and a child lying on its belly at his feet. The artist had a definite gift for injecting life into the wood. The man's face was alight with enthusiasm for the story he was telling, the wisdom of past generations evident in the old man's expression, while the boy seemed mesmerized by the story being told. A small cardboard placard, carefully lettered, simply read "Grandfather."

Anna walked to the back of the room, where the final piece stopped her cold. As she stood there, her heart jerking strangely against her ribs, her throat suddenly dry, Wheeler came up beside her.

"Are these new?"

"Lucas brought 'em by last week."

"They're amazing."

Wheeler nodded. "I get that reaction a lot, and they've been moving. The sculptor is a local man, Lucas Swift-Water, a friend of mine and the next great New Mexico talent. He's catching on fast, and I predict big things in his future, once he breaks free of the local market and goes national. Nothing Lucas does has time to collect dust—except for this piece. It's called 'The Drifter,' and nobody seems to want it." He reached out and repositioned the carving in its spotlight to provide a different perspective. The figure was seated on the flat surface of a bunk, his head lowered and shoulders slumped as he stared at Anna in abject misery. "I tried to tell him it might not sell. That he should stick with the feel-good stuff—hell, most of my customers are tourists. They want to take home some crisp air and sunshine, a little piece of New Mexico, not some piece of dark history better off forgotten."

Anna barely heard him. Her immediate shock had softened, replaced by a deep melancholy. She had to have it. No way was she leaving him here. "What's the asking price?"

Wheeler was skeptical. "You're kidding, right?"

She shrugged. "I'm interested, but there's a catch."

"Lemme guess. You want to sleep with me." He grinned a half-assed grin, a good-looking guy in his mid-twenties who held no interest for her at all.

"I want to meet Lucas Swift-Water, and you're gonna make it happen."

"Now?"

"Now." Anna handed him Carlotta's personal check for the microbrew, then followed him out of the gallery. Black Raspberry and Ginger Peachy beer that Wheeler whipped up in his brewery didn't appeal to Anna, but they played amazingly well to the suburbanites who trickled through Coyote Moon during the week, looking for a change of pace from their normal day-to-day of driving kids to soccer practice and Saturdays at the mall.

Wheeler loaded the crates into the back of the van, locked the gallery door, and climbed into the passenger seat. "Take a left at the end of the lane, and watch the ruts."

El Propios Del Diablo had been a Tucson gang since their inception. Minor players as far as bangers went, they dabbled in drugs but never seemed to corner the market on anything but dissension and internal conflict. Several leaders had come and gone in rapid succession—one or two carried out of abandoned buildings or alleyways in body bags, victim of a brother's ruthless ambition. Then one day Joaquin Aguilar drifted in from San Diego, a charismatic young man with a good head for business and an unquenchable thirst for power. Because Joaquin had served a stint in San Quentin, he had more "juice" than his predecessor. Young bangers looked up to him, and within six months after hooking up with the Diablos, he'd risen to a position of leadership.

Joaquin brought West Coast know-how to the desert, and immediately there was a spike in the city's crime statistics. Robbery, break-ins, drugs, and prostitution. He extorted protection money from local businessmen and they paid without objection, because the alternative was having no business at all. To cross Joaquin was to see your dreams go up in flames, and it took only one or two examples of how deadly opposing him could be to get the word out on the street.

Deke remembered the day Joaquin took over the Diablos because it was the day his life had shifted and started its long downward slide. He'd been working Narcotics for a couple of years, and he liked the work.

Most of his time was spent on the street; a constant stream of prostitutes, junkies and dealers paraded through his workday, and he thrived on it. There was something about living on the edge that appealed to his dark side. He got off on the thrill of being out there alone, of being so chameleon-like that the players never suspected there was a cop in their midst.

It sure hadn't hurt that he had the right look. Dark hair and eyes, brown skin and Spanish so fluent he could have passed for a Chicano. And he knew how to keep his wits about him and his mouth shut. He was so successful, so good at infiltrating life on the street, that when Lieutenant Silvio agreed to head up the gang task force it was with the understanding that Detective Deke Call came in on the ground floor with him.

There had been several months of preparation in which he'd undergone intensive training. A gangbanger who'd managed to escape the Diablos with his life had shared a safe house with Deke and given him an in-depth education on gang culture. Finally, he was ready. On a moonless night in mid-November, the task force got an anonymous tip that a rival banger was planning a meeting with one of Joaquin's lieutenants in which he'd take the banger out, revenge for a murder Joaquin had ordered a few weeks before.

A light rain had fallen earlier in the evening, and a thready fog formed watery green halos around the street lamps. Disreputable in a threadbare jean jacket and fingerless gloves, Deke leaned in a doorway, wondering if the meet had been canceled. As he fished his pack of smokes from his breast pocket, headlights turned a corner and edged slowly along the street. It was an older model Coupe de Ville, black as night, gaudy with chrome. The driver killed the lights as he swung the car into the entrance to Edgebrook Park. At the same time, Deke tucked the pack of cigarettes back in his pocket and left the doorway, moving quickly through the shadows, taking a different route than the young men leaving the car.

Timing was everything. He had to get close, yet not so close that his interference smacked of anything but sheer coincidence. He was in the right place at the right time, that was the extent of it. It all came down in a flash. Eduardo Cruz was moving toward the man they called Switch, reaching his hand out. But Switch had murder on his mind, not reconciliation. The knife appeared almost magically, just as Deke emerged from the shadows. He stepped between them, shoving Eduardo back and grappling with Switch for the six-inch weapon. Switch jerked back, the knife blade biting deep into Deke's hand before he blocked it. It went clattering to the pavement. Success came at a definite cost. He was bleeding badly, but he'd gotten his intro into the Diablos. The hitter ran, another of the Diablos attempting to run him down, but Deke stood his ground.

"Shit, man, that motherfucker meant to take me out," Cruz said angrily. He got over it quickly, an ingrained suspicion at Deke's motives for saving his ass settling in. "*Quién el infierno es usted?* Who the hell are you? And what'd you do that for?"

"I need a reason?" Deke said in fluent Spanish, blood dripping from his fingertips. "Don't worry, man. It was an accident. I thought I saw a brother in trouble. It sure as hell won't happen again." He turned away, but he was anything but calm. The adrenaline was surging through his veins and arteries, and his pulse was pounding in his temples. He was wired, and it would be a few minutes before he came back down to earth. The stab wound,

numb until now, was coming to life. It smarted like a
son of a bitch, but he couldn't allow the discomfort to
shatter his focus. The danger was far from over. Cruz
sure didn't trust him—it was never that easy—he could
decide to do anything, from letting him go to finishing
him off with a knife in the ribs. Everything hinged on
whatever action Deke decided to take, and the banger's
reaction to it. "Sure as hell don't need this shit," Deke
muttered. "I'm outta here." He turned his back and
started walking, but he hadn't gone far when Cruz
grabbed his arm.

Deke's reaction was instinctive. He crouched and
spun, a switchblade in his left hand where no knife had
been a second ago.

The banger spread his hands with a nervous laugh.
"Easy, *Chaca*. Easy. I owe you, that's all. You got
nothin' to fear from me. I'm Eduardo Cruz, 'Little Eduardo' to my *cholos*. You got a name, I'd like to know
what it is."

Deke's blade retracted. He relaxed just enough to
allow an unrestricted breath. "Call. The name's Call."

"Call, eh? I think I like Chaca better. *Chaca*—you
know what that means?"

A jerk of his head. He was losing blood and as the
adrenaline receded, he wavered slightly on his feet. His
hand was throbbing, and he was making small talk with
Eduardo Cruz, Joaquin Aguilar's right-hand man, while
he dripped blood all over the sidewalk. He should have
sought some medical attention, but the truth was, he
would have bled out right there on the street before
throwing away what might prove to be a golden opportunity. "Indian warrior."

"You are, right? Indian? You sure got the look."

"I'm Navajo."

"Thought so," he said. "I got a sixth sense about that kinda stuff, you know? So, listen, Chaca, you bleedin' bad. You from around here?"

Deke shook his head and his world spun. "Just hit town last night. No crib yet."

"That right? Guess you'd be in sad shape if I walked away now. Lucky for you I take my debts seriously. Relax, man. Lil' Eduardo, he's gonna take care o' you." He turned and whistled sharply. The young Latino who'd attempted to run down the would-be hitter trotted out of the darkness to where they stood. "Well, don't just stand there, *stupido!* Get the wheels! C'mon, *amigo,* we'll get you patched up."

Little Eduardo drove Deke to an apartment on the West Side. Located on the fourth floor, the place was not only clean, but surprisingly elegant. Deke took in every detail, from the ambient lighting to the massive flat-screen HDTV mounted on the wall above the fireplace in the living room. "Nice digs, man," he heard himself murmuring, and he meant it.

"I do okay," Little Eduardo said. "Bathroom's through there, man. Angel! Angel, get your ass out here and give me a hand!"

A young woman emerged from the darkened bedroom. She was young—nineteen, twenty, maybe. Honey-haired and beautiful, fashionably thin, she had expensive taste in clothing and pinpricks for pupils. As she approached, she staggered slightly. "You shootin' up?" Eduardo said, grabbing her chin, jerking her face up to the light. "What the hell's wrong with you?"

"I'm just havin' a little fun," she said. "I'm bored when you're away."

"How much smack'd you go through last week? How many nickle bags? Shit, why am I askin'? You don't even know." He grabbed her arm, gave her a push through the bathroom door and she stumbled, landing on the tile in a pretty but disheveled heap. "I'm sorry," she said. "I won't do it again."

"Get him cleaned up," Eduardo ordered harshly. "I'll get the kit."

Little Eduardo's bath was bigger than the living room and dining room combined in the small house Deke and Melissa had bought a few years ago. Deke took off his jean jacket and sat down on an elaborately carved bench.

The girl, Angel, knelt beside him with a clean cloth and a bottle of alcohol. "It'll sting, but I have to do it." Her voice was soft and apologetic. Deke watched her while she dampened cotton pads with alcohol and cleaned the blood from his hand. She had fine features, delicate bone structure, creamy skin. It was a good guess that she came from money, and he wondered how the hell she'd ended up here.

She trembled a little as she threw the blood-soaked cotton in the trash and reached for another. Deke took it from her hand. "Leave it. I can manage."

Little Eduardo came with a small leather bag. Inside was an amazing array of first aid equipment. It wasn't quite what he would have found at the emergency room, but close. Eduardo looked at the wound, then pulled it together with a butterfly bandage. He fished a small plastic vial from the bag, handing it to Deke. Deke shook his head. "I don't use, man. I've seen what it can do."

"Relax, Chaca, it's antibiotics. Joaquin, he's got connections."

"Sounds like this Joaquin thinks of everything."

"He's got it all right here," Eduardo said, tapping his

temple. "Smart, educated, and he's got a plan. You play your cards right, you might even get an introduction."

Deke said nothing. Too much interest, and he might arouse suspicion. "Who's the chick? She your old lady?"

"Angel?" Eduardo snorted. "She's just a hooker. Part of Joaquin's stable. She's just here till somethin' better comes along."

Just a hooker. . . .

Deke let the memories shred, torn away like smoke on the wind. It was over and done with and there was nothing he could do to change it. Angel was dead, Joaquin and Eduardo both in prison, and all that was left was to find some way to try to live with the role he'd played in the outcome.

Trying to figure out what was really going on with Lucas took top priority. It had been reason enough for him to stay the night on the old man's sofa. Malevolent spirits and owls who delivered messages, missing sheep and a bullet wound. Deke wasn't sure where he stood on the validity of the traditional beliefs. The cop that remained in him was skeptical of anything he couldn't see . . . yet he respected his uncle, and he knew that he was no fool. If he believed it, then there must be something to it.

Lucas emerged from the house with a steaming mug of black coffee. He handed it to Deke. "You know, I'm kinda glad you stayed over. It's nice havin' someone to talk to." He glanced at Deke and nodded, apparently satisfied with what he saw. "You're lookin' a little better today. Rested. Must be the air out here. Less exhaust."

"A little carbon monoxide never hurt anybody," Deke said.

Lucas shook his head. "You know I been tryin' to get a tenant for that loft above the studio. You might move in, if you've a mind to. Sure beats that place where you're stayin'."

"It's called a hotel."

"Hotel. I guess I forgot. They take down the 'condemned' sign yet?"

"Good one." Deke took a swallow of coffee. "Thanks for the offer, but it's too quiet out here. I'd never be able to sleep."

"Well, it's somethin' to think on," Lucas told him. "Guess I'll go to the workshop and check on things. Breakfast is on the stove, in case you're interested."

"Maybe later," Deke said. He finished his coffee, then went up onto the ridge to have another look around.

Chapter Three

Anna drove five miles headed east along an unpaved road. Dust billowed up in buff-colored clouds behind the van. She'd questioned Wheeler, but he knew little about the history of the haunting sculpture she'd just purchased, except that Lucas drew his inspiration for his work from life. She couldn't wait to meet him.

At Wheeler's direction, Anna hung a left onto another dirt road. She thought the countryside looked vaguely familiar—then she remembered the reason for this feeling of déjà vu. They weren't more than a mile or two from the aging wreck where the Call mass murder had taken place. It had been dark when Sheriff Rudy drove her there the day before, but she still remembered passing by the battered mailbox that marked the end of Swift-Water's lane. The driveway was unpaved, the ruts deep. Bordered by a fence that ran the width of the narrow canyon, the pasture was dotted with curly horned Churro sheep. With the pine-capped ridge looming in the near distance, and beyond that the Sangre de Cristo Mountains, hazy blue and snowcapped above, the view was breathtaking. "This place has been in Lucas's family for a couple of generations," Wheeler told her. "The neighbor to the north is a rancher, big-time cattle, and he's been after him to sell it so he can expand. Needless to say, the man's not interested."

"I can see why he'd be reluctant to part with it," Anna replied.

The lane ended in front of a one-story clapboard structure with a shady porch across the front and a pair of beechwood rockers. In one of the chairs was a broad-shouldered man with long booted legs propped up on the porch rail and a fedora tipped low over his face. His blue denim shirt was unbuttoned, and a generous strip of smooth bronze skin was clearly visible from throat to the waistband of his jeans. Anna's heart did a small half skip in her chest, and she felt an unwelcome heat rise to her cheeks. She parked the van and Wheeler stepped out.

"Hey, bro," Wheeler said.

"Dobbs, how am I supposed to work on my tan with you blockin' the light?"

"You seen Lucas?"

"He's inside, takin' a nap," Deke said, his face still hidden under the fedora. "Some stupid son of a bitch shot him, so he ain't feelin' too good. Doc wanted him to rest. Since he says the spirits are responsible, I'm guardin' the door against any *chindi* dumb enough to try and finish him off. You can pull up a chair, as long as you don't flap your jaws. I hear spirits like quiet, and damned if I don't wanna catch me one."

"*Chindi,* huh? My guess is you're not buyin' it?"

"Jury's still out on that one," said the man under the hat. "He believes it, so I guess it can't all be bullshit— and the slug Doc dug out of his shoulder was real enough."

Wheeler turned a questioning gaze on Anna. "You wanna wait?"

"Some other time, maybe," she said. "I wouldn't want to disturb Mr. Swift-Water if he isn't feeling well, or keep Mr. Call from his beauty sleep."

At the sound of her voice, Call's lean brown fingers grasped the crown of the fedora, sliding it up and off of his face. His dark eyes were heavy lidded, but he'd scraped the bristle from his upper lip, cheeks, and chin. "Well, now, there's a surprise," he said, his voice lazy and warm. "Either fate's tryin' to tell us somethin' or, baby, you're followin' me."

His dark gaze slid over her, lingering on her blue-jeaned hips, and her body's response infuriated her. She'd gone through her bad-boy phase in her late teens and given her aunt more worries than she deserved, but eventually she'd outgrown it. Or at least she'd thought she had. Then she met Deke Call, and suddenly all bets were off. From the gold loop earrings that glittered against thick dark hair to the tattoos she knew lay hidden under the denim shirt—he might as well have been wearing a flashing neon sign that warned, "Play at your own risk."

For a moment, she contemplated that, thought about straddling those long legs, running her fingertips over that smooth bronze skin, tasting that hard chiseled mouth. Then she gave herself a mental shake. She was human, and it was damned hard to look into those fathomless black eyes without at least speculating on what it would be like—but speculating was as far as the fantasy could go. "That's some ego you've got there, big boy. What possible reason could I have for following you?"

"Don't know. Maybe I got somethin' you want."

He was infuriatingly sure of himself, and for just a second, Anna wondered if he'd read her mind. "I don't know either," she said softly. "What I'm lookin' at seems kinda used and abused. Not sure I'd be willing to risk it."

"Oh, ouch," Wheeler said. "I'm sure as hell glad that one was aimed at you and not me."

Call seemed to take it in stride. He was unruffled, relaxed, and seemingly unaffected. "I ain't no virgin, that's for sure," he said, and his grin said he suspected that she wasn't either. "You'll come around."

She glanced at Wheeler. "If Lucas is under the weather, maybe we should come back some other time."

"You should've told me we had comp'ny, Deke."

"They were just leavin'."

Lucas Swift-Water was tall and barrel chested with thin gray braids that hung well down on his chest. His gaze was sharp but friendly. "Afternoon," he said to Anna. He walked to where Deke still sat with his feet propped up, and his chair tipped back on its rockers. "Mind your manners, nephew. There's a lady present. Pretty one too."

Anna couldn't quite conceal her surprise. "He's your nephew?"

"I'm afraid so," the older man said. "I hope it won't put you off none."

Deke snorted. It was Wheeler who stepped neatly in. "Lucas, this is Anna Sandoval. She just bought one of your pieces, and she liked it so much, she insisted I make the introductions. Anna, Lucas Swift-Water."

Lucas took Anna's hand and shook it. "If you don't mind my askin', which piece struck your fancy?"

"'The Drifter.' I was very taken by it. I don't believe I've ever seen such naked emotion captured by an artist before. Wheeler tells me you draw inspiration from life. Maybe you could tell me about it?"

"You hear that?" Lucas said to his nephew. "I told you somebody'd like it."

Deke pushed off the porch rail. His boots hit the floorboards with a thud. "Time for me to take a walk." Settling his hat firmly on his head, he left the porch without a word, moving across the yard to the sheep pens where he leaned against the fence to watch the sun fade.

"Don't mind him," Lucas said. "That sculpture's been a sore subject ever since I finished it. I guess it brings back bad memories for him. I thought maybe he'd gotten past it all by now, made peace with it. But it looks like I was wrong."

"Mr. Swift-Water—"

"Call me Lucas. Everybody 'round here does."

"Lucas," Anna said, careful to keep her tone level. She feigned the interest of a buyer taken by a piece of sculpture without arousing the suspicion that she was anything more. It had been a stroke of luck that Wheeler had been in the brew house when she'd stumbled upon the sculpture. If he'd seen her face in that moment, she would have had a hard time explaining her visceral reaction. "I don't get it. How can a sculpture bring back unpleasant memories?"

"It's the model, not the work. He hates Juan Martinez."

At the mention of the name, Anna's heart skipped a beat, seeming to fall in her chest. "That was his name? The inspiration for this piece?"

A nod. "He was an illegal who stole across the border a number of years back and found himself in a lot of trouble. He said he wasn't travelin' alone, but there was never no evidence to prove that story."

"What sort of trouble?" Anna asked, hanging on his every word.

"He was accused of murderin' a family—a daddy and his little girl. Deacon's family. Deacon found them, dead on the kitchen floor. Matthew beat so bad his face was almost gone, Delia smothered. Maddy, his mama, was gone—vanished. Nobody knows what happened to her. Martinez was arrested a little while later, not far from the scene. There was blood on his hands and on his shirt, and the deputy who picked him up was able to match the blood types to the ones at the crime scene. That was a little before all this DNA stuff. His finger-prints were there too. It all looked real bad for him."

"All circumstantial," Anna said.

"Most of it. He confessed," Lucas said, "but I just had this weird feelin' that there was more to it, so I went to the jail to see Senor Martinez and decide for myself." Lucas stared off into the distance, but Anna knew he was looking into the past. "I looked in his eyes, and I knew he didn't do what they were saying. He was guilty of bein' in the wrong place, that's all. But no one believed him who mattered. Then, next thing I knew, Martinez was dead."

"I don't understand," Anna said. "Why would an innocent man kill himself?"

"I never said he committed suicide," Lucas said with a mysterious smile. "I said he was dead. It's anyone's guess what happened that night. I never bought into the explanations, but I happen to like conspiracy theories," he said with a shrug. "He's haunted me ever since. That's why I did the sculpture—sort of an exorcism."

He sighed, a soft sound filled with resignation. "Guess we're all haunted by somethin'."

Anna's gaze drifted to Deke standing alone by the fence. She could feel his loneliness, his quiet desperation, and she wondered if he'd pulled himself back from the edge. Or was he a ticking time bomb, poised to go off without warning? Deke Call intrigued her, there was no denying, and she wasn't sure she liked that.

"Guess I answered your questions," Lucas said. "Now, maybe you'll tell me why you really want that sculpture. For a newcomer, you seem awfully interested in this man, Martinez, and the murders. Most young folks couldn't care less about somethin' that happened more than a decade ago. You couldn't have been more than a tadpole when it all went down."

"I was twelve," Anna said, "and the sculpture spoke to me. I just couldn't leave it there."

"That's what I like to hear," Lucas said. "It means I did my job. Well, Anna, it's been nice talkin' to you, but it's time for me to visit Obee." He went down the steps and turned slightly. "Hey, you two want to stay for supper? Deke's cookin'. 'Course, he don't know it yet."

"No thanks. I need to be getting back. The microbrew's been warming too long as it is."

"Some other time, maybe." The old man turned his back and walked to a large stone set into the ground with blue columbine planted around it.

Wheeler stepped up beside her, a little too close. Anna stepped back. "Obee was his sheepdog. He took off mysteriously a few weeks ago. When Lucas found him, it was too late. He sure misses that old dog." He sighed. "Listen, you ready to take off?"

Anna said nothing, just walked toward the van's driver's side door, her thoughts filled by Lucas Swift-

Water and the man leaning against the fence, watching the van while it drove away.

It was nearing the end of a long day, and Sheriff Harlan Rudy had barely made a dent in the stack of paperwork on his desk. He gave the wobbling white paper tower a disgusted glance and reached for the folder on top. "Swift-Water, Lucas" slanted across the manilla paper in his deputy's neat hand. He opened the folder and read the report, then got up and opened his office door. "Whitlow? You wanna get your ass in here?"

Harlan resumed his seat and a balding younger man in crisp khaki paused in the doorway. "Sheriff?"

Harlan waved his deputy into the room. "You wrote the report on Lucas Swift-Water this morning?"

Whitlow nodded. "Yes, sir, I did. At least what I could pry out of him. I interviewed him at the clinic, since he wasn't likely to come in on his own, and I knew you wouldn't want me to let it slide."

"Well, you're right about that," Harlan said. "We can't have a man gettin' shot on his own land, without getting to the bottom of it now can we? You want to fill me in on the particulars?"

"It's all right there in the report, Sheriff—"

Harlan rubbed his closed eyelids with a finger and thumb. It had been a bitch of a day. First thing that morning he'd gotten a tip that Lonnie Peale and his two air-headed brothers were back in the methamphetamine business and had a cookhouse somewhere south of town. Unfortunately, Nazareth sat smack-dab in the middle of the county so "somewhere south of town" covered a lot of ground. He'd been in the car on his way to an accident when the call came in that Josie Cellars had beaten the living hell out of her husband, Jake. Jake was pressing charges, and though Whitlow was on scene, Josie was inside their mobile home with a hand-gun refusing to talk to anyone but the sheriff.

After talking the seventy-nine-year-old Josie into sur-rendering, he'd gone home to a cold supper and a colder wife. He didn't know what ailed Ginny lately, but she'd been distant and preoccupied, her temper hair-trigger sensitive. Maybe it was the whole midlife thing. They said it made women crazy, and lately, crazy sure fit the bill where she was concerned. It was just one more thing to juggle for a man with far too many balls in the air. Damned if he wasn't out of patience with every-thing. "Was that what I asked, son?"

"No, sir, Sheriff. Sorry." Whitlow sat a little straighter. "From the little bit I could drag from him, the victim was up on the ridge that borders his place, and a turkey hunter nailed him. It seemed pretty cut-and-dried."

"A turkey hunter? Is that right? Swift-Water said this? And you believed him?"

Whitlow shrugged. "I couldn't find a reason not to, sir. Lucas is a straight shooter. Always has been. It isn't every day a man gets shot. Why would he want to lie about it?"

"Good question." Harlan laced his fingers through one another, keeping his opinions to himself. He and Lucas Swift-Water went way back, and their as-sociation hadn't always been amicable. "Was the shooter identified?"

"No one came forward, but it could be that they had no idea an accident had even taken place. I collected the bullet from Doc Webster's and sent it to the lab for bal-listics analysis."

"Ballistics," Harlan said. "You're on the ball, that's for

sure. We can get the report back and shove it in a drawer somewhere on the off chance that we find a gun to compare it to."

Whitlow had begun to sweat. It wasn't uncomfortably warm in the office, yet a light sheen of perspiration popped on his forehead. Harlan remembered being Matthew Call's deputy and didn't have an ounce of sympathy for him.

"I went out to the farm to have a look around, and Deke showed me a bootprint they found up near the pines. Other than that, there's no evidence. No spent shells, no nothing."

Harlan passed a hand over his face. "Jesus Christ. If you're gonna let Deke Call lead you around a crime scene by the dick, could you at least keep it to yourself? If there's anything I hate, it's a goddamned civilian fuckin' up a crime scene."

Whitlow turned beet red. "He's not exactly a civilian, Sheriff."

"Not exactly? What the hell is not exactly?" Harlan shoved back in his chair, and the tear in the vinyl seat tweaked his ass cheek. The not-so-subtle reminder that his office was hard put budget-wise and holding together by a thread didn't help to cool his rising temper. "Was he wearing a uniform, Deputy? Did you happen to see a shield in evidence?"

"No, sir. I just meant that he knows his way around a crime scene—that's all."

"Experience in the field ain't everything," Harlan said, finally taking pity on his deputy. "That's all I need for now. Go on, get out of here."

Whitlow left the office. The door closed. Harlan thought about the frustrations of the day, about Lucas Swift-Water getting shot. Lucas didn't have a lot of enemies. In fact, most folks seemed to like him. His nephew, Deke, now that was another matter. Deke Call had left Nazareth to become a small-town hero, and he'd returned a different man. In just about every way imaginable, he was unrecognizable as the clean-cut young man Maddy had adored. He was long haired and belligerent, and as far as Harlan was concerned, he'd committed the one unpardonable sin: he'd walked away when he was winning.

If the reports Harlan had gotten wind of were true, the boy had a drawer full of commendations, and he was here in Nazareth, haunting that damned house on Echo Canyon Road and looking like a graduate of the Hell's Angels' school of hard knocks. Maddy's son, damn it. It sure as hell burned Harlan's ass.

After hesitating for a few seconds, Harlan took the key from under his desk blotter and unlocked the second drawer on the left-hand side. The Polaroid photo had yellowed around the edges, and there was a slight crack in the lower right corner. She'd been little more than a kid when the photo was taken, a Navajo beauty on the verge of becoming a woman, with a smile that had set Harlan's world on fire. All this time, and when he thought of her, she looked just like the girl in the photo.

Damned if Deke didn't have his mother's eyes, Harlan thought. Probably the reason he couldn't look at him without being reminded of Maddy.

He fished in the drawer one more time and poured scotch into a shot glass, downing the liquor with a flick of his wrist. One more time, and he put it away. The photo he held onto awhile longer. "Damn it, Maddy . . . what the hell happened?"

* * *

Deke braced a boot on the bottom rail of the fence and watched the night come down. The sky was fading into black, the stars bright points of pure blue-white light stretching from horizon to horizon. In the near distance, the pine-capped ridge reared up, dark and ominous. The place where Lucas had seen the Ridge-Walker . . . where someone had tried to kill him. But who would want to hurt Lucas, and why?

He watched the dark treeline for a while, but nothing moved. And the only noise was the soft wind moving in the treetops. He glanced back at the house as the screen door opened, and Lucas ambled across the yard toward him.

"Brought your jacket. You left it in my truck the last time I took you home. Thought you might welcome it. Nights out here are still kinda cold."

Deke took the denim jacket and slipped it on. "Much obliged." He glanced at his uncle. There was a stiffness in his movements that had been absent earlier. "How you feelin'?"

"Stiff and sore," Lucas said. "Other than that, it hurts like a sum'bitch. How 'bout you?"

Deke considered the question but didn't answer. He didn't feel much, besides a vague uneasiness that Lucas was in bigger trouble than either of them knew. And then there was the leggy dark-haired fox intent on digging into the past, things that were better left alone. "You have the pain pills Sarah gave you," he said. "Maybe you should think about takin' one."

"I did think about it, then I decided not to. I took in enough chemicals unintentionally in 'Nam to last me a lifetime. It's always best not to pollute the body with poisons when it can be avoided."

It was a jab at his drinking. "Everybody needs a hobby," he said.

Lucas snorted. "That your way of tellin' me to mind my own business?"

"Think it'll work? You know, I'd forgotten how peaceful it is out here. So damned quiet a man can hear his own heart beat."

"They got stars in Tucson, too, I hear."

"Do they? I wouldn't know. I didn't spend a lot of time lookin' up."

Lucas digested this information, saying nothing. "That Anna, she's real pretty. I like that challenging look in her eyes—shows she's got spirit. She seems smart too."

"Shit. Who you tryin' to kid, old man? You're just flattered because she liked your work." But in his mind's eye, he saw her secretive smile and knew it would not have taken much of an effort on her part to seduce him as well. He wasn't sure he'd ever met a woman who'd had quite that effect on him, the ability to drag him so totally out of himself that he felt a little unsettled by it. Melissa hadn't had that kind of power, and Angel— Angel had needed a savior. Unfortunately she'd pinned those hopes on the wrong man.

Unaware of his nephew's dark thoughts, Lucas laughed. "Gotta admit, it sure didn't hurt. You think you'll see her again?" Deke shook a cigarette from a half-crushed pack and offered one to Lucas. "Don't mind if I do," Lucas said, bending to accept a light.

Deke drew smoke deep into his lungs, waiting for the nicotine to smooth the ragged edges of his nerves. "I reckon so. It's a small town. We're bound to run into one another."

Lucas smoked in silence for a little while, then

crushed the cigarette out on the fence rail, pinched off the end, and put the unused portion in his shirt pocket. "Everything in moderation, nephew. You comin' in? I got a little fire goin' to chase the chill. Ridge-Walker, he ain't gonna show tonight."

"How do you know?"

"I got a feelin', that's all."

Deke accepted his explanation without comment. "Think I'll stay awhile. Enjoy the quiet."

"Think about how you're gonna resist Anna when she comes lookin' for you?"

Deke grinned. "Who said I was gonna resist?"

Lucas was still chuckling when he walked back to the house. Then the door closed, and Deke was once again alone with the night. Thoughts of Anna Sandoval lingered long after his uncle's house lights dimmed, as tantalizing as the smell of wood smoke drifting on the chill breeze. He had the distinct impression that there was more to the lady than met the eye. A lot more.

Glossy dark hair that hung past her shoulders, smoldering dark eyes, and a mouth that brought salacious thoughts to a man's mind. She was leggy and gorgeous, and he got hard just thinking about her. What was she doing now? Was she helping Carlotta close at Coyote, or was she hard at work digging into his past, stirring up trouble that had never really gone away. "There are things in this life that are just better left alone," he murmured to the night at large. Yet, from the look in Anna's eyes that afternoon as she spoke with Lucas about that damned statue, he knew that it wasn't gonna be that simple.

He smoked, and he watched the ridge where Lucas had seen his *chindi,* where the shooting had occurred, but the silence was as profound as it was unbroken, and

the only ghosts abroad this night were the same ones
who'd haunted Deke daily for the past twelve years.

On Friday mornings, Carlotta's daughter, Francine,
sent the kids off to school and made the short drive from
her split-level home on the west side of town to Coyote
Moon to help with the lunch crowd. According to
Francine, the few hours during which she bitched at her
mother, rearranged work schedules, and bullied the staff
were a huge sacrifice. As a newly remarried mother of
two she was very much in demand. Nathan Jr.'s little
league team had made the playoffs, and she'd been
asked to help organize and chaperone an all-day outing
for Suzie's swim team the following week. Her second
husband, Harold, was on a golf weekend and would be
calling promptly at four, and the noise from the bar was
irritating.

Carlotta was filling a dozen shakers with salt and getting more jittery with every passing second. Francine
leaned on the opposite side of the bar, watching with a
critical eye. "Really, Mother, how long are you going to
insist on hanging onto this albatross?" She barely
waited a half beat before suggesting, "You should put it
on the market. There's good money to be made in real
estate, and you could make a bundle."

"Sell it and do what?" Carlotta demanded. The salt
overflowed the last shaker, and when she jerked back,
the box bumped shakers three and four and knocked
them over, the last of which teetered and fell onto the
floor. "Damn it," Carlotta said, pinching some of the
white granules between thumb and forefinger and tossing them over her left shoulder.

"You could stop driving yourself into the ground, for

one thing," Francine pointed out. "You're seventy-three, for God's sake! Women your age don't work, they relax and enjoy life."

Carlotta's penciled brows flattened. "That's seventy-two, and you really don't need to remind me how old I am. I'm not senile." She snapped her gum, then continued chewing ferociously. "Coyote's mine, Francine, and I'll decide when it's time to bail and head off to the raisin ranch. If I sold this place, I wouldn't know what to do with myself." She shook her red head. "Look, honey, I know you mean well, but for Christ's sake, don't help me. I can't afford it."

Francine was the polar opposite of Carlotta, mousy and plain with bobbed hair that wasn't brown and wasn't blond, nonvisible makeup, and a perpetually dissatisfied expression on her face. Her clothing was expensive but modest to the point of being frumpy. An ecru shell and matching long-sleeved cardigan, beige slacks and Italian leather flats. Carlotta knew it was an unspoken editorial on her own flamboyant style and for just a second wished Francine were more like Anna— pretty, caring, and polite enough to mind her own business.

"You're my mother," Francine said. "Of course I want to help you." She forced a smile, and it was probably as close to genuine as Francine ever got. "There's a nice little retirement community just a half-mile from Eagle's Nest. I've checked it out myself, and you could be very comfortable there. It's five minutes from the house, and the children and I could visit every weekend."

"Did it ever occur to you that I don't *want* to be comfortable?" Carlotta shot back. "I've worked all my life,

Francine, and I want to continue to be useful! Not that you'd understand the concept."

"What was that supposed to mean?"

Carlotta rolled her eyes to the smoke-darkened ceiling. She'd had enough. "God help me," she said. "I need a cigarette." She took the pack from under the bar and lit up, jabbing two red-lacquered nails in her daughter's direction. "Don't you dare say a word!"

Francine clamped her lips shut but waved a napkin in front of her face to dispel the smoke; furious, Carlotta abandoned the saltshakers and stormed out, brushing past Anna, who turned to watch her go.

"What was that about?" Anna asked Sandy, placing the stack of freshly laundered table linens on the bar. When the ex-marine wasn't manning the grill, he helped out in the bar, sweeping the floor or mopping up, getting ready for another day. The cook's gaze shifted to the woman leaning on the bar a few stools away.

"Enough said." Anna started covering the freshly wiped tables, until Carlotta's daughter caught sight of her.

"Anna? I'd like a word with you."

"I'm kind of busy. Can't it wait?"

Francine's thin cheeks flushed a dull red. "As a matter of fact, no, it can't."

"Somebody's gotta get this place ready to open," Anna said.

"You'll have time for that when I'm through."

Anna gave the woman an assessing glance. If she was pissed at Carlotta and bent on taking it out on someone, then she really needed to find another target. Anna wasn't in a mood to take it. "If you want to talk to me, then you'll do it while I work," she said, then turned her back and walked away.

Francine followed. "I'd like to know how long you intend to stay in Nazareth."

Anna shrugged, smoothing the white broadcloth over one of the tables. It was one of Carlotta's quirks. Linens during the day, but during the lull at six P.M., the lights were dimmed and all pretense of refinement abandoned. Somehow Coyote's dual personality only added to its charm. "I haven't decided, not that it's any of your business."

Francine stuck out her chin. "Everything that concerns my mother concerns me. With a little work, the apartment you have could bring in twice what it does now. When Mother retires, she's going to need the extra income."

Anna straightened, facing the older woman squarely, glare for glare. "I see you've got her life all planned out for her. Should I even ask how Carlotta feels about this or doesn't it apply?"

"When the time comes, Mother will make the right choices."

Anna braced a hand on her hip. "The right choices for her? Or for you? Your husband's a developer, isn't that right? I bet he's got ideas for Coyote. We're not that far from Taos. With the right ambience, it could become *the* nightspot . . . and all it would take is the right investors and an unlimited supply of cash. So much for your concern."

Francine lashed out, her palm connecting with Anna's cheek, and at the same time Carlotta came through the door. "Francine!" Carlotta cried. "That's enough! Go home!"

"You're not going to take her side over mine!"

"I pay Anna to help out here, and she's the best waitress I have. I'd like to keep her, if you don't mind. And if you do mind, well, I really don't give a damn. Go home, Francine," she said again. "You've helped me enough for one day."

Carlotta helped Anna dress the rest of the tables. Anna smoothed the creases from the white cloth. "She does have a valid point, you know."

"Francine, a valid point? Now this I gotta hear."

Anna shrugged. "There could be worse things than dumpin' the workload into someone else's lap so you can enjoy life for a change. And, if you played your cards right, you could turn a nice profit on this place."

Carlotta just shook her head. "My Al worked his tail off to buy this place, and I stuck by him through it all—right up until the day he died. He loved it here, and so do I. It's a lot of work, but I just can't imagine doin' anything else. Besides, can you picture me livin' out my golden years in some fancy retirement community? It'd be like tryin' to squeeze an elephant's ass into a size 5 pair of panties. It don't matter how hard you try, there's no way it's gonna fit. Listen, honey, why don't you take the rest of the day off? Go someplace and relax, or work on that book you're supposed to be writing. You've earned it."

"If you're giving me time off because of Francine, you don't have to do that."

"No, I don't have to. I want to. A little time off with pay is the least I can do. Don't worry about it bein' busy. I've got lots of help this mornin'. We can handle it just fine. Now go on. Get the hell outta here."

Anna left Coyote, but she didn't go home. She walked to Harlan's office across the street instead. Dixie was off that day, but the sheriff's deputy was at his desk. Anna knew him from the few times he'd stopped by Coyote to pick up an order of hot wings for his very pregnant wife. Seth Whitlow was a nice guy, quick with a smile, with clear brown eyes and a frank expression. He ended a phone call, glancing up. "Hey, Anna. Somethin' I can help you with?"

"Hey, Seth. Is Harlan in?"

"You just missed him," Seth told her. "Trouble at home. There was a water main break, and his wife called him home. I'm holdin' down the fort, so to speak. Is there somethin' I can do?"

"Maybe you can help out, save Harlan the trouble. I need to ask some questions for the book I'm writing. Do you know anything about the Call murder case?"

"I don't think there's anyone who owns a TV or reads the papers that doesn't know about that. I wasn't much more than a kid at the time, though. Same age as Deke, Matthew Call's son. In fact, we went to school together."

"Really?" Anna's pulse pumped a little faster. "The man Harlan arrested that night—he would have brought him here for processing and to be held for arraignment and trial."

Whitlow nodded. "Yes, ma'am, they've expanded a bit since then, but the original cell is still there. Right through that door."

"Could I see it?" Anna asked, trying to contain her excitement. "If it wouldn't be too much trouble, that is. I need to fix the scene in my mind. Writer's quirk."

If he had any qualms at all, he forgot them the moment she smiled. "Well, it is kind of slow this mornin', so why not? We're not holdin' anyone right now, so there's no danger involved." He got up and walked to the door he'd mentioned earlier. "The cells are open so we can see at a glance what a prisoner's doin'." He opened the door with a key from the ring in his pocket and allowed her to precede him into a small

enclosure. A quartet of steel cages stood side by side,
each with a stainless sink bowl and toilet of the same
material, a low bunk bolted to the wall, and an air vent
high in the back wall. "It's number two," Whitlow said.

Anna reached out and grasped the bars. The steel was
cold against her hands. Such a small, cramped space.
Dingy and depressing. She drew a breath to steady herself, and in the outer office, the phone began to ring.
"I'd better get that," Whitlow said. "You'll be okay here
till I come back?"

Anna nodded. She didn't trust herself to speak. Whitlow's footfalls moved away, then faded, and a low-voice
conversation ensued. Anna paid no attention. Her focus
was limited to the six by eight cell where Juan had been
caged . . . no better than an animal.

It wasn't hard to see it all, the young Mexican man
seated on the bunk, his head in his hands, just like
Lucas's sculpture. It was strange, but she could feel his
desperation. She closed her eyes as a torrent of emotion
surged through her. He'd left a child in the wildness outside of town. He was terrified. If he told the authorities,
they would take her away, send her back to Mexico. If
he kept quiet, she could perish.

An agony like nothing Anna had ever experienced
seemed to permeate that small place—as if it had
seeped into the concrete walls, the floor, the ceiling and
bars. Overwhelmed, she leaned her brow against the
bars, fighting a wave of deep melancholy, struggling to keep the hot, liquid emotion from escaping her
closed lids.

She heard someone pause in the open doorway.
"Anna?"

Anna turned. Harlan Rudy, Sheriff of Alamance
County, stood in the doorway. Anna pulled herself

together, stepping back from the bars. "Harlan. I'm glad you're here. Do you have a few minutes?"

"I'll give you the time you need if you tell me what you're doin' in a restricted area of my jail without my permission."

"Deputy Whitlock was kind enough to show me the cell where Mr. Martinez ended his life. Maybe you could tell me what happened that night?"

"It's not all that complicated. Martinez was apprehended less than a mile from the scene of the murder. He was covered in blood and dazed, which made him suspicious. There were bloody prints all over the scene—we had a match, so I read him his rights and took him into custody."

"The reports I read indicate that he confessed?"

"He did."

"You interrogated him?" Anna said.

"With the aid of my acting deputy, Quincy Bell."

Anna frowned. "Bell? I haven't heard that name before."

Harlan leaned an arm against the bars. "Quincy was Matthew's deputy before I got here. He retired soon after—health problems. That night, I needed somebody at my back, and Quincy answered my call. I owe him for that."

"Did you strike Martinez during the interrogation?"

"What are you suggesting, Anna?" Harlan looked amused. "That I coerced a confession from him?"

"Did you?" She watched him intently, but his gaze never wavered.

"Of course not."

"What about Bell?"

"Bell kept an eye on him while I was at the scene. As

for exactly what happened in my absence, I'd suggest you talk to him. Anything else you'd like to know?"

"Just one more thing," Anna said. "Who, besides you and Quincy Bell, had access to this cell?"

Harlan's smile faded. "If I didn't know better, I'd think you were castin' doubt on the prisoner's suicide. Why all the interest in Martinez? I thought you were gonna write about the murders."

"What happened to Juan Martinez is an important part of it. You didn't answer my question."

He shrugged. "Matthew's son, Deke Call. He was in and out of here as a kid, and he knew where the keys were kept. Did he use 'em? You've met him. What do you think?"

She knew instinctively what he was driving at. Had Call been responsible, he wouldn't have bothered to make it look like a suicide. His method would have been a lot more direct, a lot more violent. "I'd like an intro to Deputy Bell. Can you arrange it for me?"

He nodded. "I go every Saturday mornin', just to make sure he doesn't need anything. Come back then, and I'll take you along."

Chapter Four

Anna was at Harlan's office at eight sharp Saturday morning for the drive to Red Butte Personal Care Home. The home was neat and well cared for, airy and bright. They entered through the main entrance and a lobbylike reception area, down a short hallway to the day room.

"He's got a bum hip and had it surgically replaced a few years ago, but it didn't take. Since then, he's needed this assisted livin' setup." Harlan opened the door to the day room and indicated that she should precede him. "His mind's clear, though, and in my book that's what really matters."

Several older gentlemen had gathered to watch TV, but Quincy Bell was seated in a wheelchair at a table near the window. A gardening magazine was open in front of him. He looked up as they approached. "Ginny know you're steppin' out on her, Harlan?"

"Now, what would a pretty young thing like Anna want with an old warhorse like me?"

"Good point," Bell said, waiting for the introductions to begin.

"Quince, this is Anna Sandoval. She's interested in the Call case, and she asked me to introduce her. Anna, Quincy was my strong right arm that night. I couldn't have managed without his help."

"You're right about that," Bell said. Belatedly, he remembered his manners and took Anna's hand. "Pleased to meet you, miss. Mind if I ask why you're looking into a closed case? I know those murders had some amount of sensational value, but it's been over and done with years ago. What's the point in rehashing it now? Unless you're some sort of cop groupie and you get off on that sort of thing." He gave her a broad wink, but Anna wasn't fooled. He might seem charming, but a man had been hanged in a jail cell that he was supposed to be supervising, and it remained to be seen whether he'd had a hand in Martinez's death.

Anna smiled, as much to hide her thoughts as anything. "Actually, I'm a writer, and though I've researched the case over several years, I thought it might help to get a firsthand account of what occurred once Mr. Martinez was taken into custody."

Bell shrugged, shifting in his chair. "Once he was in custody, it was mostly routine. Harlan was elbow-deep in blood and gore, so he passed the prisoner off to me. I saw that he was photographed and printed, and as I recall, I took his initial statement, or tried to. I don't speak much Spanish, and he was jabberin' like some magpie, a mile a minute. All I could catch was something about a kid."

"Can you be more specific?"

A shrug. "He was agitated. Kept saying something about a *bambina.* There was no kid with him when we picked him up, so I turned a deaf ear."

The statement cut Anna to the marrow, and it was a

real struggle not to show it, to pretend objectivity when she had none. "Do you remember the interrogation, Mr. Bell?"

"About as well as any of it. Harlan here handled the talkin'. He's got the lingo. Except for a few words, I never learned."

"Anna wanted to know if I struck Martinez at any time during the interview," Harlan put in. He wore a slight smile, like the thought amused him. It was the same expression she'd seen that day at the jail, and Anna would have liked to wipe it off his face.

"You mean the black eye?" Quincy said, glancing first to Harlan, then to Anna. "That wasn't Harlan's doin'. Martinez fell gettin' into the patrol car. Caught his toe on the pavement and went headlong." The old man snorted. "I don't doubt both of us would've liked to have a turn at him, but nobody laid a hand on 'im that I'm aware of."

Anna wasn't sure she believed him, but she was more concerned with what came later. "Every account I've read indicated that Mr. Martinez took his own life. I'm aware that during the time when he was arrested and when he was found, Lucas Swift-Water came to see him. Was there anyone else at the jail that night?"

"One or two people, as I recall," he said, his eyes narrowing slightly. "You sure do ask a lot of questions."

"Which is it?" Anna asked, completely unfazed by the criticism. "One? Or two?"

"Carlotta McFadden showed up. I never did find out what she said to him. I asked once where she learnt so much wetback, but she wouldn't answer me."

Anna's hackles rose at the derogatory term. "There was someone else?"

"Yep. Deacon Call. Stood for a long while, just staring

through the bars. I kept an eye on him, 'cause I wasn't sure what he might do, his pa being killed and his mama missin'. Must've stood there for twenty minutes without sayin' a word, then Lucas come and talked to him, and dragged him out of there. I never did like that kid much." He closed his magazine and released the wheelchair's brakes. "I hope you got what you wanted, 'cause that's all I got to say. Good to see you, Harlan. I appreciate you comin'."

As he was wheeling away, Anna couldn't resist one more try. "Mr. Bell? Did Deke Call return to the jail that night?"

Bell didn't answer. The interview was over.

A little while later, Harlan parked in front of Coyote Moon and got out of the Jeep truck, opening the passenger door for Anna. "You get what you wanted back there?"

Far from it. She'd hoped Matthew Call's former deputy could shed some light on what had really happened to Juan Martinez, and instead, he'd muddied the waters even further. He did provide one lead she hadn't had before. She'd known about Carlotta's visit, and Lucas's, but Deke had been there too. "Deputy Bell's an interesting man."

Harlan gave her a level look. "He's a cop, through and through, and he doesn't like Mexicans much."

Anna watched him. "What about you?"

He just laughed. "This town's a good 50 percent Latino. As I see it, they're voters, and at least half the reason I get to keep my job."

Boots scraped on the sidewalk. A slow, even tread headed straight for where he and Anna stood. Harlan glanced up.

Deke Call. Jesus, he looked rough, a real hard case,

and he wondered what Maddy would have thought of how he'd turned out. She'd always had a soft spot for her oldest child, despite his bent for pushing the boundaries, and pushing his old man's buttons. Deke and Matthew had butted heads from the first time he'd laid eyes on the boy, and it had only gotten worse as Deke got older.

For Maddy's sake, and everything Deke had meant to her, Harlan took a deep breath and held tight to his temper. "Somethin' you want, son? Or'd you just come to cast a shadow so we could have a little shade?"

"I want to talk to you, Harlan."

"Then stop by the office during business hours," Harlan suggested. "You know where it is."

"I ain't in no mood to wait. It's about Lucas." That dark, pupilless stare flicked up and stayed, steady, unflinching. "Somebody's been prowlin' around his place, killin' his animals, stealin' some too, and now he's been shot. I'd like to know what's goin' on out there, and what the hell you're gonna do about it."

Harlan looked at the young rooster in front of him. Deke was judging him. He could feel it. Weighing the position of a county sheriff against a big-city cop and finding him lacking in every respect. Harlan's temper began a slow simmer. "The shooting at Lucas's place is an ongoing investigation, and it's my policy to give out information on a need to know basis. You're a civilian. Enough said."

"What really burns your ass, Harlan? Me bein' an ex-cop? Or that I was better than you without even tryin'?"

Harlan met him stare for stare. "I'm gonna pretend I didn't hear that, since I suspect it's anger talkin', but if you're fool enough to want to continue this conversation, you'll pick a better time, and come to my office, and maybe—just maybe—if I *don't* have anything better to do, I'll discuss it with you." His gaze slid to Anna. "I gotta get back. If there's anything else you need, don't hesitate to call."

Anna watched the sheriff leave, then turned to Deke, whose unfriendly gaze followed the same path hers had. "What was that about?" she asked.

"Nothing that concerns you," he said shortly. "Stay out of it."

"You said someone's targeting Lucas," Anna persisted. "I thought the shooting was an accident."

"You thought wrong." He stepped off the curb and into the street, heading toward a dark-colored sports car.

Anna stalked after him, catching his arm as he reached for the door handle, a move that surprised them both . . . Call because she'd dared to touch him, Anna because his skin was smooth and warm, his muscles tense and hard. Potent electrical current leaped between them. Anna felt it sizzle and spark, and a slow, liquid heat crept along her nerves. So strong, so alarming, she couldn't seem to move, couldn't breathe. "Are you saying that someone's trying to kill him?"

Something in his eyes changed. The lids lowered slightly, partially masking their dark gleam. He turned and half-sat on the fender of the car, though he remained tense. A deep marine blue, it had a black leather interior and four on the floor. It screamed speed, a recklessness she could relate to, and which she'd always found irresistible. "Shouldn't you be at the sheriff's office warming Harlan's lap?"

"Harlan? You've got to be kidding."

He shrugged and the muscles under all that ink rippled. "You showed up at the house with him before daylight. I saw him put his arm around you as you left the house. Looked to me like he was staking a claim, and I sure didn't see you tell him to back off."

Anna smiled. She could play the game as well as he could, the verbal thrust and parry, score a point with a heavy jab and then step back and circle round to see the effect it would have. Somehow, it didn't lessen the sexual tension between them—in fact, if anything, it underscored it. "What bothers you more, Deke? That Harlan has something I want? Or that he's willing to pony up?"

"You got something he wants all right. Jokes aside, Anna, be damned careful where he's concerned. The man's got a lot of sway in this county, and that's not necessarily a good thing. Power's an aphrodisiac, but it's dangerous, too."

So was his nearness. She was standing just inches from him, so close that she could feel the subtle heat radiating from him, smell the scent of soap and tobacco that clung to his skin. Anna breathed him in and felt herself weaken. One step and she could close the space between them . . . one step and she would ruin everything. "Thanks for the warning. I'll keep it in mind."

"You'll keep it in mind," he said softly, "then you'll keep on doin' whatever it is you're doin'. No matter how dangerous, no matter how reckless, because you can't resist, and you can't back off, even if it's the only smart thing to do—"

"I wouldn't be too comfortable making assumptions, if I were you. You don't know me at all."

"Don't I?" he said, reaching out to touch her, to tuck a strand of dark hair behind her ear, to trace his thumb along her cheek. Slowly he leaned in, still caressing her cheek with the pad of his thumb. "You sure of that?"

His mouth was a mere fraction away, so close she

could feel the leap of the electricity she'd noticed before conducting between them, skin to skin. Anna met him halfway. The kiss, as he took her lips, was slow and sensual, a steadily deepening exploration of lips and tongues that robbed Anna of breath and began a gradual disintegration of her will. Her hand crept up and around his neck, burying itself in his thick hair, so cool and silken . . . and when he broke the contact and opened the car's passenger door, she didn't argue, just slid into the soft bucket seat and braced for the ride of her life.

Anna had done her homework. She'd had an infinite amount of time to look into every aspect of the Call murders, to dig into the backgrounds of everyone involved. Every little detail. She knew Harlan Rudy's preference for green chile stew, and she knew that his wife nagged him. He liked his shirts light on the starch, and if rumors were true, he was something of a lady's man. He had a ring on his finger, but it sure hadn't stopped him in the past. As a deputy, he'd had an unshakable loyalty to Matthew Call, and the two had been friends off the job as well. When Call was murdered, Rudy had taken it personally. He'd sworn that he'd find the person or persons responsible, and the majority of the county's citizens thought he had done just that.

What she didn't know was how far Rudy would go to avenge the murder of a good friend, the disappearance of Call's wife, the death of his daughter. Would he break the law he'd taken an oath to uphold? Had he killed the accused in his cell to avenge the murder of Sheriff Matt Call?

The question haunted her, because she'd been in Nazareth for weeks and she still couldn't answer it.

Then there was Deke, in the midst of it all. He'd been seventeen at the time of the murders and, by all accounts, reckless and temperamental. A real risk taker, headstrong and wild. All indications were that some dark current existed between the boy and his adopted father, that there had been constant strife, and possibly even violence. He'd been devastated by the death of his sister, but it had reportedly been his mother's disappearance that had affected him most of all. Then, at eighteen, he'd graduated from high school and dropped below the radar. It had taken some really intensive digging to find out where he'd been.

Anna knew something of the boy he'd been but very little of the man she led up the stairs to her apartment. It was midafternoon, and Mrs. Bookwalter would be watching the alley from the shade of her back porch. Before they locked the door and pulled the drapes, the news that she'd invited a rough-looking young man into her apartment would be circulating through the neighborhood. Yet as she unlocked the door and stepped into the cool shadows of the kitchen, Anna didn't care.

Deke paused on the threshold for a few seconds, as if giving her a chance to end this craziness, then when she started to unbutton her blouse, he stepped inside and closed the door, leaning against it.

It was craziness, a headlong fall before mad impulse that would find her picking herself up from the emotional bottom once it was over, questioning everything and filled with regrets.

So why go through with it? the logical part of her whispered.

Why not stop now, offer an excuse—any excuse—and escape with her last shred of self-respect?

Because as insane as it seemed, the impulse to grab

whatever pleasure he would give her was far stronger than her sense of self-preservation. Because if she didn't give in, the chance to be in this man's arms might not present itself again, and she would always wonder if she'd made a mistake.

He was dark and he was mysterious—as intriguing as he was a danger to himself. She recognized the need in his eyes and she responded to it because she felt it too. As she undid the last button, he pushed away from the door and closed the distance between them. "Baby, you take playin' with fire to a whole new level. You doin' this to get your story or for some other reason I ain't figured out yet?"

"Now there's an angle I hadn't considered," Anna said. "If I thought it would work, I might just try it. Are you telling me you're willing to talk to me about it?"

"Talk won't change shit," he said.

He was right about that, Anna thought, and at the moment, talking was the last thing on her mind. There would be time for that later. *Much later.*

His worn denim shirt was already unbuttoned. Anna slid her hands underneath, her fingertips grazing silky skin as she slid it off his shoulders and down his arms. It fell with a barely discernible whisper, making a soft puddle at his booted heels. He was tall and broad shouldered with taut pecs and a stomach that rippled with muscle. Adonis would have been envious. As she drank in the sight of him, Anna sucked in a shuddering breath, then before she could change her mind, she stepped closer, framing his hard face with her hands, pulling him in for a long and seductive kiss.

It was a long while before she broke the contact, leaning back just enough to gaze up at him. "You don't have to remind me that this is dangerous. I've been telling myself that since that first day in that wreck of a house. Either it hasn't sunk in or it doesn't matter."

Another kiss, initiated by Anna, but he quickly turned the tables, deepening the contact, his tongue moving past her lips to dominate hers.

Anna caught her breath. Blood pushed through her veins at an alarming rate; her heart hammered against her ribs as she sank into his hard body, an attempt to get closer, closer. . . .

Without a word, he whisked her blouse away, then her black lace bra, leaving only her jeans and panties. His head dipped and he teased her nipple, a long, scorching kiss that had her shuddering and pressing closer—and all the while, his hands never rested. She felt his knuckles graze her belly, and the rivet at the top of her low-rise jeans released with a soft pop. A slow insistent tug and the zipper opened, inch by torturous inch. His thumbs hooked into the denim at the waistband and tugged them down and off, revealing curves masked only by a few scraps of satin and lace.

Anna slid her hands around his neck and clung to him while he opened his jeans and slid them down. She felt him press her soft flesh, bullet hard, ready for anything. "Go on, baby. Tell me to stop," he whispered against her ear.

In answer, she molded her hand to his erection and kissed him hard. It was too late to retreat. She'd reached the point of no return on the street moments ago. One kiss and she'd been lost. There was a hellish irony in that realization. A woman of experience reduced to a hot puddle of desire with almost no effort on his part—but maybe her history was the key to her reaction to Call. She'd had lovers, powerful men in high places during her time in D.C., a crusader or two whose zeal had proved irresistible—but no one who'd struck at her core like he had. With no effort at all, he'd penetrated her protective shell—one brooding glance from a lost soul had cut to the quick, leaving her wide open, vulnerable. "Stop now and I'll make you regret it."

Hooking her thumb in the narrow lace that encircled her hips, she eased her panties down, catching her breath as he found and filled her. Braced against the corner of the kitchen cabinets, Deke's forearm cushioning her back and one leg wrapped around his lean hips, Anna released her last remaining inhibition and gave the moment her all. He rode her hard, and she egged him on, digging her fingertips into his glutes while she glided against his smooth, deep strokes. On and on, deeper and more forceful with each thrust of his hips, the building tension proved unbearable. Her arms around him, she felt his muscles grow rock hard and sensed that he was holding back for the purpose of her release. Selfishly, she delayed, slowing the pace just slightly, reluctant for it to end . . . until finally he grew impatient with her tactics and wrested control, taking her mouth in a hard kiss as he brought the interlude to a shattering, ecstatic conclusion and Anna went limp in his arms.

Covered in a light sheen of sweat, Deke pulled back just enough to right his jeans, then lifting her, he coaxed her legs around his hips and carried her to the bedroom.

He looked like he belonged in her bed, long, lean, and naked—perfectly at ease. Stretched out on his back, his head dark against the wealth of white Egyptian cotton, he watched her through slitted eyes as the fingertips of one hand traced patterns on her bare skin. They'd lazed away the afternoon, making it on the cool, damp sheets, and Anna was more sated than she'd ever been. Her head resting on his bare shoulder and his arm curved around her back, she watched him and wondered how the hell they'd ended up here.

As soon as the passion faded, regret came pouring in. Well, not regret, exactly . . . it was more like doubt. She honestly didn't regret a moment of the past few hours, though she knew she *should* have.

He'd been too good for that, and just looking at him lying there, his tattoos a livid contrast to the sumptuous bed linen, she wanted him all over again—Deke Call, poster boy for reckless behavior. Anna knew it was part of his allure, and she should have known better than to fall for it. When it came to recklessness, she was no better than he was.

"Chaca . . ." she said softly, tracing the ink that circled his biceps. "That's some interesting piece of artwork. I've seen similar tattoos but nothing quite so elaborate. The double-strand barbed wire's a favorite of some of the smaller Mexican gangs in the Southwest. You a banger, bad boy?"

The hand tracing patterns on her skin never hesitated, just kept up the slow, seductive movement. "How does a waitress become an expert on gangbangers?" he asked.

"I wasn't always a waitress," Anna said, but she left it at that. A little mystery was a good thing, but not when it went two ways. She needed to know what she was dealing with, and she couldn't get answers soon enough. "I've asked around about you," she said, tracing a fingertip along the hollow of his cheek. "I wanted to find out what would make a man with so much going for him want to put a gun to his head and end it all."

Something dark and unsettling flickered in his eyes, though he said nothing, and Anna knew it was something he wouldn't discuss. Maybe he couldn't afford to revisit that moment for fear he would find himself reimmersed in the hell that had driven him to the edge. "Askin' questions is a risky business. Sometimes you get more than you bargain for."

"Which means?"

"That you're puttin' your pretty nose where it don't belong."

Anna arched a brow at him, far from discouraged. "I like to know the man in my bed, who he is, what he's capable of, where he's been."

"I'm right here right now, baby," he said, swiftly putting her on her back beneath him. "As I see it, that's all that matters."

He braced on his forearms. Anna reached up and touched the cleft in his chin, the legacy of his unknown father? "Maddy, your mother. Delia, your sister. So tell me, Chaca . . . who's Angel, and how'd you come by this?" Her hand slid around to the inside of his arm, down onto his lower right ribs where a heavy ridge of scar tissue had yet to lose its angry purple color. It was more than a surgery scar. It was jagged, like he'd been knifed by someone other than a surgeon.

She'd taken him by surprise. She could see it in his face. "Just part of the price I paid for bein' where I've been. A walk on the wild side don't always come cheap."

"Not much of an answer."

"I don't like to talk about it."

"And Angel?" she asked, not ready to let it go.

"She was someone who needed more than I was willing to give. Don't worry that she's competition. The women I care about don't tend to live too long.

Maybe you should think about that and cut ties while you still can."

"Maybe," Anna said, but she wasn't willing to commit. She didn't have what she wanted, and she wasn't through with him just yet. "What did you mean before about someone killing Lucas's animals? Is he in some kind of trouble?"

A slow, deep breath as he weighed how much to tell her. He was as expert at keeping secrets as he was at pleasing a woman, and she could only wonder what he had to hide. Had he gone back to the jail the night of the murders like Harlan had suggested? Had he played a role in Juan Martinez's death? "Looks like it," he said. "There's some weird shit goin' down out there. For a while I wondered if he was readin' too much into it . . . then he got shot, and the theory that he was seein' things that weren't there was pretty much blown to hell."

Anna frowned. "So, you really think someone's got it in for him?"

"It's one explanation. Lucas says he saw someone up on the ridge that borders his place. He seems to think it's a malicious spirit . . . a *chindi*. He puts a lot of stock in traditional beliefs."

"What about you?" Anna wondered aloud. The feathers on his arm, the name Chaca . . . it all meant something. "What do you think?"

"That nothing's ever that simple."

He was right about that. Life was unbearably complex. Bad things happened to good people, and innocent men took the blame. Lucas Swift-Water was a good man, and she could only wonder where the events swirling around him were leading. She liked him, and she hated to think that he was in trouble. "At least he's got you."

Those words bit deep, taking a chunk out of Deke's hide. *At least he's got you.* Like he could stop what was happening . . . just like he'd stopped the murders . . . like he'd been able to save his marriage or keep Angel from self-destructing. *Take this money,* he heard himself say, *but no H. Buy yourself somethin' nice. Get your nails done.*

Thanks, Chaca. She'd smiled, but her eyes were little girl lost, her essence ransomed by something much bigger, more powerful than her. *I'd die without you. . . .*

She'd died because of him.

Because she'd been too wrapped up in him, or at least in who she'd thought he was, to see the danger coming. Reality was a hell of a lot more grim. He'd used her, from the first day, and any feelings he might have had for her, any urge to protect her, was second to getting the job done.

Earn their trust. Get the goods. Take 'em down.

Who could have guessed that the price he'd paid personally for a job well done would be so enormous. Or that months after it ended, the repercussions would still resound through his life with such devastating effect.

The alarm on the wristwatch lying on the dresser bleated twice in quick succession. Anna reached up for a lingering kiss, then slid from beneath him and got out of bed. "I need to get moving. Gotta grab a shower. My shift starts at six." She didn't ask if she would see him again. On some level, Deke was relieved. Better to keep things loose. No promises he couldn't keep. No expectations. No strings. "There's beer in the fridge if you want one. Do you mind dropping me off? It'll save me a few minutes."

"No sweat." He waited until she closed the bathroom door and the water was running, then he got up and slipped into his jeans. It didn't take much of a search to find the notebook computer. It was stashed in a leather tote under the bed. He sat down on the bed and powered the unit up, then quickly scanned the files. Just the basics. A word-processing program and a few assorted documents, but nothing pertaining to her manuscript. If those files ever existed, they'd been scrubbed. The shower stopped running. He clicked onto the e-mail program and scanned the contents, but it had been wiped clean too. Nothing in the deleted file, no folders, nothing to indicate that she was who she said she was. He even checked the instant messaging program, but the archives were accessible by password only. He'd never met a novelist, but he'd known a few reporters from Tucson and they'd been creatures of habit, with littered work spaces and notes scribbled on everything. Anna didn't fit the stereotype. Yet that didn't mean she was lying.

He flicked off the power and placed the computer in its case, slipping it back under the bed. A second later, the bathroom door opened. She looked fresh and sweet in tight jeans and a snug white T-shirt. "You ready?"

"That depends on what you've got in mind," Deke said, following her from the apartment.

Chapter Five

Later that evening John Miller swept up the broken glass and carried it to the construction dumpster parked on the front lawn. He'd hired a couple of guys to help out with the repairs. One spoke enough English to negotiate wages and take instruction, but the other spoke only Spanish. There was a good chance they didn't have a work visa between them, but John didn't ask. They knew what they were doing, the price was right, and that was all that mattered. The three of them had been working since early that morning, and the last of the broken windows had been replaced and the new front door swung smoothly on its hinges.

Standing back to check out the progress, he found he was pleased with the results. It was sad how quickly an abandoned house fell into disrepair and how just a little TLC quickly breathed life back into it. Some new glazing and a fresh coat of paint, and it would barely be recognizable as a house purchased for delinquent taxes at a sheriff's sale. The door opened and his wife, Corrie, stepped out carrying a tray with a pitcher of iced tea and a trio of glasses. There were cobwebs in her dark hair and a smudge on the end of her nose, but her brown eyes danced with delight. She served the workers first, accepting their murmurs of *gracias* with a nod and a smile, then handed John a sweating glass, setting the tray down on the plank that rested between two sawhorses, craning for a look around him. "Looks like we've got our first visitor," she said. "I'll go get another glass."

John stopped her with a hand on her arm. "Let's see what he wants first."

The stranger was tall and lean; his jeans were worn through at the knee and his denim jacket had a ten-inch slice in the sleeve. He caught sight of the ink under the denim, the hair that touched his collar, and reined in his enthusiasm. "Afternoon," John said. "Can I do something for you?"

"I was out here a few days ago, and I left somethin' inside. The sheriff told me somebody bought the old place. I didn't expect the renovations to start so soon."

"We should be in by dark. It's gonna be a work in progress for a long time, but Corrie's got the worst of the dirt under control on the inside, and we can rough it for a few weeks. At least the glazing's in place, so nothing from the outside can get in unless we want it to." John's eyes narrowed. "You said you'd been out here. You mind if I ask what you were doing on my property?"

"Revisitin' the past is all. I lived here when I was a kid." He glanced at the house, at the upstairs windows, then turned to go. "Good luck with the place."

"Thanks." John breathed a sigh of relief as the rough-looking visitor walked toward the car, but before he could get in, Billy came barreling around the corner on his bicycle, nearly running the man down. He screeched to a stop, staring up at him with widening eyes. "Is that a real tattoo?" Billy asked, mesmerized by the ink clearly displayed by the tear in the sleeve of the jean jacket.

John watched the man drop onto his heels in front of his son, and for an instant, that cold black gaze softened. "It's real, all right. You wanna see it?"

A quick nod.

He pushed back the sleeve, revealing a few inches of the intricate artwork.

"Cool!"

The exclamation took Deke back years in a single instant. He remembered what it was like being a kid. Everything looked bigger from that perspective—the highs higher, the lows a devastating crash. Maddy's voice echoed inside his skull, panicked, full of sorrow. "My God, Matthew! What have you done?"

Matthew was winded from the thrashing he'd given Deke. "He's spoiled, Maddy. Too damned bullheaded for his own good. Somebody's got to instill the fear of God in him. . . ."

Deke shook the echoes off, focusing on the present. "Let's talk cool, my man. What's that you got there?"

"Ma says it's a harmonica. I found it. She says I can take lessons."

"Lessons are a good thing," he said, getting to his feet. "You take care now, and mind your folks."

Deke was opening the driver's door when John Miller called to him. "Hey, mister. Aren't you forgetting something? You said you left something inside."

"I guess I was wrong about that," Deke said. "I hope you're happy here." *I wasn't.*

* * *

Anna tallied the cash drawer, locked the money in the safe, and closed and locked the doors for the night. Carlotta hadn't been feeling well and had gone home an hour earlier. It wasn't unusual for Anna to close, and she actually welcomed the short walk through the alley and down the block to the apartment. At three in the morning the streets were deserted, the town silent, sleeping. The cowboys and the rowdies from the bar had taken themselves off to parts unknown, and with the day finally behind her, she had the time and luxury to just breathe, without the constant pressure of keeping up the pretense, the secrets, the lies.

After the noise of the bar, the quiet was intoxicating, and she lingered on the street corner outside of Coyote for a few minutes, gazing at the stars and seeing instead a similar night sky twelve years ago. With the silence of the sleeping town all around her, Anna saw her father's face above hers in the darkness. Heard his earnest whisper. "Stay right where you are, and don't move until I return. I'll only be a little while."

"Papa, please. Let me come with you."

"Ssssh. You'll be safe here, and I'll only be gone a little while." Huddled under the overhanging bank of a dry creek bed, a frightened kid with very little English and a heart full of hope waited for her father's return.

Years later, when Anna closed her eyes, the dank odor of the earth in the roots overhead filled Anna's nostrils. The memory remained fresh, as if it had happened yesterday instead of twelve years before. She remembered cowering there, anxiety slowly building in her solar plexus as the hours passed and night bled into day, and day into night again. The taste of fear was so strong it was almost overwhelming.

She had emerged only when thirst drove her to it. The

creek had receded to the point where the water no longer flowed. Water bugs skated over the surface of the few shallow holes remaining. They were filled with tepid tea-colored liquid she'd dipped out with a small, cupped hand and drank greedily. On the bottom of the puddle, half-buried in the soft brown-green silt, lay the body of a rattlesnake. It had been there a long time, because the skin was starting to come off.

Anna remembered crouching on the rocks to vomit up all she drank, then she crawled back to the dirty haven under the bank where she hugged her knees and wept. The next morning, the woman came. With fluent Spanish, she coaxed Anna from hiding, offering her half of a peanut butter sandwich and some bottled water.

Anna, fevered from the water she'd consumed, had thought that she was dreaming. She'd never seen hair that flaming red before.

From then on, the memories grew soft and hazy. There was just a sense of sadness, mixed with the smell of clean sheets and as much chicken soup as she could eat. . . .

Carlotta had nursed her back to health, but every time Anna asked about her papa, she changed the subject. Contacting Juan's sister in California, she'd even checked them out, making sure Teresa Sandoval was on the up-and-up before turning Anna over to her. Years later, when she was old enough to understand, she'd learned the details of what happened that night in Nazareth, New Mexico—the night her father went out to steal a loaf of bread and was framed for a murder he didn't commit.

Anna took a deep breath of the cool night air and slowly exhaled, finally turning the corner and heading home. The apartment she leased from Carlotta was situated on the backside of State Street, a mere block from

Cottonwood Alley. The place was small, just three rooms and a bath above a garage Carlotta used for storage, but the price was right and the offbeat location afforded her a level of quiet she might not have had living along the main drag.

The street lamp outside her apartment was on the fritz again, and the shadows its absence cast were dark and deep. Broken glass crunched underfoot, glass that hadn't been there earlier in the day. Some kid with a pellet gun, most likely, and too much time on his hands.

The thought didn't ease the creepiness of a dark alley and darker stairwell or keep the skin at Anna's nape from crawling. It was weird, but she could have sworn something waited in the shadows between the buildings, crouching as it watched and waited, biding its time, malevolent in spirit, murderous in intent.

Anna shook off the anxiety. It was just the combination of the broken street lamps and her own imagination running away with her. She walked this same street every night after closing, and she'd never had a single incident. She was as safe walking home as she was waiting tables at Coyote Moon. Somehow, the reassurance fell flat, and she couldn't quite banish the eerie feeling that tonight was somehow different.

She quickened her steps, her pulse picking up its pace along with the increased adrenaline flow. Something separated from the base of a telephone pole, the threatening dark shape of a man.

"Anna." Harlan's voice sounded steady but far from reassuring. "I was beginnin' to think you weren't comin' home. The bar closed forty-five minutes ago. Everything all right?"

"Yes, why do you ask?" Anna struggled to contain the urge to turn and walk away. It was late, and though she wasn't sure why, his sudden appearance raised her hackles.

He shrugged in his jean jacket. He was off duty, and he should have been at home with his wife. "Just checking. Seth Whitlow happened to drive by your place earlier, and he mentioned that Deke Call's car was parked outside."

"Your deputy was watching my apartment?" That got Anna's back up.

Another shrug. He drew on a slim black cigar and blew smoke at the night sky. "No need to be upset, Anna. It's just a precaution. It's my job to keep a lid on things around here. Pretty girl like you sometimes invites trouble without meanin' to. Take Deke Call, for instance. You might want to tread carefully where he's concerned. That boy's a loose cannon. You can see it in his eyes."

"I appreciate your concern, Sheriff, but I can take care of myself. I don't need anyone looking out for me."

He smiled around the cigar. "That's good to know." He took a folded slip of paper from his jacket pocket and handed it to her. "My cell phone number. In case you need it. Get some sleep, Anna."

He turned and walked slowly away. Anna stood in the dark alley, watching until he was out of sight, but it was several minutes before she calmed enough to turn and mount the stairs.

Turning the key in the lock, she went inside and turned the latch, but she didn't turn the lights on. Instead, she went to the cabinet and took down a bottle of whiskey, splashing three fingers into a highball glass. She added some cream soda and sipped, breathing a tired sigh.

It sure had been a bitch of a day, and she had a feel-

ing of deep dissatisfaction gnawing at her that wouldn't
let up and wouldn't go away. The interview with Quincy
Bell, Matthew Call's former deputy, hadn't yielded
much in the way of leads. He'd claimed the bruises on
her father's face had been accidental, but Anna still had
cause to wonder. The mistreatment of a prisoner wasn't
something any cop was likely to admit to, especially
when that prisoner had turned up dead while in custody.
Bell had been present when Harlan interrogated Juan,
but neither man had admitted to anything, and since
it had been a joint venture, they would cover for one
another.

Of course, the possibility existed that Harlan was
telling the truth. There had been a few incidents over the
years in which detainees had complained about rough
treatment, but the complainants had impressive rap
sheets, and with no witnesses to back them up, the
charges were deemed unfounded.

Then there was the question of that night. When she'd
asked who had access to the cell, one name had come
up most often. Deke Call.

Deke was definitely a hard-ass, and she suspected
that he was capable of taking a life. But had he somehow managed to take Juan's, then make it look like a
suicide?

Anna's doubt kicked in. She could imagine him
taking revenge for the murders, but he wasn't exactly
the backdoor type, and making it look like a suicide was
a little too subtle to suit Deke's style.

Of course, if she were totally objective, she *had* slept
with him—a huge mistake but one she couldn't say she
wouldn't make again—and the memory of his arms
around her, the heat in his kiss, was still vivid. He'd
been so good, but had he killed her father? And if she

found out that he was responsible, could she drop a dime on him and make him pay?

One thing has nothing to do with the other, and yeah—if he did this, I'll drag his ass through the courts and see him put away. Anna sipped her drink and felt her momentary anger fade. It was crucial that she maintain a measure of objectivity and not allow her anger or her attraction to Deke to get in the way. She had no proof that he was responsible. Nothing but a retired deputy's word that he'd stood outside Juan's cell, staring through the bars and not saying a word. And what about the Call homicides? She knew Juan was innocent, which meant the murderer had never been caught.

It could be that the two incidents were directly related, that the person who'd shattered Deke's life had wrecked hers as well. The most frightening thing about that possibility was that she was the only one who realized it.

It was sobering how much Joaquin Aguilar and Deke had in common. Under ordinary circumstances, they might have been friends. Aguilar wasn't a product of the streets. He'd come from good family in a small Mexican border town, but when his father was killed at thirty-nine, Joaquin had been forced to assume responsibility for the family. Times were tough in portions of the Southwest, but it was worse in Mexico. A man couldn't make a decent living unless he had connections or could manage to cross the border and find work in the U.S. Opportunity was more plentiful there, Joaquin knew, so he made the decision and took the leap along with fifty-three others—men, women, and kids.

Joaquin paid the smuggler fifteen-hundred dollars

and was packed into an airless trailer along with the others. But the truck broke down in the desert, and the driver, panicked by the prospect of being discovered by the border patrol, abandoned the truck and left the illegals to die. By the time they found a way out, the women and kids had succumbed to heat exhaustion and perished. Five out of fifty-three survived, Joaquin among them. With his family in his thoughts, he melted into the desert and never looked back. But the American dream proved illusive, and Joaquin had his sights set higher than a job cutting some rich guy's grass. He drifted to southern California where he was introduced to gang culture.

He learned quickly that if a man was careful, there was serious money to be made on the shady side of the law. And money mattered more than anything. Over the course of five years, he worked his way up on the inside of a Mexican gang, until the rivalry between him and the second in command turned bloody and he was forced to run. He moved east to Tucson and found what he was looking for in the Diablos. Within months, he had assumed the position of command.

By the time Deke walked into the warehouse the Diablos used as headquarters, Joaquin's organization had taken on the well-oiled look of a mini-mafia. Little Eduardo preceded Deke past a pair of gang members guarding the door—beefy, early twenties, and heavily armed with automatic weapons. Deke didn't acknowledge that they were even there. He kept his cool, aware that all eyes were on him, assessing whether he posed a threat. Eduardo clasped hands with two of those gathered, but it was a dark-haired man about Deke's age he addressed. *"Ese,* man. What's up? Hey, Joaquin. This is the dude I was tellin' you about. His name's Call, but Chaca fits him better."

Aguilar didn't approach. His gaze was curious but cold. "Pat him down," he told the goons who guarded the door. "He's got to be carryin'. No man's fool enough to come onto Diablo turf unarmed."

Deke held his arms out at his sides, submitting to the search for weapons. They took the 9mm he'd bought at a pawn shop on the other side of town and planted, along with his switchblade. Everything was riding on this moment—success, survival; no banger worth shit would walk the streets unarmed. Better to be seen as hostile than weak. The weak sure as hell didn't live long.

Aguilar was surprisingly well spoken, an intelligent man in a unique position. "Eduardo says you're new in town. That you're on your own."

"I blew in about a month ago," Deke said. "I've got family in Albuquerque, but they got nothin' more to do with me."

"What do you do, Chaca?" Then, when Deke didn't answer, "How do you live? A man's got to do something to make money."

A shrug. "I do what I have to do to get by, until somethin' better comes along. You thinking of makin' an offer? I'm all ears."

Aguilar smiled. "Could be. I could use a good man, in case Eduardo does somethin' stupid, like getting whacked. But I'm careful about who I let in, so we'll see." He turned to Eduardo and the smile faded. "Keep him close. He doesn't breathe that you don't count the breaths. I'll be in touch. Now, get him outta here. We got business to discuss."

He turned his back, dismissing Deke, but it wasn't

until he walked out into the cool December air that he realized he'd been sweating. . . .

The cell rang and Deke opened his eyes. He'd stretched out on the bed, fully clothed, but he hadn't slept more than an hour since coming in at midnight. Most nights were hell. He lay awake, the past playing in his head like an R-rated movie. The mistakes he'd made, the price everyone had paid, and was still paying.

Darkness came and the haunting began.

He glanced at the alarm on the bedside table. Four forty-three. The sun hadn't begun to rise yet, but it would before long. He rolled over onto his right side and felt the usual hitch in his ribs. Anna had questioned him about the livid scars, but he'd avoided telling her anything. It wasn't in his nature to answer questions. He'd spent too much time keeping everything in to share himself with anyone. It had been part of the job. A crucial part. One leak, one stupid misstep, could cost him his life—and almost had.

It was different with women. In his experience, secrecy was something they just didn't understand. But as the thought gelled and he reached for the phone on the nightstand, it occurred to him that Anna was different. The girl had secrets of her own she was keeping.

The phone continued to bleat. He checked the number, but it was blocked. Unidentified caller. No data. Few people had his cellular number, so he picked it up. "Call."

"Deacon." An icy bolt shot through his vitals. "Oh God—Deacon . . . I'm in trouble. . . ."

Deke ran a hand through his hair. He was sitting on the edge of the bed in the seedy hotel room he rented, the wallpaper faded and colorless in the predawn gloom, and he was barely able to breathe. "Mama?"

"Deacon . . . God help me," she said, and the phone went dead.

Dread surged up from the pit of his stomach, crowding his heart and lungs so that he fought for every breath.

It couldn't be.

It was some sort of sick joke.

It had to be. Yet even as he tried to talk himself out of this feeling of urgency, Deke knew his mother could still be alive. There had been no blood evidence at the scene to negate the possibility that somehow Maddy had gotten away, that somehow she had survived the carnage.

It was a scenario he'd replayed in his mind a million times since that night, always searching for answers to the nagging questions that arose from it.

How had she survived?

Where was she?

Why had she stayed away all these years?

And the most troubling question of all . . . *Had she been involved in the carnage?*

Could the mother he'd loved his entire life, who'd been so giving, so caring, so protective of her family, have been a party to their destruction?

No. It wasn't possible. She would have died protecting them.

Never in a million years could she have harmed a member of her own family.

Yet there were times when he couldn't prevent the cop from creeping in, when he couldn't keep the things he'd seen from jading his view of everything, even Maddy. A man didn't see the things he'd seen and remain untouched, untainted by it. Mothers who sold their children to pedophiles or put them in dumpsters, as if they were

trash. Suburbanites who kept up appearances on the outside while hiding a cooler in their attic containing the
body of a three-year-old who they'd starved to death.
Shit happened, and seemingly normal people did crazy
things for no good reason, plunging in an instant to a
subhuman level.

*Oh God, Deacon . . . I'm in trouble. . . . Deacon . . .
Deacon . . . Deacon. . . . Oh God, Deacon . . . I'm in
trouble. . . .*

Deke's gut wrenched, tension coiling so tightly he
couldn't bear it a second longer. If she were alive, if
she'd somehow found her way back here, if she needed
his help, there was one place she would go—one. Grabbing his keys and putting the phone in his jacket pocket
before he could talk himself out of it, he went out.

Every window in the farmhouse blazed with light.
Deke tried to tell himself that there was nothing abnor-
mal about that, but the front door hanging ajar triggered
an involuntary tightening of his stomach muscles, and
the hair rose on the back of his neck. It didn't take much
to flash back to that night twelve years ago, the night his
world shifted on its axis and everything changed. . . .

Another predawn. He was late coming home. Curfew
was midnight, but he couldn't help pushing the old
man's buttons. Maybe it was because he was such a disappointment, or the fact that he was somebody else's
kid, but Matthew Call had ridden him like a rented mule
since the ink dried on the marriage license. He knew
other kids his age who had the same sort of shit to deal
with and just put up with it. Go along to get along. But
Deke's heart was as hard as his head, and the more
Matthew Call applied the spurs, the harder he bucked.

He didn't have it in his nature to do otherwise, but he did have one regret—it put his mother square in the middle.

She'd be waiting up now, he thought, praying he'd get home before her husband so she could smooth things over . . . just like always. Only that night it was different. All of the house lights were on, blazing footlights for the gruesome scene that greeted him when he went inside. . . .

Deke took the Colt from the glove box, slipped it into the waistband of his jeans at the small of his back, and walked cautiously up the sidewalk. He shouldered the door to avoid leaving prints, and it swung silently open. "Hello?" he called out.

No one answered.

Nothing moved, nothing breathed.

The house seemed to be holding its breath. The tension in his gut kept building. Every nerve sang, every cell screamed. Details leaped out at him, surreal in their similarity to that other night. The overturned chair in the living room, the broken lamp, the afghan lying in a soft puddle on the floor. The sense of sorrow and loss that seemed to seep from the paneled walls, from the newly carpeted floors—but was it real? Or just his imagination?

"Maddy?" Deke called his mother's name, aware that she might not recognize him. "Maddy Call?"

Nothing but stony silence, punctuated by the distant howl of a coyote outside.

His pulse hammering in his ears, Deke walked toward the kitchen, just as he had that night. He could see the toe portion of a small bare foot protruding just beyond the doorway.

Jesus.

"Maddy?" he tried one more time. Then, "Mama, it's Deke. You called and I'm here. Whatever's wrong, I'll make it all right. Just come out, please."

He reached the doorway to the kitchen, and his breath froze in his lungs. The boy, Billy, lay on his side. His eyes were closed, his face unnaturally pale. The harmonica lay inches away on the linoleum. Deke picked it up and put it in his pocket, then lay two fingers on the boy's carotid artery to confirm what he already knew. On the other side of the overturned table was the boy's father, his face so beaten, so bloody, it was unrecognizable. The tension that had been steadily building inside Deke tied itself into a large knot as he took out his cell phone and dialed.

"Alamance County Sheriff's Office. This is Dispatch. What's your emergency?"

"Dixie, this is Deke Call. Find Harlan and tell him to get out to the Miller farm right away. Somethin' really bad's gone down out here."

Harlan was dreaming of Anna, and he resented the hell out of being dragged awake by a phone call. The numbers on the digital alarm on the bedside table glowed a fuzzy red. He fumbled for and found his glasses. Five minutes after five. He'd been home for an hour and asleep for half that, he thought, grabbing the phone while rubbing the sand from his eyes. "Sheriff Harlan Rudy—"

Harlan listened as Dixie rattled off the information, which wasn't much. "I don't know more than that. He identified himself, said there was a situation at the Miller farm, and that I was to notify you right away."

"Give me the caller's name again." He'd heard it

clearly the first time, but some perverse impulse made him ask anyway. For some weird reason, he needed to hear it again.

"He said it was Deke Call, Sheriff."

Deke Call. The last time Deke called the sheriff's department had been an early morning call too. He'd been seventeen then, a little wild, a lot good looking, and hell with the young ladies.

Not much had changed as far as Harlan was concerned. That night, he'd been reporting the double homicide he'd walked in on after coming home from a late date. There had been a few times over the years when Harlan had wondered if the possibility existed—when doubts about the boy's involvement crept in. Just as quickly, he shut them down. There hadn't been a single shred of evidence to support such a theory, and he couldn't afford to admit—personally or professionally—that the possibility that Martinez had been an innocent man existed. "I'll get right on it," he said, and hung up the phone.

Beside him, Ginny stirred, her sleep mask reminding him of the black-and-white westerns the local TV station played sometimes on Saturday mornings. All she needed was a white hat and a friend named Tonto. "What's wrong?" She sounded drugged; the sleeping pills she took religiously hadn't worn off yet.

"I don't know yet, but it's probably nothin'. Go back to sleep."

"You're going out again? You just got in a little while ago." It was amazing how she could fly from a dead sleep and into a full state of fuss at the thought of him leaving the house before the sun came up.

Jesus Christ, you would think she would have gotten past it by now. His affair with Maddy had happened thirty years ago. He and Ginny had married fresh out of high school. Three years into it, they'd run into some really rough waters, but instead of bringing them closer, it drove them apart. She'd gone home to her parents for a while, and he'd really believed it was over. He hadn't planned on falling in love again, but there was no way he could avoid loving Maddy. She'd brought a shining light into his life that he'd never imagined was possible, and for the first time he'd felt free. But Ginny had come home again, and Maddy moved on to greener pastures. That had ended it. He'd never mentioned Maddy again, though he'd never forgotten her either.

Harlan sighed. It was bad enough he'd be sleep deprived, he didn't need her giving him the third degree on top of it. "It's my job, and some night's are like that. After thirty-three years of marriage, I'd think you'd get used to it."

But she had never gotten used to not knowing where he was, or what he was doing, or who he was with.

"Can't you let your deputy handle it?"

"No, goddamn it, I can't!"

She stiffened beside him, as cold as an iceberg in that moment. "Whitlow is a newlywed with a baby on the way. He pulled the late shift all last week. I'm not waking him so I can stay here and fight with you." Reaching out, he squeezed her shoulder, a lame attempt to pacify her. "I'll call you at nine, just like always," he promised, deliberately softening his tone. "Just go back to sleep. It'll be all right." But he wondered as he left the house if it would ever be all right again.

When he arrived at the old Call place, Deke's car was parked at the berm in front, as if he belonged here. The man himself leaned against the back bumper, his arms crossed, waiting. From the garish tattoos that covered his arms, to the long hair and twin gold loops in his ears, Deke Call was the personification of all Harlan's many prejudices. Damned if he didn't look like he belonged in a street gang. And he'd been a cop. It was damned hard to imagine.

The glare Harlan shot the younger man brimmed with malice. "This is the second time I've come out here before dawn and found you on the premises. Exactly what the fuck is goin' on?"

"You need to go inside and see for yourself, but take your cell phone. You're gonna need to call the state boys for a forensic team."

Harlan started to argue, then thought better of it. He walked to the door and shouldered it wide without putting a hand on it. Then gingerly, he stepped inside while Deke waited by his car.

He was in the house for ten minutes. As first officer on scene, he would have to do the preliminaries himself, noting every detail that could be caught at a glance, how the bodies were positioned and anything out of place. That was just the beginning.

When finally he emerged, his pique at having his wrinkled old ass dragged out of bed had vanished. That kind of sight was always sobering, and he'd taken on the same no-nonsense persona he'd worn the night of the first murders. "I need answers, son—before this place is swarming with outsiders. Suppose you tell me what the hell you're doin', callin' in a double homicide—again?"

"I drove past and somethin' didn't look right, so I stopped," Deke said. "As for why I called it in—why the hell wouldn't I? Somebody had to."

"What are you doin' out in this neck of the woods at the crack of dawn?"

"I was on my way to see Lucas—and it may be early to a white-eyes sheriff but not to Lucas. He greets the sunrise with a ritual most mornings."

Harlan's blue eyes hardened. "I'd watch the native shit if I were you. For all you know your daddy was a white-eyes."

Deke answered with a glare.

"So you passed by, in the dark, and noticed that somethin' wasn't right. Was this some sort of gut feeling left over from your glory days?"

"There wasn't any glory in it," Deke said calmly. It didn't matter that he didn't like the man questioning him, he knew the drill, and he knew that Harlan was a cop to the bone. He would say anything to get under Deke's skin, to piss him off, get him to say the wrong thing. "The lights were all on, and the door was open . . . just like it was that night. So I called out, then walked in—"

That got the older man's back up. "You walked in? On a crime scene?"

"That's what I said."

"You touch anything? Disturb anything? Remove anything?"

"I checked the kid's carotid to see if he was still alive. He was already gone, and starting to lose his warmth. Then I used my phone to call your office." Deke waited a few seconds, then asked, "You notice how it looked in there? You see the similarities? It's been staged perfectly, right down to the last detail." It was enough to make his skin crawl.

Harlan said nothing, but Deke could read his thoughts. *Where was the woman, Mrs. Miller?*

"You done with me?" Deke said finally. "I got some place to be."

Harlan nodded. "I'm done with you—for now." He let Deke get as far as the driver's door of his car. "Deke?"

Deke met his gaze, careful to give nothing, show nothing.

"Why'd you quit? You had everything goin' for you."

Because he could no longer look in the mirror without hating the man looking back at him. Because the price he'd paid for success had been too damned high. Because if he lost one more person he cared about, it would kill him. He said nothing. He just got in the car and drove away, aware that Harlan watched him until he was out of sight.

Chapter Six

Somewhere in the back of Harlan's mind, Maddy still lived, just as beautiful and full of spark as she'd been that long ago summer, before she'd crushed his dreams by telling him she was pregnant by another man. If he allowed his focus to turn inward, she'd be right there, lying in the tall grass by the shores of Mirror Lake. Lucas had worked hard that summer, but they'd still had plenty of time to spend together. For a split second, he saw a youthful version of himself smiling as he watched her, so full of love for her that he thought he'd bust wide open. Then he pulled himself out of the fantasy and back to the present.

Deke's taillights faded into the early morning mist, a grim reminder of just how disappointingly the dream had ended. There had been a time shortly thereafter when he'd asked himself if it was possible that Maddy had lied to him about the boy's paternity—but he just couldn't imagine her ever being that cruel. Having a child with her would have changed everything. It might have been difficult for a while, but he would have extricated himself from his marriage to Ginny. In fact, he would have given up everything if only—

Whether it would have been better for Deke to have a father who'd loved him instead of one who despised him was pure speculation. He'd never been a father, so how the hell could he know?

It had all come down differently. Maddy had cut him off at the knees a few days after Ginny returned from her parents' by telling him she'd been seeing someone else and was having the man's baby. She'd gone away for a year or so, staying with friends, he'd heard, and when she'd come home, she'd had the black-haired, black-eyed boy who looked nothing at all like Harlan. She took a job waiting tables at Café Matamoros, raising the child with Lucas's help, and life went on in Nazareth.

Harlan had asked her once, and only once, why the boy had no father. She'd shrugged, saying that life had come apart at the seams while trying to make a go of it with Deke's daddy, but everything was okay now that she was home. She and her son were happy. She'd never have done anything to upset that. Harlan's hand had rested on her wrist as he looked down into her eyes, and that was how Ginny found them.

Ginny hadn't said anything in front of Maddy, but he'd paid for it many times over. He'd spent the next six years trying to put their marriage back on solid ground, pretending that he didn't know anything genuine or giving existed. In the meantime, his Maddy started seeing Matthew, and Deke's long slide began.

Harlan settled his hat more securely on his head, putting the past aside, getting down to business. He'd just finished a careful inspection of the area when the patrol car nosed in behind his pickup. Whitlow looked rested, his uniform crisp and clean. By comparison, Harlan had thrown on the jeans and striped shirt he'd worn the night before, but with lack of sleep turning his eyes sandy and his temper frayed, he felt as old as Methuselah instead of fifty-one.

Police work was a thankless job, with too much stress and too little pay. Watching Whitlow drag the crime kit from the trunk of the car and carry it to the sidewalk, he wondered if it might not be time to hang it up and go fishing. Leave the job to a younger man. Some fool fire-eater who was eager for it. He had enough time logged for his pension and a nice little nest egg to tide him over till the monthly checks kicked in. If he was careful, he could swing it. Maybe with some time alone, he and Ginny could heal the rift between them and make something decent from what remained of their marriage. Maybe . . . but definitely not today.

"Two bodies inside," Harlan told his deputy. "Looks like John Miller and his son, Billy, but I can only be sure about the boy. I did a cursory search from attic to basement, and there's no red flag as to Mrs. Miller's absence. Could be she's with friends, or away, or maybe she ran—"

Whitlow frowned. "You think she had something to do with this?"

Harlan shrugged. "It's a possibility, but I haven't drawn any conclusions yet. We need to put some feelers out, see if we can locate her—then, if we fail, an APB and missing persons."

"Boy, I sure don't like the way this feels, Sheriff. With what happened here before—" He was staring up at the house, remembering the grisly details of the Call case. "They never did find Deke's mama. Not a trace." He shuddered. "Jesus. You don't suppose it could happen again?"

"Don't go there until you have to, son. Let's concentrate on what we need to do. Get the tape up and cordon off the area. Then photograph the outside. Check the vehicle too. It's on the south side of the house. Don't overlook anything. We'll get it hauled to impound before we leave. I'm goin' back inside." He handed the deputy one of the two cameras that were department property and a half-dozen rolls of film. "If you run into trouble just give a yell."

With Whitlow overseeing the operation on the outside, Harlan returned to the house. Deke had immediately picked up on certain similarities between the original crime scene and this one, details that leaped out at him too. Deke had pointed out that the scene had been perfectly staged, down to the last detail, and he was right.

The chances of that occurring naturally were practically nil, which left one possibility. Someone with intimate knowledge of the Call murders had killed Miller and his boy, then set the stage to mimic the first crimes.

Down to the last damned detail. Definitely a scream for attention. That raised Harlan's hackles.

Call had strongly advised him to call in the state police, but Harlan had his own way of doing things, and he wasn't ready to have uniformed troopers stepping all over his turf. This was his ball game, and he'd handle it until he decided he no longer could. It was a matter of pride, and more than that, it was personal. Once word of this hit the wires, it would be broadcast and print news far beyond the state lines, and when that happened, there were going to be comparisons and questions.

Harlan bristled at the thought. He didn't like being

questioned, but it was bound to happen and he needed to be ready for it. When the questions came, he'd have a handle on it. With that thought uppermost in his mind, he rolled up his sleeves and dug in.

The boy lay closest to the interior wall. He was curled on his side, his eyes closed, and except for the stark white of his skin and his blue-tinged lips, he might have been sleeping. His freckles seemed abnormally dark postmortem, black dots on skin as pale and fragile as parchment. Harlan photographed the room, then the kid and the area around him, careful to get shots from every angle. In his notepad, he drew a brief sketch of the room and noted the positioning of the bodies in relation to the room and each other, then took measurements and made more notations, and then moved onto the second victim.

Was it John Miller? Damned if he could tell. The victim had been felled by a blow to the throat, then beaten as he lay on the floor. Multiple blows had cut flesh and shattered bone, leaving a mass of pulpy flesh, drying blood, and bone fragments but nothing recognizable as a human face. Holding a ruler a few inches above the floor, he angled the camera to shoot both it and the pool of blood congealing under the man's head. Then he concentrated on the blood spatter. Ceiling, refrigerator door, cabinets. It was everywhere. Overkill, and he strongly suspected the vic had already been dead when some of the beating had occurred.

When he finally left the house, the day was pretty well spent and Harlan's ass was dragging. Whitlow leaned against the fender of his squad car, chatting with the two ambulance attendants. The medical examiner was just pulling in. Harlan sat down on the car's fender, trying to concentrate just on filling his lungs with untainted air. It felt good, but he knew from experience that nothing would chase the metallic smell of coagulating blood from his nostrils and throat but a full twenty minutes in a hot shower.

Levi Grant grasped Harlan's hand and shook it. "Sheriff. I got your message. It sounded important. What do we have here?"

"Two victims, homicide, and it's a bad one. The scene's been processed, but I'll go over it again once the bodies are removed."

"Then let's get to it," Grant said. He motioned to the pair of attendants, who broke off their conversation to join him on the sidewalk. The trio moved forward single file, stopping at the door to don disposable paper booties before entering the house. Harlan followed close behind. The ME bagged the bodies, and he and the attendants exited the scene, careful to backtrack in their own footsteps.

"High priority," Grant promised. "I hate it when kids are involved."

"Me too," Harlan agreed. The last thing he did was to screw a heavy hasp onto all three entrances and padlock each one. *No one intrudes on my crime scenes unless they are invited in, invited to give their input. No one, that is, except Deke Call.*

Harlan's right palm itched ferociously, as it always did when he was annoyed. Deke Call had been a thorn in his side ever since he hit town, and given this morning's phone call, it wasn't likely to change.

By the time Deke got to Lucas's place, the sun was starting to rise. The eastern sky above the Sangre de Cristo range was tinged with rose, a lovely contrast to the deep mysterious gray of the white-capped mountains. There was nothing pretty about the morning so far, however, or about Deke's mood for that matter. As he got out of the car, he felt ragged and worn, so edgy that any quick movement would have him coming apart at the seams.

The house lights were on, but that didn't mean much. The house lights had been on at the Miller place. They'd been on that night twelve years before too. Somehow, it almost made it worse. It signaled to Deke there had been no attempt to hide the dark deeds, and from a psychological perspective, it might even be seen as highlighting the killer's work.

Take a good look at what I've done. It was the message he got from it. *Aren't you impressed? You should be. I've taken great care setting the stage.*

And he had—taken great care. Down to the most minute detail. It was a clear statement. Bold to the point of being brazen. Whoever did the Miller homicides wasn't worried about getting caught. Either he was insane or he was accustomed to killing.

Neither scenario eased Deke's mind. He'd been shaken enough by the phone call to abandon any pretense of caution and go out there, but the moment he'd stepped into the house, he'd had the weird notion he was stepping into the jaws of a trap.

When he'd seen the harmonica lying beside the boy, he'd had little choice except to take it. His prints were all over it, and maybe his saliva too. He didn't want Harlan to know he was at the house earlier, for obvious reasons, and he might not buy the excuse that it had been left there before the Millers moved in, even if it was the truth. It wouldn't matter that he barely knew the victims and didn't have a motive. He'd taken evidence from a crime scene, and he'd deliberately lied to the investigating officer. That was damning enough to land him at the top of Harlan's suspect list, and it sure as hell didn't help that they hated one another.

He was two steps from the porch when a sharp whistle brought him around toward the mountain range. Walking across the dew-laden meadow was Lucas, rifle in hand, looking healthy and fit. Deke let go of the breath he'd been unconsciously holding, turning and walking toward him. They met at the sheep fence.

"You're up early," Lucas said.

"I could say the same for you. Everything all right?"

Lucas nodded. "Doin' a little reconnaissance. I feel better, keepin' an eye on things. Been quiet, though, since that turkey hunter nailed me. I did hear an owl night before last, but it was a distance away. Maybe that *chindi*'s decided to go play tricks on somebody else."

Deke was quiet, ominously so. Lucas could tell something was eating away at him, something more than his usual restlessness. It would do no good to question him, so he didn't. He just allowed the peaceful silence of the morning to settle in between them. He'd talk when he was ready, and not before. They watched the sun rise above the ridge, painting the earth and trees in a soft hazy pink. "Pretty morning," Lucas said after a while. "It's always been my favorite time of day."

A muscle jumped in the younger man's cheek. "You never said much about Mama—about what you thought had happened. About where she went, or why she never came home."

Lucas sighed. "Some things are better left unsaid. There was nothing to confirm what I thought, and at the time you had enough to deal with, just gettin' your life pulled back together. I didn't see any point in addin' to it."

"You think she's dead." There was an edge to the statement that sent a chill through Lucas's insides.

"Don't you?"

"For years I thought so, but I don't know what to believe anymore."

Lucas watched the morning unfold. "It don't really matter what a man believes, as long as he believes in somethin'."

Deke released a breath, but it didn't seem to lessen the tension that rolled off him in waves or ease Lucas's concern for his nephew. "I got a phone call a couple of hours ago," he said. "It was Mama's voice. She called me by name, and she said she's in trouble."

Lucas digested that, or tried to, but he was unsure what to say. He'd always known his sister Maddy was dead. Otherwise she would have found a way back, or a way to contact them, to let them know she was okay. She'd had an unbreakable connection to this place, and to her family. "Sounds like somebody's playin' a prank. The mean-spirited kind."

"That's what I told myself," Deke said. "But the possibility existed, and no matter how remote, I had to find out for myself."

"So that's why you're up with the sun," Lucas observed.

"I drove to the house. I knew that if she were alive and found a way back here, that's where she'd be—" He broke off, the muscle working furiously in his cheek. "The door was open when I got there, so I called out and went inside. They were lying on the kitchen floor. The boy didn't have a mark on him, but I'm just about certain he'd been smothered. His old man's face had been beaten in, and the boy's mama—"

"Nowhere to be found." Lucas asked his ancestors to put the right words in his mouth, the words Deke needed to hear. But when the old ones remained ominously quiet, he sighed. "So, it's happened again. I wish I could say I was surprised. I've felt the clock ticking ever since they closed the books on the original case. I even told Harlan it was just a matter of time before the real murderer resurfaced. He called me a fool. Said it was over and done with. I'd say he was dead wrong."

Deke shook a cigarette out of his pack and offered one to his uncle. He knew what Lucas was about to say, and he wasn't ready to hear it. This was a copycat crime, he was convinced of it. Anything else was unthinkable.

"The arrest came too quick, too easy, and the fact that Martinez never lived to recant that confession made everything suspect. Awfully convenient, to have it over that quick—convenient for one man—Harlan."

Deke shook his head. "I don't like Harlan Rudy any better than you do, but the fact remains that Martinez confessed, and I'm not so sure I believe he was fond enough of his predecessor to kill his prisoner in cold blood and make it look like a suicide."

"You're a cop. You know better than I do that evidence can be manufactured. Harlan had a huge mess dumped into his lap, the biggest crime this county had ever seen. He needed to solve it, and fast. He'd been salivatin' over the job for years, you know. Not that he had any hope of ever winning that office—not so long as Matthew Call was alive. Then, all of a sudden, Matthew's dead and the roadblocks are gone . . . he's got what he wanted all along, but he can't afford to look incompetent if he wants to keep it. Folks around here needed a scapegoat, and Harlan provided it for 'em. Some would consider that good business."

"I'm an ex-cop," Deke insisted, for what seemed like the millionth time since he'd dumped his career and come home. On some level he knew that Lucas had a valid point. He just wished the older man weren't so free at speaking his mind. The sheriff was ass-deep in a murder investigation, and Deke knew how fast loose talk could turn on you. If Rudy learned that Lucas had been expecting something bad to happen at the scene of the first murders, it could easily translate into the suspicion that somehow Lucas did something to make it happen.

You're a cop. You know better than I do that evidence can be manufactured.

Deke frowned. He *did* know. He'd seen it done. He'd seen officers lie during interrogations to make a suspect think that indisputable evidence existed linking them to the crime, when the cops involved had little more than a hunch to go on. Hints of a phantom eyewitness, fiber evidence that didn't exist or hadn't been found, endless pressure applied over as many hours as it took to wear the suspect down physically and psychologically and to force a confession . . . *just tell us what we want to know and you can go home.*

As bad as things could be in any police department in any city, at least some parameters existed, boundaries within which officers were forced to work to avoid a case being thrown out because a suspect was denied his rights. It was different with someone like Harlan. He ran the county as he saw fit, and few people dared to question him openly.

The man had connections. The county prosecutor was Harlan's wife's second cousin, and Judge Riley Oscar and he went way back. Aside from being poker buddies, they shared the same hardline, zero-tolerance, throw-the-book-at-'em philosophy that stopped just a few notches short of turning the county into a police state, or at the very least trying to.

Not that Deke could afford to hurl accusations. He'd done a lot of things that couldn't withstand a close scrutiny from an ethical standpoint. Things he didn't like to remember but couldn't seem to forget.

"Be careful what you say," Deke warned, even though he knew Lucas wouldn't listen. "Harlan'll be lookin' for somebody with motive, and remarks like that'll put you square in his sights."

"Maybe I got a lot less to hide than he does," Lucas suggested.

"If that's true, then it makes him twice as dangerous." A flash of reflected sunlight caught Deke's attention, the kind that shot off a windshield and chrome. Shielding his eyes, he watched Carlotta's old van round the bend in the lane. Its driver conjured up images of damp tangled sheets and a shadowed bedroom, the acrid but not unpleasant smell of hot sex and the light sheen of sweat on her upper lip as she lay beneath him. "Kind of early for company, ain't it?"

"That's not company," Lucas said. "That's Anna, and I been expectin' her. I invited her to breakfast. She wants to interview me for her book."

"Is that so?" Deke said nothing as he watched her park the van and get out. She wore a tight red T-shirt with a deep U-neckline that ended a good three inches from where her cleavage began; the sight of her made his mouth water. Sometimes it took a while for attraction to dim, but sooner or later he'd tire of seeing her. Or at least that's what he told himself.

It was purely physical. Hot sex without the painful relationship dance most women insisted on doing and which he wanted no part of. Mutual indulgence without any emotional strings. It was fine to be intrigued by her—and he was—as long as he didn't allow himself to get dragged in. Keep it casual and nobody got hurt. He was no damned good at long-term anything. "You gonna talk about that night, maybe I should sit in."

"I thought you didn't want any part of this," Lucas said.

He hadn't wanted any part of it, but things had changed when he'd walked into the house that morning and found the Miller boy and his old man dead on the kitchen floor. The similarities in both crime scenes were too obvious to miss. Something weird was going down, something he couldn't afford to ignore. If Anna was who she claimed to be, then she'd been researching the original murders for some time. Could be she had information he didn't have, information that would tell him if there was a viable link to past events and present, other than some psycho's sick need for déjà vu. "I changed my mind."

Lucas looked amused. "This have something to do with that tight top she's wearin'?"

Deke pushed away from the fence and started toward the porch. "It sure as hell don't hurt."

"She sure is pretty," Lucas said, catching up. "Too bad she's not twenty years older. Woman like that's enough to make a man want to give up his wild ways and settle down."

It wasn't the reaction Deke had to her, but he kept his thoughts to himself as she approached.

Lucas's invitation had seemed like the perfect opportunity, the very one Anna had been hoping for. She'd thought about Lucas a lot since their last conversation.

Not only was he a fascinating character, they shared common ground. They both believed in Juan Martinez's innocence, and possibly his murder. So when the older man called and invited her to breakfast, she'd jumped at the chance. Had she known that invitation would include his nephew, she might not have been so quick to accept it.

She'd been hoping to let the dust settle before seeing him again. The heat they'd ignited between the sheets had barely begun to fade. One glance at him, leaning against the porch support, his hands stuffed into the pockets of his jeans and his arms bare to the chill morning air, was enough to shake Anna's confidence, and the restless certainty that she'd made a huge mistake stirred to life within her once again.

She'd thought she could handle this, handle him.

She'd told herself sleeping with him one time wouldn't change anything.

She'd sworn that the job she had to do was too important, too sacred to allow anything to interfere.

And it was crucial, but the fact remained that no one handled Deke Call. He was as secretive as he was dangerous, unpredictable, and wild. Not only could Anna not anticipate his next move, she couldn't say with any certainty that it would only be one time.

"Mornin'," Lucas said, grasping her hands and lightly kissing her cheek.

"I hope I'm not interrupting," Anna said, her glance sliding to the younger man leaning against the porch.

"Nope," Lucas replied. "Your timing's perfect. I was just about to fire up the griddle. How's stuffed French toast sound?"

Anna smiled. "Sara Lee?"

Lucas just chuckled. "The Swift-Water special,

actually. I do cook occasionally. Come on in, make yourself comfortable."

Anna preceded Lucas into the house and took a moment to look around. The place was surprisingly spacious. The living area and kitchen had the feel of a mini great room, with a rustic stone fireplace against the western wall. The furnishings were sturdy and comfortable looking, the artist's only attempt at embellishment a few framed photos on the mantle and a bright woolen rug on the hardwood floor in front of the fireplace.

Anna wandered into the living room, stopping in front of the mantle to look at the photos. She was aware that Deke had entered and stood watching her from the doorway. "Do you mind?" Anna asked Lucas, indicating the photos.

"Not at all. Deke? You want to do the honors? I got my hands full out here."

The first photo was an artistic shot of Lucas and a hound of undetermined age. Lucas, seated in his rocker on the front porch, stared off into the distance while the dog stared adoringly up at Lucas. "That's Obee," Deke said, his voice low and very near Anna's ear. His nearness, the sound of his voice, and the tickle of his breath against the hollow beneath her ear raised a shiver that chased down Anna's spine.

Anna admired the photo for a few more seconds, then moved on to the young man in uniform. It was a snapshot, not the typical formal shot with dress uniform and stoic expression. The jungle setting was foreign, the M16 rifle he carried and his alert, war-weary expression testament to the danger he was facing. "It was taken in '68," Deke offered. "Good luck askin' him about it, though. He doesn't like to talk about it."

"Like uncle, like nephew," Anna murmured. His gaze

clashed with hers, impenetrable black with soft, chocolate brown, and she caught her breath.

"That would depend on what it is you want to talk about," he said. "I got a lot to say about some things."

"Such as?" Her voice had taken on a teasing quality. He responded with a smile. It was amazing how the simple lifting of the corners of that hard mouth changed his face, brought a warm glint to his eyes, the suggestion of the blatant sexuality Anna had already sampled. As that familiar warmth pooled in her belly, she suspected that a mere sampling wasn't nearly enough. The thought was terrifying.

He glanced at Lucas, but the older man was tending the griddle. "Like what you had in mind by comin' out here."

"Lucas invited me to breakfast," Anna said. "And I accepted. It's that simple."

"I get the feelin' that nothin' is ever simple where you're concerned. Take that book you're supposed to be writin'. Why is it there's nothing pertaining to it on your computer's hard drive?" Deke waited for her reply, wondering if he'd played his hand too soon, carefully weighing her reaction.

"You searched my files?"

Annoyance but zero surprise. She'd been expecting him to get around to it, but the question remained: what did she have to hide? "I do my homework. Mystery woman arrives in town, askin' a lot of questions for a book that may or may not exist. Makes a man curious. You haven't answered the question, Anna."

Reaching into the front pocket of her jeans, she extracted a small metallic key with a USB connector on one end. "A flash drive, the paranoid writer's best friend. I don't like to share my work with anyone, and a girl can't be too careful. You'd be surprised how many people there are who don't respect a simple right to privacy."

She'd gotten her jab in and seemed content to let it go at that. Reaching out, she lifted the last photo from the mantle, studying it a long time before looking back at him. "She was so young," she said.

"She turned nineteen two days after I was born," Deke admitted. It was strange that he could even say it, that telling her about Maddy would feel almost—natural. He wasn't the kind of man who shared himself with anyone, and for a few seconds, he almost wished that he could take the admission back.

"Your father wasn't around?"

"You askin' for the book or for yourself?"

"I don't know. Maybe both."

At least she'd been honest. "There's little to tell on that score. She never talked about him. Didn't matter how many times I'd ask, I never did get an answer. Maybe she thought I was better off not knowin'. Then she met Matthew, and he played the big man and gave me his name."

"You didn't like your adopted father?"

"No love lost, either way, believe me. We never got on, and coexisting for her sake was pure-D hell. What about you? You must have an interesting story to tell . . . I mean, there are a lot of crimes out there to pick from. Why'd you want to write about this one?"

She shrugged. "It caught my attention years ago. I'm not so sure I believe that Juan Martinez was guilty. What makes a better read than the destruction of an innocent man's life for the sake of ignorance and prejudice?"

"Prejudice?" Deke said. "Give me a fuckin' break."

"Martinez was an illegal alien. Lot of people don't like Mexicans sneaking in, taking their jobs. Deputy Rudy's boss is dead, and he's suddenly thrust into a position of power. He needs a suspect, and he needs an arrest, fast. The sooner he makes an arrest, the better he looks, and who's gonna argue—or even give a damn? A drifter . . . with no family, no connections, no money—"

"You've been talkin' to Lucas." Deke didn't buy it. "Martinez had blood on his clothing. He left a palm print at the scene. There was trace evidence all over the kitchen and pantry, and if that wasn't enough, he confessed."

"All circumstantial evidence, except for the confession, and that could easily have been coerced." She took a step closer and lowered her voice, obviously hoping to convince him. "How much digging have you done into this case? Did you bother to look into the suspect's background?"

He said nothing. He didn't need to. The evidence had been enough to convince him, and he'd been focused on other more important things, like Maddy's disappearance.

"No?" she continued. "Well, I did. Martinez was a devout Catholic. He never would have taken his own life. Not under any circumstances. It's a mortal sin."

"Maybe, but so is murder." They were standing almost toe to toe, and she was breathing a little harder from the stress of their argument. Staring down at her, Deke could only think how pretty she was—misguided, wrongheaded, determined to believe something he didn't even want to consider, but lovely. Reaching out, he traced a finger along the deep U of her neckline, savoring the softness of the exposed flesh. "You better come up with a new argument. I'm afraid it's gonna take more than that to convince me that Martinez was innocent."

"You're wastin' your breath on Deke, Anna. I would've bet that after what happened this mornin' he would've changed his way of thinkin'—"

Deke threw his uncle a dark warning look. "Is that your breakfast burnin'?"

"Have it your way," Lucas said with a shrug. "She's gonna find out anyway, as soon as she gets back. It might be a whole lot better if she heard it from you."

"Heard what?" Anna asked. Her gaze shifted to Deke's, and it lost that melting, sexy quality. "Deke? What did he mean by that?"

Deke turned without a word and walked from the house, unable to stand being indoors another second. He could feel the tension building, and the walls started closing in. He went as far as the porch, where he stopped to light a cigarette. He'd barely sucked the smoke into his lungs, breathed a sigh of relief as the nicotine kicked in, when she appeared at his side.

"What was that all about back there? What did Lucas mean that it might be better if I heard it from you? Heard what?"

"The family that bought the house—Miller and his kid. I found them this morning— both dead. A double homicide. The woman wasn't there—or at least, she didn't seem to be."

It took a moment for it to register, for the color to drain from her face, the horror to sink in. "Another family at the house where your family was killed? My God. When did this happen?"

"Sometime during the night," Deke said. He didn't mention that he'd gone there after he'd dropped her off at Coyote hours before the killings, that the family had been intact and very much alive when he left there. "The kid was cold when I got there. I didn't bother to check his old man, but with his face beat in, it was pretty fuckin' obvious that he was dead."

She didn't wait to hear more. "I have to get back," she said suddenly, heading to the van. "Tell Lucas I'm sorry—I'll explain later."

Lucas came out of the house in time to watch the old black van rattle down the drive. Shading his eyes against the sun, he sighed his regret. "And here I thought things were goin' pretty well. Guess she wasn't very hungry."

"Guess not," Deke said. "Murder sure has a way of spoilin' an appetite."

Chapter Seven

Anna powered up the notebook computer and logged onto the Internet. Almost immediately, the instant messenger sent up a flag that "Felix" was buzzing her.

"Are you there?" came up on screen, all lowercase letters, no punctuation. Felix spent too much time dotting i's and crossing t's to bother with punctuation in e-mail.

"Yes," Anna keyed in.

ANNA: I just got in. There's trouble here—as in MAMMOTH.
FELIX: You found a Woolly Mammoth?
ANNA: Check the wires. All HELL just broke loose—as in déjà weird—as in another double HOMICIDE. It's damned creepy. The family that bought the Call place. I swear, that house is like the freaking Bates Motel.

She paused for a second, wondering how much to relate, then plunged on.

ANNA: Deke Call found the bodies. No official ID yet, but it appears to be a father and son, and the woman is

missing. Explain to me how the hell something like
that happens twice to the same man.

FELIX: Easy enough if he's involved. Tell me you're not
trying to get information from him. Okay, sweet
cheeks . . . time to abandon the quest and come
home.

"READ CLOSELY," Anna wrote, realizing that she
didn't leap to Deke's defense—perhaps because on
some level she'd had the same thought a few dozen
times since their conversation that morning.

ANNA: If this went down the way it appears, then the
real killer's still out there. I can't come back. I have to
see this out.

FELIX: Anna, get a grip. You're the best the paper has.
We can't afford to lose you.

ANNA: I'm not going anywhere, and you aren't going to
lose me. I just need more time.

An emoticon with a serious pout appeared.

ANNA: Give me three weeks.

FELIX: Three weeks? HAVE YOU LOST YOUR FUCK-
ING MIND?

ANNA: All right, two weeks, and stop screaming at me.
C'mon, Jay (she pleaded, abandoning his screen name
for the real deal). You've been my editor for four
years. I need to know you got my back on this thing.
Please. I NEED to do this. For the sake of my sanity.
For Dad's memory. I can prove he had nothing to do
with the Call murders—I know I can, and I need to find
out what really happened in that cell that night.

FELIX: Anna.

ANNA: He didn't kill himself. He never would have abandoned me.

FELIX: All right. All right, two weeks, but I want you to know you've got my blood pressure soaring. If I stroke out, it's your fault.

ANNA: Your mom's ninety-three and in perfect health. You'll be fine.

FELIX: One last thing . . . does anyone know who you are yet?

ANNA: No, and I intend to do everything I can to keep it that way. Listen, I gotta log off.

FELIX: Anna—just be sure you keep in touch. I won't be able to concentrate on anything if you drop off the radar.

Anna clicked off, slipping effortlessly into the files she kept stored on her flash drive. Double-click on photos, and a parade of images began. A grainy black-and-white image of a young Deke Call taken by some reporter on the day of the funerals and published in the local paper. A color shot of her aunt crooning to her mixed-breed dog Chi-Chi. The mug shot of the accused murderer, Juan Martinez, which had also appeared in the papers, one eye swollen shut, his lip cut. He barely resembled the last shot . . . the photo of a young Juan holding a little girl in his arms and smiling for the camera.

Anna touched a finger to the screen, to the face of the handsome young man. She'd been far too young to remember the photo being taken, but she remembered him. The way he'd looked, the kindness in his voice, the love in his dark brown eyes. All he'd wanted was a chance to make a new start with his little girl. When he'd crossed the border, he'd had twenty

American dollars in his pocket and his good name, nothing more. When Nazareth was through with him, he'd been stripped of his honor, his dignity, his child, and finally his life.

"Somebody's gonna pay for this, Papa. I swear to you. I'm gonna make that happen."

It was six that evening when Harlan left the office and made the two-mile drive to the house he and Ginny had bought on the outskirts of town a few years back. It was bigger than the first place where they'd started out, a sprawling raised ranch, stuccoed in light terra cotta so that it blended nicely with the landscape. It had a three-car garage, a small stable for Ginny's Arabian mare, and more landscaping than his modest income would allow. It was the envy of the neighborhood, but there was something cold and lifeless about the place. Since it seemed to please her, he said nothing, but it just didn't feel like home. More often than not, when he looked back to the happy days of his marriage to Ginny, he remembered that modest little four-room house they'd bought before she got her trust fund.

The first two years of their marriage had been good, but that was before she'd lost all hope of having a child. Things had been so much better back then, and he wondered how not being able to have a baby of their own could have made such a difference. He would have been lying to himself if he pretended that it hadn't gotten to him on some level, but eventually he'd gotten past it and found other things to focus on. For Ginny, there seemed no getting past it, and she'd somehow gotten it fixed in her mind that it was the stick by which everything was measured.

Damned if he understood how being physically unable to reproduce made him less of a man, or her less of a woman, and he was sick to death of feeling guilty because of it.

Harlan pulled into the cement-paved drive flanked by a pair of ornamental pole lights, and parked on the right side of the drive, outside the garage. He killed the motor and got out, glancing up at the kitchen windows before lifting the garage door and pulling the tarp off his baby. The '36 Packard Victoria convertible was showroom shiny. He'd bought it years ago for a couple of hundred, a rusty wreck on rotting tires, and then spent all his spare time restoring it. From the toothy chrome grill to the white sidewall tires, it was every antique car buff's wet dream. Harlan admired it for a few minutes, then headed for the stairs.

Ginny was in the kitchen, scouring the sink. It was one of the many things that had attracted him to her in the first place, the fact that she never hesitated to dirty her hands. She'd come from money, but while growing up on a thriving ranch, she'd worked as hard as her brothers. It had been expected of her, and he'd respected her for being a hands-on kind of girl. She didn't bother to glance up when she heard him come in. "Leave your boots, Harlan," she reminded him. "Rosa did the floors today."

Harlan broke the cardinal rule, crossed the kitchen and turned off the faucet, thrusting a hand towel at her.

"Harlan, what on earth?"

"Dry your hands," he said. "We're takin' a ride."

She furrowed her brow at that, and the angry vertical crease formed in the center of her forehead, detracting from a face that once had seemed so damned pretty. She was still attractive at fifty, with a rounding of all the sharp edges, a ripeness she'd lacked in her youth, and for a few seconds he imagined that if he could just get her out of here, convince her to let her hair down, he could blow off a little of the steam he'd built up over this long day.

She shoved the towel aside and turned the faucet back on. "Have you lost your mind? It's after six, and dinner's in the oven. I can't leave it or it'll be ruined."

"Screw dinner. We can grab a bite at the café before we head home. C'mon, Ginny," he said. "I'll put the top down on the Packard. You used to like the wind in your hair."

A dry little laugh. "I used to like a lot of things."

Harlan took a step closer, putting his arms around her, feeling her stiffen. "Harlan."

He tried to kiss her and she turned her head. "Harlan, for God's sake, *don't*." She reacted so quickly he barely anticipated the shove she gave him, then, as he stepped back, she said, "Excuse me, but aren't you the same man who came in long after midnight, with no indication as to where you'd been? Then, you go out again? It isn't that easy, Harlan."

"With you, when has anything *ever* been easy?" Harlan asked, his tone a low growl.

Throwing down the towel, she stalked from the room.

Harlan clenched one fist, then brought it crashing down on the counter, rattling dishes and making the silverware she'd laid out dance. For a few seconds, he stood there, half-tempted to go after her, to have this out once and for all. As the seconds ticked by, the impulse faded, and he turned and went out the way he'd come in, got in his cruiser, and headed to Mirror Lake.

Ginny stood in the bedroom window, watching him

leave. When the truck was out of sight, she went to the garage and opened the Packard's trunk. The crowbar was under the mat, at the very rear of the trunk. She took it out and for a moment just held it in her two hands. The weight of it was strangely satisfying. The cold steel warmed quickly. Odd, how an inanimate object could allow her to feel more powerful than she was. She felt better just having it close, but where could she put it? A few minutes of indecision, then she lifted the covers on the bed she shared with her husband and slid it between the mattress and box spring.

There was close to an hour of daylight left when Harlan parked the truck and walked to the water's edge. A sheer incline, still stark from a harsh winter, rose sharply from the opposite shore, a dark backdrop for a pair of soaring hawks. Harlan drew a shuddering breath and released it with a measured slowness that was foreign to him, but the tension twisting his insides into tight knots stayed.

Normally, when he drove out here, he came with a rod and reel, to relax, to slough off the mantle of sheriff for a few delicious hours, to forget about everything and everyone in his life and just exist. Tonight he wasn't capable of shedding any of it.

The scene with Ginny in the kitchen was typical, and though it chafed, it wasn't what rode him so relentlessly. It was the summons to the Miller place that had his insides in a vise. He'd known when he took the oath of office for the first time that keeping the peace wouldn't be easy. He'd been Matt Call's deputy for a good ten years, and when he'd been called to the scene of the first murders, he'd truly believed he'd seen the worst that could happen. It went without saying that crimes would come and go, that he'd see things that would be hard to take, but he'd seen nothing to rival the Call murders. Every cop had at least one case that refused to let go, and he'd been goddamned sure that was it for him.

Then he'd answered the call from dispatch before daylight this very morning. Another double homicide. Same MO, same house, and he was guessing roughly the same time frame. The stage had been set as carefully as if it were some sort of bizarre play—furniture tipped over, props positioned carefully, and a woman missing. After leaving the crime scene, Harlan had started making calls, asking questions. He'd begun the process of looking into John and Corrie Miller's backgrounds while locating and notifying next of kin.

Miller's brother Vince lived in Santa Fe, and he'd held it together long enough to provide Harlan with a few facts. The couple had been living in Vale, Colorado, but when Miller's company downsized and he found himself out of a job, they could no longer afford to stay. Vale's cost of living had skyrocketed when Hollywood moved in. They'd come to New Mexico for a new start, and the price was right on the Call place.

As for Corrie Miller, she had a sister in Michigan, but her parents were deceased. There were a few friends from Vale she kept in touch with, but the brother-in-law didn't know their names offhand. She was supposedly clean as a proverbial whistle, no booze, no drugs, few if any bad habits—the perfect wife and mother.

Vince Miller and his wife were driving up first thing tomorrow for a face to face and to make the necessary arrangements, but he'd already indicated there was little or no marital strife between the deceased and his missing wife. Harlan wasn't sure he believed it. He knew firsthand that things happened between husbands and wives that never reached the light of day, so as far as he was concerned Corrie Miller would remain at the top of his suspect list until he could positively rule her out.

Harlan took a cigar box from his coat pocket, took a cigar out, and lit up, turning up the sheepskin collar of his coat. Not even sunset and the air had taken on a bitter chill. It got damned cold after dark.

As the sun slipped behind the sheer cliffs, the water's surface turned a dull pewter. At the other end of the valley, the lights of a house flickered on and glowed brightly. Lucas Swift-Water's place. He thought about driving over to check on him but just as quickly decided against it. He wasn't exactly welcome there, and if anything happened, he'd get wind of it soon enough. Besides, it had been a long day. Time to go home and at least try to get some sleep.

The shearing shed had chinks between the planks for ventilation, but by late afternoon of the following day it was nonetheless stifling. Lucas's recent "accident" had him temporarily out of commission. He watched from his position at the fence as Deke manhandled the sheep, a job he'd been doing since he was twelve. It was hard but simple work. He cut a few select ewes from the flock and herded them into a smaller holding pen, then one by one guided them down a chute and into the shearing shed where Hank Redding waited.

A wiry man in his late seventies, Hank had been shearing sheep for forty-two years and had a skill that was unequaled in all of New Mexico; his calendar was always booked during the spring of the year.

Working with shears that were mounted on braces and powered by a motor from a 1933 Maytag washer, Hank waited for Deke to subdue the struggling ewe and flop it onto its backside, then with practiced ease, Hank stripped the pregnant ewes of their fleece. "Just like runnin' a hot knife through warm butter," Hank said with a grin.

The shearing served a dual purpose. Not only did it prepare the sheep for the coming of warmer weather, but without their heavy wool, the ewes would seek shelter to lamb, and their young stood a greater chance of surviving if born in a lambing shed.

"That's number nineteen," Hank said, straightening to relieve the crick in his back. "What've we got left, Deke?"

Deke swiped the sweat from his brow with a bare forearm and paused to catch his breath. "Arlo."

Hank laughed silently, his weather-browned face dissolving into a sea of deep troughs and furrows. "Lucas's pride and joy."

"And a major pain in my ass," Deke said.

"Saved the best till last. You gonna need help wid 'im?"

"I'll manage," Deke said. When he walked out, Lucas was hand-feeding the ram, scratching his chin and talking to him in low-voiced Navajo. Arlo rubbed his head against the older man's leg, playing the pussycat, but Deke wasn't having any of it. He'd spent countless weekends as a kid helping out at Lucas's place, and he'd learned damn quick that you don't turn your back on a ram. Especially Arlo, King of Contrary. The ram might look harmless, but he could knock a man into the next county just for the sheer hell of it. "What are you givin' him, *Shi-Da?*"

Lucas glanced up, shading his eyes with his hand. "Fudge. He's like me. He's got a bit of a sweet tooth."

"Jesus. Ain't that little son of a bitch trouble enough without giving him a sugar high?"

"Who, Arlo? Why, he ain't no trouble." Reaching over the fence, Lucas lavished his favorite with attention. "Don't let him hurt your feelings, boy. He's obviously got you confused with some other good-for-nothin' sheep."

"Okay, Arlo. Time to go," Deke said, stepping onto and over the fence rail. As bullheaded as his owner, the ram didn't go willingly. He kicked and he fought and he struggled until Deke wrestled him to the ground, then picked him up and carried him to the shed. A few minutes later, a less-dignified Arlo dashed down the chute into the holding pen, minus his shaggy coat.

"That's the last one." Deke walked to the hand pump and, after several cranks, stuck his head and torso under the cold stream. He had bumps and bruises on his bumps and bruises, and he'd be sore as a son of a bitch come morning, but the water felt almost as good as the hard day's work had.

Lucas opened a cooler and handed him a beer. "Wheeler's comin' by later with a friend. We're gonna play some poker. Might as well hang around—unless you got plans, that is."

Deke popped the top and took several long swallows of ice cold beer. No specific plans . . . though he couldn't seem to get Anna out of his thoughts. The coolness of her hair caressing his face as she leaned down to kiss him, the smell of sandalwood with an underlying hint of citrus that surrounded her like an exotic cloud, and the immediacy of her response as his hand found her sex all lingered teasingly in the back of his mind.

It didn't seem to matter how often he told himself he was treading dangerous ground. That he knew nothing about her. That he was allowing his libido to rule his head. It was almost a given that nighttime would find him at her door. "Gotta go home and get cleaned up. Damned if I don't smell like a sheep."

Lucas leaned on the fence. "Oh, I don't know that any of the sheep smell that bad. See you at eight?"

"Hell, why not?" Deke said. It would provide a distraction, and maybe that was what he needed to keep him from doing something exceptionally stupid, like seeking her out again so soon.

"Mr. and Mrs. Miller," Harlan said with a nod. "Please, come in and sit down. I appreciate the fact that you've granted me this interview. It's a difficult time, and I realize that. Unfortunately, I know very little about your brother and his wife, them bein' new here, and it doesn't give me much to go on."

"I'm not sure we'll be much help," Miller said. "John and I didn't talk often."

Harlan glanced up over his reading glasses. "I take it you weren't close?"

"It wasn't an estrangement," Karen Miller hastened to say. "More like a lack of common interests. John's ex-wife, Linda, and I are very close."

"Second marriages are common enough these days," Harlan said. "Was the divorce amicable?"

"As amicable as it can possibly be when there's cheating involved." Karen Miller's tone was bitter, and Harlan got the idea that Vincent Miller, who squirmed in his seat, had paid in spades for his brother's decisions—justified, or otherwise, he was no one to judge.

"It got pretty messy," Vince said. "Linda took him for everything he had. He started over with nothing, though Corrie never seemed to mind. She was pregnant, and for a long time, everything was okay."

"This ex-wife have an address and phone? I'd sure like to talk to her."

"She's in Africa," Karen put in eagerly. "She works for a humanitarian aid organization."

Harlan sat forward and the tear in the seat of his chair tweaked his ass cheek. He'd intended to mend it with duct tape, but he hadn't the chance. "Any idea how long she's been out of the country?"

"Eighteen months."

Harlan made a note to check on Linda Miller, then moved along. "You said you weren't close to your brother and his wife. Did you know Corrie Miller very well? I'd like to get some idea as to what kind of person she was. What she's capable of."

"If you're asking if she killed John, I just can't see it. As for the boy—spoil him? Maybe. But hurt him? No way."

He had the brother's input, but the man's wife was a bit more reticent. His gaze fell on her, questioning. "Mrs. Miller?"

She sighed. "As much as I'd like to say otherwise, I just can't imagine Corrie killing anyone. Stealing someone's husband? Now that's another matter. The woman's definitely a hypocrite—all that holier than thou crap—but I'm not sure that's punishable by law."

"If it were, I know a lot of folks in Washington who'd

be in hot water," Harlan said. "If there's anything else you can think of that might be useful in this investigation, you'll be sure to call me?" He stood, ushering them out.

When the door closed and the office was quiet once again, he returned to his desk. He double-checked the ex-wife's whereabouts, and Karen Miller's statements were verified. She had nothing to do with it, unless she'd hired someone. But the divorce had taken place a decade before, and she appeared to have moved on in a very big way. For now, he'd leave it at that.

Besides, it wasn't a home invasion scenario. No forced entry, no damage to doors, and no broken windows. Whoever had gone into that house had talked their way in.

It was either someone they knew or someone who convinced them he could be trusted.

It gave Harlan a lot to think about. He got up and went out. "Gonna grab a bite at the café, Dixie. Call my cell if you need me."

"You got something goin' on with Lucas I should know about?" Wheeler asked the question without glancing at Anna. "Cause if that's the case, it'll be a hell of a blow to my fragile ego."

Anna snorted. "If your ego were fragile, you would have stopped asking me out after the first time I said no. As for Lucas—he's colorful, he's interesting, he's smart, and he's a gentleman. What's not to like?"

"Okay, I got it. You're a closet lesbian."

A jaded look. Anna shook her head. "You really are hopeless. I'm not looking for a lover. Period. It complicates everything, and at the moment, I have other, more important things to think about."

And she meant it. The time she'd spent in Deke's arms had been a result of an instantaneous mutual attraction that would die out before either one of them could figure out why it had happened in the first place. It had been a momentary madness, a much-needed release from the unbearable tension resulting from living a lie.

Not that there wasn't a damn good reason for the deception. Yet justification didn't make it any easier to carry it off. One slip of the tongue, a single misstep, and she would blow whatever chance she stood of proving that not only had her father been innocent of the Call murders, he'd been every bit as much a victim as Deke's family.

Getting involved with Deke Call, sexually, emotionally, wasn't a part of the plan. It had simply happened. And if Anna were being perfectly honest with herself, there was a damn good chance it could happen again. The attraction between them was strong. In fact, just thinking about him made her want him all over again.

"You sure you want to go through with this?" Wheeler asked. "It's a big step, and I don't know if he's ready yet. He was awfully close to Obee."

"I'm sure," Anna said. She got out of the van and took the bundle from Wheeler, who fell into step behind her. As they reached the porch, the door swung open.

Lucas glanced at the wriggling bundle in Anna's arms. "Hey, Anna. What you got there?"

"It's a thank-you gift," Anna said, unfurling the blanket. The mixed-breed puppy shivered and whined. "His mama's a Border Collie that belongs to my neighbor. His daddy—it's anybody's guess. A litter of six, and he's the only one left. They were talking about taking him to the shelter."

Lucas smoothed his big hand over the pup's small black and white head, then tilted its chin up so he could look in its deep blue eyes. "He's got an intelligent look to 'im, doesn't he? Herd dogs have a keen intellect, you know. Obee was bright—real bright. Knew what needed to be done almost before I did, and he didn't just keep an eye on the lambs. He kept an eye on me too. He was a good friend."

Anna's tone softened. "He's no substitute for Obee, but with some work, he might catch on."

"Oh, no, he could never replace Obee. He was one of a kind." He chuckled, but there was a note of sadness in it. "Dogs are like people, you know. No two are exactly alike."

"Would you mind holding him for a minute? I left my bag in the van." Anna placed the puppy in the older man's arms and walked to the van, where she pretended to search for a handbag that was in its usual place between the bucket seats.

"You're good, I'll give you that." His voice was as soft as it was unexpected, and a chill rippled along Anna's spine. "You sold him a bill of goods on that dog, and he swallowed it all, hook, line, and sinker."

"Bill of goods?" Anna repeated innocently. "I don't know what you're talking about."

He handed her a folded yellow paper. "Does Drummond's Pet Store jog your memory? You dropped it when you got out of the van." He watched as she pocketed the pet store receipt, his expression one of curiosity and doubt. "That dog cost you a hundred bucks. Waitresses don't make much, yet you can buy a sculpture on a whim and a dog for a man you barely know. You never did say you had a publisher for the book you're supposed to be writin'. So where's all this money comin' from?"

Anna's gaze was speculative. "For a man who jealously guards his own past, you sure do ask a lot of questions."

He shrugged, and the uppermost thorn on the tattoo seemed to prick deeper into his flesh. She could have sworn the drop of scarlet beneath it was real instead of art. "Lookin' out for my own, that's all. I'm willin' to admit that you made his day, but what's in it for you?"

"Most good deeds don't have a tangible payoff."

"So you bought him a sheepdog and made up a sob story he couldn't resist."

Anna smiled. "Every puppy deserves a good home. It's a victimless crime, Deke. As a former cop you should get that."

The change in him was subtle yet evident. His muscles tensed, his expression hardened, and his tone revealed his wariness. "Looks like I'm not the only one askin' questions. You find out what you need to know?"

"Not really. I know that you worked for the Tucson Police Department for a number of years, yet the only listing I could get was your rank, Detective. That's a little unusual, to say the least." She let her gaze slide over him, from the hair that brushed his collar to the gold earrings and livid tattoos. "But then, undercover cops don't usually advertise the fact that they're working for the good guys, isn't that right?"

He didn't answer directly. "Is that a guess? Or'd you bribe somebody at the TPD?"

"Bribery?" Anna clucked her tongue. "Are you always this suspicious?"

"Baby, I was born suspicious." Smooth and easy,

undeniably provocative, like a lazy afternoon spent with him between the sheets. The comparison brought back memories, made her long to repeat it, and to hell with the risks involved. "It don't pay to be otherwise."

"Maybe." It was as much as she was willing to give in that moment. Maybe he was right to be suspicious. In his position, she would have been wary too. A man caught between two multiple homicide investigations, past and present, and somehow he had stumbled upon both sets of victims.

It was downright spooky.

"If you tell him about the pet store, he'll give it back." She took a step closer and put her hands on his chest. She loved the feel of hard muscle under her fingertips, the heat that immediately ran through her at his nearness. "You should have seen him, Deke," she said, looking up at him. "All alone in that little wire cage, so hopeful and sad. Those big blue eyes met mine and I just couldn't resist. He was begging to be rescued, to be taken home, to be loved. All I did was listen. We all need to feel loved at one time or other. Don't you agree?"

Deke glanced up over Anna's shoulder, watching as Lucas offered a shallow bowl of bread and milk to the puppy. His smile was wide and genuine as he observed the pup lap it up.

Say anything to wipe that smile off his face?

No fucking way. It looked like she was gonna get exactly what she wanted—this time.

Anna dropped Wheeler at his place at half past twelve and drove home alone. Strangely charged after the confrontation with Deke, she decided to take the long way home, down Echo Canyon Road, past the scene of the most recent homicides. The house sat eighteen feet off a road that was crisscrossed at intervals by smaller interlocking byways. Some were unpaved, dirt and rock base overlaid with loose gravel, and others were oil and chip, less expensive than asphalt but with the same general effect—all could have provided an easy access for someone wanting to come and go without being seen.

Word had it that Sheriff Harlan Rudy was pulling round-the-clock shifts to try to get a handle on this case, and Anna knew for sure that he wasn't talking to anyone, because she'd tried unsuccessfully to see him that morning. As a reporter she knew that his silence could mean a lot of things, from simple strategy to investigating style. Yet she was skeptical.

Harlan certainly hadn't been reticent about the hasty press release he'd sent out after Juan Martinez was taken into custody. Anna's gut instinct told her he didn't have crucial evidence, he didn't have a witness, and there was no suspect, yet. Rudy was scrambling to get a grip on his investigation, and he was doing his best to avoid comparisons between this investigation and the Call case to keep the press from asking uncomfortable questions.

Anna didn't have to question anything. The link existed. She was certain of it.

As she neared the Call house, she slowed. The yellow crime scene ribbon strung from tree to tree around the perimeter of the grounds fluttered in the night breeze. It was stunning to see the improvements the Miller family had made and to think how abruptly and violently their new start had ended. New glass in the windows and an oak entryway door only added to the haunted air of the place.

Anna cruised past and did a double take, certain she'd seen a glimmer of light in a downstairs window. An arc of pale illumination, there one second, gone the next. She braked to look again, more closely this time.

Imagination gone wild? Maybe.

She couldn't deny being spooked by recent events, but she wasn't exactly alone in that one. She had a pretty good idea from the conversations she'd over-heard since the news broke that a lot of folks shared her uneasiness.

She had just passed the property when she caught sight of a blur in her peripheral vision, something moving fast outside her passenger window. Anna gasped and slammed on the brakes, her heart nearly stopping as the yearling doe dashed headlong in front of the van. The animal never slowed, frightened by the figure lunging from the weeds.

Dressed in dark clothing, with a Halloween *Scream* mask covering the face, he swung the head of a long-handled flashlight, smashing out one of the van's head-lights. Anna swore and slammed the column shift into reverse as he took aim at her windshield, stepping on the gas. The van's 350 engine sent it rocketing back-ward. Anna took her eyes off the man in the road in time to avoid a culvert, and when she looked back, the wind-shield exploded in a million tiny Herculite glass cubes. She screamed, throwing up an arm to protect her face. Out of control, the van's rear passenger wheel slid into the ditch, sinking into soil gone soft from recent rains.

Anna applied the gas and spun deeper. Her attacker was closing in. She clawed for the door handle, shoving the driver's door open and preparing to jump, when at the same time headlamps bounced over the rise a hun-dred yards back.

The dark-dressed figure hesitated, then turned and

broke for the trees, quickly melting into the woods by the side of the road. Shaking, her heart a deafening thunder in her ears, Anna opened the driver's door and stepped out onto the side of the road to flag down the driver who'd quite possibly saved her life.

Chapter Eight

The vehicle came into view, a dark-colored sports car. It slowed, then stopped, and the passenger window whirred down. Anna breathed a sigh of relief. "Oh, thank God it's you!"

"Hey, baby, somethin' wrong?" Deke leaned over to open the door, and she collapsed into the bucket seat.

The adrenaline rush was ending, but she was a little afraid she might crash land. She was shaking, her breath coming in labored gasps. She had to put forth a concentrated effort to calm.

Deke waited till his curiosity got the better of him. "Anna, the van's in a ditch. What's goin' on?"

Anna shook her head. "I thought I saw a light inside, so I slowed down. A deer jumped off the bank in front of me, frightened by something—or rather, *someone*. That someone came right for me, carrying a flashlight. Before I knew what was happening, he smashed the headlight out, then the windshield. When you topped the rise he ran off into the woods."

He parked the car and set the parking brake. The motor was running. Anna tensed. "Call me a coward, but I'd really rather you not go out there just yet. At least not until I stop shaking."

He reached behind his back, and retrieved the Python, pressing it into her hand. Its steel was warmed by his body heat, but it still failed to lessen her nervousness. "The safety's off. All you have to do is squeeze the trigger—just be damned sure who it is you're aimin' at. I'm gonna take a quick look around."

He got out of the car, moving first to the van, then, following the general direction her attacker took, he disappeared into the dark timberline. Anna clutched the .357, but it was cold comfort in lieu of what had just happened.

She'd been attacked, the van damaged, and if Deke hadn't come along when he did—she shuddered, unwilling to speculate on what could have happened. Another minute. Then two. Anna watched the digital clock on the dash. It felt like an eternity, sitting along a deserted country road, alone, terrified, waiting.

Movement in the brush. She slipped her forefinger through the trigger guard . . . then Deke stepped into the headlights, and she breathed a sigh of relief. He opened the driver's door and slid behind the wheel, tossing something onto her lap. The empty black sockets stared unseeing, the hideously distorted mouth mocked her. Anna swept the mask off her lap and onto the floor.

"Look familiar?"

A nod. "Yes. That's what he was wearing."

"He?" he repeated. "You sure it was a man?"

"Yes—no," Anna said. "I think so." She shook her head, stunned at how rattled she'd allowed herself to become. She'd been through tough situations before, but nothing quite like this.

Deke put the car into gear, releasing the parking

brake. "Whoever it was, he's long gone. Probably dropped that thing so he could run without breakin' his neck in the underbrush. Nothin' to be done about the van tonight. Charlie Brill has twenty-four hour towing, but he's in the hospital with pneumonia. His boy's due in from Oklahoma City tomorrow, I hear. Gonna run things till Charlie's back on his feet. I'll give 'im a call in the morning."

"Thanks, but I'll take care of it." She'd slept with him, but she was vastly uncomfortable letting him handle what amounted to her responsibilities. She'd gotten herself into this mess by taking the long way home past the scene of a recent murder, very late and alone. She'd get herself out. He'd done enough for her already.

He drove to her apartment, but instead of letting her have a clean getaway, he killed the engine, the leather bucket seat creaking softly as he turned to face her. "So, you gonna invite me up for coffee? Seems like an appropriate thank-you for a lift home."

"You sure you don't have someplace else you need to be?" Anna asked.

"There's an upside to not havin' anybody in your life who gives a damn," he said. "I come and go as I please. Do what I want when I want . . . see who I want to see." He smiled to soften the remarks, but there was something in his dark eyes that warned her that if she followed his suggestion and invited him in, it would involve a whole lot more than just coffee and casual conversation. Despite her insistence, there was nothing casual about this thing they had going on between them.

Maybe her adrenaline rush hadn't faded completely. Her blood seemed to thrum through her veins, heightening her senses, rushing to her extremities and back to her heart again. Every cell seemed to tingle, scalp to toes. She drew an unsteady breath and offered a smile. "Would you like to come in—for coffee? It's the least I can do for you giving me a ride home."

Deke got out and opened her door, helping her out, then Anna took his hand, leading him up the stairs.

Inside, Deke reached for her, and Anna didn't hold back. He unbuttoned her blouse and slid it off her shoulders, his hot, hungry mouth following in its wake. Anna caught her breath as his beard abraded her flesh. Soft yielding to hard, forceful persuasion followed by the ultimate surrender. Her zipper slid effortlessly open, and his hand found its way into Anna's jeans. She'd had lovers who had been unpracticed, and at least one jackass who had been unabashedly selfish about his own needs. A few had been good in bed, one or two just adequate enough to satisfy, but nobody compared with Deke Call.

He knew exactly what he wanted and he knew how to get it without neglecting her desires. In fact, that was a big part of his allure. When she was with him, Anna had no doubt that it was all about her. How she looked, the softness of her skin, the way she clung to him when he rose above her. He wanted *her*. It was that simple. Got off on being with *her*. And damn, that was sexy.

Hooking his thumbs in her waistband, he peeled her jeans down, and she stepped out of them. They landed in a crumpled heap on the kitchen floor. His shirt came next—she liked him best this way, all that gleaming bronze skin and intriguing body art. The barbed wire and the roses and thorns were like a flashing neon sign proclaiming, "I'm dangerous."

Sinking into a kitchen chair, he freed his sex from concealment and pulled her down onto his lap, finding her wetness with his fingers, a prelude to pave the way for bigger, better things. A deep, long kiss, and Anna sighed. The suggestive movement of her tongue deep in his mouth conveyed without words what she wanted from him, and he gave it to her, cupping her ass with his large, strong hands and impaling her with a single thrust.

Her hands on his silken skin, Anna pushed him back against the chair. She wanted to lead. She needed control. Didn't want to think beyond this moment.

From the instant he filled her, she could feel the ecstasy threaten . . . that telltale thrill that sang wildly deep in her being, that demanded a rush to completion she had no will to resist or deny, and she was rewarded more quickly, more powerfully than she could have ever imagined.

When Deke felt her melt against him and knew she'd gotten what she wanted from him, he lifted her and sat her down on the table's edge, spreading her knees with his hands. Reaching up, she ran her hands down over his ribs and the ridge of scar tissue on his right side. Then, before she could question him, before she could say a word, he maneuvered her hands above her head and held them there. Then, covering her mouth with his kiss, he finished what she'd started.

"I don't even know how you take your coffee," Anna said. "But then, there's a hell of a lot I don't know about you. Like how you came by those scars below your ribs. You never did say. Somebody try to off you recently?"

"Not in a couple of months. On the job accident, that's all." Evasive. Anna cut him a glance. His expression was closed. He didn't want to talk about it. So maybe that was okay, given she wasn't exactly willing to share either.

Pouring coffee into a matte black mug, she paused with a questioning look. "Black, no sugar," he responded.

He was leaning against the sink, inches away. Jeans and no shirt. Warm, sexy, accessible. It was weird, but in a way it seemed almost natural, making coffee after sex. The hard part of the process was keeping her hands off him long enough to measure the aromatic grounds into the filter.

He seemed to be having the same problem, only he didn't try to resist but ran a finger down her bare arm to her wrist. He took her hand, her left hand, in his. "No wedding band. That's a relief."

"I don't have time for attachments." His glance said "my kind of girl." Anna smiled and shrugged, offering no excuses. She was wearing an oversized T-shirt with nothing beneath but a pair of boy-cut panties. Her hair was loose and rumpled from a leisurely romp on the bed, and she felt more relaxed than she had since the last time they'd been together. She thought about the things they'd done to one another and shivered.

What did she know about this man?

He was a stranger.

And she was thoroughly mesmerized by him.

Anna didn't even want to think about how dangerous a position she was in. *Better not to think at all right now. Anyhow, it's a little too late for using my head where he's concerned.* "What happened? Between you and your wife? Or is that too personal a question for a casual acquaintance to ask?"

He waited till she'd taken a sip before pulling her in to nuzzle her neck below her left ear.

He nibbled his way down her neck, and Anna closed

her eyes. "Damn it, Deke," she said with a groan, "you sure don't make it easy on me." She stepped back in an effort to clear her head. Logical thought was impossible with him coming on to her all over again.

"Easy ain't all it's cracked up to be," he said, but he gave it up for the time being, picking up his mug. "Sure smells good, Anna. You know your way around a coffeepot."

Coffee . . . the staple of the newsroom. As an intern, she'd had two choices: learn to drink the acidic brew scorching on the hot plate for hours or make it herself. It had been a matter of basic survival. "You didn't answer my question. If it hit a nerve, then tell me it's none of my fucking business. If not, I'd like to know."

"Irreconcilable differences," he said with a shrug. "My concept of art didn't jibe with hers."

Anna knew there had to be more to it than her objecting to his tattoos, but she didn't pursue it. He wasn't the only one in this room who had a past, so maybe it was best just to leave it at that.

He went to the table and sank into a chair. Anna moved no closer. Safer that way.

"How long you been in Nazareth?" he asked.

"I blew in the last week of March."

He took a sip of the hot coffee and sighed. "Three weeks. Anybody been harassin' you at work?"

Anna shrugged. "It's a bar," she said. "I deal with drunks every evening. Sometimes a cowboy gets a little out of line, but it's nothin' I can't handle, and most come back and apologize once they sober up. What's that got to do with anything?"

He lifted his gaze to hers. "That asshole who busted out your windshield tonight wasn't just fuckin' around, Anna. He meant business."

Anna chafed her arms, frowning at the memory of shattering glass. "It was just a random act of somebody trying to scare the piss out of me. Cheap thrills via vandalism. A lot of kids do it." She sounded so convincing—so why did she still feel so uneasy about it? "Besides, no one knew I was going to be driving down Echo Canyon Road in the middle of the night."

His eyes narrowed slightly. "You never did mention what you were doin' way out there."

It was the sort of question a cop would ask. Anna glanced sharply up. "I could ask you the same thing, Call. You were on the same road I was at the same time of night."

"Yeah, but my windshield's still in one piece."

Anna laughed uneasily. "I guess that's the luck of the draw. Maybe next time it'll be your turn." She shrugged it off as nothing, but after he was gone and she was alone in the dark apartment, Anna wondered if Deke was right.

Corrie Miller huddled in the darkness and tried to focus on her breathing. It was the only thing that allowed her to cling to consciousness, helped to combat the excruciating pain. That pain rippled through her skull, settled in a dull throbbing along her spine, where she felt certain several vertebrae were cracked if not broken, and radiated from her broken wrist and mangled fingers.

So much misery . . . but she could endure far worse if it meant she could somehow get back to her husband and son.

Thoughts came and went. She drifted in and out of a thick red haze.

How long had it been?

One day? Two?

No way to tell. Not a speck of light penetrated the thick tape over her eyes. She had no idea where she was or how she'd come to be here. The last thing she remembered was leaving the grocery store in Hardwick. It was a twenty-five minute drive, but she preferred to shop there because she could buy in bulk for less money. She remembered unloading the cart into the trunk and buying a can of soda for the drive home. She'd pulled into her usual parking space a few dozen feet from the front door, and they were waiting.

Lights blinded her and Corrie flinched, bracing for more punishment, but it was only in her mind. *Headlights. Brighter than anything she'd seen before. She raised her hand to shield her eyes, and then nothing.* As the memory faded, she couldn't quite stifle a sob.

She thought about John and Billy. They must be frantic by now.

John was such an impatient man. He wouldn't be content to sit around and wait for something to happen. He'd be out searching, driving the sheriff crazy with his demands. And then there was Billy. He was such a sensitive child, frightened sometimes by things he couldn't see, easily hurt. Was he crying? Did he believe that she'd come home to him or had he given up?

If only she could send a message. If only there were some way to let them know. . . .

But there was nothing but the darkness and the unrelenting sea of pain.

Lucas had forgotten how a young dog could brighten a morning. Quick little paws padding at his heels, the insistent tug on his pant leg when the boy wanted to play, and the endless search for something new to chew. Every waking moment was rife with adventure, from chasing circles around the old Bantam hen to nosing the pickup's tires. Lucas watched him for a while, then when he'd run some of the silliness out of him, he hooked Obee's old leather lead to his tiny red collar and coaxed him toward the sheep pen. "We got to find a name for you, don't we? Can't just go on callin' you *boy*." He whistled softly, and the pup pricked its black ears. "C'mon, then. Let's go meet the sheep."

The puppy pulled on his lead, but Lucas barely noticed. His attention was focused on the ewes and lambs, which huddled tightly in a corner of the night pen. Piney and Trudie were always the first to break for the fence when they saw him approaching, eager for their morning grain ration. This morning they hung back, unusually skittish. He was a few yards from the pen when the stench reached him.

The metallic taint of blood.

The odd smell of a body's interior, closely associated with and unique to slaughtering.

Lucas picked the puppy up and walked the rest of the way to the fence. Poor old Arlo had fallen beside the watering trough. His double horn on the left side of his head was shattered, his skull smashed in and his eye distended from the socket. If that wasn't enough, a jagged incision split the proud ram, and his intestines had been pulled out and draped over the carcass like grotesque streamers. . . .

Lucas forced himself to turn away. There was nothing he could do for Arlo now. Too late for that.

The puppy whined and Lucas rubbed his chin, as much to comfort himself as the young dog. "It's all right, boy," he said, taking the cellular phone out of his coat pocket and dialing the emergency number. "Hey, Dixie. It's Lucas Swift-Water. Could you send somebody out to my place? Somebody killed my ram."

When Deke got to Lucas's, the white Jeep pickup Harlan used for official business was parked in the drive. The two older men were on the porch, Lucas seated in the rocker with the dog in his lap, Harlan standing by the porch rail. Except for the reading glasses which rode low on his nose, the sheriff was holding his own against the ravages of time, though this morning, Deke wasn't willing to cut him a break. As Deke mounted the steps, Harlan looked up from the small spiral notebook he held. "Mornin', son."

Even the greeting, cordial enough, grated on nerves as tautly drawn as skin on a drum. "I ran into Whitlow a few minutes ago. He said there'd been trouble out here. What the hell's goin' on?"

"They got Arlo," Lucas said. "Smashed his head in with a sledge. Poor old sheep. He probably walked right up to 'em, thinking they'd have fudge or a chin scratch for him."

Deke turned and started down the steps. He would have headed for the fence if Harlan hadn't stopped him. "Look, Deke. Give it a few minutes, will you? I know you're pissed, and I can't say as I blame you, but I haven't been over there yet, and I need to see it all more than you do."

"You're sure takin' your time about it, Sheriff. Not that it's all that unusual where you're concerned. Seems like you take your good old time about most things these days. Guess I shouldn't wonder. Everything slows with age."

Harlan took a deep breath and sought a measure of calm he sure didn't feel. He'd spent half the night going over his notes from the Miller case and the other half trying to find a comfortable position on the old sofa in his office. He'd decided on the way home from Mirror Lake to give Ginny time to cool off. A night at the office might not help, but it'd give him breathing room. Or so he'd thought. Then Dixie woke him to take Lucas's phone call, took one glance at the whiskey bottle on his desk, and pursed her lips in disapproval.

By now it would be all over town that he and Ginny were on the outs because of his drinking, and it wouldn't matter than nothing could be further from the truth. Facing down a day full of headaches, the last thing he needed was Deke Call's attitude. "I'm not so slow or decrepit that I can't recognize a man lookin' for trouble when I'm lookin' at 'im. I'll get to the ram *after* I talk to Lucas. I'm gonna get as much information from your uncle as I will from the sheep pen, and that carcass ain't goin' nowhere. His recall is fresh right now. Could be he'll remember somethin' that'll tell us who's behind this vandalism. Now, are you gonna let me do my job or do I have to spend half the mornin' explaining something to you that you should already know?"

Call crossed his arms over his chest, returning Harlan's hard stare. He could see his contempt for a backwoods cop he considered beneath him. It was written all over his face. "I know about police procedure, old man. I know a department that's in trouble when I see it too."

"You don't know shit."

Deke snorted. "You got a double homicide and a missing persons on your hands, and beside the vandalism here at the ranch, Anna was attacked last night on her way home."

"Attacked?" Harlan glanced sharply at the younger man. "What are you talkin' about?"

"Somebody jumped off the road bank as she passed the Miller place and smashed out her headlights and windshield. She threw the van into reverse but slid into the ditch. If I hadn't been a couple of minutes behind her, ain't no tellin' what might have happened."

"And why the hell isn't she the one tellin' me this?" Harlan demanded. "Why do I gotta hear it from you?"

"You don't exactly inspire confidence in a body, Harlan. Maybe it's time to think about hangin' it up, givin' that shield to somebody who can still cut it. Somebody who gives a flyin' fuck about what goes on in this county."

Harlan's gaze narrowed. He'd had just about as much from Call as he was going to take. "It's a damn shame your mama ain't around to see how her little boy turned out," he said. "I bet she'd be real proud."

"Fuck you, Sheriff," Deke said, unfolding his arms, stalking off the porch, heading for the sheep fence. "You find who's doin' this or, by God, I will." He glanced at Lucas. "Do what you gotta do, *Shi-Da.* I'll go dig the hole."

Harlan pushed the breath from his lungs. "What the hell put the burr up his ass?"

"Funny you should mention Maddy. He got a call from her night before last." At his sharp glance, Lucas nodded. "Yeah, you heard right. That's why he was at the Miller house and why he found the latest victims. She called his name and said she was in trouble."

"You know as well as I do that it wasn't real," Harlan said. But his mouth had suddenly gone dry.

He would have known if she were alive.

He would have felt it.

Lucas met Harlan's gaze. "I know it and you know it. He ain't so sure."

"Why the hell didn't he say somethin'?"

Lucas sighed. "'Cause he don't trust nobody these days. Maybe not even himself."

"Yeah, I get that," Harlan said, and maybe on some level he understood it. Law enforcement demanded a lot from a man under the best of circumstances, and he'd long suspected that it may have taken more from Deke Call than the man could afford to lose. He didn't know it for sure, because the man wouldn't talk about it. In a way, maybe he understood that too. "Tell me about last night, will you?"

"Nothin' unusual, really. I invited Wheeler and Anna to play some poker, and Deke was here."

"Deke and Anna. Those two seem to be spending an awful lot of time together," Harlan observed.

"Yeah, and I'd like to see it continue," Lucas countered. "He needs somethin' positive in his life."

Maybe, Harlan thought, but that didn't mean he had to like the idea of those two together. Deke Call and that pretty little dark-haired girl. It just seemed off somehow, but he was wise enough to keep his thoughts to himself. "What time did the evening break up?"

Lucas shrugged. "I guess it was around midnight. Anna and Wheeler left together. He had his truck repo-ed, so she gave him a lift. Deke stayed for a while, then he went on home. I took the dog out for a walk, then we turned in."

"You didn't hear anything unusual? Notice anything?"

Lucas shook his head. "It's still too cold at night to

have the windows open, and the house is well insulated. So, no, I didn't notice anything until this morning. I went over to the fence, like always, and that's when I found him."

Harlan was quiet for a moment, then he sighed. "You and I go way back, Lucas, and I've never known you to have trouble with anyone—except maybe with me." He chuckled low. "Guess I can't fault you for that."

Lucas stared off into the distance, and Harlan wondered if, like him, he saw the past. "You were married, Harlan. Maddy deserved better."

"No argument there," Harlan said. "We all make mistakes, I guess, and I sure made some big ones." With a sigh, he dragged himself back to the present. "About this mess with the sheep . . . did you maybe have words with someone? Notice anyone actin' strange around you? Anything that would make you suspicious?"

"Nobody human," Lucas replied. "I'm sorry I can't be more help, Harlan. You want to have a look at him now?"

"Yeah. S'pose so."

Harlan left the ranch with a large lump of dissatisfaction lodged stubbornly in his solar plexus. Deke's acid comments had hit their mark, even if pure hardheadedness kept him from admitting that the younger man might be right. He had a full plate right now. The murders loomed as the largest and most pressing problem, but Lucas's problems seemed to be escalating, and that had him worried. Someone was targeting him, but why? Was it a grudge? Or was it something far more complex?

There hadn't been much in the way of evidence at the scene—a half print of a boot and a discarded nine-pound sledge, the business end of which had been covered with blood and pale fibers that appeared to match those of the animal. Harlan had bagged the weapon and made a plaster impression of the print. Everything by the book. He'd do his best to get what he could on it, but there was no guarantee he'd find the answers. Sometimes he got lucky and the actor turned out to be a complete fool, someone who left prints everywhere and all but wrote his name in the dust. He just didn't expect this to be that easy.

That was the trouble with everything right now, Harlan thought as he made the right turn onto Hazen Street and drove the last leg to the house he and Ginny owned. There were no guarantees about anything. The film was back from the lab, so he had the crime scene photos, and two full bags of hair, dirt, and fibers collected from the surfaces of the Miller place had gone directly to the lab for detailed analysis. The interview with the Millers the day before had roused his curiosity about Corrie Miller, so he'd run a list of Corrie Miller's friends, taken from an address book he'd found at the house, but nobody had seen or heard from her in several months, before they moved from Colorado. Every single one of her friends had been eager to talk, so Harlan had a wealth of secondhand information about the missing woman.

Most parroted what he'd learned early on: the woman was happy in her marriage, a devout, straight-as-an-arrow, stay-at-home mom with zero skeletons in her closet. One woman in the circle of friends had put a different spin on it, admitting that Corrie Miller had some psychiatric problems a few years back, bad enough to land her in a psychiatric ward in Colorado—something about a chemical imbalance, aggravated by alcohol . . . but from all accounts she'd recovered and hadn't had anything stronger than a Diet Coke in six years. Susan Warren described her friend

Corrie as the perfect wife and mother. Still, Harlan had to ask. "In your opinion, could she have killed her husband and son?"

"Corrie? Oh God, no."

"A lot of marriages go through periods of stress," he'd countered. "Could she have snapped?"

Susan Warren had laughed cynically. "Sheriff, John was a prince compared to my ex, and I haven't killed him yet. Believe me, Corrie had no hand in this."

Her friends swore that despite her emotional problems, Corrie Miller wasn't the type to kill her husband and son and split.

No? Then where was she?

That was the sixty-four thousand dollar question. The blood at the crime scene had been analyzed, and it belonged exclusively to John Miller, a scenario that had proven hauntingly familiar. There hadn't been any trace of Maddy's blood at the Call crime scene either. If not for Juan Martinez, Harlan would have had to examine the possibility that Maddy had been involved in the killings. He would not have been given a choice. Thankfully, it hadn't come to that.

Corrie Miller was a different story. There were no other immediate suspects. He'd lifted hundreds of prints, but none that were a surprise. Corrie, John, and young Billy. Then there was Deke, who'd been in the house prior to the Miller's recent renovation. No surprises. No red flags. Not even a hunch so far.

Of course, it was possible that Susan Warren was wrong, that Corrie Miller's emotional trouble had resurfaced worse than before, that she'd lost it and offed her family, then disappeared. It would account for the boy's condition. Whoever had ended his life had done it as gently as possible, if there was a gentle way to kill someone.

The ME had called that morning. Cause of death: asphyxiation by suffocation. No struggle, no bruises, no marks, aside from the petechial hemorrhage in the inner lining of his eyelids. Examining the crime scene, Harlan had had the distinct impression that the person or persons responsible had felt an immediate remorse upon killing Billy, a remorse that was totally lacking when it came to John Miller.

John Miller had been beaten about the face and head with an unknown object with such ferocity that every facial bone had been crushed and his nose had been driven into his brain. *An act of uncontrolled, excessive rage to the point of overkill.* That was how Harlan read the man's death. *The doer had taken his violent emotions out on Miller yet been sufficiently collected not to leave a blazing trail of evidence behind.* But there *was* one other thing. The ME had found metal fragments, almost microscopic in size yet large enough to analyze. The filings had gone directly to the state lab. He had no clear idea when he'd get the results.

Harlan made a left into his drive and shifted into park, pausing long enough to look up at the house before turning off the ignition, pocketing the keys, and opening the main door leading into the garage. Ginny's Tahoe was in the garage in its usual spot. He went in quietly, through the garage as he always did, and for once kicked off his boots.

"You takin' your shoes off, Harlan?" Her voice sounded hollow and watery, issuing as it did from the shadows near the top of the stairs. "How long have I been tryin' to get you to take off those damn old boots?"

Harlan sighed, pausing at the bottom of the stairwell.

"Too long. Maybe I'm just thickheaded for it to take so long, but it finally sunk in." He laughed low, but there was no humor in it. "Don't worry. I'm not stayin', so I won't be in the way. I just need to get a change of clothes before I head back to town."

A weird sound escaped her as he started up, like a half-strangled gulp. "No," she said. "Don't."

"Ginny." It was a plea for peace, for one last chance to salvage something from thirty-three years together.

She didn't seem to have it in her to relent, and he wondered for the thousandth time how the hell they'd gotten to such a pathetic point when once it had all seemed so promising. As he reached the landing, she stood, catching his shirt to try to hold him there, dissolving against him in a flood of incoherent crying.

"I'm sorry. I'm sorry, I'm sorry, I'm sorry—"

"Ginny. C'mon, Ginny please don't do this."

"Don't leave—please—don't—" She clutched at him, catching his shirt, tearing the tails from his trousers. One of the buttons went flying, landing on the steps and bouncing. Her hands were on him, touching where he had ached to be touched for so long, and he reacted. "Don't leave me, don't leave me, don't—" She unbuckled his belt, opening the button at his waistband and his fly, manipulating him into a frenzy with her hands.

Harlan said nothing. He was afraid to speak for fear the sound of his voice would shatter the moment, that she would turn angry, turn inward, turn away . . . but she only braced her weight against the banister, pushed down jeans and panties, and spread her legs for him.

He needed no further encouragement, entering her, drawing a shocked breath at the sudden sensation of heat. It had been so damned long he'd almost forgotten. She was crying and hanging onto his shoulders, as frantic for him as she'd been in the early days—then before he knew it, it was over. She struggled briefly in his arms, her body going tense, and Harlan held her all the harder. "No, Ginny, no. Don't do this—don't push me away—"

She shook her head, violently. "No! I can't—I just—*can't!*" She disengaged, righted her clothing, and sank onto the step, curling into a miserable ball.

Emotionally wrung out, his frustration running at high tide and his ego in shreds, Harlan zipped his fly over a withered erection and went past her up the stairs to gather his things, too numb to examine what had just happened.

Chapter Nine

On Wednesdays Coyote Moon didn't open until two. It was a long-standing tradition and the only time Carlotta let her hair down and just relaxed. As a lady of leisure for a few hours, she slept late, read the paper in her satin pajamas, and drank herbal tea till it threatened to come out of her ears. By noon, she was usually so fed up with relaxing that she would complain to Anna she could hardly wait to get back to work.

This particular Wednesday was very different. The herbal tea was steeping and Carlotta wore her royal blue satin pajamas and Chinese silk robe, but the mood in her kitchen was far from relaxed. "Are you sure you're all right, honey?" she asked as she laid a small spread of apricot–cranberry bread and poppy seed rolls. "Maybe we should get you over to Doc Webster's and have you checked out. You could have lost an eye with all that flying glass."

"Well, I didn't, and thanks for the concern, but I don't need a doctor." Even as Anna said it, she was fully aware that she had Deke to thank for it. If he hadn't come along when he had . . . Maybe it was better not to think about that right now. "I just wish the van hadn't taken the brunt of it."

Carlotta flicked a red-nailed hand in a dismissive gesture. "That old rattletrap ain't worth much. Been ready for the junkyard for years, and it'd be there right now if you hadn't bought it from me. Don't you give it another thought. This was vandalism. The insurance'll cover it." She put down her best French-white china, then turned away for the teapot. "I'm a lot more concerned about this happenin' at all. What the hell's goin' on around here, anyway? Used to be a woman could walk the streets at three in the morning stark naked and nobody'd dare say boo to her. Now there's a murder every other week it seems, and you can't drive home without having some jerkwater bust out your windows! It's always been a decent little town, and it really burns my ass that somebody's workin' so hard to fuck that up." She poured steaming liquid into both cups, pausing to light a cigarette before she sat down. She looked haggard in the light pouring through the French doors. It seemed strange, seeing her without makeup. "You get a look at this guy?"

Anna shook her head. "No, I wish I had, but it was impossible. His face was covered—a Halloween mask. I had the impression it was a man though."

"Well, there's a shocker," Carlotta said, shooting a stream of smoke toward the ceiling. "Men do stupid shit all the time for no good reason. Most women are more practical. Take some chick's boyfriend, she'll pull your hair and slap your face, but she isn't likely to smash out your headlights on a lonely back road." Another drag on her cigarette and she crushed it out in a glass ashtray. "You didn't happen to take some girl's man, did you, honey?"

"Not lately," Anna said. As far as she knew, Deke was unattached, and had been since his divorce.

Carlotta sipped from her china cup. "You never mentioned how you got back home. With the van disabled and all."

Anna took a breath, and sipped her tea. *Now, how do I answer this one?* "A car came along and scared the guy off, and they gave me a ride."

Nothing escaped Carlotta's notice, and she seemed to sense Anna's reluctance. "Them?"

Anna rolled her eyes. "Deke Call," she admitted, wincing at Carlotta's loud hoot.

"Deke Call! Lucas Swift-Water's nephew? Now there's a story waitin' to be unraveled. You said he took you home . . . you didn't say whether you invited him up."

"Carlotta McFadden! You should be ashamed of yourself for asking!"

"Yeah, I know. It's none of my business." Another sip. "Well . . . did you? Man, I hope so! It'd be a damn shame to pass that one up."

Anna hid her smile behind the rim of her cup. It was just one of the things she liked about her friend and employer. Another sip, and Anna seized the opportunity to get her slant on the mystery man. "You've known him a long time?"

Carlotta shrugged. "All his life—until he went away, that is. That was after the murders. I heard he'd graduated college, and then the police academy, though he don't look much the part, that's for sure. Everything I've heard was based on gossip, and nothin' came from the man himself. Men like Deke Call don't talk about themselves, as a rule."

"I suppose not," Anna said. "What was he like, before he left?"

"He was pretty wild as a kid, as I recall . . . rebellious, you know? Always seemed to be buckin' the system. Challenging authority, and at that time the authority around here was Matthew Call. If those tattoos are any indication, I'd say that rebellious streak hasn't gone anywhere."

"I kind of got that," Anna agreed. "He didn't get along with Matthew?"

Carlotta's smile turned wry. "That's an understatement. Matt was a real hard case. He was the Law, and he made sure everybody knew it. From what I heard back then, he was no softer at home . . . except maybe with Maddy and the little girl. It must've really rankled a man like Matt that he couldn't get Deke to bend. I saw bruises on the boy more than a few times, but who's to say Matthew put 'em there?" She tucked her chin against her thin chest, looking up at Anna as her voice turned cynical. "Not one person insane enough to ask the most powerful man in the county if he beat his boy—yours truly included. And that ain't somethin' it pleases me to admit."

Anna frowned, her thoughts with a battered boy who must have felt he had nowhere to turn. "Do you think he had anything to do with Matthew Call's murder?"

"Honey, isn't it a little late in the game to be questioning the character of the man you're screwing?"

"Carlotta!" Anna said, then, "That wasn't an answer."

"Do I think Deke was angry enough to kill the weathered old son of a bitch?" A sigh. "Yes, I think he may have been. But kill his little sister?" She shook her head. "No. He loved that child, and he watched out for her. I think he would have sacrificed himself to keep her safe, had it been necessary. And whoever killed Matt killed that child too. I'd stake my life on it." She lit another smoke, her motions angry and impatient, though none of it was aimed at Anna. "Sets the hair on the back of your neck on end, don't it? The idea that if Juan didn't do it and Deke didn't do it there's a killer still out there."

There was a soft tap at the back door. Carlotta got up to answer it. "Well, if it isn't the sheriff! I'd like to say I'm surprised to see you, Harlan, but givin' that this county's goin' to hell on a handcar—"

"Always a pleasure, Carlotta," he said, neatly cutting her off. "Anna." He gave a nod of greeting and took off his hat, fixing Anna with that penetrating blue gaze of his. "I was hoping I'd find you here." He pulled out a chair and sat down directly across from her, making it impossible for her to avoid him.

"Well, pull up a chair, Harlan," Carlotta said sarcastically. "Make yourself at home."

He flicked a glance at his hostess, and a frown of displeasure settled over his rugged face. He wasn't Anna's type, but she couldn't deny he was still a good-looking man. "I hear you had some trouble last night near the Miller place. Maybe you'd like to explain what you were doin' out there and why I had to hear about it from Deacon Call."

Anna didn't understand the dynamic between Deke and Harlan, but it was obvious they disliked one another, and she could only imagine what might have been said. Yet, before she could answer, Carlotta stepped in. "It might be because Deke Call's more likely to do somethin' about it than you."

He gave Carlotta a look. "Do you mind givin' us some privacy? As much as I enjoy your company, I'd like to get to the bottom of this."

"Whatever you say, *Sheriff,* but only cause *I* want you

to get to the bottom of it too." Carlotta uncrossed her arms. "I'll be upstairs, Anna, honey. Just yell if you need me."

"Lucas says you were at his house last night and that you showed up with Wheeler Dobbs. Did anyone know your whereabouts last night, besides Deke Call?"

"I didn't exactly announce it, if that's what you mean."

"What about Dobbs? Did you happen to mention which way you'd be heading?"

Anna shook her head. "Wheeler needed a lift because his truck's been repo-ed and he has no other transportation. If he couldn't get to Lucas's, how could he have gotten to the Call place before I did?"

He said nothing, but Anna knew he hadn't let go of it, and she wondered if she'd ever met anyone quite as hardheaded as Harlan Rudy. Aside from Deke.

It was nearly the same question Deke had asked her a few days before about Harlan. "You seem to spend a lot of time at Lucas's ranch. Is there a reason for that?"

"I'm not sure how that pertains to what happened to Carlotta's van, or what business it is of yours, Sheriff."

Harlan's expression hardened subtly. "Everything that goes on in this county is my business," he assured her. "Make no mistake about that. I went to Echo Canyon Road to have a look at the van after leaving Lucas's this morning, and I saw the shattered glass from the headlight and windshield. It was just yards away from the same house where a double homicide occurred days ago, and a woman is still missing. If that isn't serious, then I don't know what is. Now, how about you tell me what happened." He lowered his head, looking up at her from under sandy brows. "And do me a favor, Anna. Don't leave out any details."

Anna took a deep breath and gave him what he wanted, starting with the drive home and ending with Deke's arrival.

"Deke Call," he muttered under his breath but loud enough for Anna to hear it.

"You have a problem with Lucas's nephew? Is it personal or professional?"

"Oh, it's personal, all right. Every damn time I look up, that boy's standin' in my way. That's a tendency that can get under a man's skin real fast. But I'm guessin' that's somethin' you understand . . . Call gettin' under your skin. . . . "

Anna refused to answer, asking instead, "Level with me, Harlan. What's really going on here? Two cases of multiple murder in the same house? Two women disappear? Even a dozen years apart, that's hardly a coincidence."

He pushed back in his chair. "Did I say it was a coincidence?"

"You haven't said much of anything that I know of. I'd like to have your take on recent events, on the record. Who killed Miller and his son, and why? And where is Corrie Miller?"

"If I knew, I wouldn't tell you. This is an ongoing investigation. As a crime writer, I'm going to assume you know what that means."

"Oh, I know what it means. You mentioned being at Lucas's this morning. Is everything okay out there?"

"As a matter of fact, it isn't. Somebody killed his ram last night and strung its guts out like toilet paper streamers at Halloween. It was anything but pretty. Looks to me like somebody's got it in for him, and it's my job to figure out why."

"My God," Anna said beneath her breath.

He pushed out of his chair with Anna still reeling from the news about Lucas.

"Tell Deke to stay out of trouble," he said, but what he meant was *tell him to stay the hell out of my way.*

He went out onto the porch, and Anna, standing by the door, noticed the short blonde paused on the second step. Ginny Rudy was middle aged but attractive, without the stuffiness or affectation of her friend Francine. She glanced at Anna, then at Harlan, and turned sharply, starting back down the steps she'd just mounted. Harlan's spine stiffened and he ran a hand through his hair before seating his Stetson on his head, but he didn't attempt to stop her.

"Well, well. Looks like a storm's brewing in the Rudy household," Carlotta said. She'd appeared so fast on the sheriff's heels that it was obvious she'd been listening. At Anna's questioning glance, she inclined her head at the sheriff's wife getting into an SUV parked at the curb. "I'll have to give her a call later and see what she wanted."

Deke had a feeling that something big was about to happen. It was gut level and immediate, impossible to ignore. Little Eduardo showed up at the door of the flophouse where he'd been staying, dragging him from a half sleep. "Get dressed, man. Joaquin says you gotta come with me."

Deke knew better than to ask questions, but the skin at the top of his spine did a slow crawl, and it took every ounce of will he had to maintain a convincing level of don't-give-a-damn attitude. Tonight was the night, the litmus test that would mean acceptance or expulsion. The success or failure of the entire TPD task force was riding on his acceptance into the Diablos. If Aguilar turned him out, they'd be back at square one and the last five months would have been wasted, but he couldn't afford to think about that now, so he threw on a shirt and the denim jacket that had seen some rough usage and followed Little Eduardo out into the night.

Eduardo usually ran at the mouth. Quick with a joke or stupid chatter about any number of things, tonight he was uncharacteristically reserved, almost to the point of being withdrawn. "Hey, man," Deke said, skating a glance in his direction. "You sick or somethin'?"

"What? Hell, no. I'm better than okay." He glanced from the highway to Deke and back again. "I gotta keep my mouth shut, but I can tell you this—it's your big night, man. The moment of truth has arrived, Chaca. Just keep your head. Stay cool. No matter what happens."

They pulled into a parking lot on the west side of Tucson, and the banger killed the headlights. He opened the door, hesitating, then offering his hand. Deke took it. "Good luck. My money's ridin' on you." He got out and, as Deke followed suit, escorted him to the abandoned building. The ground level had been used for storage and was wide open except for some empty crates stacked along the perimeter of the room. Something stirred in the shadows, to the left, to the right, straight ahead. He turned slowly, his pulse kick-starting.

Six hard-core *cholos* moving simultaneously into the half light. The man to his immediate right hit Deke with a sucker punch, just below the ribs. Pain exploded in his midsection as the breath was driven from him. A banger named Jewels threw a hard right, connecting with his left cheekbone. Unsatisfied, he hit Deke again, and a third time apparently just for the hell of it.

Each of the six bangers took his turn, and Deke didn't

lift a finger to defend himself as he was "beaten" into the Diablos. A kidney punch knocked him to his knees, where he wavered. Blood streamed into his right eye, blinding him on that side. The left was swollen nearly shut, but he saw Joaquin snap his fingers and the bangers move back to let him through.

Aguilar stopped in front of Deke and, reaching down, patted his cheek. "Congratulations, brother," he said, his voice echoing weirdly in Deke's head. "You're in." Then Aguilar walked away, exiting the building.

It was over, Deke thought, his breath coming in sickening gulps between spasms. He'd succeeded. He'd just been welcomed into the Diablos. Now if he just lived to make use of that connection.

Little Eduardo was kneeling in front of him. "You made it, man. Jesus! You made it!" He shook his head, sounding relieved. "How you feelin'? You need a doctor?"

"No doctor," Deke said, pushing to his feet. His lower back burned like fire, and he knew there was a damn good chance he'd bruised a kidney. "Can you give me a lift back? I'll be okay."

"To that rat hole you call home?" Eduardo said. "Shit, man! That was okay before you were connected, but you're a Diablo now—a brother. You're comin' home with me. In a day or two, you'll feel better, eh? Then we'll find you someplace new. Someplace upscale."

Deke didn't have the strength to argue as Eduardo opened the car door and Jewels practically poured him into the passenger seat. Streetlights overhead were an indistinct blur as he drifted in and out of consciousness. Eduardo kept up a running chatter as he drove, but Deke wasn't sure if it was directed at him or the silent man in the back seat. A few minutes later, Deke was dragged from the car and hustled through a side door and into a private elevator. For the second time in five months he found himself in Eduardo's posh apartment, only this time he was in no shape to appreciate his surroundings.

He didn't remember much of what followed, but he had the vague impression that he'd fallen, and he suspected he must have passed out on the way in. When he woke, Angel was there. He could hear voices—Eduardo's, Jewel's—and knew they must be in the next room. "You make a habit of this?" he managed to whisper. His lower lip was split and swollen, and he had a chipped incisor. It hurt like hell to talk.

"Only when Eduardo asks me to," she said in a dreamy little girl voice. He was lying on a bed in what must have been a guest room. It was just as elegantly furnished as the rest of the apartment. Eduardo lived high and had excellent taste, and Angel was no exception. From the looks of the alcohol and bloody cotton pads piled in the wastebasket near her, she'd gotten the worst of it taken care of. "Eduardo's protective. He doesn't like me putting my hands on other men. For some reason he's made an exception where you're concerned. I guess he thinks I'm safe with you."

"I'll try not to disappoint him," Deke said, wincing. He should have been relieved to know he had gained the other man's trust. He wasn't. It was far too early in the game to relax. But he meant what he'd said to the girl. Christ, she was just a kid, and he wasn't stupid enough to get involved with another man's woman. It was asking for trouble in the most mundane circumstances. "It's Angel, right?"

A bare nod.

"Angel, could you get me some water?"

She left the room and came back with an icy bottle. Deke thanked her, then took a careful sip. The liquid slid down his throat, sending his aching stomach into renewed spasms. She held out a colorful capsule, slipping it between his teeth when he asked, "What that for?"

"It's just Percocet. For the pain. It'll help you sleep. I take them all the time."

Deke took the pill and downed it with a swallow of water. "Thanks. You mind if I ask you somethin'?"

She snorted. "You can ask. I may not answer."

"How old are you?"

"Old enough," she said. Her hazel eyes were sad, almost as empty as her smile. "What about you?"

"Twenty-eight. How long have you been using?"

She took the pack of cigarettes off the bedside table, confiscated his lighter, and lit one, taking a long, sensual drag before offering it to him. "Using? I don't know what you're talking about. Eduardo was just kidding before."

"Yeah, you do. The heroin chic, the track marks— it's impossible to miss." Reaching out to take the cigarette, he caught her slim wrist between finger and thumb, slowly sliding her long sleeve up as far as her elbow.

She snatched her wrist away. Deke held his breath. He was taking one hell of a chance with her. According to gang culture, she *belonged* to Eduardo, and if he overstepped the boundaries it would mean trouble. The Percocet was kicking in, though, and it lowered his natural inhibitions just enough to encourage him to ignore the danger and attempt to satisfy his curiosity.

"What do you care?"

He shrugged. "I had a little sister once. I guess you just reminded me is all."

"Once?" she said. "What's that supposed to mean?"

"She's dead," Deke said, and his own voice was faint and far away. The pain of the beating was fading; his

grip on consciousness was sliding fast. He heard her
sigh as she stood, heard Eduardo's voice as he confronted her.

"You take care of Chaca, Angel?"

"I took care of him."

"He gonna be all right?"

"I don't know." A pause. "He's big, strong. I think so."
She moved past him and exited. Deke knew when she
left the room, because the brooding disquiet in the
atmosphere shifted, dissipating. It was calmer now, the
bed on which he lay softer than anything he'd ever slept
on. His muscles released and he relaxed, sinking further, and everything faded to gray. . . .

The memory slipped from Deke's grasp. He leaned
on the handle of the shovel and drank in the clean, cool
air. Rain wasn't far off. He could feel it in the chill kiss
of the wind on his exposed skin. The new leaves had
gone belly-up, a good indication that the barometric
pressure was dropping. "Think maybe we should get
him placed and covered over," Deke suggested gently.
"Gonna rain before nightfall."

Lucas gave the ram's shaggy coat one last stroke, said
something close to the animal's ear Deke couldn't hear,
and got to his feet with a groan. Lucas wasn't a young
man, and it was impossible to ignore the toll recent
events had taken on him. He still carried himself
straight and proud, but the lines around his eyes and at
the corners of his mouth seemed deeper and more pro-
nounced, and he moved a little slower than he normally
did. "I s'pose you're right. No sense in delaying any
longer."

Together they wrapped the ram's carcass in an old
woolen blanket, and Lucas watched as Deke laid him in
the grave. Then, Lucas stood by while Deke covered it

Zebra
Contemporary
Romance

Zebra Contemporary

Whatever your taste in contemporary romance – Romantic Suspense... Character-Driven... Light & Whimsical... Heartwarming... Humorous – we have it at Zebra!

And now Zebra has created a Book Club for readers like yourself who enjoy fine Contemporary Romance written by today's best-selling authors.

Authors like Fern Michaels... Lori Foster... Janet Dailey... Lisa Jackson...Janelle Taylor... Kasey Michaels... Shannon Drake... Kat Martin... to name but a few!

These are the finest contemporary romances available anywhere today!

But don't take our word for it! Accept our gift of FREE Zebra Contemporary Romances – and see for yourself. You only pay $1.99 for shipping and handling.

Once you've read them, we're sure you'll want to continue receiving the newest Zebra Contemporaries as soon as they're published each month! And you can by becoming a member of the Zebra Contemporary Romance Book Club!

As a member of Zebra Contemporary Romance Book Club,

- You'll receive four books every month. Each book will be by one of Zebra's best-selling authors.

- You'll have variety – you'll never receive two of the same kind of story in one month.

- You'll get your books hot off the press, usually before they appear in bookstores.

- You'll ALWAYS save up to 30% off the cover price.

  SEND FOR YOUR FREE BOOKS TODAY!

To start your membership, simply complete and return the Free Book Certificate. You'll receive your Introductory Shipment of FREE Zebra Contemporary Romances, you only pay $1.99 for shipping and handling. Then, each month you will receive the 4 newest Zebra Contemporary Romances. Each shipment will be yours to examine FREE for 10 days. If you decide to keep the books, you'll pay the preferred subscriber price (a savings of up to 30% off the cover price), plus shipping and handling. If you want us to stop sending books, just say the word... it's that simple.

If the FREE Book Certificate is missing, call 1-800-770-1963 to place your order.

FREE BOOK CERTIFICATE

Yes! Please send me FREE Zebra Contemporary romance novels. I only pay $1.99 for shipping and handling. I understand that each month thereafter I will be able to preview 4 brand-new Contemporary Romances FREE for 10 days. Then, if I should decide to keep them, I will pay the money-saving preferred subscriber's price (that's a savings of up to 30% off the retail price), plus shipping and handling. I understand I am under no obligation to purchase any books, as explained on this card.

NAME _____

ADDRESS _____ APT. _____

CITY _____ STATE _____ ZIP _____

TELEPHONE (___) _____

E-MAIL _____

SIGNATURE _____

(If under 18, parent or guardian must sign)

Offer limited to one per household and not to current subscribers. Terms, offer and prices subject to change. Orders subject to acceptance by Zebra Contemporary Book Club. Offer Valid in the U.S. only.

Thank You!

CN086A

Ill..l..lll....llll....ll.l.l..l..ll.l..lll.l..ll.l..lll...l

Zebra Contemporary Romance Book Club
Zebra Home Subscription Service, Inc.
P.O. Box 5214
Clifton NJ 07015-5214

PLACE
STAMP
HERE

over with the displaced earth. He returned the spade to the toolshed and followed Lucas back to the house. "The offer for the apartment above your studio still open?"

"That depends on who wants to know," Lucas said. "You wouldn't be thinkin' of leavin' that palace of yours for better digs?"

Perching on the banister, Deke lit a cigarette, cupping his hands around its tip to shield the flame from the rising wind. "I might be, if the rent's right."

Lucas snorted. "How's three-thirty a month sound?"

"Like extortion, but I guess it'll have to do."

Deke drove back to town, crammed his stuff into a duffle bag, and settled the week's rent with the manager. Within the hour, he'd relocated and stashed his clothes in the closet. The apartment was clean and spacious, three rooms and a bath above the studio where Lucas worked. Not a single cockroach, and the place had a private entrance. Damned if the phone wasn't turned on, and there was beer in the fridge.

What more could a burned-out ex-narc ask for? he thought, emptying his pockets onto the top of the bedroom dresser. *Some peace, maybe? A shred of happiness? Contentment?*

"Peace? Not likely. You reap what you sow, man. You reap what you sow." With Little Eduardo and his woman still in his thoughts, Deke pulled the harmonica from his shirt pocket—the same harmonica he'd taken from the crime scene. He'd dusted it for prints after he'd got back home but found only the boy's and his. Putting it to his mouth, he pulled a string of notes from it, a sad, jazzy melody he remembered from somewhere but couldn't quite place.

Where would Angel be right now if she hadn't had the

misfortune to cross his path? To get in the way of his fucking ambition? He would have preferred to think that it wouldn't have mattered, but deep down he knew better. She'd been in a hell of a bad way when he first met her, and getting involved with him had only made things worse. Like just by existing he'd made things worse for his mother. Somewhere in the back of his mind he heard Matthew's angry growl. . . . *Fuckin' little bastard! You'll mind me or else!*

Then Maddy's shrill, *Matthew, no! Please! For God's sake, he's just a boy!*

Dark emotion surged up from his boot tops, feelings repressed for what felt like an eternity, blotting out every speck of self-worth he'd ever known, every ounce of physical sensation. The raw emptiness screamed, a voiceless howl that echoed through every cell, every atom of his being.

He glanced at the pistol lying on the dresser. It was fully loaded, but one slug was all he needed.

One to end it.

To quiet the roar, to put the pain to sleep.

One instant, one shot, and it would all be over. . . .

And he wouldn't have to think, to feel, anymore.

One . . . one . . . one. . . .

It would be so easy. So goddamned easy.

Death was seductive, a siren's song with an irresistible allure. . . . He stared at the heavy steel frame for a long time, his mouth as dry as dust, thinking about the darkness that awaited, the quiet, thinking about his uncle . . . about the hurt his escape would bring. He thought about his mother, about the possibility that she was still out there, somewhere . . . about the boy he'd found lying in the same spot he'd found his little sister twelve years before.

He stared longingly at the Colt, then turned and walked through the sliding glass doors and out onto the deck. The lowering clouds scudding across the sky suited his black mood, and as the first fat raindrops splashed around him, Deke filtered his pain through the harmonica, an offering to the approaching night. He let the rain wash over him. The cold discomfort was nothing. He didn't feel a thing.

The haunting melody drifted on the damp breeze. Lifting her face to the rainy dusk, Anna followed the sound to its source and found herself at the top of a long flight of stairs. He was leaning against the wall, eyes closed, pouring everything he had into the melody as the rain sluiced over him, unaware that he was no longer alone.

Heart in her throat, Anna watched him.

It hurt to witness it, the intensity with which he laid his soul bare, the expression of exquisite pain on his dark, handsome face.

Anna went to him. She couldn't seem to help herself. She framed his face with her hands and kissed one cheek, then the other. He hadn't shaved, and as he dropped the harmonica and buried his face in the curve of her throat, his stubble abraded her sensitive skin. His arms closed around her, the ferocity with which he held her a little frightening—fear, not for her own well-being, but his. Looking over his shoulder, through the open doors, she saw the revolver lying on the dresser and suddenly understood how unrelenting the demon that drove him really was. "Jesus, Deke. What happened to you?"

He held her for a few more seconds, and Anna had the

impression that he needed to memorize that moment, imprint it onto his cells, burn it into his brain, then he released her. "If you came to see Lucas, he's not home. He took off a while ago. Somethin' about business with Wheeler. Guess you should come back another time."

"I didn't come to see your uncle," Anna said, admitting it to herself for the very first time. "I came to see you. I stopped by the hotel. Millie said you'd moved out."

"Yeah. Lucas needs help, and at the moment I'm all he's got."

Rain dripped off his dark hair, ran down his face in thin runnels, but he made no move to go inside, and there was no way she was going to leave him. Something was dreadfully wrong. She sensed it, felt it, right down to the soles of her feet. "You're soaked. Why don't we go inside?" Voice soft, she tugged at his hand.

Catching her fingers, he brought them to his mouth, kissed them gently, sadly, then released her. "Go home, Anna."

"Go home . . . because you don't want me here? Or because I might get in the way if you decide to pick up that gun and do something insanely stupid?"

His mouth quirked at one corner, an odd little half smile that didn't touch his eyes or lessen the severity of his expression. "Baby, you don't know shit about me, and if your luck holds, you'll never learn."

On the crime beat, she'd been persistent in the extreme, and she was no less so now. It was the only way to get answers.

Give up, give in, back down . . . get nothing.

"I know that there's something dark inside you, something that makes you go to extremes. If I was to guess, I'd say it had something to do with this. . . ." She ran a finger down the arm with the trailing roses. "And this," and she touched the word *Chaca* emblazoned on the opposite bicep. "I asked before, and had it meant nothing, you would have told me."

The gaze he turned on her was hard and cold, and it chilled Anna more than she was willing to admit. She was on the right track, and she knew it. His self-destructive streak had to do with his past, with Angel, and the others, but he was just as hardheaded as she was, and the more she pressed him, the more securely he closed down. "Then why the fuck are you askin' again?"

The ensuing silence between them was shattered as a freak bolt of lightning struck in the distance, high atop the ridge. A second later thunder rumbled through the ground underfoot. Storms were rare this early in the year. "Because as dangerous as it is, as stupid, I care about what happens to you."

She might as well have slapped him hard. He drew in a sharp breath, looking away to the ridge and beyond, to the past. "Then I pity you. Close to me ain't someplace you want to be. You'll end up getting hurt, or worse, and I've done enough damage already. Go the hell away, Anna. For Christ's sake. Just leave me be."

"Leave you be . . . so that you can finish what you intended to do that first night at that damned house, before Harlan and I walked in."

His silence was an affirmation on its own.

Lightning flashed again, lighting up the night, searing her senses. It cast him in a blindingly white light for a split second, so that the misery in his eyes was stark and unavoidable. A muscle worked violently in his cheek, proof of some inner struggle that eluded her, that she wanted as desperately to understand as he wanted out. In that instant, she would have said anything, done anything just to reach him, to break through the granite wall he'd erected between himself and the world. "Why didn't you do it that night, Deke?" she pressed, an ache in her tone she didn't want to identify but couldn't seem to control. "After we left—why didn't you pick up the gun and finish it?" When he refused to answer, she hit him with both fists, an action conceived in frustration and born of a sense of unshakable impotence. The blow caught him midchest but didn't seem to faze him, so she hit him again. "Why, damn you! Why didn't you do it then? Goddamn you, Deke Call, answer me!"

Another blow, and he caught both fists, forcing her hands up, pinning them close to her body between them. "Because of you," he said. "Because of you."

The fight left Anna, and she went limp against him. Slowly, he released her wrists, and as he put his arms around her a sigh rippled through him. Reaching onto her toes, Anna kissed his cheeks, his chin, then with a hand at his nape pulled him into a long, deep kiss. With their emotions running high, the contact was explosive. Cold wet skin met cold wet skin, and despite her best efforts, Anna shivered.

She sensed that the crisis had passed. "Let's go inside."

He led her through the dark apartment to the bathroom and closed the door, then, turning on the water, adjusted the shower and closed the glass doors. The sodden shirt and jeans were peeled from her body, and Anna didn't protest. As he stepped under the steaming jets and pulled her against him, she found his lips again, barely coming up for air. How could it feel so right after everything that had just happened? Steam rising around them, Anna watched, mesmerized as he knelt before her, and guiding her legs apart, worshipped her body with his mouth. Sensuous heat . . . earth-shattering ecstasy didn't wipe away the frightening fact that she might be all that stood between this enigmatic man and sure disaster. . . .

A little while later, Anna curled against his side. Her hair was still damp from the shower, but she was warm from their recent sexual activity and, with the rain still falling outside, reluctant to stir from the comfort of Deke's bed. He lay very still, eyes closed, but she knew he wasn't sleeping. "Harlan stopped by Carlotta's house today."

"Good ol' Harlan," he said, his voice rough from disuse. "I suppose he filled you in."

"He told me what happened, yes," Anna said. "How's Lucas?"

"Upset. Tryin' to act like nothin's happening here."

Anna frowned. "What *is* happening, Deke? Lucas is so kind. Why would anyone want to hurt him?"

"Baby, I don't have the answers," he told her. "Because they could, and because it meant a lot to Lucas. That old ram was so tame he'd almost forgotten how to be a sheep. I checked out the area, and there was one set of footprints that didn't match mine or Lucas's. There were only a few prints inside the fence. He walked right up to them."

"Did you check outside the fence?" Anna asked, knowing the answer.

"I tracked the bastard across the valley grass. They crossed the ridge and disappeared at the blacktop road. Whoever killed that old ram came part of the way by vehicle, then walked in using the same route along that ridge that Lucas's Ridge-Walker uses."

"Ridge-Walker?" Anna frowned at him. "I don't get it. What's a Ridge-Walker?"

"Lucas says somebody's been prowlin' the ridge above the pasture. Says it's a *chindi,* but it's superstition talkin'."

"*Chindi?* You mean, like a ghost?"

"Somethin' like that. It's the Navajo version of the dearly departed, comin' back to wreak havoc on the livin'."

Anna frowned. "He thinks he's got a ghost. What do you think?"

"I think it's gettin' late and I should probably take you home."

"Time to throw me out," Anna said. "Before I start asking questions, before things get too uncomfortable." She smiled, bending to tease the dark nipple that capped his pectoral, then ran her tongue down the center of his chest to the place where the sheet covered him. "You sure you want me to go?" She slid a hand under the sheet and his erection sprang to life again.

In less than a heartbeat he'd flipped her onto her back and filled her. "Maybe it won't hurt, playin' with fire . . . just this once."

Anna woke to the ringing of the cell phone Deke left on the nightstand. Rolling over, she reached for Deke and discovered that the bed beside her was empty. The sheets were cool, and for a few seconds she fought a sudden surge of panic. She sat up, glancing at the dresser across the room, catching a glimmer of blued steel, breathing a sigh of relief. The phone continued to ring. Anna got up, throwing on her shirt, padding to the bathroom, then the kitchen. "Deke?"

Silence. The phone gave one last bleat before she picked it up and flipped it on. "Hello."

There was a brief pause, then someone took a shuddering breath. A woman's voice, small and quivery, "D-Deacon." The caller stammered as she spoke his name.

"Who is this?" Anna had the impression that she was uncomfortable with what she was saying. A sob, half-stifled, and she continued. "Oh God—Deacon. I'm in trouble. Deacon . . . God help me."

"Who is this? Who's calling?" Anna demanded. An audible click, and the line went dead.

Chapter Ten

Wheeler Dobbs paced the floor, pausing just long enough to down another shot of vodka before resuming the restless walk. Four in the morning and the crazy bitch was starting to look like a no-show, but instead of saying to hell with it and going back to bed or diving headfirst into his latest project, he was doing a damn good job of wearing a threadbare path in the carpet. "What the fuck is wrong with this picture?" he said, splashing Absolut into a water glass and crossing to the door to gaze at the night for what seemed like the millionth time since midnight.

No headlights.

No movement.

No nothing. Just pure, deep darkness and the light, chill fog that followed an early spring storm. "If you had a damn bit of sense, you'd dump this shitbag town and move on."

Christ, the thought was tempting, and he clung to it for a few minutes, letting himself consider where he would go and what he would do next. California was always a possibility, or the Seattle area. Maybe even

Alaska. An artist of his caliber might eventually make a name for himself there, but that would mean cutting his losses and leaving everything behind. His guts roiled at that.

It had taken him four years to build his business here, and though he hadn't exactly hit the big time, every day brought another opportunity for a potential patron of the arts to walk through the door, preferably a rich older woman with a deep bank account and a fondness for fast-talking, good-looking rogues. To cut and run now would mean giving up everything he'd worked for and starting over . . . and it didn't matter anyway. He was in too deep, and she was far too dangerous to double-cross.

He'd managed to get clear of New York without losing his precious freedom. But one word in the right ear and it could end in a heartbeat. Not only did the lady have a psychotic streak a mile wide, she had powerful connections.

Unable to sleep, Deke got dressed and went out into the night. The rain had passed, and a thready low-lying fog crept in. Sufficient to obscure details without providing total cover, it nonetheless made for an eerie atmosphere. Lucas's windows were lightless, the house quiet. Nothing stirred. He stopped at the sheep pen and, leaning against the fence, lit a smoke and thought of Arlo. The ewes and last year's lambs were huddled together in one corner of the fence, bewildered without their protector. It was obvious they missed him and, in a way, so did he. Like Lucas, he'd been a fixture at the ranch. It didn't seem right that he was gone. But nothing seemed right these days.

Deke turned to stare into the darkness and wondered why he was so restless. An evening with Anna should have had him feeling relaxed and complacent. The dark-haired beauty in his bed was intriguing, and he was anything but bored by her interest in him.

But maybe that was the problem. It had been six months since he'd been involved with any woman and longer than that since he'd been in a serious relationship. Not long enough to dim the memories of Angel's betrayal and Melissa's disappointment in him.

The timing of Anna's appearance in his life couldn't have been any worse if he'd set it up himself. Yet it had happened, and now he couldn't seem to get enough of her. He could have insisted it was just sex, nothing but mutual need, but he'd stopped lying to himself after his world fell apart for the second and last time. In his mind he saw Silvio's round face directly above him, the lights of the hospital corridor casting a florescent halo behind his shaven head. "We got 'im, Call. We got Aguilar and three of his inner circle, including Little Eduardo, and it looks like he's ready to roll over on Aguilar."

Attendants rushed the gurney down the corridor to the OR, Silvio running alongside. Deke grabbed his lieutenant's T-shirt, trying to pull himself up, getting in his lieutenant's face. "The girl," he ground out. "Angel. Where is she?"

"I'm sorry, Deke. There was nothing anyone could do. She was dead at the scene." The look on his face said there was a lot he wasn't saying. "You did a good thing, Deke. You helped get Aguilar and his punks off the streets. You remember that! You hear? You remember it!"

Deke rubbed absently at the furrow between his brows

and willed the memory away. "She's not Angel," he insisted. Anna wasn't using, and she wasn't fragile. . . .

That didn't mean the lady didn't have a hidden agenda, one that somehow involved him, or Lucas, or both. Past and present melded in a suspicious swirl. There was no doubt that he was more than a little paranoid—a man couldn't go where he'd been and not be a little wary. Given everything going on around here, he'd be a damned fool to trust anyone.

The stakes were just too high.

Lucas's computer was in his office, at the rear of the studio. The door was locked, but Deke knew where his uncle kept the key, and he let himself in. The room was dark, several of Lucas's current projects, in various stages of completion, were cast in mysterious shadow. Wood shavings covered the concrete floor, silencing the sound of his footfalls. The door at the back of the room was open, the ghostly blue of the monitor's screen saver the beacon that drew him.

Deke sat down and logged onto the net, typing Anna's name and starting a search. Forty-five minutes later, he picked up the phone and dialed an exchange in Tucson. *One ring . . . two . . . three.*

"Silvio." The voice on the other end of the line was weary but wide awake.

"Hey, Sil . . . it's Call."

Something creaked, and Deke got the impression the lieutenant had shifted forward in his chair. "Call? Jesus. Is that really you? I was beginnin' to think you'd dropped off the planet."

"Yeah, well, it's been kind of crazy here," Deke said. "Listen, Sil, I need a favor."

When Deke left Lucas's office, light flooded from the windows of the apartment. The sliding glass door was open and Anna was dressed. She met him at the door with a cup of coffee. "I have to get back to town," she told him, "but first, we need to talk."

One more sleepless night, and Harlan was as grouchy as an aging bear with a sore ass. By the time Whitlow arrived he'd had too much coffee and too much time to stew over everything. On a caffeine rush, he barely gave the younger man time to cross the threshold before he was barking his name.

"Morning, Sheriff."

"Have a seat, Deputy." He glanced up. "You want some coffee?"

"Decaf?"

Harlan gave him a look that suggested he'd lost his mind. "Thanks," the younger man said. "I think I'll pass. Caffeine gives me the jitters—Cindy thinks I should give it up completely."

"Cindy's a nice-enough girl, but you'd be a damn fool to let her lead you around by the nose. You start that, it won't ever end—you can take my word for it." Harlan realized he sounded harsh, but he wasn't in a habit of backing down, and no way in hell would that start now. "Suit yourself," he said, grabbing another cup himself, then taking a seat in his chair. The cushion tweaked his ass and he shifted his weight, bellowing over his deputy's shoulder. "Dixie!"

"I'm not deaf, Sheriff, and if you would just push that little red button on the intercom, you'd save yourself from havin' a stroke." A dark-haired, forty-something woman glared at him from the open door. Dixie Zane was almost as big around as she was tall, and she served double-duty as dispatcher and receptionist. For fifteen years, she'd managed every technical detail needed to run a smooth operation, and she was the one person in the office Harlan couldn't intimidate. He respected her for that, even though this morning her attitude rubbed a hide that was already raw.

Harlan took a gulp of scalding black coffee. "I'm glad you brought that up," he growled. "Maybe you can explain why I have a working intercom but can't sit down without making mincemeat out of my ass with this goddamned piece-of-shit chair?"

Dixie crossed her arms across her chest and looked sour. "Because when the subject of updating office furniture came up last year you said it was a stupid idea? Because you said you liked that old chair, that it had sentimental value because it belonged to Matthew? Shall I go on?"

Harlan gave her a flat look. "Don't you ever forget anything I say?"

"No, sir, I don't. It's all right here." She tapped the side of her head with a brightly lacquered nail. "Anything else you want to know—Sheriff?"

"Just get a new chair in here by lunchtime," Harlan said sourly. "Something that won't chew the hell out of my backside. Unless you have some objection?" He leaned forward on one forearm, knowing he looked fierce as hell, waiting for her to deny his sorry ass a little comfort.

"Any particular fabric suit your fancy—sir?"

"I'll leave the details to you, just no decorator sissy stuff. Now, leave us alone, would you?" Dixie stalked out; Whitlow looked everywhere but at Harlan. "Would you knock that shit off, Deputy? I don't need anybody to tippy-toe around me. If you got somethin' to say, then say it."

Whitlow cleared his throat. "I think I changed my mind about that coffee." A short row of mugs marched across the top of the table where the coffeepot sat. One for every member of the department. Whitlow's had a photo of Teddy, his Golden Retriever, on it. A silent apology to Teddy, and he filled it with the acid black brew. Resuming his seat in front of Harlan's desk, he took a sip and grimaced. "You know, sir, I don't even like decaf." A sigh. He raised his gaze to Harlan's. "Sheriff—meaning no disrespect, but are you okay?"

The question grated. Whitlow's neatnik appearance grated. *Shit.* Everything grated. Harlan took a breath and made a vain attempt at lowering his blood pressure. He took a gulp of coffee, then put down his cup, running a hand through his hair. At fifty-one, he had very little gray, a fact he took pride in, yet given recent events that probably wouldn't last. "No, son, I am definitely not okay. I've been up all night going over the details of the murders, and I got a weird feelin' about this whole damn thing."

Whitlow spoke over the rim of his mug. "Has there been any word about the Miller woman?"

"Not a damn whiff of anything." Harlan shook his head, feeling his frustration mount again. "Credit cards, bank accounts, there hasn't been any activity, and their van is still in the drive. It's like she fucking disappeared into thin air."

"What was the determination on the blood at the scene?"

"O-positive. It belonged to Victim B. His wife's AB-negative." He stared into his mug and saw his frown reflected on the oily black surface of the cooling coffee. "ME says that the murder weapon was something heavy but thin, with a crooked end."

"Like a crowbar," Whitlow said.

"Could be. We can't really be sure, though, unless we find it." Harlan sighed. The weapon from the Call murders had been very similar in nature. *And* it had never been found. Harlan's palm itched, and he rubbed it absently on his trouser leg. Deke Call's derision of the previous morning came back to haunt him, mocking him for what he was thinking but wasn't ready to admit. "The reports are in from the ME. As for the boy, he was definitely suffocated. Under magnification, Grant found some cotton fibers in one of his nostrils. They've gone to the lab for identification, but I'd lay money on it being a match with the bed pillow they laid him on."

Whitlow frowned. "Just like Deke's sister."

"I already caught that," Harlan assured him. "Everything's the same, right down to the last detail, and it chews my ass almost as much as this damned old relic of a chair. I sure as hell want to believe this is a copycat crime."

"But you don't." There was no judgment in Whitlow's clear brown eyes.

"No," Harlan admitted. "No, I don't, and neither does Deke Call." Deke had found his stepfather and sister a dozen years before, and he'd managed to stumble onto the Millers as well. So how the hell did one man get to be so unlucky?

Or was it something besides luck, Harlan wondered, having no basis for suspecting Deke other than his innate dislike of what he'd become. Deke seemed genuinely pissed about what was going on at his uncle's place, but the possibility that it was all an act existed. In fact, what better way to throw Harlan off the scent than to create problems at Lucas's ranch? Could be he was reaching. Then again . . .

There had been motive enough for Call to kill Matthew, but it had been proven he wasn't involved when Martinez confessed.

"Did you process the footprints you found at the crime scene?" he asked Whitlow.

"Photographs and dental stone. The casts are in the filing cabinet." Whitlow got up, sensing their conversation was winding to a close. "Anything you need me to do?"

"As a matter of fact, there is. Put your civies on and go have lunch at Coyote Moon. I'd like to know who's talking in town and what it is they're saying."

"Yes, sir."

Whitlow went out, and Harlan opened the filing cabinet, retrieving the plaster cast of the bootprint found outside the Miller house. Then, opening the bottom drawer of his desk, he retrieved the cast he'd made at Lucas's and placed them side by side. One was large, the other smaller. The differences were so obvious that it took little more than a glance to determine they belonged to two different individuals. "Well, so much for that," Harlan said, and put the cast from the sheep pen away, removing a thick folder from the same drawer and tossing it on the desk blotter next to a pile of paperwork that had been whittled down to head height, but which was growing again. The manilla was yellowed with age, the label written in Harlan's own hand: "Call Homicide."

He opened the folder and reviewed the photographs, hoping to see something, some difference that would disprove the niggling doubt rising in his mind about the Call murders. Martinez had killed Matthew and the girls. He'd never been more certain of anything in his entire life.

So what the hell was going on here?

Was this some run-of-the-mill wacko's idea of getting attention?

Of shaking things up?

Or something even crazier, more sinister?

Maybe there was a connection—but not the connection he'd been thinking of. Maybe the connection was purely personal. Someone connected to the Calls . . . or to Martinez. . . .

Harlan frowned. Martinez must have had family somewhere. He remembered the man mentioning his little girl, but no trace of her had ever been found, and Harlan had dismissed the prisoner's ramblings as a bid for sympathy he didn't deserve. Could be he'd been wrong after all, and though the girl being involved in the replay of the original crime was certainly a long shot, it might not hurt to look into it. He closed the folder for the time being, but he left it on his desk beside a hastily scrawled note: *Martinez's family.*

Careful to ease out of the chair, Harlan stood and picked up his hat on his way out. "Dixie, I'm goin' out for a while," he said, passing by the dispatcher-slash-office-mainstay's desk. "I need to talk to a man about a van. If anything comes up, call my cell phone."

"I don't get it," Anna said. "Is this some kind of sick joke?"

Deke ran a hand through his dark hair. "Damned if I know. If anyone finds this funny, it sure ain't me."

Crossing the room, Anna sat across the table from him. "It sounded scripted to me, forced. Like she didn't feel comfortable saying it, yet had no choice."

Deke shook his head, frowning. "It isn't the words.

It's the misery, the fear—either it's real or she deserves an Academy Award for her performance."

"She says my name, then she pauses," Deke said. "Like she's looking to somebody else for direction, or approval."

"So you've heard it before," Anna said.

Deke nodded. "The morning of the murders."

Anna met his gaze. "I got the impression she was being coached . . . or threatened. She sounded stressed—worn out, and I have a feeling someone else was in that room with her."

Deke was silent. "Who would do something like this?" Anna wondered aloud.

A shrug. "I can't be sure, but the Miller woman's still missing."

"The Miller woman? You think someone's holding her against her will, that they forced her to call?"

"I think it's a possibility. It would explain why she disappeared, why she hasn't resurfaced. With someone else controlling her every move, she couldn't make contact. Hell, she may not even know her family's gone."

Anna's disbelief was written all over her face. "I don't get it, Deke. Why call you? Did you know her?"

He snorted. "Baby, it ain't about her. It's about who's got her." He got up and walked to the sliding glass doors. They were open to the morning. The low-pressure system had moved off to the east. The morning was clear and dry, the sky an unbelievable blue, but Deke couldn't see past his mounting problems to the stark beauty of his surroundings. He went out, leaning his forearms on the deck's handrail as he sought to make sense of the confusing swirl his life had become.

Anna crossed the threshold, joining him on the deck. "But why call you?"

"I don't have a clue," he admitted. "My guess is someone gets a hell of a kick out of watching me dance to their tune. That other call I mentioned—it was my mother's voice on the phone."

"Your mother," Anna said, barely breathing. It was all the proof she needed, corroboration that the psycho who'd killed his family was still out there. Still operating. And the two crimes weren't just connected, they were connected to Deke. Someone was playing with him, using his love for a mother who'd vanished over a decade ago to torment and manipulate.

Maddy Call *was* dead, she thought. She had to be. She remembered the photograph at Lucas's, the sweetness in her expression. From everything she'd learned about her, everything Lucas had told her, she'd been devoted to her children and very close to her only son. Not only did she find it impossible that she would walk away, she wouldn't stand by and allow Deke to be tormented like this.

The look on her face must have clued him in to what she was thinking. "I know how crazy it sounds. Everybody thinks she's dead—even Lucas. But they never found any evidence to make it a proven fact, so when I heard her voice—"

"You had to find out for yourself," Anna finished for him.

"Somethin' like that." He leaned a shoulder against the door frame, watching her watching him. "You think I've lost it, and maybe I have. The cop I once was knows how far-fetched it is that she could have survived that night."

"I'm not sure what to think right now, except that we need to try to find out who's behind it all."

"There ain't no 'we' about it, Anna. No way am I

gonna let you get involved in my business. I had the first call traced. The number matched the pay phone on Delano Avenue. It came from Nazareth. Somebody in this town is bent on makin' my life a livin' hell, and I can't be sure how far they might be willin' to go to get what they want. If I'm right, then they've already done murder. I don't want you puttin' your life on the line for no good reason—that means you steer clear of this, clear of me, and let me handle it my way."

If he imagined for a nanosecond that she was willing to do what she was told, then he didn't know her at all. "And if I don't like that idea?"

Reaching out, he stroked her cheek with his thumb. "Nobody said you had to like it. Just make sure you do it—until this is over. I don't want you hurt, or worse."

"We don't always get what we want," she told him. "And I prefer to keep my options open." The alarm on her wristwatch beeped a high-pitched tattoo, and she beat a hasty retreat. "I have to go," she said, and he didn't even try to stop her.

Wheeler checked out his new digs, a high-tech loft with a wall full of glass overlooking Fisherman's Wharf. A twenty-year-old with a set of headlights a man could drown in and her own personal pharmacy was sleeping it off in his bed, while her twin sister had her hands all over him and wouldn't stop, even when he asked her to. He'd just started thinking there really was a God when the hammock he was snoozing on did a 180 and he was dumped on his face in the dirt.

He came up to an elbow, sputtering, ready to defend the big-screen TV from the repossession Nazis if necessary, and instead came face to face with Harlan Rudy.

For a half second, he lay there, a growing sense of panic gnawing ratlike at his insides. Then his sense of self-preservation kicked in, and he picked himself out of the dirt and acted like a man with nothing to hide. "You could've knocked, Sheriff."

"I could have," Harlan said, "but then I'd have missed the chance to survey your little paradise at my leisure. This is some setup you've got here, son. You're selling Lucas's work and takin' a cut, you got that scientific shit in the back where you make that pansy beer, and if your credit report's any indication, you can barely keep the lights on. Lost your truck last week, that right? Boggles the mind."

Wheeler got to his feet, dusting off his T-shirt and jeans. "Sheriff, is there a reason you're puttin' your nose in my personal business? Because if there is, I guess I need to know it."

"Me, nosin' in your business? You got it all wrong, son. I'm just an observant man, that's all. It's a nasty habit, I suppose, but it sure has come in handy over the years. If you keep one ear to the ground, you sure do learn a lot." He glanced around and sighed. "I can't get over what you've done with this place. Take that building, for instance."

"It's a gallery," Wheeler said.

Harlan smiled, but it didn't ease Wheeler's unease one iota. "Yeah, I got that," the sheriff said. "What's a building that size go for these days?"

"I don't really remember."

"No shit? I got every receipt from every improvement I've made to my place. Takes a long time to make a decent home on my salary."

Wheeler's irritation ramped up considerably. "That's as good a reason as any to marry into money, I guess."

The look Harlan gave him was cold as ice, and Wheeler could have swallowed his tongue. His tone when he answered was a little less conversational. "Guess you've been pickin' up on a few rumors yourself," he said, then shrugged. "Well, I shouldn't be surprised. It's sure no secret that I married up. But like you say, it's *her* money, not mine." He settled his booted feet a little farther apart, took a cigar from his pocket, and lit it. "So, how's a poor boy from Missoura finance an operation like this? The stainless in that brewery must have set you back fifty grand, without the cost of the building itself and the labor to put it up. That's where you said you were from, right? Missoura?" He shook his head. "I gotta give you credit. I couldn't afford somethin' this expansive unless my wife paid for it. You got it all goin' on, that's for sure. Nice piece of real estate, interesting friends—"

"As far as I know, none of that's against the law." Wheeler grinned, hoping to lessen the tension a little. "Now, if you don't mind, I have a few things that can't wait."

"No, I don't mind," Harlan said. "As a matter of fact, I have a few pressing cases too, so how about I just cut to the chase. You were at Lucas Swift-Water's place Saturday night, that right?"

Wheeler started to sweat. "Yeah. Yeah, as a matter of fact, I was."

"And it's my understanding that after an uneventful evening, Anna drove you here and dropped you off."

Wheeler's eyes narrowed. "I'm without wheels at the moment. Anna gave me a lift."

"What'd you do when she dropped you off?"

"I don't know what you mean," Wheeler said.

"Then why don't I clarify; you go anywhere else after Anna Sandoval left here?"

Wheeler's expression darkened. "On foot?"

"On foot," Harlan said. "Or maybe somebody else picked you up?"

Wheeler felt the sweat begin to pop. "Look, Sheriff, I don't know what you're drivin' at, or why you're hell-bent on jerkin' my chain, but I have nothing to hide, and no, I didn't leave again that night. I was right here, all night, alone. I heard about what happened to Anna, and I didn't have anything to do with it. She's a nice chick and a good friend. Why would I do anything to hurt her?"

"Good question," he said. "I can't see a motive from where I'm standin', but that doesn't mean one doesn't exist. And one thing I've learned over the years is that the criminal mind doesn't always differentiate between friends and potential victims." Harlan pulled one last drag from the cigar, then dropping it in the dirt, he ground it out with the toe of his boot. His gaze drifted downward, and that same tight smile appeared beneath his mustache. "Nice boots, Dobbs, but it looks like you got somethin' on them."

Wheeler glanced down and shrugged. "It's paint," he said. "My sprayer got clogged."

"Well, son, I'm glad you shared that," Harlan said. "Otherwise I might have mistaken it for dried blood spatter." He turned and started to leave, but at the corner of the trailer, he turned back. "I don't suppose you have any ideas as to who killed Lucas's ram?"

Wheeler shook his head. "None."

The sheriff touched the brim of his hat, a one-fingered salute. "See you 'round, Dobbs. If I have any more questions, I'll be sure to let you know."

"Thanks," Wheeler said, expelling a breath from his

lungs when Harlan turned the truck and headed to the road. When he was out of sight, Wheeler took off his boots and put them in a garbage bag.

Anna locked the apartment door, threw down her keys, and powered up the laptop. She had the day off from Coyote Moon, and she meant to make the most of it. "Felix," Jay Goldstrom's screen name, was displayed in bold black, which meant he was online and available.

ANNA: Jay? You there?
FELIX: Thank God you're alive! I've chewed my nails down past the first knuckle. Where the hell have you been? Did I not ask you to check in, and did you not swear to me that you would? Anna, I've been FRANTIC.
ANNA: Jay, you're such a drama queen.

She intentionally omitted telling him that he might have every reason to worry, rationalizing that she was still on the fringes of the bull's-eye and not dead center like Deke and his uncle. Until that changed, she'd be damned if she'd panic. Her ultimate goal was too important—she wouldn't back down any more than she could back off.

FELIX: Someone has to worry, YOU OBVIOUSLY DON'T. Sorry if I'm a bitch. I get that way when the people I love ignore me. Why don't you fill me in on what's going on before my colon goes into complete spasm?
ANNA: It's getting weirder by the minute. I spoke to a woman who called Deke this morning. It was a plea

for help from this unidentified woman—he seemed to
think it might have been the missing wife of the latest
murder vic.

FELIX: Back up a second. Deke? As in Deacon Call?
The same Deacon Call you aren't involved with? The
guy who has a knack for finding dead people? Anna,
for God's sake. He sounds like the prince of darkness. Tell me you aren't falling for this guy.

Anna bit her lip. She and Jay had been friends for
five years, since she'd landed the job at the *Post*. To say
they were close was an understatement. He'd been her
editor, her pal, her drinking buddy, her confidant and
advisor; the relationship worked because they never
lied to one another.

FELIX: Jesus, Anna!
ANNA: I'm not falling for anyone (she told him, and
prayed it was true). I'm here to find out what the hell
happened at the Call place in '93. Which brings me
back to why I logged on. Can you hook me up with a
good PI? I need someone to do some digging for me,
ASAP. I want to know everything there is to know
about Maddy Call—starting with her birth records.
FELIX: Call's mother? She's a missing person, right?
So doesn't this fall under police jurisdiction?
ANNA: It would if I felt the local police could be trusted.
As things stand, I'm not so sure. So, can you hook
me up?
FELIX: Are you going to explain that last comment?
You know I hate cryptic, Anna, not to mention that it
flies in the face of what I've heard about Sheriff Rudy.
My source swears he's a real hard-nosed Western
lawman type—the original Marlboro Man.

Describing Harlan was almost as hard as describing Deke.

ANNA: He's at least half right. At the moment, Harlan isn't the problem. Let me get back to you on it.
FELIX: Sigh. Do I have a choice?
ANNA: NO (Anna wrote, and threw in a widely grinning emoticon). I have to cut this short. I'll be waiting to hear from you.
FELIX: BE CAREFUL.

And he was gone.

Anna powered down the computer, but the conversation with Jay wouldn't leave her. Eighteen hundred miles away and he somehow managed to pick up on what she'd been working so hard to deny, and still wasn't ready to accept.

The thing with Deke *was* moving too fast. She hadn't realized she was in too deep until she'd walked onto the deck last night at the apartment and found him struggling to hold the jagged pieces of his soul together. Seeing him that way, on the edge of a dark precipice, emotions raw, tormented by something she couldn't understand and he refused to discuss—he'd really gotten to her. His predicament had touched her on a level that no one had reached before—not since Juan Martinez.

At that moment, she would have done anything to help pull him back from the edge.

Anything.

The realization was every bit as terrifying as the certain knowledge that the situation's outcome was completely beyond her control. With a last glance at the laptop, she headed for the shower. Until she heard from the private investigator about Maddy, there was nothing to do but wait.

Chapter Eleven

Whitlow spent the day drinking coffee and picking up on bits and pieces of various conversations, just as the sheriff had suggested. He'd always been an amiable sort, with the kind of looks that helped him blend in. Dressed in civilian clothes—jeans, boots, and a plaid Western shirt—folks tended to forget he was Sheriff Rudy's right-hand man, and he became just plain old Seth Whitlow.

That didn't mean he'd picked up a wellspring of information—at least not the caliber of information the sheriff had been hoping for. A half hour before his shift ended, he paid for his coffee and walked across the street to headquarters to report in before he headed home.

The sheriff's desk looked like the all-you-can-eat buffet at a Chinese restaurant. Eight take-out cartons crowded into the small space between stacks of case files and legal pads scrawled with notes on every case still open, and one that wasn't. The folder for the Call murders was displayed prominently by his boss's left elbow, and pillows and a thick throw lay forgotten on the old sofa. Whitlow did his best to ignore that and took a seat when asked to.

"Deputy," Harlan said, leaving the plastic fork standing upright in a container of Mu Shu Pork. "You hungry?"

Whitlow shook his head. "Too much coffee. I started to vibrate like a tuning fork a half hour ago. Cindy's gonna be so pissed."

"Suit yourself. There's plenty. Figured I'd order enough to have some left over. Always gotta have that midnight snack."

Seth shot a glance at the uniforms hanging on the back of the door, the overflowing wastebasket, his boss's two-day growth. "You sure everything's okay, Sheriff?" he said in a sheepish voice, then immediately started to justify the inquiry. "I kind of noticed that you hadn't been home."

"Heavy caseload, that's all," Harlan said. "It always gets to me, and Ginny has a sleep disorder. My being up prowling around the house all night long just makes things worse, so I figured till we put this case to bed, it might be best if I camped out here."

Whitlow recognized the lie, and his mouth hung slack.

Harlan's glance turned cutting. "Well, what the hell are you lookin' at? A man can't show his wife a little consideration without causin' a stir?"

"No, sir! I mean, that's a nice thing for you to do for her."

Harlan picked up the Mu Shu Pork, shoveling through it with the fork, then with a sound of disgust, he made an overhand throw onto the wastebasket. The carton teetered there for a few seconds, then toppled to the floor. "Jesus Christ," he ground out. "I got fed up and I walked out."

Whitlow said nothing.

"I'm too damned old for so damned much bullshit," Harlan said. "And that's a hell of a lot more than you needed to know. Now, wipe that idiotic look off your face and tell me what you have for me."

"Folks are talkin', all right, but it's mostly scared talk. Pete Delano, the salesman from the used car lot, had a few too many on his lunch break and he started spoutin' some nonsense about it bein' an outlaw biker gang that murdered Miller and his kid. Said he saw the woman talkin' to someone who fit that profile the afternoon before the murder, but the weird part of it was, he wasn't ridin' a motorcycle, he was drivin' a sports car—a sports car he recognized. Said it had Arizona plates."

Harlan's head came up. "Lemme guess—dark blue paint job? Lots of chrome, and a driver with a ton of attitude."

Whitlow shifted in his chair, suddenly uncomfortable. "You picked up on it too, I see."

Whitlow sighed. "I wish I didn't. Sheriff, I know you don't like Deke, but him and me, we go way back. I ain't claimin' he's a saint, but I don't believe he has it in him to hurt a child."

"People do crazy things," Harlan said, "and everything about Deke screams trouble. Maybe it's time I had a little talk with him, on the record." Another jab-fest with Deke Call—who said he had nothing to look forward to?

Harlan allowed the notion to gel, savoring it for a few more seconds before setting it aside. "You know Wheeler Dobbs. What's your take on him?"

Whitlow shrugged. "He's an okay sort, I suppose. Why?"

"You think he has it in him to kill a man's sheep?"

Whitlow frowned. "You think he's behind Lucas's problems?"

"Not only do I think it," Harlan said, "I'd bet my Packard on it. He had rusty brown spatter on his boots. Said it was paint, but I'd been all over that place and I sure as hell didn't see anything that came close to that color."

"Are you gonna have the boots tested?"

Harlan shook his head. "I could have asked him to hand them over, but without a warrant, I couldn't force the issue. I made sure he knows that I know. Maybe it'll be enough to keep him from doin' any more mischief. Sure would like to know why he did it, though. It bugs the hell out of me when people do shit I can't understand."

"What about Miss Sandoval's incident on Echo Canyon Road?" Whitlow wanted to know. "You think Dobbs is behind that too?"

"No clue. Like the homicides, it's still wide open. Could be it was random—just a prank, and she was just plain unlucky to be there when she was. Or it could be that Anna has an enemy." Harlan stared glumly at the mess on his desk, wishing for answers. Most of the cartons hadn't even been opened, yet he'd suddenly lost his appetite. "Your wife like Chinese, Whitlow?"

"A little too well, sir. She woke me at three A.M. last Saturday to get takeout. Ever try to find a Chinese restaurant open at that hour? I sure will be glad when this baby finally gets here."

"I can't imagine," Harlan said. "Listen, how about doin' me a favor and takin' this stuff with you. I was kiddin' myself when I ordered all this. Ain't no way I'll eat it, even if I do end up pullin' an all-nighter."

"You sure, Sheriff? I wouldn't feel right about takin' your supper."

"I'm sure." He glanced at his watch. "Five o'clock. Shift's over, son. Go on home, and you be sure to give Cindy my regards." Whitlow put the cartons back in the bag and left. The squad car's engine revved to life, and then it was quiet again.

Footsteps as Harlan sank back in his new leather chair, loving the fact that his ass cheek was safe from being tweaked into sheriff-burger. He sighed as Dixie appeared in the open doorway. "You approve, I take it?" she said, crossing short arms over a large bosom.

"Approve of what?" he said, for the sake of being obstinate.

She made a disgusted noise, glaring at him for a full minute before she spoke again. "Harlan, you and I have known one another for a long time—too long to mince words."

"Dixie, you have *never* minced words with anyone. You just don't have it in you. And yes, I like the chair. It sure beats the hell out of havin' my ass chewed to bits by that old man-eater Matthew used. Guess I'm not really such a hard-ass after all, huh?" He winked. "Thanks for takin' care of it for me. Appreciate it."

"You're welcome," she said. "Now, when are you gonna swallow your pride and go home? You and Ginny have weathered a lot of storms in thirty years—surely this time is no worse than any other."

Harlan took a deep breath, resisting the urge to snap. She meant well. He knew that, but she had no idea—nobody did. "Yeah, we've weathered a hell of a lot, but old boats are a lot more fragile, more likely to spring a leak. I don't know if this can be fixed, and right now, I don't even want to think about it."

She seemed to understand that it was a little more serious than a run-of-the-mill quarrel, and though he could see she didn't like his answer, she accepted it. "Good night, Harlan."

"Night, Dixie."

Dixie turned and walked away, and the office settled into silence. Alone again, Harlan resisted the urge to unlock the drawer and take out Maddy's photo, instead dragging the case file for the most recent homicides to the center of the blotter and looking through it one more time.

Anna's day off didn't last long. At half past five, Sandy called, and he sounded superstressed. "I'm sorry, darlin'. I know it's supposed to be your day off, but Evie didn't show, and we're busier than we've been in a month. I don't suppose you could drop whatever it is you're doin' and come on down here to sling a little hash? I'm afraid with the workload that Carlotta'll have a coronary. I told her not to go tryin' to do everything, but it's like talking to the wall, and she's really lookin' ragged lately. I hate to admit it, but I'm worried about her."

Anna frowned. She'd noticed how tired the older woman seemed. Not that she would admit it. She prided herself on being tough, and she would have torn out her own tongue before complaining. It showed in her slower pace, however, and in her face too. She looked worn around the edges, and the fatigue was noticeable enough that even the best department store makeup couldn't hide it. "How's ten minutes sound?" Anna asked.

"Sounds like you're a lifesaver," Sandy said. "Thanks, Anna."

"Don't mention it." There was precious little she wouldn't have done for Carlotta. She owed her more than she could possibly repay. Not only had she saved her life and reunited her with her only remaining family, she'd kept her secret all these years. Anna hung up the phone, remembering the cold spring night when she found herself at Coyote Moon.

She'd often thought of the woman who'd saved her life all those years ago, wondering if she would even recognize her. Yet as she approached the bar and saw the energetic redhead serving drinks to the ranch hands and farmers, she realized she would have known her anywhere. "Carlotta McFadden?"

"I'm Carlotta," she'd said. "Who wants to know?" Before Anna could answer, her eyes narrowed. "I'm imagining things—" She faltered. "It can't be—but you've got her eyes. I could never forget those eyes. Anna?"

Anna nodded. "My God," she'd said. Dropping the glass she'd been wiping, she hurried around the bar, wrapping Anna in a tremendous hug. "My God. It really is you. I just can't seem to believe it." She wiped a little moisture from her cheek. "Ah, honey, lemme look at you! You're all grown up. No little girl anymore."

"No little girl," Anna had agreed.

"You're a beauty," Carlotta said with a warm smile. "But I always knew you would be. It was part of the reason I couldn't rest until I knew you were safe. Beauty's a two-edged sword, Anna. It cuts both ways, and there are men out there who would have taken advantage of you without considerin' that you were just a child." She called Sandy to watch the bar for a few minutes, then took

Anna's hand, pulling her to a nearby table, urging her to sit. "What on earth brings you back here? I didn't think I'd ever see you again."

"I had to come back," Anna said. "I have to know the truth. I have to know what really happened here that night." Anna shook her head. "There's a shadow over my heart," she said, "and I can't live like this any longer. I need the truth." She gripped both of Carlotta's hands, her gaze locking with that of the older woman. "I'm going to find out who killed that family and what happened to my father, only I can't do it alone. I need help. I need a cover. . . ."

Anna had asked, and Carlotta had folded her into her life, her business, providing the half truth that Anna was the daughter of an old friend to whoever would listen, and no one had questioned it.

It was getting dark as Anna left the apartment and went down the stairs. The street lamps were just coming on, but the watery blue-green halos couldn't penetrate the dusk. She thought about driving the rental car she'd gotten to replace the van to Coyote, but it was only a couple of blocks away and the evening was mild. She could be there in five minutes if she cut through the passageway between Mrs. Bookwalter's house and Wind Horse's Mercantile. The passageway was wide enough to accommodate a few garbage cans and the larger dumpster belonging to the mercantile and still allow two pedestrians seeking a shortcut to bypass one another without touching.

At this hour, it was deserted, the shadowed space between the buildings dim and gray as only twilight can be. Anna held tight to the shoulder bag slung over her left shoulder, her keys palmed in her right. Normally she would have avoided a close, dark place like the alley. It reminded her too much of the space she'd occupied under the river's bank after her father left her. Yet, with Carlotta in her thoughts and Sandy awaiting her arrival, she needed to make time.

Passing the dumpster, she caught the sound of something stirring in the shadows. A black rectangle interrupted the long brick wall of the building on her right where the dull white paint of a service door should have been. Anna's skin crawled, but she kept walking, picking up her pace. As she passed the dark doorway, a sibilant hiss stopped her dead in her tracks. Hair prickling at her nape, she turned to look back and caught the lighter outline of the figure hunched deep in the lightless hallway. Anna's mouth went dry. "Who is it? Who's there?"

No reply. Nothing. But she could feel eyes boring into her and knew whomever it was, they watched and waited.

"Who are you? Why won't you show yourself? Let me see who you are."

A dark fury rolled from the doorway in waves. Anna felt it and took an involuntary step back. It was cold and black and ugly. "*Pretty girl.*" A breathy whisper of sound. *"Pretty girls aren't pretty when they're dead."*

Anna turned and ran, barreling from the alley, colliding with something warm and solid and male. Twilight had fled while she stood in the alley, facing down the faceless threat, and for the space of a heartbeat, as he reached out to steady her, she thought it was Deke. Then, glancing up, she saw her mistake. "Harlan. Oh, thank God."

"Well, there's a first. It isn't often anyone's so glad to see me that they involve the Almighty. Especially someone so pretty."

The word *pretty* sent a shudder through her.

"Anna, you all right? You're shaking."

"No, as a matter of fact, I'm not okay," Anna said. "Someone was in the alley just now, hiding in the shadows of the doorway."

"It's probably just Ben Livingston. He gets a head of steam up and a bellyful of beer and he seems to think it's a men's room. I've busted him so many times I'm thinkin' about installing a revolving door on the cell."

Anna shook her head. "It wasn't Ben. I would have recognized his voice from the bar, and there's no way he'd ever try to frighten me. The service entrance to the mercantile was open."

Harlan sobered. "They tried to frighten you?"

"They said, 'pretty girl'," Anna said. "'Pretty girls aren't pretty when they're dead'."

"You headed to work? Then go on." He inclined his head toward Coyote, a half block away. "You'll be safe enough there. I'll go have a look." He turned, melting into the lightless canyon between the buildings.

"Anna?" Sandy stood in the doorway of the bar, wiping his hands on a hand towel. "Jamie Turner said he saw you talking to the sheriff. Everything okay?"

"Yeah," Anna said, reluctant to talk about what just happened. Sandy and Carlotta had enough to handle without her adding to their worries. "Everything's fine."

His hair still damp from the shower, Deke grabbed his keys and went out. He stopped by Lucas's place before heading to the car. The door was unlocked, the puppy curled on the rug by Lucas's favorite chair. It picked up its head and whined softly but remained where it was, waiting for its owner's return. The TV was on, the volume low to keep the canine company, and Lucas's rifle was missing from the gun cabinet.

He was out, positioned, armed, and watching—unlikely to return for hours. Deke was unsure that the old man's quiet vigil would solve anything, but he knew what he was doing, and with the right cover, could position himself so stealthily that a man could pass within a few feet of him and not even notice he was there. Oddly, he was probably safer out in the open than in his own house, at least until they figured out who the hell was trying to sabotage the operation and destroy his peace of mind.

That grated. His uncle had worked to build up his place, and he'd done it on his own. It pissed Deke off that somebody was trying to ruin it for him. But who?

He made a mental tally of possible candidates. It didn't come down as much to a list of the old man's enemies as it did to who stood to profit from Lucas's problems.

Astor Cox's land bordered Lucas's spread to the north. Wealthy enough to buy and sell Lucas several times over, Cox had tried to convince Lucas to sell out, and Lucas, of course, had refused. There hadn't been any animosity in the process, as far as Deke could tell, and they remained civil, if distant. But appearances didn't mean shit. He'd learned in his first few months on the streets that to get to the truth, you had to dig a little deeper.

Deke had heard rumors recently that Cox had grabbed land from another neighbor with financial difficulties at a less-than-fair price and was planning to expand his twelve-hundred acre spread even farther . . . but did he want Lucas's land badly enough to try and run him off?

Damn good question. And then there was Harlan. He

was what passed for the law around here, but cops became corrupt. It happened, and as far as Deke recalled, Lucas had never had anything good to say about the man; it was plain that the feeling was mutual. If Harlan was somehow involved in what was going on out here, it would certainly explain why he was making little headway with the investigation . . . but whatever lay between the two men, was it enough to make him want to destroy Lucas?

Deke didn't like anything about Harlan Rudy, but he still didn't think so. Somebody had shot Lucas using a .22-caliber rifle. Fired from a distance, a weapon like that was unlikely to make a clean kill. It was possible, but the odds would be much better with a high-power rifle. Either the shooter was unfamiliar with weapons, he'd meant to wound and not kill, or it really had been an accident.

Deke's gut told him the first scenario was far more likely than the other two, which ruled Harlan out hands down. Whatever the man was, he knew his business, and he knew weapons. Had he picked up a rifle with the intention of killing Lucas, Lucas would be dead.

Which brought him to Anna. She was a newcomer who'd met Lucas through Wheeler and had immediately insinuated herself into his uncle's world. She seemed to be genuinely fond of Lucas, but was it really genuine?

Or was it all an act?

And just what could she possibly hope to gain from gaslighting an old man?

Was she capable of that kind of deception? Could she really be involved?

He thought about her sudden appearance at the house that first night, and again last night. She'd somehow managed to show up when he needed her most, and she'd reached down into the darkness, taken his hand, and guided him toward the light again.

He thought about the sheepdog puppy and the lie she'd told to convince Lucas the dog needed him as much as he needed it.

He thought of her softness when she opened to him, welcoming him in, her willingness to go to great lengths to please him, her fearlessness when it came to getting tangled up with him.

He found it hard to imagine a day without her in it, yet what did he really know about her? She claimed to be a writer working on the story of the murders . . . but he'd run a search on Anna Sandoval, and he'd come up empty-handed. No bibliography, no reviews, no articles. And no real evidence that she was who she said she was.

Deke opened the car door and slid into the bucket seat. He started to reach for the keys and heard the ominous dry rattle from the passenger seat. The car's interior was dark, but he didn't need to see to know he was in a shitload of trouble. He froze, shifting his gaze slowly to the source of the sound without moving his head; the snake's gray-brown body was as thick as his wrist. He could see the darker diamonds on its back, the arrow-shaped head, and black and white stripes on its tail.

A Western Diamondback, venomous enough to kill, poised and ready to strike. If he was any judge, the snake was easily five feet in length. In the close confines of the car, there was no way to avoid it. Any sudden movement and it would strike.

Slow, controlled, shallow breaths.

A fine sheen of sweat popped from his pores. Death faced him, its tongue flicking out to pick up the vibrations emitted by his pulse, his breathing. If he grabbed for it, he'd suffer a painful, perhaps deadly bite. If he stayed still, his odds weren't a whole lot better. As he weighed his options, his gaze fixed on that arrow-shaped head, he caught a blur of movement in his peripheral vision, right beside the passenger window . . . then Lucas opened the car door, and as the snake arced toward this new threat, Deke struck. All the pent-up energy went into the grab.

No room for a mistake.

The lunge was fast, but Deke didn't feel that. The threat to him, to Lucas, made everything slow to a crawl. His heart squeezed out a beat. His hand opened, arm extending as the snake lunged for Lucas. In painfully slow motion, he closed his fist around its body, just behind the head, cutting off its strike . . . then, as it writhed and curled itself around his wrist, he blew the breath from his lungs.

The car door swung open. His uncle surveyed the scene for a few seconds, then shook his head. "If you want a pet, we'll find you a nice dog. If you want, I'll ask Anna. She seems pretty good at it."

"I'm glad you think this is funny," Deke grated out. Still gripping the snake, he opened the door and got out. "You got any idea who did this?"

Lucas shrugged. "I saw Anna leavin' earlier, but I can't think she'd want to do anything like that. She seems to like you well enough."

"Anyone else around today I don't know about?"

A shrug. "Wheeler dropped by this evening for a consult. He's got some ideas on how we can increase sales."

"Wheeler?"

Lucas frowned. "Yeah, Wheeler. Blond hair, lives in a mobile home a couple of miles over that way. You sure you didn't get nailed? You sure are actin' funny."

"No, I didn't get nailed. But somebody's about to. You still got those half-gallon jars under the sink?"

"Couple of 'em. Why?"

"Because I want one."

Wheeler entered through the back door of the trailer and headed straight for the can. He'd downed a six-pack after coming back from Lucas's place, and too much beer always gave him a raging case of the shits. It didn't help that he was nervous. He'd waited at their rendezvous point for two hours, and she'd stood him up again.

Why the fuck did he bother with the manic bitch? He asked himself that same question a hundred times a day, then she'd call and he'd go right back for more.

He was like a dog after a bitch in heat, even though she had him by the balls. He couldn't seem to stop himself, and maybe he didn't want to. Being involved with a woman like her, the wife of a powerful man, was something of an aphrodisiac to a risk-taking, hedonistic leech like himself. And it sure as hell eased the pain when she turned the screws that she had money and was willing to share.

He undid the rivet at his waistband and unzipped his fly, shoving his jeans to his knees as he reached down and lifted the lid. He was squatting within inches of a comfortable seat when something brought him up short. Half-crouched over the toilet, he glanced down between his knees, saw the snake coiled in the white porcelain bowl, and let out a scream. "Jesus Christ!" He did a perfect double axel, caught his boots in the tangle of his half-mast jeans, and sprawled in an undignified heap halfway out the bathroom door.

A few feet away, the man leaning against the wall in the hallway struck a match. The tip flared, illuminating Deke Call's face, turning his features demonic. "Stops the heart, don't it?" he drawled, hanging a cigarette on his lower lip, touching the lighter's flame to the tip.

"Deke," Wheeler said again, gaining his feet, restoring his dignity. "If that's your idea of a joke, man, it sure as hell wasn't funny."

"No joke." He paused, dragging smoke into his lungs, shooting a pale gray stream into Wheeler's face as the younger man struggled up, righting his jeans, redoing his fly. "The asshole who put that big boy in my car wasn't tryin' to be funny. He meant business. I was just returnin' the favor."

Wheeler laughed, bracing his hand on his hip. "Wait a minute, Jack! You think I put that snake in your car? Shit! We're buddies, man, *amigos*. Why the hell would I do somethin' that crazy?"

"Good question," Deke said, and his burning black eyes bored into Wheeler's. "Why don't *you* tell *me?*"

Wheeler shook his head. "Look, man. You believe what you want to believe. I don't know shit about snakes, especially rattlesnakes! Christ, my idea of the great outdoors is an afternoon in my hammock with a couple of cold ones."

Deke's eyes remained hard and cold, and Wheeler realized he didn't believe a word he was saying. With his guts roiling and a porcelain bowl full of trouble, he felt his grip on reality slipping.

He was dreaming.

That was it.

He'd fallen asleep and was having a nightmare.

"You behind the shit that's been happenin' to Lucas? When somethin' bad happens, Wheeler Dobbs has been hangin' 'round. You were there the day he found Obee and every time he found a lamb missin'. You came out there with Anna the night before the old ram was killed, and today before the trap was laid for me. Either you've got some rotten timin' or you're involved in what's goin' on. Either way, it's unhealthy."

If it was a nightmare, then it didn't really matter what he said. "Now I get it. You been talkin' to Harlan." He ran a hand through his hair, trying to conceal the fact that it was shaking. "You forgot one thing. I wasn't there the morning your uncle got shot. Lousy timing? Yeah, you could say I've got lousy timing, but Lucas is a friend of mine, and you can think whatever you want, but I'd never do anything to hurt him."

Deke stepped close, dying his cigarette out in the sink bowl, an inch from Wheeler's hand. His gaze never left Wheeler's. "Lucas means everything to me," Deke warned quietly. "You mess with him and trouble's gonna rain down on your pretty-boy head like nothin' you ever seen."

For one second, Wheeler was sure he'd shit himself. Then, when he was sure Deke had gone, he made a mad dash for the scrub outside his door.

Chapter Twelve

"My God, it's hot in here." Carlotta filled a mug with draft, letting the head swell right up to the rim before sending it sliding down the bar to Ted Nearly.

Nearly was wearing jeans and checked flannel and looking comfortable. Carlotta was breaking a sweat and about to crawl out of her skin, but she never slowed her hectic pace, and Anna suspected she was running on sheer determination alone. "Carlotta, why don't you take a break? I can handle the bar."

She looked at Anna like she'd lost her mind, and she poured another beer. "Two-for-one Happy Hour, and it'll go at this pace for another forty minutes."

John Blessing leaned on the bar, waiting for the whiskey he'd ordered ten minutes ago. "Hey, sweet cheeks, d'you forget about me?"

"Now, how could I forget a good-lookin' cowboy like you?" Carlotta quipped. At the same time, Sandy shoved two plates over the service window and bellowed for Anna. "Pick up for table two!"

Carlotta gave Anna a look. "They're lookin' for some

sanity because of what happened at Hell House, and honey, we're it. I'll turn up the air, and I'll be fine."

"If you say so," Anna said, skeptical. "But you've earned a break. You want me to call Francine? Maybe she can lend a hand for a couple of hours."

The glare Carlotta shot back answered the question, but Anna wished she'd relent and take her up on it. Francine was a pain in the ass sometimes, but she did care about her mother, and in one respect, she had a point. Carlotta worked too hard.

On nights like this, Anna couldn't help but wonder how long she could keep it up. Six days a week, fourteen-hour days, one day off a week. It was a grueling pace that would have broken someone half her age. Lately, she'd looked older, more worn than ever. There were circles under her eyes, and while her cheeks were flushed, the rest of her complexion had taken on an ashen cast. Anna had tried to convince her several times to go to the clinic, but Carlotta was stubborn, and she refused to listen, insisting nothing was wrong. But the assurances had a hollow ring to them, and Anna wasn't convinced.

The double doors opened and Harlan walked in. Heads turned, and not a few people murmured his name as he passed. He nodded an acknowledgment, touched the brim of his hat, and took a stool at the end of the bar. "Coors," he told Carlotta, "bottle, not draft."

Carlotta opened the bottle and set it in front of him. "Harlan, you look like hell. You gettin' any sleep at all these days?"

A jaundiced look. "Thanks, and no, as a matter of fact, I'm not. Anna, mind if I have a word?"

Carlotta said nothing, but she watched them walk to a table near the wall. Her scowl indicated she wasn't happy. "Thanks for keeping it quiet," Anna said. "I'd like to keep her out of it. She's got enough to handle without me adding to it."

A slight shrug, just a movement of his broad shoulders beneath his Levi's jacket. "I'm nothin' if not discreet." A smile crinkled at the corners of his blue eyes. "I found the door unlocked, just like you said, but whomever you heard was long gone. The building was empty. I called the owner and got him over there. We checked all three floors—even went down to the basement."

Anna stiffened. "So, you don't believe me?"

"That's not what I said. This isn't the first time you've been the target of something questionable. You had problems with anyone recently? You turn someone down who might take it personally?"

"Wheeler, but he's not exactly a threat."

"And you know this how?"

"I just know," Anna insisted. She'd worked with a lot of men over the past few years and she'd gotten to be a pretty good judge of character. It was usually easy to spot the guys she could trust and the ones it was healthier to avoid.

Harlan took a long swallow. "I wouldn't be too sure if I were you. Sometimes it's the folks you think you can trust you should be watching out for. Take Deke Call, for instance. You came to Nazareth to research the murders for a book, then you ran into Deke, and your focus suddenly shifted."

Anna didn't deny it. It wouldn't do any good to try. "What's that got to do with me having a stalker?"

Harlan's smile faded, but he didn't lessen his hold on her. "That's a good question, and I don't have an answer— yet. Could be nothing—or it could be everything. What I do know is that trouble seems to follow that boy. Not your typical bar fights, or DUIs, mind you, but murder. Lucas is having trouble, and so are you. Think about it, Anna. What's the one thing you and Lucas have in common? You're both closely connected to Deke. Now, as I see it, either he's a target or he's involved. Either way, it'd be a damn sight healthier for you if you took yourself out of the line of fire."

"Are you insinuating that Deke had something to do with the first murders?" she asked, narrowing her gaze.

"It's crossed my mind."

"You made an arrest and closed the case, Harlan. What are you saying? That you made a mistake when you arrested Juan Martinez?"

Harlan sat back in his chair. "I'm not sayin' anything. It's an observation, that's all. Like you said, it looks like you've got yourself a stalker. How long's this been goin' on? A week? Two? Since you started visitin' Lucas and seein' his nephew?"

"You've already tried inventing a connection where none exists," Anna told him. "It won't work. Deke had nothing to do with any of this."

"But you don't know that, do you, Anna? Any more than I know for sure he had nothing to do with what happened at the Miller place."

"I know that it's the same MO," Anna said. "And I know that Martinez was innocent. Two crimes, one killer, Sheriff. But you'll never find out who did this if you keep looking at Deke."

A shrug. "This is a copycat crime, Anna. Deke was seventeen when the original murders took place. In fact, he was the one who walked into that kitchen and found 'em, the kid laid out like she was at a sleepover. And Matthew—he'd been beat so bad his face looked like fresh ground hamburger. It was hard for me to see it, a grown man—what do you suppose somethin' like that does to a seventeen-year-old mind? Maybe somewhere in there re-creating the original murders makes sense to him. Maybe it's a cry for help."

"He isn't crazy," Anna insisted, the images of the gun lying on the dresser at the apartment and Deke leaning against the wall in the driving rain flashing behind her eyes. There had been an unmistakable desperation in the way he'd held her.

"You sure about that?" Harlan asked. "You're takin' a hell of a risk, and if you're wrong, it could cost you your life."

"It's a risk I'm willing to take," Anna said, looking into Harlan's blue eyes. She wished she could tell him about the phone call Deke had received. She was certain that someone was working hard to push Deke's buttons, to drive him over the edge, but it went hard against her grain to confide anything in Harlan Rudy.

She couldn't be sure how far he'd go to solve the Miller homicides, and she wasn't willing to chance it. Would he take his suspicion and run with it? Her father's face wavered in her mind's eye—not the handsome man in the photo on her laptop but the face of the drifter Lucas remembered and immortalized in his art, brutalized in body, his spirit ragged and worn—devoid of the smallest shred of hope.

The man now questioning her about Deke had taken a young man's hope and crushed it, grinding it to nothing in a matter of hours because the pressure was on and he'd needed a scapegoat. Anna knew it could happen again, if she let it.

"This old man botherin' you, baby?"

"Well, well," Harlan said with a grim smile. "Speak

of the devil. Have a seat, son. We were just talkin' about you."

Deke's black glance slid from Harlan to Anna and back again. "I think I'll pass," he said, all business. "But I do have a question for you, Harlan. What's Wheeler Dobbs got to do with the shit goin' on at Lucas's ranch?"

"Wheeler and your uncle?" Harlan said. "I don't know what you're talkin' about. They're tight, business partners, ain't that right? What makes you think Dobbs is involved?"

"I had a little talk with him this evenin', and he happened to mention your name, Harlan. If you've got information, you need to spill it."

A hard smile, not at all friendly. "Let's talk about spillin' information," Harlan said. "I hear that you were at the Miller place the afternoon before the murders. I have an eyewitness. Yet you didn't see fit to tell me. What were you doin' there?"

"Haven't you heard?" Deke said. "I'm a card-carrying member of the welcoming committee."

Harlan laughed, a sharp bark of sound, full of disbelief. "And you want *me* to give *you* information when all you give me is a load of shit? Whose town is this anyway? You're nothin' but a civilian. Ain't no such thing as professional courtesy between a career cop and a major fuckup."

The muscle in Deke's cheek convulsed. Tension crackled in the air between them, but he said nothing, made no attempt to deny it or to defend himself. So Harlan pushed a little harder. "You think I don't know that you graduated first in your class at the academy? You think I didn't ask around? That I don't know that you made detective in record time?"

Deke planted a hand on the center of the sheriff's

chest, grabbing a fistful of shirt, leaning into his face. His expression was as hard as granite, his dark eyes cold as ice. A tremor ran through him. He was itching to lash out, to wipe that nasty grin off the older man's face, but he didn't say a word as the sheriff continued, "Why'd you quit? Why the hell'd you walk away?"

The twitch in his cheek was nonstop, but he wouldn't give Harlan what he wanted. Refused to rise to the bait. "Lucas is family, Harlan. You got any idea what that means? Somebody's fucking with his operation, fuckin' with me. If you've got information about the man responsible, then I need to know it." The fist that held the sheriff tightened.

A soft, almost imperceptible click sounded under the table. The old-fashioned five-shot .38 sidearm Harlan carried was missing from its holster. Anna held her breath.

"I get your upset, son, but if you don't back off I'll have to put a bullet in you. Do you really want that? Hasn't your uncle seen enough trouble?"

"Deke, for God's sake, let him go," Anna pleaded.

His fist clenched, then released, but he didn't back down or move away, and his expression was no less menacing. "Why does Dobbs think you suspect him?"

"I got nothin' to say to you, Call," Harlan said, bringing out his piece and laying it on the table between them. "You're a loose cannon, son, and the last thing your uncle needs right now is to have you in my lockup on an assault charge—or worse." He flung a bill on the table and stood. "Anna, if you want to talk, you know where to find me." Then, picking up his revolver, he turned his back and stalked out.

Deke followed. Anna caught him on the sidewalk, grabbing his arm. "What the hell is wrong with you?"

she demanded. "He could have killed you just now, and he would have been justified."

"He could have, but he didn't."

The red light from a neon beer sign in Coyote's window washed over him, accentuating the hunger on his features, the hollowness in his dark eyes. Anna wanted to shake him, to frighten him half as much as he'd frightened her, to make him angry—anything but what he was in that moment. "He thinks you're this close to losing it," she said, holding up finger and thumb. "Even worse, he thinks you're involved in the murders . . . that you were damaged somehow by what happened in the past."

That dark gaze shifted, his thick lashes at half-mast, partially concealing the emptiness in his eyes. The fist at his side unclenched. His hand came up. One finger grazed a strand of hair that brushed her cheek. "What do you think?"

Tension rippled through Anna's five-foot-seven frame. Her instincts screamed at her to turn and walk away. Better yet, to run. But she couldn't listen. The loneliness she saw on his face held her there. "I don't know what to think," she admitted. "I can recognize the truth in what Harlan says . . . then I think about you, about the way you are when you're with me—" Breaking off, she shook her head. "But there's something there, Deke, something that haunts you. It's the reason you don't care if you live or die. It's the gun on the dresser, and you standing alone in the rain. You have to level with me. I need to understand."

He didn't flinch, didn't acknowledge her statements or give validity to her suspicions, but he didn't deny it either. "Don't," he said, a quiet plea, the fingers of that same hand threading through her hair, so tender, so loving.

Harlan was wrong.

He wasn't capable of hurting her.

She would never accept that.

"I have to ask," Anna said.

"You want answers," he said softly, that familiar, tantalizing ache in his voice. "Well, *querido,* so do I. Why don't you start by tellin' me why it is that the writer Anna Sandoval doesn't exist?"

The commotion inside the bar spilled out through the open doors, a woman's startled cry, several male voices, then John Blessing pushed through the doorway and onto the sidewalk. "Anna, you'd better come quick. Carlotta passed out."

"You think I should call Francine?"

Carlotta threw a dark look at Sandy for the suggestion. "Don't you even." She was on her feet again a few seconds after her collapse, irritated by all the attention and trying to pretend nothing had happened. "Back off, all of you. I haven't seen this much enthusiasm in a crowd since that carnival rolled through town a few years back with Joey, the three-breasted Hootchie-Cootchie."

Anna watched Carlotta closely. Her color had returned, and other than being a little more angry than usual, she seemed almost normal. "Did you have anything to eat today? And I don't mean coffee and a cigarette."

Carlotta rolled her eyes toward the ceiling. "I had an omelet and a slice of buttered toast."

"When was that?"

"Oh, for heaven's sake—"

"When?" Anna persisted.

"Five-thirty."

Anna glanced at Sandy, who hustled to the kitchen. "I'm right on it," he said. In two minutes, he'd returned with a sandwich and a glass of juice.

"Can you handle last call?" Anna asked the cook. "We're closing early. She needs to get some rest."

Sandy nodded and did as Anna requested. Anna took a seat across from her employer and friend. "Who's runnin' this place anyway?" Carlotta groused between bites.

"You are," Anna said, "and I'd like that to continue. We all would, but you're going to have to start taking better care of yourself, Carlotta."

"Don't give me the speech, Anna," she said with a sigh. "I get it often enough from Francine. I sure don't need to hear it from you."

"I want you to see the doctor, first thing tomorrow," Anna said. "Don't worry about the morning rush. We can handle it." Carlotta didn't argue, but her expression changed; the heat seemed to go out of her in that moment, and she looked ten years older. "What'd Harlan want with you this evening?"

"It's nothing to worry about," Anna began, but Carlotta cut her off.

"It was too long a talk to be nothin'. Don't try to bullshit me, child. It ain't gonna work."

Anna shrugged and did her best to downplay the frightening episode in the alley. "Someone was in the doorway of the building when I walked through, and they gave me a scare. I bumped into Harlan, and he checked it out. He was filling me in—then the conversation took a turn—"

"To Deacon Call," Carlotta guessed. "Those two are

like a couple of hounds circlin' one another, fangs bared
and hackles up. I wonder what Deke's mama would
make of it, if she were here to see it, her precious boy
and Harlan at each other's throats."

There was something in the way Carlotta said it that
brought Anna's gaze sharply up.

Carlotta waved a thin hand in dismissal. "Don't go
lookin' like that. I've always been suspicious, but I can't
prove anything. Can't say I didn't wonder, though, why
Maddy refused to name her boy's daddy. It ain't like
we're livin' in the Dark Ages. Pregnancy outta wedlock?
Happens every day. But if the daddy's a married man?
Well, that might be a different story."

"Harlan and Maddy Swift-Water?" Anna shook her
head.

Carlotta shrugged. "He sure was sweet on her. Didn't
hide it very well either. As for Maddy, stranger things
have happened. There's no greater allure than a powerful man. Maddy had a thing for power—after all, she
married Matthew. As for Harlan, that's easy enough to
figure out. Maddy was young and beautiful, dark and
vibrant—everything Mrs. Rudy could never be. Kinda
like you, honey. Could be part of the reason Harlan
looks at you like he does."

"Harlan? You're hallucinating," Anna said with
a laugh.

"I see a lot more than you think," Carlotta assured
her. "There's a softness that comes into his eyes when
he looks at you. He used to look at Maddy that way too.
Now, Deke. . . . Deke's a different story. His eyes show
the ache, the emptiness inside him. It's like he's broke
somewhere you can't see. Maybe he can be fixed,
but then again, maybe he can't. I don't know." She
reached out, taking Anna's hand in hers, and Anna was

shocked at how thin it was. "Good or bad, Deke Call's a thrill ride."

And a worry.

Anna couldn't anticipate his next move, and that was unnerving. He'd been checking up on her, delving into her past . . . or trying to. How long would it take for him to uncover the truth? And what would happen if he did?

Carlotta finished the juice, but she left half the sandwich. "What do you say to drivin' an old lady home? My car's in the parkin' lot. I don't want you walkin' home, and I really don't feel like doin' the drive, even if it is just half a mile. You can swing by in the morning and pick me up."

The crowd had thinned to a few diehards, and even they were down to the dregs of their beer and preparing to leave. Anna signaled Sandy, who'd been keeping an eagle eye on his boss from his position at the bar. "Will you close? I'm gonna drive Carlotta home."

A grim nod. "Sure thing."

Anna brought Carlotta's coat and put on her own black leather jacket. Carlotta grimaced as she got up. "Don't get old, Anna. It sure ain't for sissies."

A few minutes later, Anna parked the car and walked her to her door. "Are you sure you're okay?"

Carlotta smiled. "I'm tired, that's all. A good night's sleep, and I'll be good as new. Good night, honey. You be careful goin' home."

Anna climbed behind the wheel, waiting until the door to the house closed and the light went out. Then she drove home to her apartment.

Corrie Miller heard a footfall and shivered in anticipation. The drugs brought vivid disjointed dreams,

frustrating because they kept her from fully compre-
hending anything—yet existing without them was
unbearable. Something heavy covered her eyes and the
bridge of her nose. Sticky and too tough to resist, it kept
her in a state of perpetual darkness, dreadful because
she feared most of all what she couldn't see.

The loose-fitting dress she'd been wearing when she'd
been taken was unsuitable for the conditions in this
place. Its worn cotton was too thin to hold in her body's
warmth, and worse, it was soaked with her own urine.
The air was sour with it, pungent with the smell of pine
and something else, something she had never before
recognized—fear.

Her bones ached from the beatings she'd received;
there was a painful lump on her jaw but she kept gnawing on the duct tape wound around her wrists. It was
tight, so tight she'd lost the sensation in her hands long
ago. Ratlike, she chewed and kept chewing, tugging
against the fibers, bit by bit. She had no idea how long
it took, but when she tested the binding for what seemed
the millionth time, it loosened just enough to allow her
to pull her left hand free.

Pain shot up her arms, and Corrie gasped. She shook
her hands, limp on her wrists, and they pricked painfully. Feeling returned, and she tore the tape from her
eyes and blinked at the darkness. No light, nothing at
all. Just varying degrees of black. Darkness overhead,
criss-crossed by darker stripes. Somewhere in the distance, she could hear water dripping.

"Oh dear God. Where am I? What is this place? I
want to go home! I want to go—home."

But would she ever go home again?

Something deep inside, some small voice whispered
that she wouldn't, that they would be coming back, and

without a way to defend herself, she would die here in this dank, lightless place. She thought about her son, Billy, her husband, John, and the house that would never know the wonderful smell of fresh-baked bread if she didn't do something to get away.

On hands and knees she inched her way around the floor, the sharp stone shredding her flesh, feeling for anything she might use as a weapon. Circle after circle, around and around, and she found nothing. "Please, God, please! It can't end this way! It can't!" Her right palm came down on something sharp. She ran her hands over it, frantic now.

It was a rock. Just a rock, slightly larger than the palm of her hand. She grabbed it, clutching it tightly with both hands. Crying hysterically, Corrie collapsed.

A foot scraped the ground outside. She curled in a fetal position, turned her face away, and held her hands close to the front of her body. Air rushed in, cool and refreshing, washing over her exposed skin, raising gooseflesh along her arms. The one who entered edged closer. She could feel their eyes upon her. A foot prodded her spine, and she stayed still as death, waiting, waiting. A match struck, a bloom of yellow light. A face loomed over her, and Corrie struck. The rock was sharp, cutting flesh and wringing a howl from her tormentor. Too late, she saw the pistol, heard the sickening "pop," then her world went black.

Bridgeton Avenue was the main artery in Tucson's worst neighborhood. Running east to west, it was the warehouse district, far enough away from Diablo turf to make the meet between Deke and his contact safe. He'd chosen a good vantage point in the shadows of a doorway from which to watch and wait. Ten minutes to midnight and his contact still hadn't shown. Rain had been falling steadily since early afternoon, and the asphalt streets had taken on a greasy sheen that mirrored the glare of the headlights of an approaching car.

Deke's pulse quickened. Lounging in the doorway, he struck a match and lit a smoke, but instead of shaking the fire out, he held it for a few seconds, then flung it onto the sidewalk. It made a small golden arc, then fizzled out, and the ratty old Ford pulled silently to the curb. Deke emerged from the doorway, opening the passenger door, leaning down to stare in. The driver was alone, no visible firepower, the backseat empty. "My mother likes red candles," the man at the wheel said, eyeing Deke skeptically. "You know where I can get one? Tomorrow's her birthday."

"Red candles are bad luck, man. But there's a store on Ivy."

"Show me."

Deke got in without saying another word, and the man drove to a parking lot. "You Deke Call?"

"That's me."

"Paris, Johnny T." He stuck out his hand, and Deke gripped it, banger-style. "I'll be reporting back to Lieutenant Silvio as soon as we're through. What'dya have for me?"

Deke filled Paris in on the Diablos' operations and a major delivery Aguilar was expecting soon. "The shipment's comin' in from a Colombian cartel, to San Diego. Joaquin has connections there, and his man'll meet the coke, make the payment, and arrange to bring it here."

"You got details, man? Don't hold back. Give 'em to me."

Deke gave Paris a long, measuring look, and the man

knew he didn't fully trust him. He could see it in his expression. "Aguilar's tight-lipped. He don't say much he don't need to, and he don't tell anyone everything. He's that smart—and I don't ask, 'cause I like to live, and I ain't stupid."

"How long you been with the PD, Call?" Paris asked.

"Eight years. You?"

"If I make it to January, it'll be fifteen. We don't know one another, and I should keep my mouth shut, but I'm not goin' to. You get off on the undercover thing, that right?" When Deke said nothing, Paris continued. "You don't need to say shit. I got a good handle on most people I meet, and I've seen guys like you. You're in deep with the Diablos, maybe you even begun to think of these punks as *familia,* but they're not. They'll cut you down in a heartbeat if they think there's a chance you'll interfere with business as usual. You'll do well to remember who your real friends are."

"That all?" Deke asked. The man's advice rubbed. He was the one living the life, on the street, in the trenches, and he didn't need anyone telling him how to handle it. He glanced in the side mirror, and seeing a clear street, stepped out of the car, watching as it rattled off into the misty night. If he was damned lucky, someone else would meet him next time.

But he hadn't seen the end of the interference. The next day, his lieutenant caught up with him. Deke was grabbing scrambled eggs with green chiles at a local haunt when his cell rang. He fished it out of his denim jacket and checked the number. It came up with no data, but very few people had his number. "Chaca," he answered without even thinking.

"In the alley around the corner, two minutes," the voice on the other end of the line said. "Be there."

Deke paid for his meal, tipped the waitress, and made the rendezvous. Lieutenant Silvio Carrera was waiting, and he looked anything but happy. "Call. I haven't seen much of you at the precinct lately. What's it been, two months?"

"More like three." It had been three months since he'd been "beaten into the gang," and he'd been too involved in the work to come up for air. "I haven't exactly disappeared, Lieutenant. I'm doin' what you sent me here to do. I collect info and I meet with my contacts. If I want to keep the Diablos' trust, there ain't time for much else."

"So I hear. No time for family either, I suppose?" He crossed his arms over his chest. He was shorter than Deke by several inches, and he was forced to tilt his bald head back and look up to meet his gaze. "How's Melissa?"

Deke shifted his stance. He wasn't comfortable sharing his personal life with anybody, no matter how well meaning he might be.

Silvio was as persistent as he was pissed. "Have you seen her lately? Talked to her?"

Deke's look discouraged further questions. "My life's my business, Lieutenant."

"She called me last week, Deke. Despite the divorce proceedings, seems she's concerned about your grip on reality. I thought it was a cop's wife's fear talkin', until Paris came to see me this morning. He tells me he's got a real bad feelin' about you. He tells me he thinks the lines are startin' to blur where you're concerned. That you're holdin' out on him."

"You want to know what I think?" Deke said. "That Paris is fried. A half-hair from a ledge. He's jittery, and makin' rendezvous with someone that on edge puts me at risk of havin' my cover blown."

"So your story is that he's full of shit."

"That's pretty much it—Lieutenant. And the fact that my marriage is over doesn't have a damned thing to do with it. How many men who do what we do manage to hold it together?"

Silvio, himself divorced twice, said nothing. "Give me one good reason I shouldn't haul your ass in and force you into a desk job?"

"You need me to be right where I am," Deke said. "Force me in and you'll blow the chance to take Aguilar and his operation down." He could see from the change in the man's expression that he was right. He turned and left the alley without another word, but he was aware of the lieutenant's stare boring a hole between his shoulder blades until he hung a right and was out of sight. . . .

Years later, Deke could admit that Johnny Paris had had him dead to rights. One ten-minute meet and he'd recognized the danger in what he was becoming. He'd described the contact as a man on a ledge, but it had been him and not Paris with a ten-story drop between him and the cold concrete.

Overhead, the black canopy of the night sky had cleared, and the stars were huge and too numerous to count. A sliver of white moon hung suspended just above the horizon, cold and aloof, despite being surrounded by millions of points of glimmering light.

Deke watched the constellations and wished he didn't know how that felt. Surrounded by people but nonetheless alone. While working for the task force, he'd kept his secrets in order to survive. These days, he did it out of sheer habit, and the certainty that something dreadful would happen if he let go for even a second.

"Pretty night, ain't it?" Lucas's voice emerged from the shadows before he did. "Too bad you can't see it. When you gonna get past this thing, Deacon? Whatever it is that's been eatin' away at you?"

"I don't know if I can get past it," Deke said. It was the most honesty they'd had between them since he came home from Tucson—two months out of the hospital, healed in body but feeling like one of the walking dead. He'd had a decent chunk of severance pay and a monthly pension. Enough to get him a car and keep him in whiskey.

Nothing else had mattered.

"Then I'd say you got a problem," Lucas said, his voice strangely calm. Had he known what Deke had been thinking, he might not have been so serene, but he'd always trusted him, and it was apparent that much hadn't changed. "You'll solve it," he said with the confidence of one who knew. "You always do."

"I wish I believed that." While working undercover, he'd lost perspective, and it had cost a young girl her life. The lines really had blurred, until in the end he'd very nearly lost his grip on reality, unable to distinguish between good or bad, right or wrong. He couldn't afford for that to happen again. There was too much at stake.

A moment passed, then two. Deke breathed the cool night air and wished he had a little of his uncle's wisdom. "What do you really know about Wheeler Dobbs *Shi-Da?*"

"Wheeler?" Lucas leaned against the porch railing so he could look his nephew in the eye. "He's an okay sort. Eccentric and unorthodox, but artists are like that." A shrug. "People expect it. Makes us seem more romantic, I guess. Why do you ask?"

"I'm just wonderin' how he fits into all of this. He

was here tonight when the coon-tail rattler showed up in my car and the night Anna was attacked in Carlotta's van. Anytime something bad happens, Wheeler's not too far behind."

Another shrug. "Okay, but just 'cause he's around don't mean he's involved. I just don't see him tryin' to hurt Anna. They're friends, you know."

"I didn't say he meant to hurt her," Deke said, bending his head to light a cigarette, offering one to Lucas. "Could be he meant to frighten her."

"But for what reason? Don't you cops need a motive in order to suspect someone?"

This time he didn't argue the cop thing. It never seemed to get him anywhere with Lucas. Besides, he couldn't seem to shed the thought process no matter how much he wanted to, and lately he'd been acting more and more like one. "I don't need a motive to suspect him. The suspicion just about always comes first."

"It precedes the snake in the john, I guess? You scared him good, you know that?"

"I meant to," Deke said.

"He said you're crazy, and he was talkin' about pressin' charges." Lucas snorted. "Assault with a deadly reptile. He said you threatened him."

"If I'm right and he's responsible for what's been happenin' 'round here, then he's got reason to be scared shitless," Deke said.

"I still don't see it, Deacon," Lucas mused. "My star's on the rise, and he gets a cut. Why mess up a good thing?"

"I don't think any of this is about money."

Lucas shook his head. "You kiddin'? With Wheeler, it's always about the money. The dollar's his main motivator.

He's always lookin' for an angle. The man's got a taste for the good life."

Deke snorted. "The good life? They re-poed his truck, and he's livin' in a tin can."

Lucas shrugged. "Maybe his sugar mama ain't come through for him yet."

Deke raised his gaze to his uncle's. "Dobbs is hooked up with a rich bitch?"

"Sure sounded like it," Lucas said. "I overheard him on the phone one day when I stopped in. It was an impromptu visit—unannounced. Sounded to me like they're pretty hot and heavy. He mentioned her old man, so I'm guessin' she's married."

"That, or jailbait," Deke said. "I wouldn't put anything past that son of a bitch. What else do you know 'bout this?"

"That she's crazy," Lucas told him.

Deke frowned. "How so?"

"She floated him a loan for the microbrewery equipment, and the building too. Ain't no way he'll ever turn enough of a profit to pay back her investment."

"So he's an expensive piece of ass," Deke murmured.

But what else was he?

And why would he target Lucas?

What the hell could he hope to gain from it? It couldn't be money. Most of his uncle's assets were securely wrapped up in land and Churro sheep. His nest egg wasn't huge, and even combined with his army pension and the profits from the sale of his sculptures, he wasn't exactly rolling in it.

But maybe it wasn't about what Lucas had.

Maybe it was about who he was.

Think about it, Deke. The shooting, the dead ram,

the attack on Anna, the phone calls, maybe even the murders. . . .

It all had one common denominator.

Him.

He was the only apparent survivor of the killings that night, and he was closely connected to both Anna and Lucas. Even Miller and his kid were loosely associated to him through the house on Echo Canyon Road. It made sense, at least from the standpoint of explaining why Lucas had been targeted and Anna attacked. Was Wheeler behind it all? And if so, then just how far would he go with all of this? As far as cold-blooded murder?

"So you think that Wheeler is somehow tied in with what's going on around Nazareth?"

"I don't know what to think," Deke admitted. "Draw a connecting line to everything that's happened so far. The weird shit here at the ranch, Anna getting her headlight smashed out, both murders, and it comes straight back to me. I walked away that night, the only survivor."

"Yeah, but it's been quiet for twelve years."

"And it starts again a couple of months after I come home."

Lucas nodded. "I know you ain't very good at makin' friends, but who hates you enough to want to do somethin' like that? And why not just come after you? It don't make sense, especially if the man who killed Matthew and the girl is already dead. He's got no family—"

"He's got family. In fact, he's got a daughter." The light clicked on in Deke's head. Silvio had run Anna's name, and he'd come up empty. Or, at least, he'd run her alias. "I need to use your computer," he said. "There's somethin' I need to check out."

"Don't go to no porno sites," Lucas warned. "Last time, I got a virus."

Deke gave him a look.

Lucas shrugged. "Hey, I was just lookin'. I might be old, but I ain't dead."

"And I'm sure as hell gonna try to keep it that way," Deke muttered, heading for his uncle's office.

Chapter Thirteen

Harlan made a walk-through of the business district before turning in, but it was more formality than necessity. There hadn't been a break-in for six weeks, since Willie Redwing broke the lock on a storage building behind the hardware and built himself a small fire to keep warm. Trouble was, Dan Tremaine, the old tightwad who owned the hardware, had a pile of oily rags and several large cans of turpentine stored there, among other things, and Redwing started a three-alarm fire.

Tonight was quiet, though perhaps deceptively so. The hardware store windows were dark, with an illuminated clock on the back wall the only visible light. Down three doors was Vella's Floral Shop and its colorful spring display bright with white twinkle lights, then farther down, Coyote Moon. The CLOSED sign was turned out, even though it was barely two o'clock, and when Harlan glanced in, he saw Sandy putting up chairs. He rapped on the glass with a knuckle, and the ex-marine came to unlatch the doors. "Everything okay?" Harlan asked.

"Just gettin' ready to close the doors for the night, Sheriff, but thanks for askin'."

"It's kinda early for that, isn't it? There's always one or two you gotta roll out the door at closin'."

"Carlotta wasn't feelin' too well," Sandy admitted. "Passed clean out. I'm bettin' it's a bout of the flu. She's been lookin' pretty run-down lately. Anna drove her home. Pushes herself too hard, she does."

Harlan touched a finger to the brim of his hat. "She does, at that. Well, I sure hope it's nothin' serious. Night, Sandy."

"Night, Sheriff." Sandy turned the lights out and locked the door. Harlan walked on.

First the voice in the alley, and now Carlotta. Anna had had quite an evening. After turning down the alley, he walked past her apartment. Carlotta's car was parked outside. The lights were on, but everything seemed okay. At least there was no sign of Deke Call.

A ten-minute stroll, but everything seemed normal enough. When he opened the office door, the phone was ringing. Normally, Nancy Wheaten worked the night shift, cleaning the office and answering the phones, but Nancy had a week's vacation, and since Harlan was sleeping on the sofa, there was no sense in looking for a temp to fill in. Reaching the dispatcher's desk, he grabbed the receiver. "Alamance County Sheriff's office."

Dead air. The caller had already hung up.

"Well, now I guess I've seen everything," a voice said from the open doorway. "Answering your own phone, Harlan? What's the world coming to?"

Harlan straightened slowly, facing her. "Ginny." Normally he would have felt the need to answer for his absence, let her know where he'd been and what he'd been doing in order to avoid her asking. She'd always been possessive, and he knew that his affair with Maddy had somehow justified within her the need for control. He'd grated at the questions, the attempts to turn the screws of his guilt, and sometimes, fed up, he'd cut loose completely and done things he shouldn't have done. It was a sick cycle that would have ended a long time ago if they'd both been a little less stubborn. "It's late for you to be out. Is somethin' wrong at the house?"

"Other than my man not bein' there? Not a thing." A small, nervous laugh. "The house feels empty, and I keep listening for the truck to pull in the drive." She shook her head in disbelief at her own admission. "How long are we gonna do this dance, Harlan?"

"Is that what this is?" Harlan said with a harsh laugh. "A dance?"

A sigh, and her voice cracked. Harlan looked for tears, but to his relief, he didn't see any. "I know I've been a bitch," she said. "I'll try to do better. I promise, I'll try. Can't you just come home so we can talk about it?"

Harlan closed his eyes, massaging his lids with fingers and thumb. "Ginny." It was a plea, and that rankled somehow. For years, he'd felt the need to "manage" her. Conversation was limited to the subjects that wouldn't ignite the powder keg, every effort made to keep the marriage on an even keel—because he'd cheated and she knew it. Ironically, the extreme maintenance of marriage to Ginny had been the thing that had driven him into Maddy's arms.

Wild, sweet Maddy—she'd been so young, and he should have been horsewhipped for foolin' with her, but he couldn't have resisted her. Like a breath of fresh spring air, she blew through his life, made him feel alive again, blessedly free.

"It's her, isn't it? The pretty young girl I saw you with at Carlotta's? Are you sleeping with her, Harlan? Or merely hoping to?"

Harlan's voice tightened, his muscles tensed. "I've got an investigation goin' on," he heard himself say. "I'm under a lot of pressure, and I just don't have the time or the patience for this right now."

"You don't have the time, and it seems I have nothing but." She leaned a shoulder against the door frame and lit a slim black cigar, neat and attractive in a white shirt, jeans, and ostrich-skin boots. "Thirty-three years, and I really do deserve the dignity of an answer. It's something you haven't afforded me much of—dignity."

She was at it, and she would keep at it until he gave her what she wanted. "Her name's Anna, and no, I'm not sleepin' with her."

"Not yet, anyway," she said, the cigar sending a trail of blue smoke curling up into the air in front of her blond head. "I'm sure you'll get around to it." A knowing smile. "Anna. I knew it was something common. You know, in a way she reminds me of Maddy, Matthew's wife."

The "Matthew's wife" was added for his benefit, and Harlan knew it. Always a twist of the knife, and he wondered why he hadn't seen it years before. Her vindictive streak. Was it a result of some innate character flaw? Or the fact that she'd been rich and spoiled?

"There's something in the way she carries herself, like she's got the world in the palm of her hand and she knows it. Does she remind you of Maddy, Harlan?"

Everything reminds me of Maddy, Harlan thought. He thought of her a hundred times a day, at every turn.

Dreams of her kept him from sleeping peacefully, and had since the night she disappeared. He saw her face in everything, and everyone, and it had gotten worse since Deke came home. With the Miller killings and another woman missing, it was nearly unbearable. "Now that you mention it, yeah, she does," he said. "I haven't forgotten her, and I never will. That should make you happy, Ginny. You been after me for years to admit it."

Her face registered the pain he'd inflicted, but her eyes were flat, cold. "Well, congratulations, Harlan. You been cattin' around all these years, lookin' for a substitute. Looks like you finally found one." She pushed away from the door frame, turned silently, and was gone.

Harlan thought about going after her, but the phone rang, and he answered it instead. "Alamance County Sheriff." He listened for a moment, then hung up.

"Wrong number?" Anna watched him from the open doorway.

He took a deep breath, glancing up. "No one there. I've been gettin' a lot of those lately." A nod of greeting and he smiled. "Anna. I'm surprised to see you here."

"I didn't think I'd be here," Anna admitted. She came into the room, slowly and deliberately. "I bumped into your wife on her way out. She seemed upset."

"Ginny's made a career out of bein' upset. She's perfected it so well, it's damn near an art form where she's concerned. Best thing is to try and pay her no mind. That's what I do." He moved to close the door, then half-sat on the corner of the receptionist's desk. "What brings you here so late, Anna? You didn't come over here to talk about my wife."

"Actually, I came to talk about Deke, and his mother, Maddy."

That surprised him. He braced a hand on the desk. "This for the book?"

"It's for my clarification," Anna said. "Carlotta tells me that Maddy Call was involved with a mystery man before she married Matthew Call, and information I've received leads me to believe that that mystery man was you." She had expected him to deny it, to stonewall, anything but what she got.

"Information? I'd like to ask your source."

Anna shrugged. "I hired a P.I. to look into Maddy's past. Is it true?"

"It seems to be a night to talk about Maddy." He sounded tired, and she remembered his admission to Carlotta that he was losing sleep. "Carlotta's got a keen eye, but there's a lot she doesn't know."

"You're admitting that you were involved with Deke's mother?"

"Not just involved. I was in love with her." He ran a hand through his hair. "Hell, there's no 'was' to it. I've never gotten over losing her. Maddy was unforgettable, a real fireball." He watched her steadily. "Now, you're thinking that Deke's my son, but you'd be wrong. By the time she got pregnant, there was another man in the picture."

"Who?" Anna asked.

"She wouldn't say—I guess she was afraid I'd meddle, and she was probably right. I would've done anything to keep her. But she swore the baby belonged to him, not me, and Lucas backed her up."

"And you believed her?"

"I had no reason not to. Maddy never lied to me. Then she left town, and by the time she came back, Ginny and I were trying to make a go of it—somethin' we've been doin' ever since. Then she got involved with

Matthew, and they got married, and that was really the end for me."

"That must have been difficult for you," Anna said, "given how you felt about her."

"Like I said, by then we were a long time over. Besides, I had obligations of my own to satisfy." His brow furrowed. "And that's about as personal as I intend to get. You mind tellin' me what this is about? My affair with Maddy had nothin' to do with the murders."

Anna wondered if she could believe him. Deke's paternity wasn't the issue—or was it?

What if he was lying?

What if he'd known that Deke was his son?

Seeing Maddy marry the man he worked with every day would have been tough. Watching his flesh and blood mistreated at the hands of that same man might have proven impossible. And Deke was the only one to survive that night. "How did you feel about Matthew? He was your superior, incredibly powerful, undeniably abusive. He must have made her life hell, considering how she felt about her only son."

His expression darkened. "I'm not gonna deny it bothered me. I don't hold with grown men bullyin' kids—"

Or killing them?

"I offered once," he said. "I could have found a way to get her out of there, and the kids. They would have been safe. I would have seen to it. She turned me down flat."

Anna took a deep breath and took the plunge. "You wanted her safe, but how far were you willing to go, Harlan? Would you have been willing to kill to protect her?"

Harlan laughed, but there was no humor in the sound. "So that's what this is about. You think I killed Matthew."

Anna shrugged. "Maybe you'd finally had enough. Every man has his limits. Maybe you decided to confront him. Maybe things got out of hand."

"Maybe," he said. "But what about the child? You really think I'd go that far?"

"I don't know what to think," Anna admitted.

"Well, it's a good theory, I'll give you that, except for one thing . . . I would have given my life for Maddy. Nothin' in this world would have been worth hurtin' her, and she loved Matthew and that little girl more than she ever loved me." A grim smile. "Are we through here, 'cause I've had enough talk for one evening. I'd like to get some sleep."

"We're through," Anna said. "For now."

Late the following afternoon, Carlotta made an excuse and left the bar in Anna and Sandy's capable hands. She'd told them she had errands to run, then she got in her car and drove. She hadn't seen the property since the night she'd found Anna, huddled under an overhanging lip of earth in the dry riverbed that bordered her daddy's old homestead.

On that particular day, she'd been hoping for an epiphany too. Frank had died a few months before, Francine and Steven were grown and gone, and she'd never felt so lost, so rudderless. Maybe it was a worn-out cliche, to return to the place where it all began when life got tough, but it was her way of handling things. When faced with the hard choices, she came out here to this barren little plot of land and all its memories. Like her daddy, the house where she'd grown up was long gone, nothing but a pile of rotting timbers on stone, with a few ragged pieces of tar paper clinging to what once had been the roof.

She surveyed the scrub, one hand shading her eyes, and thought that her daddy must have been crazy when he bought this plot of land. When he'd looked at it, he'd seen potential, and he spent the next eighteen years trying to make it pay off. "You always were a dreamer," Carlotta said. "And where'd that get you? Six feet of earth and debts you could never repay."

Years later, Carlotta had bought the valley—not with the intention of developing it, but as a reminder where pure-D stubbornness and the adamant refusal to face reality could get you.

Now, she was here again, troubled and looking for direction. She'd gotten the results of the tests two weeks ago, and she'd been doing her best to ignore them ever since. How could she do anything else? Her relationship with Francine wasn't the best, but how was she going to break it to her little girl that she was dying? And how could she tell Sandy, or Anna, when she couldn't seem to grasp it herself.

As crazy as it seemed, she'd thought that if she just kept doing what she'd always done, everything would work out all right. Staying busy helped, and during work hours, she didn't have to face the grim reality of the next couple of months. But when the bar was closed, the fear closed in. Last night had been the proverbial wake-up call, and suddenly it was appallingly clear that she couldn't ignore this any longer.

"Oh God, Frank," she said. "I don't know if I can do this. I'm not strong enough."

There was so much to consider. So many details to take care of, and she couldn't put it off any longer.

Her eyes stung, and she squeezed them shut, fighting back unaccustomed tears. When she opened them again, her vision swam and the pain in her chest intensified. She could hear the doctor's voice so clearly, a respected surgeon from Santa Fe. "There are masses in both lungs, Mrs. McFadden." He pointed to the dark spots on the X-ray. There were thirteen, of various sizes. Her stomach fell, the sensation as sickening as the vertical drop of a speeding roller coaster. "I'd like to do a biopsy, and we can't afford to delay."

"A biopsy," her own voice echoed in her head. "That's just a formality, right? I mean, you and I both know what we're lookin' at."

"A necessary formality," he'd said, "I won't lie to you. I've seen enough of these cases to be concerned. That's why I'd like to schedule the biopsy. Then, when we know what we're dealing with, we can discuss treatment options. . . ."

She'd called Francine and Anna and pretended that everything was fine. She'd bumped into an old friend and they were going to dinner that evening. She'd return late the next day. It had worked. No one had suspected. The results, however, had just served to confirm her fears. Small-cell cancer—the most difficult to treat—in an advanced stage, involving both lungs. Worse, the surgeon had ordered a CT scan, and it wasn't confined to her lungs. She had the option of chemotherapy and radiation, but there were no guarantees, and her odds of survival after treatment, barring a miracle, were in the lower two digits. Without treatment, she'd have a few months.

Carlotta didn't like her options. "I worked hard all my life, and this is the thanks I get." She kicked at a stone with the toe of her shoe, forgetting it was light canvas.

Pain shot the length of her big toe, into her instep; as she stooped to rub at it, she noticed the deep red stain next to her foot.

Blood. Large, fat drops splashed on the rocky ground. Her stomach in a tight knot, Carlotta followed the fresh trail. It led to the hillside, to a rough wooden door nearly covered by undergrowth. Daddy's root cellar. Abandoned too many years ago to even count, she'd completely forgotten it even existed. A hasp closed over its loop—surprisingly new, but there was no lock. Carlotta flipped the hasp over and pushed on the rough panel. It opened silently. . . . A tarp covered everything but the woman's bare feet. A foot away, the remnants of rags had disintegrated and hung, tattered from the bony rib cage of what once was a human being. Carlotta looked closer. Matted, long dark hair cushioned the skull. "Lord, God almighty," she said. "Maddy—is that you?"

She ran back to the car, fumbling in her purse for her cell phone. She flipped it on and dialed. One ring, two. . . .

"Damn it, Dixie, pick up!" She didn't see the shadow loom over her until it was too late.

The crowbar fell, then fell again. Carlotta didn't hear the sickening crunch of the repeated blows that followed after she'd fallen. Winded, her attacker took the phone from her hand. "911." The dispatcher's voice came through the receiver. "What's your emergency? Hello?" And closed the phone. . . .

Angel's enthusiasm was rubbing off on Deke. She tugged at his hand as they emerged from the elevator, urging him down the hallway, then covering his eyes as they neared the apartment door. "No peeking," she said.

"Not even a little? How about one eye open?"

She swatted his arm playfully, and Deke felt something soften deep inside his solar plexus.

Little Eduardo had insisted that it would simplify their working relationship if he found digs nearby, and on some level, it had. At first, Deke had worried about the pressure of living as Chaca 24–7, yet he was stunned at how easy it had become.

Too easy, maybe?

The thought came and went away. He didn't want to believe that Silvio was right about him. He was doing his job, and that was all that mattered.

Focus on the goal, man.

It was all about getting there. The path he took didn't count for shit.

"It's supposed to be a surprise!" she said, putting on a little girl pout.

He sighed. "All right, Angel-baby. When you look at me like that, how can I say no?" He closed his eyes, listening as she unlocked the door. Then she slipped her hand into his and pulled him inside.

"Are you ready?"

"I got a condom in my pocket, sweetheart. I'm always ready."

She laughed, a bright, sexy sound that rippled over him like a beguiling wind. "C'mon, Chaca. It's your new crib," she said. Check it out."

"Shit!" Deke said, softly. "Baby, I can't afford this."

"Eduardo said to find you someplace nice, and I aim to please." She smiled, and those strange eyes of hers—eyes with pinpicks for pupils—twinkled. It was a little amazing that she could shoot up and seem so normal. She'd told him she was trying to get clean and confessed that she used just enough to keep the withdrawal at bay.

He didn't buy it. An addict was an addict. It was all the same.

Take away her smack and she'd be on her knees and ready to do anything for a fix in twenty-four hours. He knew it, and it still wasn't enough to ward him off.

His instincts whispered that he should stay away, yet something about her spoke louder, drowning out the warning. It was the glint in her eye, the hint of seduction in her smile, the invitation in her lingering touch—her vulnerability. Without saying a word, she cried out to him, and something deep inside, something he couldn't, or didn't want to, control answered the call.

"You haven't seen the best part," she said, her smile widening, more playful. She pulled him through the plush living room and down a short hallway to a door on the left. Stepping inside she flicked on the soft, ambient lighting for the full effect. Pot lights shone down on a huge bed, spread with silks and brimming with throw pillows of various shapes and textures. "Check this out," she said, grabbing the remote from the nearby shelf and pushing a button. The top of the black lacquer cabinet opened and a huge TV screen materialized. "We can catch up on the latest when I come to visit. And you know the coolest part? If you lie down in the middle of the bed and look straight up? That's where I'll be sleeping—just one floor up—" Her fingers glided over his forearm, caressing the petals of the roses, the vines, leaves, and thorns. "So when you're lying here . . . you can think of me."

"Of you, and Little Eduardo," Deke found himself saying. "A threesome, it just ain't my style."

The bald statement didn't have any lasting effect as she stepped closer and rose on her toes to kiss him. "It doesn't have to be a threesome. Eduardo, he's done a lot for me—but he doesn't love me. He's not like you, Chaca. He doesn't have it in him to love anyone. . . ."

Deke's eyes opened, and for a few seconds, he expected to feel her breathing beside him. Then the disorientation melted away, and he remembered where he was, who he was. Deke Call. Chaca was dead—as dead as Angel, and he had bigger problems than the persistent echos of his not-so-distant past.

His involvement with Angel had never gotten beyond the first few heated weeks. It hadn't been about love. Sure, he'd found her attractive, despite her dangerous lifestyle—or maybe because of it. He'd been playing fast and loose for months, sinking deeper and deeper with the Diablos. He'd taken the new apartment and all the frills that went with it, because he didn't dare do otherwise. The bangers weren't fools, and he was always aware that someone was weighing his actions, judging his loyalty, watching his every move.

Someone was judging him now too, watching and trying to fathom just how far they could push him before he snapped. Only this time, there was no role to play, and the only goal in the end was survival.

He sat up on the sofa, passing a hand over his eyes, his thoughts shifting to Anna. There were no similarities between her and Angel. She was older than Angel, more poised and self-contained. She wasn't looking to trade up, and she sure as hell didn't need a savior. In fact, she knew exactly what she was doing.

There was no denying that the woman had an agenda. He'd sensed it immediately and found it incredibly intriguing. But as the intrigue surrounding her deepened, he wondered just how far she'd go to get what she wanted.

Was that why she'd gotten involved with him? Why

she'd slept with him? Was she using him, as he'd used Angel?

The sliding door opened, and Lucas leaned into the room. "Thought I'd see if you wanted some supper. Beans and biscuits—you interested?"

"Think I'll pass," Deke said. "You mind if I borrow your rifle? The one with the infrared scope?"

"That depends on who you're gonna shoot," Lucas said.

"Nobody—yet."

"That's comforting, Deke. It's over at the house. Come by and get it—just watch the dog don't take your leg off. He's a ferocious one. Tore my slipper all to pieces, and I wouldn't want to see you get hurt."

"I'll keep that in mind," Deke said. Then he went to the kitchen and made a thermos of coffee. It'd be dark in a couple of hours, and he had someplace to be.

Harlan was grabbing an exceptionally late lunch when Dixie tapped on the door. With a mouthful of hot sausage and fried jalapenos, he mumbled an invitation to enter. "I'm glad to see you're gettin' some real food into you instead of that junk you've been eating. Ginny bring it by for you?"

"It's Matamoros takeout, and Ginny had nothin' to do with it."

She digested that without comment, crossing to his desk and sliding a piece of paper in front of him, then watching as he put on his reading glasses. "It came in a few minutes ago, but since the call was never completed, I took the liberty of running it down before I brought it to you."

"Cellular call, routed from the Red Butte tower."

Harlan glanced at her over his glasses. "What about the number?"

"Blocked."

"That doesn't give me much to go on. They say anything at all?"

"Not a word. Could have been a prank call—or a mistake. I just figured you needed to know."

"Thanks, Dixie," Harlan said, "and my ass cheek thanks you too. This new chair's heaven."

Harlan finished his sandwich and left the office. His conversation with Anna last night had left a bad taste in his mouth, and it wasn't likely to go away until he spoke with Lucas. He found the man near the sheep fence, a dog roughly the size of one of his boots nosing the ground around a ewe and her lamb. The ewe lowered its head and tried to look threatening, but the dog just circled wide and nipped its heels.

"You see that?" Lucas said. "It's instinct at work. Barely bigger than a mite and he still knows what he's supposed to do."

Harlan leaned his forearms on the fence a few feet from Lucas. "He's gonna take a lot of work."

"He'll learn," Lucas said. "Besides, I got all the time in the world to train him. That's the nice thing about gettin' old. Everything slows down, and there ain't no reason to rush things."

"It does put things in perspective," Harlan agreed, nodding at the glimmer of sunlight on water at the far end of the valley. "Take that lake, for instance. It's been callin' my name for damn near six months. If things ever slow down at the office, I just might listen."

"You come all the way out here to invite me along fishin', Harlan?"

Harlan expelled a deep breath. "No, I surely didn't. I

came because I had to. Anna came to my office last night, late. She had questions about Maddy, Lucas. More to the point, about Maddy and me."

Lucas glanced at him, his gaze unreadable. He'd always been like that, tight-lipped, giving nothing away. He'd always done his level best to protect his own, especially Maddy, who'd lived with him after their parents were killed. Harlan couldn't fault the man for it. Maddy had needed someone strong, and Lucas had unarguably been that. "What'd you tell her?"

"The truth," Harlan said. "That I was in love with her and that I'd never gotten over losing her."

"That makes two of us," Lucas said softly. "Three, if you count Deke."

Harlan watched the lake in the distance. "Deke," Harlan said, breaking out a cigar, offering one to his host. "Every damned time I look at that boy, I see her face. It would've been a hell of a lot easier for me if he'd stayed gone."

"It ain't about easy," Lucas said.

"I suppose not," Harlan said. "Level with me, Lucas. Who does he belong to?"

A sigh. "It's an old can of worms, Harlan. What do you want to open it for now?"

"Because if she lied, then I've got a right to know."

Lucas gave him a long, measuring look. "Maddy had her reasons for doin' what she did. I won't fault her for it, thirty years after the fact."

"If that's supposed to make things right, it fell a ~~bit~~ shy of the mark," Harlan ground out. "Did you ever consider for one damn minute that maybe I'd want to know? That I might have been able to do him some good somewhere along the way?" He didn't expect Lucas to answer, and he wasn't disappointed. The older man just stared off into the distance, giving nothing, while Harlan cursed him roundly for being a stubborn old fool.

"You got what you came here for," Lucas said finally. "What do you intend to do?"

Harlan gave him a hard look and walked back to his Jeep. "Damned if I know," he muttered, slamming the shift into reverse and turning. "Damned if I know."

Chapter Fourteen

The sun went down, and the evening crowd trickled through the doors at Coyote Moon. From her position behind the bar, Anna served drinks and kept a nervous eye on the door. Eight o'clock and Carlotta still hadn't returned. She put on a bright smile for the ranch hands holding down stools at the bar, but the feeling that something was wrong never left her completely.

A half hour till lights out, and Sandy emerged from the kitchen, wiping his hands on a towel. "It's been hours, Anna, and the phone hasn't rung once. I'm starting to sweat this. It isn't like Carlotta not to check in. Where'd she say she was goin' again?"

"She didn't. She just said she had something to take care of—that she'd be back in an hour or two. Maybe it had something to do with last night. I talked to her about seeing a doctor."

Sandy nodded. "I sure hope everything's okay. What say we close the doors early and make some calls? Ain't no chance of me gettin' a wink of sleep till I know what's goin' on."

Sandy manned the phone, while Anna took a more

direct route, via the van. She drove past her employer's house, but her car was gone and the house lightless, so she made the drive to Harlan Rudy's office and reported Carlotta missing.

For the second time in twenty-four hours, Harlan glanced up to see Anna standing in his office. "Didn't figure to see you back here so soon," he said. "You come up with some new angle on the Call murder case? Maybe you think my receptionist did it. She worked with Matthew, too, you know."

She stood in the doorway for a moment, then slowly entered. "Carlotta's missing. She left this afternoon supposedly to run some errands—and she didn't come back."

"You check with her kids?" Harlan sat back in his chair, a frown settling on his face.

"Sandy made the calls," she said. "Nobody's heard from her, and I'm worried."

He digested that for a moment, watching her intently, unsure what she wanted from him. "Well, I expect she'll turn up when she feels like it. Carlotta's a tough old bird. Ain't much she can't handle."

"Surely there's something you can do."

He pushed back in his chair, impatient that one more problem had been added to a growing heap with which he was already struggling. "Anna, I don't know what you want from me. I can't even file a missing persons until she's been gone twenty-four hours. Look, go home. Get some sleep. If she doesn't come home by tomorow afternoon, we'll do the paperwork. It's the best I can do."

But Carlotta wasn't back by the next afternoon, or at closing either. Anna filed the report early, then talked to the older woman's friends during her break, to everyone she could think of who might have seen her, with no results. She stayed till closing, then climbed into the van for the short ride home.

The sheriff had told Anna not to worry, and he'd gotten back to business as usual.

Easier said than done. Anna couldn't help worrying. Coyote meant everything to Carlotta. She hadn't missed a single day of work in years, and despite Harlan's half-hearted assurances that she'd "turn up sooner or later," she wasn't the type to just decide to leave town without telling someone.

But where was she?

And why hadn't she called?

Unless she couldn't call, Anna thought, remembering that last night at Coyote Moon. If she'd collapsed in a public place, they would have heard something by now. Someone would have found her identification and the authorities would have notified her next of kin. Yet no one had heard anything. Francine had stopped by the bar earlier in the day, and the woman was a basket case. Beside herself with worry. Carlotta's son Steven had phoned twice from Santa Fe to ask for news, and it killed her that she had none to give him.

Anna parked the van and got out. The stairwell was deep in shadow. She'd been so distracted by Carlotta's absence, she'd forgotten to turn on the porch light. "Hey, baby."

Anna's heart nearly stopped. Fear turned her voice impatient. "Damn it, Deke. What are you doing here?"

"Waitin' for you," he said, shooting a stream of smoke into the cold night air. "I heard about Carlotta. You okay?"

Her irritation with him fled. "I will be, as soon as she comes home."

She glanced at him. He said nothing in reply, but he

didn't have to. She could see the doubt in his dark eyes. "Don't you look at me like that," Anna said, her voice suddenly vehement. "She'll come back. I know she will." Quieter. "She has to."

"She means that much to you."

Her answer was immediate, heartfelt. "Yes." She brushed past him, making her way up the stairs, unlocking the door. She stepped inside, leaving the door slightly ajar. In a moment, he followed.

She didn't bother to turn on the lights, she just went to the cabinet above the sink and took down the bottle she kept there and two glasses. Splashing whiskey in the tumblers, she handed one to him and watched him swirl the liquid in the bottom. The shadows suited her mood; they softened sharp edges, blurred the lines between fantasy and reality, hope and despair. She sensed that he wanted the truth, and this time something compelled her to give it to him. "I was just a kid when my father and I crossed the border. My mother had been killed a few weeks before, and her family threatened to take me from him. He didn't have the kind of money and influence they had, and it frightened him, so a friend of his made the arrangements and we stole away one night. We ended up here, just a few miles outside Nazareth. All he wanted was a fresh start—a decent job—and I wanted to be with him."

She took a sip of whiskey, taking satisfaction from the surge of warmth that blossomed in her belly before continuing. "We'd been more than a day without food, and I was tired, and crying. Father found a safe place for me to hide and told me to wait. He promised he would return before the sun rose. He was just going to find something for us to eat. But the sun came up, and he didn't come back like he promised—not that day, or the next. I might have died of exposure if not for Carlotta, a friend of a friend of my papa. She was our contact here in the states. She'd been waiting for our arrival and was going to help pave the way for my father to find work and a place to live. When she heard that he'd been arrested, she went to the jail to meet with him. He told her where to find me."

"Your father, arrested for murder? So, you're Martinez's daughter?"

"Sandoval is my aunt's married name. I took it when I came to Nazareth. I couldn't afford to use the name Anna Maria Martinez. If I had, my connection to Juan Martinez might have been apparent, and I wanted answers. I had no idea that it would be so difficult, so dangerous, or that I'd meet the one person whom the Call murders had affected as profoundly as they did me."

Or come to care for him so deeply. The thought came and went, and Anna gave it very little credence. He was someone she'd slept with, that's all. She couldn't afford for it to be any more than that. An intriguing man who had entered her life and, when the time was right, would leave it just as suddenly.

He said nothing, just sat, staring into the untouched amber liquid, and for a long time there was only silence between them. "If Carlotta brought you here, why didn't she alert Harlan?"

"Because Harlan would have contacted my grandparents in Mexico, and I would have been returned to them. Papa wanted more for me than that. He made her promise to contact my aunt in California, and as soon as I was well enough to leave, they met in Arizona. By that time, my grandmother had passed on of a sudden heart attack, and Grandfather relinquished all rights. Aunt

Teresa's attorney handled all the details, and the adoption was finalized two years to the day after Papa died in Harlan Rudy's cell."

"So the book was just part of your cover?" he said.

Anna laughed softly, bitterly. "The book is real enough. I started it a couple of years ago but found I couldn't finish it without all the answers. So, now you know the truth. What do you intend to do with it? Are you gonna take it to Harlan and destroy everything I've worked for?"

He watched her for a long while, his expression unreadable, then he bolted his whiskey and placed the empty tumbler on the table in front of him. "Tellin' Harlan who you are wouldn't solve anything as far as I can see. It sure as hell doesn't change the facts, unless you're somehow involved in the Miller double homicide."

She shook her head. "I came here to uncover the facts about the original crime, that's all. I've never hurt anyone."

Deke watched her expression and knew she was telling the truth. It was too damned bad he couldn't say the same.

Allie Johannsen set out from her house at six the next morning dressed in her favorite sweats and her most comfortable pair of Nikes. She kept her pace leisurely at first. It was a joy, trotting through the suburbs as the sun peeked over the mountains, casting everything in the morning's rich, golden glow. Yet as the concrete streets and avenues became a blacktop road and the evenly spaced neighborhoods thinned to a house here and there, her pace naturally increased.

There was something about running alone that Allie found exhilarating. Her husband, Larry, said she was insane, especially since the news broke about the murders. But as a breast cancer survivor Allie had something to prove, and she had no intention of quitting. So what if she was forty-four with some stiffness in the mornings and a few more aches and pains than she'd had at twenty. She was cancer free, and she was going to participate in her first marathon in less than two weeks.

As she cleared the last cul-de-sac and the land turned rural, she broke into a run. At this time of morning, traffic was minimal. She passed a few of the regular commuters making their way into town to jobs at the school cafeteria, the courthouse, and the hardware store, and they raised a hand to wave in passing. Then, when the road was deserted again, she crossed onto the north branch of Waverly Pass.

She'd been telling Larry for a week that she intended to run the pass, and every time she mentioned it, she got the same worried look from him. "Waverly Pass is too tough, Allie. It's too steep a grade and way too isolated. If something should happen back there, you're royally screwed. It's too remote to even get a cell signal there." His expression had softened as he'd taken her hand. "Darlin', I know you want to do this, but please take it easy. It's only been sixteen months since the chemo, and it kills me to see you pushin' yourself so hard."

"Sixteen months is a milestone," she'd argued, "and I'll be fine. I promise." She softened the promise with a kiss and hoped he'd forget that she mentioned it.

The memory faded. Allie knew Larry didn't understand her newfound need to push limits she'd never considered pre-cancer, and she wasn't sure she could explain it. She just needed him to accept it, and if he couldn't support her efforts, then she needed him to stay out of her way.

As she swung left onto the north branch of Waverly Pass, Allie was smiling. The smile didn't last. Twenty minutes later, a trembling Allie ran back to the blacktop road, where she flagged down a pickup truck. "Hey, Allie," Jeff Avery said. "What're you doin' way out here?"

"Mr. Avery," Allie gasped, "thank God it's you! There's been an accident at the summit on Waverly Pass. My cell isn't working—can you get me to a phone?"

The car had breached the guardrails at the summit of Waverly Mountain, plummeting off a sheer hundred-foot drop before wedging itself against a tree. Below that tree, the hillside sheered away for another nine hundred feet. Had the driver survived, she might have been deemed lucky. She hadn't, but unless Harlan had totally lost every ounce of instinct that he'd ever had, cut it wasn't the crash that killed her.

Whitlow arrived, a few beats ahead of the tow truck. Ned Brill set the brake and let the rig idle. "Sheriff," he said with a deferential nod, "you ready for me to hook up the winch and haul it on out of there?"

Harlan gave the word but stayed with the car until Brill set the winch. He and Carlotta had been at odds for years, but animosity aside, he felt he owed her that much. When the car disappeared over the lip of the hillside, he climbed the rocky incline and waited for the EMTs.

Two hours later, he left the scene. He was covered

with grit and his jeans were torn at the knee. He looked in the rearview mirror. Tired eyes that had seen far too much stared back at him. He had at least a day's growth bristling from his cheeks and chin, and an alarming percentage of his beard was white. He needed a shower and a shave just to feel human again, but there was something he had to do first.

The thirty-minute drive to the housing development where Carlotta's daughter, Francine, lived gave him a little too much time to think, something he'd been trying to avoid since his conversation with Lucas. He'd done a miserable job, not thinking about what a goddamned fool he'd been. For almost thirty years he'd been living Maddy's lie, and as far as he could see, there was no way to fix it.

Deke Call was his son.

His flesh and blood.

It was such a shocker that he'd spent a few hours just reminding himself of the truth, and at least a few more so angry with Maddy that he could barely look at anyone. He'd snapped at Dixie and growled at Whitlow, and he'd finally gotten so disgusted with himself that he'd closed the office door and broke out the bottle of scotch in his bottom drawer.

It had helped burn away the anger, but it didn't alter his stark reality. Ginny had wanted a child, and damned if he didn't have one.

A son.

His son.

An angry, troubled man who hated the sight of him.

What the hell do you do about it? It was a little too late to change anything. Deke had grown up rough with an adopted father who'd been hard as granite. His road to manhood hadn't been an easy one—then, he'd lost the one person who'd loved him unconditionally. Sacrificed for him. Tried to shield him, to give him what he needed most—a father. . . .

"Jesus Christ," Harlan ground out, almost glad when Sycamore Circle came into view and he was forced to focus on something other than the mess his life had become. Number 521 was a beige split-level with the appropriate landscaping. Every blade of grass was trimmed, and there wasn't a single speck of dust on the BMW in the drive. Harlan climbed out of the Jeep truck and rang the bell.

Footsteps behind the oak panel, quick and light. The door opened and a red-haired little girl looked up at him through the opening. She had her grandmother's look, and there was little doubt in his mind that in a few years she'd be the terror of the neighborhood. The thought triggered a sharp twinge. Harlan swept his hat off. "Good mornin', sweetheart. Is your mama home?"

"Who is it, Suzie?" Francine came from the kitchen, wiping her hands on a towel. When she saw him, her eyes narrowed. "Sheriff Rudy? What brings you all the way out here? Is something—"

Harlan glanced at Francine's little girl and smiled. "Mornin', Francine. If you can spare a few minutes, we need to talk."

She asked him in, then took the hint and sent the child to the backyard to play.

"Francine, you might want to sit down," Harlan said. "It's about Carlotta."

It was business as usual at Coyote Moon, despite Carlotta's continued absence. Anna and Sandy kept things going, but the mood in the bar was definitely subdued.

Not a single patron walked through the doors who failed to snag Anna's arm. "Is there any news?" was repeated well into the afternoon. "What do you s'pose happened? I heard Carlotta wasn't feelin' too well the other night. Passed out right over there. Anna, darlin' how you holdin' up?"

On it went until Harlan got there. Fatigue rode him hard, deepening the lines at the outer corners of his eyes, slowing his walk. He nodded and spoke a few words to Bill Yancy, who wrung his hand before exiting. A few more similar exchanges and he sat down at the bar. "I'd like a word with you, if you can spare the time. Sandy, too, I guess, since it affects him."

Something in his tone hit Anna hard. She finished filling a pair of mugs with draft and set them in front of Alfred Jackson and his brother Jean. "Keep an eye on things for me, Al? I'll only be a minute."

"Sure thing, Anna."

She moved to the kitchen door, and Harlan followed. Sandy looked up from scraping the griddle, his hard face red with heat and exertion. Anna touched his shoulder. "Leave it, Sandy. This is important."

Sandy nodded, his expression fierce. "Sheriff. I'm guessin' you found her or you wouldn't be here."

"A jogger out for a morning run came across the car. It had gone through the guardrails and plunged down a hillside. She got close enough to see there was someone inside. As soon as I got there, I recognized the car. It was Carlotta."

"She made it, right?" Sandy said. "She's at the hospital?"

Harlan shook his head. "I'm sorry. I know how hard this must be for both of you, but she was dead at the scene. I notified her next of kin. Once the ME releases the body, she'll make the arrangements."

Anna frowned. "The medical examiner? Then, it wasn't an accident?"

"The official cause of death hasn't been decided yet. Dr. Grant's a good man, and he's put a rush on this for me at my request. I'm afraid that's all I'm at liberty to say."

"You don't need to say anything, Harlan. I can see it in your face. You found something out there—something that didn't set well with you, something that indicates foul play."

"I'll let you know when I have something more I can give you." And he walked out.

"Geez, Anna," Sandy said. "You've got this all wrong. Who'd want to hurt Carlotta?" He shook his head, and the tears rolled down his weathered cheeks.

"I don't know, Sandy. I don't know."

Francine arrived the next morning to close down Coyote Moon. She fired the employees and changed the locks on the doors. Anna had shown up while she was there. Their exchange had been brief but tense. "If you intend to tell me how sorry you are for my loss, don't waste your breath. I don't need empty platitudes from anyone, especially you."

"You're the only thing around here that's empty, Francine," Anna said. "It isn't just your loss. We all loved Carlotta."

"Oh please! She was your meal ticket." She clamped her lips together, looking more sour than usual. "That's over now—or at least it soon will be. The only thing keeping me from putting you out of the apartment and onto the street is the remaining thirty days on your lease. Consider this your notice. I don't intend to renew." With that, she slipped on a pair of dark glasses and marched to her BMW, parked at the curb.

Anna watched her go, taking no satisfaction from the certainty that the glasses were strictly for appearance's sake. Francine's eyes weren't red rimmed like her own.

Dr. Levi Grant wrung Harlan's hand, ushering him into the office and closing the door. "I appreciate that this was top priority, which is why I called you down here so early. Carlotta was important to a lot of people."

Harlan took a seat, watching as the ME flipped open the cover of a manilla folder and sat back in the high-backed leather chair. He could tell from the younger man's expression that the news wasn't good, but he'd expected as much. "Give it to me straight, Doc. This case is a homicide. That right?"

Grant scratched his head. "Three blows to the back of the head. Cause of death is definitely homicide. The skull fracture was unlike anything I've seen around here, except for the Miller case. The bone splinters were driven into her brain tissue by a sharp object. The marks are remarkably similar to something I've seen before."

"The Miller case?"

Grant shook his head. "Actually, I was thinking of the Call autopsy." He dug in a drawer and brought out another file, this one with full-color photos. "The blows to the face were too numerous to allow identification, but if you look here, at the back of the sheriff's head— two forceful blows felled him, leaving the unique wounds. Squared off, with a space between." He paused, reaching under the desk, producing a crowbar. "Sort of like this."

"You keep a crowbar under your desk, Doc?"

"I borrowed it from maintenance," he said with a shrug. "I usually try to leave the psychology of crime to the experts, but I'm gonna go out on a limb this time and guess that the person or persons you're looking for have some serious issues. I'm sure glad it's your job to find them, not mine."

Harlan stood up. He got what he'd come here for, and he was about to leave when Grant stopped him. "There was something else, though I'm not sure how it relates to your investigation, if at all."

"What's that?" Harlan asked, his hand resting on the doorknob.

"If the killer had waited a month or two, nature would have saved him the trouble. Carlotta had Stage Four lung cancer, and the hourglass was definitely running out for her."

"No kidding."

"No kidding. Now there's irony for you."

Harlan returned to Nazareth, but he didn't go back to the office. Instead, he went to the apartment Anna leased from Carlotta, climbed the steps, and knocked. It took a full minute for her to open the door. "You mind if I come in? It's about Carlotta."

Anna pushed the panel wider. Dressed in flannel pants with a drawstring waist and a cropped T-shirt, she wasn't up to company, but she let him in anyway. "You got the report from the medical examiner?"

"I got it, all right. I'm not exactly sure why I'm gonna share it with you, except that maybe you know something I don't, and given your closeness to the victim, you want this solved as much as I do."

"You're right about that." Anna sank into a chair, steeling herself for the worst, and getting it as he laid it out for her.

Homicide.

Three blows to the back of the head.

Death was instantaneous.

Part of her didn't want to absorb it, but slowly it penetrated her consciousness, turning her grief into anger.

"Anna, you may have been the last person to talk to Carlotta before she died. Did she seem at all upset to you?"

Anna shrugged. "She was distracted, and restless—like she couldn't wait to get out of there, but nothing too far out of the ordinary."

"Did she say anything to you? Was she meeting with someone?"

"She said she had something to take care of," Anna said, frowning. "And she'd be back before things got busy that evening. I took it to mean she was running some errands—business as usual."

He made a few notations in his pocket notebook and pinned her with his direct blue stare. "Did she happen to mention to you that she was sick?"

"Carlotta?" She shook her head. "No—why?"

"Doc found it when he did the autopsy. Cancer of the lung."

Anna sank back in her chair. Another blow. More to absorb, and she was already overloaded. She felt like a threadbare electrical wire, pushed beyond her limit and ready to burst into flames. "Oh my God. No, she didn't say anything. But she'd fainted the night before. After you left the bar. My God." Anna passed her hands over her face. "Who could do something like this?"

"I was hopin' you'd tell me," Harlan admitted. "She

have words with anyone recently? Any trouble at the bar?"

"Other than Francine?" Anna shook her head. "Why are you asking me this?"

"Until I know differently, I've got to go on the assumption that Carlotta knew her killer," Harlan said, his expression steady, questioning. He put up a hand before she could say anything. "Before you go off on me, I've already checked, and I know that you and Sandy were at the bar all day. An alibi isn't a consideration. I'm more concerned with what you may have seen or heard that might be relevant to this investigation. Somebody hit her from behind, then they tried to cover it up by running her car off a mountainside with her in it. Maybe they were hopin' for an explosion, but it didn't happen. Now, I can surmise that there's some serial wacko runnin' around killin' folks, but it seems more likely that she stumbled onto somethin' she wasn't supposed to see."

"You think this is related to the others. The Call murders, the Millers, and Carlotta."

He gave her a look that clearly said not to push it. Admitting that the Call murders were connected meant that he'd made a mistake, an error of judgment that had cost an innocent man his life and cost her her beloved father. And most powerful people buried their mistakes.

"Think about it," he suggested, "and if you remember anything, call me. Day or night."

Deke drank coffee from a thermos while keeping an eye on the trailer. He'd settled in just before dark, but he'd seen nothing of interest yet. Wheeler had carried the garbage to the end of the lane, placing the bags safely inside a wire cage that kept the scavengers from making a mess, he'd stretched and scratched himself, then he went back inside.

Deke remained where he was for several hours. As three A.M. approached, he thought about leaving, then he saw the glare of headlights turning off the main road and crawling slowly along the lane, and he decided to settle back to wait.

The night was cloudless, the sky a deep velvety blue, and the third-quarter moon gave just enough illumination that he was able to determine it was an SUV. The vehicle pulled around to the rear of the trailer and parked, where it couldn't be easily seen from the road. The headlights died and the driver's door opened. Deke put an eye to Lucas's scope, swearing softly as the woman walked across the pergola and opened the door without knocking.

He settled back to wait. The moon sailed across the sky. At fifteen minutes of five the door opened again and Ginny Rudy emerged, climbed in her car, and left as stealthily as she had come.

At five-thirty A.M. Deke pulled into the drive at the ranch and parked beside the van. The apartment was dark when he entered, but not deserted. Anna was curled on one end of the sofa, a pillow clutched to her chest. She'd fallen asleep, sorrow still damp on her cheeks. As Deke propped the rifle in the corner, she woke and was instantly on her feet, in his arms.

Anna buried her face in the curve of his throat. "I had to come," she said, sighing as his arms closed around her. He didn't ask why, didn't question—he just reached down, scooping her up and carrying her to his bed.

There was no argument, no conversation. Anna didn't care. She didn't want to talk, and she was sick of crying.

She needed the feel of his strong arms around her, the satin feel of his bare skin against hers. There was so much death and destruction around her that she needed to feel his heart beating in unison with hers and to know that they were vitally alive.

He took his time getting down to it, toeing off his boots and stripping off his shirt. "You sure you're ready for this, baby? I heard about what happened. Maybe what you need most is sleep."

"Don't tell me what I need," she said softly, angrily. Framing his face with her hands, she kissed his mouth, but there was no tenderness in it. When she broke the kiss, she leaned her brow against his, closing her eyes, breathing his breaths. "I don't want to sleep. I want to forget. For once, I don't want to think about who I am, or why I'm here, or what's happened. Do that for me, Deke. Make me forget."

He unbuttoned her jeans and slid his hand inside, finding and entering her warmth. He didn't say anything. He didn't have to. He knew what she wanted and he gave it to her.

Later, she lay in the curve of his arm, her head pillowed on his chest, and slept peacefully while Deke drifted from dream to dream. . . .

He'd come in later than usual, but the meeting with Joaquin had run long. A shipment was arriving in two days; Joaquin and Eduardo would meet it. Chaca would provide the muscle. They trusted him enough to allow him information and access. That was important, he told himself. He couldn't drop a dime on the Diablos until he had enough intel. So he'd been sitting in on the meetings for weeks, listening, offering his thoughts only when asked. And he still hadn't made the call to alert Silvio about the shipment.

Soon, he promised himself. But "soon" got delayed until Sil's words rang in his ears. *You're in too deep, Detective. Maybe you've forgotten just who the hell you work for?*

He hadn't forgotten. He was waiting for the right time. He'd get only one chance to break the back of the Diablos.

One.

If he could bust Aguilar on a RICO statute, he'd go down for the long haul. Little Eduardo was target number two. With Aguilar and his lieutenant off the streets, the Diablos would go back to being a minor threat. In fact, there was a good chance they'd completely disintegrate.

But he had to be careful.

He took the private elevator to his apartment and was about to unlock the door when the knob turned under his hand. By the time the door opened, he'd palmed his semiautomatic. Angel's eyes were wide, but her pupils reacted normally to the light. He lowered the handgun. "Angel, what the hell are you doin' here? Eduardo's on his way home."

She shrugged, the spaghetti strap of her tank slipping low on her arm, revealing the upper curve of a soft white breast. "I needed to see you, Chaca," she said, running her hand over his chest, down across his belly.

Deke maneuvered her inside and shut the door. "Sometimes I think you want to get caught. Otherwise you would've picked a safer mark than me."

She smiled, her eyes suddenly alight. "I know you're not afraid of Eduardo," she said. "He's small-time compared to you." Her voice grew soft and wheedling, and she put on a little girl pout. "You could take him out and no one would ever know. With Eduardo out of the way, Aguilar would make you his lieutenant."

The suggestion turned Deke's stomach. He'd had sex with her, despite the dangers involved, but he knew in that instant that it had been a huge mistake. "Time to go, Angel. And don't come back."

That night she went home and shot up, and she didn't come out of her stupor for thirty-six hours. Deke went out to a pay phone, the only safe place to make a call. He hung up the phone, and the scene morphed into something else. Something dark and dreary. A warehouse, or abandoned factory. Tiles were missing off the roof, and the stars were visible overhead. He was meeting Aguilar and a contingent of rival bangers. It was Joaquin's intention to make peace, so he'd ordered Deke to leave his weapons at home. He'd come alone, unarmed, and he hadn't even smelled the trap until he walked in and the *cholos* stepped out of the shadows . . . Diablos to a man.

Eduardo stepped up with a grin and put his arm around Deke's shoulders. "Hey, man. We been waitin' for you. Good thing you came when you did—you almost ruined my surprise."

Deke forced himself to play along. Like he had a choice. "Surprise, shit, man. It ain't my birthday."

"Maybe not, but you're gonna like it. Here, let me show you." Eduardo walked Deke to a corner where a pile of old tarps had been discarded. Taking the edge of the one on top, he pulled it away.

Angel lay curled in a fetal position. Her face and arms had been slashed. The cuts, too deep to close, gaped open, bathing her pale skin in crimson. She whimpered, holding her hands cupped before her, and Deke saw that the tips of two fingers were gone. "Don't worry, Chaca.

She's so high, she don't feel much. You ain't gonna be half so lucky."

Deke hit him, then hit him again, knocking him flat. He fell so hard that his head rang off the cement floor, and turtlelike, he couldn't rise again.

Breathing hard, Deke turned to face Aguilar, when he caught a blur of movement in his peripheral vision. The knife penetrated his right flank. Deke felt the first blow, a hard hit, like a fist, only it stung. The ones that followed seemed hazy, as if it were happening to someone else. He saw himself drop to his knees, waver for a moment, then fall onto his face. His own blood made a warm puddle in which to lie . . . and he kept thinking that he needed to get up and try to help Angel. Something moved . . . a pair of Italian leather shoes just beyond that dark perimeter of the growing puddle. Deke's ears rang, his vision swam, but he recognized Aguilar's expensive shoes. "This belongs to you," Aguilar said in a voice far away. Then something fell onto the cement, landing a few inches from Deke's face. A shining gold shield in a black leather billfold. . . .

Deke woke in a cold sweat and sat straight up in bed. It had been months since Angel's death and it was still fresh. Sometimes he thought it would never fade, never recede, that he'd be forced to relive it again and again until the thought of facing it one more time became more unbearable than what he needed to do to end it.

Anna lay awake, watching him, the sheet barely covering her breasts. "You called out her name," she said. "If I were less secure, I might be jealous."

Deke raked both hands through his hair. "Jealous of a corpse, that's a good one."

She traced the bloom with Angel's name with her finger. "It doesn't always end with death, and we both know it. You wear her name on your arm, homeboy. It's obvious you're not over it, yet."

A long shuddering breath. "She's dead because of me," he said quietly. "Maybe there ain't no gettin' over something like that."

"That's a loaded statement."

"She was a pawn in a game I was playing. And when it all came crashing down, she got caught in the crossfire." He hadn't planned to talk about it. He hadn't been able to speak about it to anyone since Silvio filled him in on what happened—but that hadn't been until later, after he was out of the ICU. Lucas hadn't asked questions. He seemed to understand instinctively that, like Vietnam, it was a subject better left alone. Somehow with Anna it was different. He gave it to her straight, everything leading up to that night. "She must have gone back to the apartment. Christ knows what she was lookin' for, but she found my shield."

"And she took it to her boyfriend," Anna said.

"Maybe she thought he'd reward her for it," Deke said with a shrug. "But bein' involved with a cop was an unforgivable sin, and the Diablos could never trust her again. Eduardo saved face with Aguilar by slicing her to ribbons." He reached for the cigarettes on the nightstand and hung one on his lower lip. "A few weeks later, I found out she'd lied about her age. She was only seventeen."

"And that's the part you can't accept," Anna said.

He didn't say anything, just dragged smoke into his lungs, then shot a stream of soft blue-gray toward the ceiling. "You've spent some time with Dobbs—did you know about him and Ginny Rudy?"

She sat back with a laugh. "Harlan's wife? You're joking!" Then, "My God, you aren't joking."

"I saw her sneak into his place by the back door tonight. Now, why do you suppose she'd be there in the middle of the night? She's old enough to be his mother, not to mention that fuckin' around with Harlan's wife could be damned unhealthy. Makes me wonder what the hell she'd want with Dobbs, and what else he's up to."

"I doubt her age would matter much, if there was a chance that she had money."

"Oh, she's got money, all right. The Sellars, Ginny's family, were big in cattle back in the day. They still own an impressive spread in the next county. She sure didn't need Harlan's income, and that's a damn good thing, 'cause cops don't make much."

"He's been spending his nights at his office," Anna said. "That's where I found him the night Carlotta went missing."

He reached out and stroked her silky hair. "Lucas said they found her in her car out on the north fork of Waverly Pass. That's some rough territory. What the hell was she doin' out there?"

Anna shook her head. It was hard to talk about it. "No clue, but the medical examiner said that she was sick—that she had lung cancer. She never let on. Why would she keep something like that to herself?"

"Maybe she didn't want to risk bein' pitied," Deke said. "Carlotta lived life on her own terms. No compromises. As I see it, that ain't such a bad thing."

It didn't surprise her that he would feel that way, but it pained her to think about it. If Carlotta had just trusted her, there might have been something she could have done to help. Instead, she'd carried the burden of a terminal illness alone. "Harlan questioned me about the hours before she left the bar. He wanted to know if anyone had given her a hard time. Pretty much the same questions he had when I heard the voices in the alley."

She felt him tense, but it was too late to take it back. "What voices?"

"That last night you came by Coyote Moon and I was talking to Harlan. I came to work through the alley, and the side door to the hardware was open, the building dark. Someone was there. I heard a voice. Harlan checked out the building, but he didn't find anyone. By the time he arrived, whoever it was had gotten away."

"You heard somethin'. What was it?"

Anna shrugged. "Nothing important. Besides, Harlan took care of it."

Deke pulled away from her and sat up. "Harlan took care of it," he said, crushing the cigarette out in an ashtray. "I'd feel a whole lot better if you stayed the fuck away from him."

She couldn't have heard him right. It was one of the reasons they were so good together. He didn't try to stifle her or hold her back, and he reserved all of his male muscle for the bedroom. "Excuse me? I can't have heard you right."

"Stay away from Harlan. He's a worn-out has-been who isn't above using you if it gives his sagging ego a lift."

"A has-been?" Anna said, wincing under the scathing criticism. She couldn't help thinking that maybe if he knew the truth— "I get that you two don't like one another, but don't you think that's a little harsh?"

"Don't tell me you're gonna defend him?" He got up, stepping into his jeans, zipping the fly.

"I'm not defending him," Anna said, irritated that they were even having this conversation. She was off the bed in an instant, finding her clothes, throwing them on. "Look, there's a lot you don't know, all right?"

"A lot I don't know," he repeated, shaking a cigarette out of the battered pack on the nightstand, lighting it. "What the hell don't I know, Anna? You got a thing for that old man now? Shit, honey, if you need another lover, the least you could do is provide a little healthy competition."

Anna hit him, an openhanded slap that stung her hand and left a scarlet imprint on his dark cheek. He grabbed her wrist, but he didn't hurt her, just held her fast to keep her from taking a second swing. "Damn you," she said, wrenching from his grasp. She was tempted to blurt it out, the truth about his parentage, but something made her hold back. She was angry with him, but not enough to want to be the one to blow his world to bits. If he learned the truth, he wouldn't hear it from her. "I need to get back," she said, voice tight. "I have a lot to do."

"It's nothin' that can't wait," he said, totally discounting her own plans. "You're not chasin' a byline this time, Anna. This is serious."

"There's the difference between the two of us, Deke Call," Anna said. "I don't play games. Especially when it comes to other people's lives." Buttoning her blouse, she grabbed her keys, heading for the door, but he beat her to it, blocking the exit. She gaped at him. "You've got to be kidding! You're gonna try to keep me here?"

"Nazareth isn't safe—not until I get to the bottom of this—"

Anna shook her head. "You still don't get it, do you, Deke? I didn't risk it all to come here so that some burned out ex-narc could get his kicks out of playing guard dog while I cower behind locked doors. I want the truth—more than that, damn it! I deserve it!"

"Don't you think I want the truth? Don't you think I want to know what happened to her? But the truth ain't gonna bring either of them back, and it's not gonna help matters if you get yourself killed—it just ups the body count."

She pushed him, then pushed past him.

He caught her by the elbow, one last attempt to make her stay. "Forty-eight hours. That's all I'm askin'."

"Thanks all the same, but I think I'll take my chances," she said as she pushed past him and ran down the stairs.

As she got into the van, she heard his angry shout. "Damn it, Anna! Don't be a goddamned fool!" Then the engine turned over and drowned everything out.

Chapter Fifteen

Deke picked up the phone and hit redial for the fifteenth time, but the phone at the apartment rang and rang. Anna's machine didn't pick up. She must have turned it off and was using Caller ID to screen calls.

Great, Deke. Just great. You blew it, big-time.

He couldn't blame her for avoiding his calls. It had been a dumb move, to push her like that, and it didn't matter that he was worried about her and just wanted to protect her. Anna wasn't an ordinary woman. Back her into a corner and she'd take your eyes out.

All of her energy, all of her focus, went into finding out what really happened to Juan Martinez. She'd taken a leave of absence from a prestigious high-pressure job, left her home and her friends, and traveled thousands of miles to the town where her worst nightmare had occurred years before. And in a moment of testosterone-laden insanity, he'd insisted she stop.

Hearing her admit that someone was stalking her had sent a jolt through him. Premonitions were Lucas's territory, but he'd known with a cop's honed instincts that he wasn't the only one who'd recognized her dogged pursuit of the truth.

Deke deliberately slid inside the killer's mind, thinking like he'd think, using his own experiences as a cop to go as deep into the darkness as he possibly could.

Twelve years and he hadn't been caught. Might as well be Christ incarnate, he could do no wrong.

The sheriff didn't have a fucking clue.

Nobody did. They were stupid—all of them.

A town full of morons.

He tips his hat to his neighbors, passing down the street with no one the wiser. No one suspects he's got blood on his hands.

He sits in church on Sunday morning, his head bowed, but prayer isn't on his mind. He's thinking about the night twelve years ago when he let his rage consume him. The night when he smothered a child and beat the most powerful man in Alamance County to death in his own kitchen.

He's thinking about how it felt, before, during, after. How he'd plotted and planned and prepared for the event, then carried it off without leaving any clues. He felt a frisson of the anticipation that had gripped him, knowing he would unleash the beast but not knowing the outcome, because Matthew Call wasn't an easy target. A ghost of a thrill chased through him when the man lay dead on the floor and he realized he'd succeeded. Then, sweet, profound release. Jubilation because of a victory. He'd won. He'd survived. He'd triumphed.

But the memories didn't compare, and as time wore on, and the boring sameness of day-to-day life kicked in, he longed to relive it in all its gruesome glory. Seeing the only survivor of that night walking the streets of his hometown was the spark to the powder keg.

Deke picked up the phone one more time, dialed, and listened to it ring. "C'mon, Anna. Pick up the damn phone."

On the tenth ring, he gave up trying, but the killer wouldn't leave him. His return had been the irritant, he was sure of it. He was the connection. He had to be. He had ties to Lucas, and to Anna, and to the Millers through the house they'd purchased. He'd been a grim reminder of what the man had accomplished, the trigger that had him wondering, could he do it again?

What better way to get the attention he deserved than lightning striking twice in the same location? It would prove that he'd gotten away with it. It would prove that Harlan was an idiot. And not even the hotshot ex-detective could catch him.

What a thrill.

Deke threw the phone, then put his fist through the nearest wall. The handset disintegrated, and the plastic pieces were still skidding across the linoleum when Lucas stepped in. "It's a good thing I asked for that security deposit on this place," he said. "Bad day, I'm guessin'?"

Deke sent him a look but said nothing.

"First Anna tears out of the drive, and then you bust up the place. You two have an argument?"

"Somethin' like that. I asked her to stay here, just till this is over, and she handed me my balls for daring to interfere."

Lucas shook his head. "Till this is over? Ease my mind and tell me that you're gonna stay outta this and let Harlan do his job."

Deke's expression was hard, full of resignation. "As I

see it, at this point, Harlan's about as useful as tits on a bull. He made an arrest after the murders, but it's pretty apparent that he collared the wrong guy. And what'd he do to find Mama? Nothin'. It might've helped if he'd given a damn. Maybe if she'd been a white-eyes, he would've had better results."

Lucas shook his head, his expression sad. "That's your anger talkin'. Harlan ain't a favorite of mine, but he's no bigot, either, and he thought the world of your mother. When he looked at her, he didn't see the color of her skin. He saw the woman he loved."

It was the one thing Deke wouldn't hear. "Go home, *Shi-Da*. There's nothin' you can do here."

"Go home. What? I'm a worthless old man now too? Maybe it's time you had your eyes opened. You don't have to like him, but you should respect him for the same reason you respect me. Because you owe it to him."

"I don't owe him shit."

"The man gave you life. You *owe* him respect."

It was the last thing he was ready to hear. "Anybody ever tell you to mind your own business, *Shi-Da?*"

"You are my business, and you've already escaped this evil once. You might not be so lucky the next time."

"Somebody's got to put an end to this," Deke told him. "It might as well be me." He took the Colt off the dresser, slipping it into his waistband.

"This came for you this morning." Lucas gave him a long look, put the package he carried on the table, then turned and went out without another word.

Deke released the breath he'd been holding. Harlan, his old man. All these years, and the truth had been right under his nose. He didn't need to do the math. Harlan wouldn't have been much more than a kid himself when he was with Maddy, but he'd been married. He must have been relieved when Maddy disappeared. With Lucas more than willing to keep the secret, the threat of the truth coming out had vanished with her. He probably hadn't given her another thought, while her disappearance was a ghost that haunted Deke to this day.

He glanced at the package Lucas brought in. It was wrapped in plain brown paper; the mailing address was computer generated. No return address. Something made him pick it up. He cut the tape with his pocket-knife, slipped the brown paper off the shipping container, and opened it. Inside was an elaborately carved rosewood box, the kind antique freaks kept treasures in, the kind Wheeler carried in his gallery. They were made by a Rosa Metcalf, who lived near Nazareth. Deke flipped the brass latch, lifting the lid. A musty odor rose from the tissue paper interior, as strong as it was unpleasant. His pulse kicking up several notches, he pushed the paper back and stared down at the box's contents.

It was black with age and decomposition, the nails shiny and dark, the knuckles large from the shrinkage of the skin. His pulse a thunder in his ears, he took a closer look.

A hand.

The left one. At one time it had belonged to a woman, but a prolonged exposure to arid conditions in a sheltered area had dehydrated it, mummified it. Had it been exposed to the sun and the insects, it would have been nothing but discolored bones by now . . . the wide gold band on the third finger would have been lost as the deer mice did their work and the joints separated.

Maddy had worn a ring just like it. Given to her by

Matthew on their wedding day. Deke replaced the tissue and closed the lid. Then, lifting the box without disturbing the contents, he took a penlight from the drawer and scanned the bottom. In the upper right corner, the initials "R. M." were clearly visible.

"Rosa Metcalf, who sells her wares to Wheeler Dobbs." It was all the proof he needed.

Deke took the macabre gift and drove to the hillside above Dobbs's place. He could walk in there and kill him, but it wouldn't help him understand what the hell was going on. Better to take his time, do this right. So he watched from the same vantage point he'd occupied the night before, until Wheeler walked across the yard to the small corrugated steel building where he created the sculptures offered for sale in his gallery. The rear door was open, and Deke could see the arc of the welder on the soft gray of the steel siding.

Secure in the knowledge that he'd be occupied for at least a brief time, Deke put Lucas's rifle in the backseat of his car and made his way to the trailer on foot. The door was locked, but he took out a credit-card-sized piece of tin and jimmied the lock. A few seconds and he was inside.

The interior of Dobbs's place was surprisingly lavish considering that he was a starving artist. The decor was Spartan black and white, but the carpet's pile was deep and the leather sofa and chairs obviously high quality. Deke didn't need to wonder about the source of his accoutrements for long. The Rolex lying on the end table told the story. Deke picked it up and read the inscription on the back. "Wheeler, all my love, G."

Ginny Rudy.

Silk sheets on the queen-sized bed and ambient lighting. A big-screen TV and a stereo system that must have laid her back a good five grand. Expensive imported beer in the fridge. So Ginny was keeping him, as well as sleeping with him.

Did Harlan know about his wife's infidelity?

Or the flow of cash from her accounts to Dobbs's?

Was that the reason for their split? And what else was going on? Was there a chance Ginny knew about Wheeler's dark side? Was that part of the attraction? Was she looking for excitement outside her marriage? If so, a murderer certainly would fit the bill. And if she had it in for Harlan and was looking to get back at him, what better way than taking up with a potential felon on the sly?

Deke had seen stranger situations while working for the TPD and was prepared for just about anything. He didn't find much inside the trailer. Nothing, at least, that confirmed his suspicions that Dobbs was somehow involved in everything that had been happening.

Coming up empty-handed didn't satisfy him. In fact, it pissed him off just enough that he redoubled his search, uncaring of the mess he created. He dug through every drawer, took them out and looked underneath, certain not only that the evidence existed but that it was close at hand.

Dobbs was a player, and he was all about deceit. He got a buzz from working the people around him. Manipulate and control. Make them believe what you want them to believe, even if there wasn't a grain of truth behind it. It was all about pushing the limits, and how better to pull off the ultimate shell game than to be sitting on the evidence that would put him away and have no one suspect his involvement? Deke had seen it hundreds of times when he was working the streets. No matter how intelligent the criminal minds, sooner or later they all made a mistake. Most of the time, it came down to a matter of giving in to ego and arrogance.

He checked the fridge and the freezer, and the toilet tank for good measure; then, when he was sure there was nothing to find, he went out, took the penlight from his pocket, and crawled under the trailer. It took an additional ten minutes, but he finally found what he was looking for. Someone—most likely Dobbs—had taken a torch and cut out a piece of the tin beast's underbelly, then they'd fastened it back in place with a few screws and some duct tape. Inside the makeshift compartment was a .22-caliber rifle, complete with scope. Deke pulled the rifle out, and a wave of cold, dark fury overtook him.

The welder at the shop ceased its bright arc. Deke lay on his back, watching Dobbs approach, but the man never looked down. Instead, he went straight inside, blissfully unaware that he was in a world of shit.

Carlotta's Buick had been towed to the impound lot, where it was processed, bit by meticulous bit. Harlan and Deputy Whitlow dusted for prints. The paint was dark, so a light gray powder was more visible on the trunk area, hood, and doors. The white vinyl interior required standard black. Harlan went over the tight confines of the interior, steering wheel, brake release, seat belt buckles, and door handles. The steering wheel and door handles had been wiped clean, but he lifted a pair of clear prints—one from the brake release, the other from the rearview mirror. Judging from their size, both appeared to be female.

When Harlan finished dusting the interior and lifting the prints, he turned the process over to Greg

Carmichael. "Go over it once and pick up what you can. Package and label everything, then tear out the seats and go over it a second time. Let me know when you're finished, and I'll have another look."

"Yes, sir. We're talkin' a few hours, at least."

Harlan promised to drop back later in the day, then left the man to his work.

Back at the office, he scanned the prints and ran them through the database, but the computer crashed as Whitlow stuck his head into the room. "I just got back, sir."

Harlan glanced up over his reading glasses. "Well, get your ass on in here and tell me what you got."

Seth came in and took a seat. "If there were prints on the outside of the vehicle, they were compromised by the elements. Nothing was clear enough to lift. Maybe you had better luck?"

"Two perfect prints, size of both indicates a small-statured female. Of course, one may very well belong to the deceased. I also happened to notice the sticker on the windshield, top left. The oil was changed the day before the homicide, by Sike's Lube. The mileage noted at the time of the oil change was eighteen miles less than the current odometer reading. Eighteen miles. That's close." Harlan measured the distance on a map at the four points of the compass with Nazareth dead center, then drew a tight circle to encompass it. The area ran from Red Butte on the northern edge to Pine Ridge in the south. The most heavily populated area was directly dead center, in and around Nazareth. Beyond the suburbs, the land was open except for the occasional spread. "Supposing you killed some old boy down on Main Street, in the middle of the day. What would you do?"

Whitlow thought for a moment. "That's a tough one. Are there witnesses?"

"None that we know of."

"I'd get away as fast as I could, try to blend in, and not arouse suspicion."

"Would you get in the vic's car and drive miles with the body to get out of town?"

"I hope I'm not that stupid, Sheriff."

"You couldn't afford the luxury of moving the car to a different location if there was a chance you'd be spotted—stopped with a body in the car—a car you have no business driving."

Whitlow shook his head. "No, sir. That's true."

Harlan drew another circle that encompassed the more heavily populated areas within the eighteen-mile radius. "All right," he said. "Here's what we're lookin' at. This outer perimeter is what we need to concentrate on."

"How we gonna handle this, Sheriff?" Whitlow asked. "It'd be pretty difficult to conduct a search on an area that large when we don't know what it is we're lookin' for."

"We can't do a search, but we can do a house-to-house. Talk to the folks who live in those areas. Start with the bigger spreads and work down, and don't miss the workers. I want to know if anyone has noticed anything unusual, especially in the past seventy-two hours. If you run into any resistance I want to know. If you get a hot lead, I want to know—"

"If I get anything at all, you want to know. I got it, Sheriff." Whitlow stood. "Is there anything else, Sheriff?"

"If I think of anything, I'll let you know." Harlan sat back in his chair, but Whitlow still hadn't moved. "Son, what're you waitin' for? Get a move on."

Whitlow grabbed his hat and went out. Harlan settled back to take care of the day's business, but the Miller homicides wouldn't leave him alone. In the course of an earlier consultation, his deputy had asked him if he'd considered they had a serial offender on their hands. The question rose in Harlan's mind again, but his gut reaction remained the same.

He just didn't think so. It was weird, but it all felt personal. There was nothing random or opportunistic about it. He lifted his coffee mug, then set it down again. He'd had three cups already, and it just got worse as it went on. He couldn't make coffee worth a damn, and maybe it was time for him to admit it. Dixie insisted it wasn't in her job description, and the café didn't deliver. "What are the odds of someone randomly picking the same location to commit a double homicide that had already seen a double homicide? Ten million to one?" He shook his head. "About as unlikely as us havin' three homicides take place in one week. One of them totally unrelated to the other two."

If they were unrelated. What if Carlotta was killed by the same doer who got the Miller family?

He sighed and tried one more time to concentrate on something else, but it really was no use. This case had him by the short hairs and damned if it would let him go. He couldn't stop thinking about Carlotta. About the grim prognosis of her medical condition. And how strangely it had ended. Had she just gone about business as usual? Or was that all just a front for what was really going on? What had she really been doing that last day? The explanation that she had given Anna about running errands didn't appear to be true. No one in Nazareth had seen her, aside from Kim at the local gas station when she'd stopped to tank up. Harlan had talked to the man personally, and he'd indicated that Carlotta had been upset enough to walk out without her credit card. He'd called after her and returned it. Her behavior had puzzled him, and he'd watched as she drove away. She'd been headed south, out of town.

But where the hell had her mind been that morning? Had it been on the fact that time was running out? And where was she headed?

"Eighteen miles. And that includes the drive to Waverly Pass."

"Talkin' to yourself, Sheriff?"

Harlan glanced up at Dixie standing in the doorway to his office.

"You feelin' okay?"

"Fine, Dixie. Thanks for askin'." He rocked back in his chair with a dissatisfied sigh. "Dixie, tell me something. What would you do if you found out you only had a couple of months to live? Would you tell somebody?"

"I suppose that depends on what kind of person you are," she said.

"Humor me for a minute and just answer the question."

"I'd tell everybody. No way could I keep somethin' like that to myself. It'd be too big a burden to carry alone, and I'd want time to say good-bye to my friends and loved ones."

"Too big a burden," Harlan repeated. She was right about that one. Yet Carlotta had kept it a secret. She'd seen a surgeon out of town and she hadn't told anyone. It seemed almost inconceivable. He tried to put himself in her place. Where would he go if he were in that position? What would he do?

He thought about Mirror Lake. A rod and reel and some ice cold beer. Because it was the most peaceful place he knew of. Because he had memories of Maddy that were connected to that lake. It was part of the reason he went back there repeatedly, because some of the best hours of his life were spent there with Deke's mama. In fact, the odds were pretty good that the boy had been conceived on the shores of that lake.

Shaking off his distraction for a second, he realized she'd gone back to her desk.

Yes, for him, it was definitely Mirror Lake. What was it for Carlotta? Where would she go to reconnect? And what had she seen there that she wasn't supposed to see?

Her wounds spoke to him. Struck from behind with enough force to crush her skull. No defense wounds, no DNA under her nails. She hadn't seen it coming, which meant it had been more of a sneak attack than a face-to-face confrontation. She had stumbled onto something big, something dangerous, and she'd paid the price. But what?

The only big thing happening in this county was the Miller homicides and the disappearance of Corrie Miller. It had been a week, and still no sighting, no activity on her bank account or credit cards. No sign of a body either. Yet, given Maddy's disappearance, Harlan couldn't look at the lack of a corpse as a good thing.

Maybe the best thing was to chuck the paperwork for now and get some fresh air. "I'm gonna step out for a few minutes," he told the dispatcher. "Give a yell on the cell if anything comes up."

Harlan reached for the door handle on the Jeep pickup when he saw Ginny's Tahoe pull in across the street in front of Coyote Moon. Abandoning his plans, he crossed the street. He hadn't seen her in several days, but she seemed to be holding up okay. She looked good in navy slacks and a khaki silk shirt, but she'd always looked good. Ginny took great pains with her appearance. It was other areas of their lives that had fallen by the wayside, then fallen apart.

"Ginny."

Her brows lifted above her dark glasses. "Harlan. You're the last person I expected to see today."

"It is my town," he said with that proprietary air that always infuriated her. She didn't mind his being sheriff as long as it brought her prestige, but she'd hated it taking precedence over her or the marriage.

No outward reaction except for the tightening of the fine lines around her mouth, and Harlan knew it must have been the Botox. "How many times have I heard that? I suppose I thought you'd be comforting Carlotta's waitress—what's her name again? I just can't seem to remember it."

"Her name's Anna," Harlan said. Maybe it was simple stubbornness to refuse to dignify the implied accusation with a clarification, but he'd played this game far too often to indulge her in one more round.

"I paid a condolence call to Francine this morning. She's planning on tearing down the bar. I wish I could say I'll miss it, but it's been an eyesore for years."

Harlan let his gaze roam over the building's facade. It was hard to imagine a Nazareth without Coyote Moon. "Not everyone feels that way." The conversation had already dissolved into a sparring match, so he decided to put it to a quick death. "I filed the papers yesterday. I thought you deserved to hear it from me."

"Is that all I deserved, Harlan?"

"You'll walk away with a fair percentage of our combined assets and you know it."

She snorted softly, shaking her head. "That's not what I meant and you know it. You never committed to our marriage—not a hundred percent. There was always something else—*someone else* in the way."

"I'm sorry you feel that way," he started to say. He saw the sudden flash of anger in her face, saw the recoil for the slap, and he caught her wrist in midair, holding it tightly enough to cause some discomfort.

Ginny struggled to wrench free of his grasp. She yanked her hand away, and the violence of the move disarranged her long bangs and knocked the dark glasses from her face. She scrambled to retrieve them, but not before Harlan got a good look at her face.

"What in hell happened to you?" he demanded, taking her chin in an ungentle grasp and tilting her face for a good, long look. The dark bruise covering the brow bone and extending into the crease of her lid had been softened with foundation, but there was little she could do to camouflage the nasty-looking gash above her eyebrow.

"Like you care," she said, shoving his hand away. Then, "I heard a noise the other night and walked downstairs to see what it was. The lightbulb was blown and I ran into the door. Now, if you don't mind, I have more important things to do than explain myself to you."

Harlan nodded, stepping back. "Take care of yourself, Ginny," he said, watching as she got into her SUV and drove away.

Chapter Sixteen

Sleeping with Ginny had been the worst mistake of his life, and Wheeler wished a few thousand times a day that he could go back to that day two years ago so that he could change the outcome.

She'd been with Francine, Carlotta's extremely anal daughter, enjoying a day of shopping and spoiled rich-bitch girl talk, and they'd bumped into Wheeler as he was coming out of the First National Savings and Loan. Francine wasn't exactly a favorite of his, and if not for the classy blonde accompanying her that day, he might have given Francine a lame excuse and made a fast exit.

Ginny had caught his interest, though. She was articulate and intelligent, and he quickly learned that she had an avid interest in the arts and artists in general. She was older than he by a good twenty years, but age mattered a lot less than a six-figure spending allowance. Prolonged eye contact and the nuances of body language were the tools of the trade as far as Wheeler was concerned. His California beach-boy looks and smooth talk had gotten him this far, and though it didn't carry any weight with the loan officer at the bank, it sure worked wonders on older, wealthy women, and Ginny Rudy fit the bill.

Pretty and blond, she'd taken an immediate interest in his plans for a gallery, and as Francine spoke to someone on the street, she'd slipped her card into his shirt pocket. "Call me," she said softly. "I'd like to hear more."

They met alone for the first time two weeks later, an afternoon rendezvous hotter than anything Wheeler had ever experienced. She'd left him drained but full of hope that his ambitious plans might finally be realized.

The fact that the woman he was screwing had a husband who could have ended it all with a hint as to who he really was and a phone call to New York authorities only added to the thrill of being with her. Wheeler had always been up for anything, as long as he wasn't required to break a sweat on a regular basis. Ginny kept him on the string with a series of small gifts—tokens of her appreciation. An expensive wristwatch, a state-of-the-art stereo system. She'd even fronted him the cash for the gallery, then the brewery—a long-term no-interest loan. She'd been generous with the bait, and he'd snatched it up willingly, not realizing the price he'd pay until he was in over his head.

It might have been okay, except for two things: Deke's return from Tucson, and Anna's arrival in Nazareth. If the two of them had just stayed away, it might have ended peacefully, though there was a good chance that the problems with Ginny would have surfaced sooner or later anyway. It was hard to keep her kind of crazy under wraps for long.

"Maybe it's time to get the hell outta Dodge," he muttered, crossing the pergola and reaching for the doorknob. "Cut my losses and run." Then he stepped inside, and the idea of escape went from a mere possibility to an absolute necessity. The place had been trashed. Drawers taken out, their contents dumped. Furniture upended. His clothing strewn from one end of the trailer to the other.

Someone had broken in and torn the place to shreds. He stared open-mouthed at the wreck his place had become and felt the cold finger of encroaching dread trace a path up his spine.

Harlan would have come with a warrant, and he'd have taken pains to tear the place apart while Wheeler watched. His insides squeezed at the thought, but the idea of Harlan doing a search wasn't half as bad as the second possibility.

Deke Call.

Harlan Rudy might bend the law, but he would stop short of breaking it. Deke, on the other hand, knew how to play dirty, and there wasn't a doubt in Wheeler's mind that he fought to win.

Panic, big-time. Moving fast, Wheeler grabbed a few changes of clothing and stuffed them into a soft-sided carry-on. He took what he needed for a couple of days, plus some of the bling-bling Ginny had given him, which he could pawn for cash. Then he grabbed the bag and left. He couldn't get away fast enough. He'd get a bus ticket for Albuquerque, and from there, he'd change directions. Alaska was looking better by the minute. There were still some jobs along the pipeline. He could pick up some work until he could re-establish himself. A new plan, a new name, and if he were incredibly lucky, he'd be able to lose himself so completely that no one would ever find him. Not Deke Call, and not Ginny Rudy.

Wheeler flung the door open and stepped out under

the partial shade of the pergola, catching a fragrant whiff of tobacco. His stomach lurched. The man leaning against the support post took a last drag from a cigarette, then tossed it into the dirt. "Goin' somewhere, Dobbs?"

"Hey, Deke," Wheeler said, faking it, though he nearly crapped his pants. "What the hell are you doin' here?"

"Waitin' for you to step outta that sardine can." Deke's shirt was open, and the ripening afternoon sunlight brought a soft sheen to the worn walnut grip of the revolver resting against the tanned skin of his stomach. He was too easy, carrying that cannon. Wheeler stared at it, a case of nerves overtaking him that he couldn't seem to shake. "Set your laundry down, man," he said. "You and I got some unfinished business."

Wheeler didn't put down his bag. He couldn't stop now. He was too damned close to getting out of this damned little shitbag town. "I'd love to hang around, but I've got somewhere to be. You wanted me gone, and you're gonna get your wish. By this afternoon, this place'll be nothin' but a bad memory."

Deke's black gaze burned into his. "You walkin' away from all this? Guess I should change that—you ain't exactly walkin', ain't that right? It's more like tuck tail and run, before anybody finds out what you've been up to."

"You know, I'm really gettin' tired of all this bullshit—" Wheeler threw the bag into Deke and made a break for it. He actually made it halfway across the pergola before pain exploded in the back of his head and the lights went out.

Deke didn't bother to try to catch Dobbs as he fell. He just watched as the man's knees buckled and he fell on his face in the dirt. "You ain't the only one tired of all the bullshit." He stuck the pistol back in his waistband, then, taking the nylon wrist restraints from his pocket, he wrenched Wheeler's hands behind his back and tightened the restraints until the discomfort brought him around; he didn't offer to help him up.

Dobbs lifted his head in an attempt to look at Deke, then groaned and lay flat. "Headache?" Deke asked.

"Motherfucking asshole." He turned his head aside and spat out a mouthful of sand.

Deke's expression was grim. "How's all the shit that happened to Lucas tie in with the murders?"

"I don't know. I told you before, I didn't have anything to do with what happened to Lucas."

"No?" Deke shoved the .22 rifle he'd found stowed under the trailer under Dobbs's nose. "What do you suppose the odds are that the ballistics from that shell Doc Webster dug out of Lucas'll match this rifle?"

Dobbs said nothing, but his respiration picked up noticeably. Ratchet it up another couple of notches and he'd be hyperventilating.

"Nothin' to say? That's all right, bro. We'll just move on. We got plenty to talk about, you and me. I got your package in the mail. Guess you must have been figuring it'd arrive after you were long gone. Funny thing about the post office. Just when you figure they'll be late as usual with deliveries, they surprise you and deliver early."

"Package? What package?"

"This package."

Deke opened the box, cleared the wrapping, and shoved the box where the rifle had been a moment ago. He caught a whiff, and his eyes bugged out of his head. Deke could tell the exact moment recognition dawned, because he screamed, bucked against the restraints, and tried to roll away.

"Jesus," he said, "oh Jesus," and vomited into the dust. "I didn't send it. I swear."

"The wooden box came from your gallery. It has Rosa Metcalf's initials carved into the bottom, and it's her work. I'd know it anywhere. She's already identified it as a piece she sold to you." It was a lie, but he didn't give a damn. All he cared about was getting results.

"She must have taken it. I didn't know anything about it."

"She? You mean Ginny?"

Wheeler gave in to the dry heaves, his body convulsing as he groaned. "Yes! She's crazy, man, and I didn't know it till it was too fucking late."

"Spill it," Deke said.

Dobbs shook his head. "I've said too much already. Not another word till I've talked to a lawyer."

Deke grabbed him by his scruff and hauled him up onto his feet. He held him fast with a fistful of shirt-front, the warm steel of the Colt Python jammed to the soft place under Dobbs's chin. "You don't get it yet, do you, asshole? Either you tell me what the fuck's goin' on or you don't live to see a lawyer." Deke cocked the hammer, jamming the short barrel of the Colt a little deeper into his chin.

It would be so fucking easy to splatter his brains all over. He could do it and not lose a minute's sleep, but with Dobbs dead, his chances of getting to the truth would take a sharp nosedive. He ground his teeth, waging the inward battle against the strong inclination to send him to hell for what he did to Lucas. But that would leave him with Ginny.

Ginny. She was the trump card, but getting to her

wouldn't be easy with Harlan standing in the way. It was easy to say that Harlan was inept, but he was still one tough old bastard. Deke had a good idea that he'd side with his wife, cover for her, if it came to that. She was kin, after all, and in his case that kind of connection meant more than sharing the same DNA did.

"What's Ginny Rudy got to do with Lucas?" When the man didn't answer, Deke prodded him with the revolver. "You ever seen what happens when a slug this big enters under a man's chin? Takes the top of the head clean off. Big mess, lot of splatter. It's like smashin' a ripe melon."

"You won't kill me," Dobbs insisted, though he didn't sound very confident. "I just might be your last chance. Besides, you're still a cop, and I don't have a weapon. Lucas says you got a commendation. You'd never shoot an unarmed man."

Deke pulled the pistol from under Dobbs's chin and fired one shot that blew a hole through the man's boot at the toe. Blood, flesh, and bone fragments flew, and Dobbs screamed, dropping to the ground and rolling around. "You're right about one thing," Deke said. "I won't blow your head off—yet. But I can work my way up. The next shot's gonna take out your kneecap."

"Fucking crazy son of a bitch!" Dobbs screamed.

Deke grabbed a stool and sat down to wait. "What's Ginny Rudy got to do with Lucas?"

"Aw, Jesus, that hurts," Dobbs moaned. The pain provided some incentive. He gulped air, sweat running off his white face. "She said to work on his superstition. To start small and work up."

"Why?" Deke asked.

"She wanted him gone."

"Why?"

"I don't know!"

Deke cocked the revolver again, and the other man started to weep. "You can kill me and it won't matter—I can't give you what I don't have! I shot Lucas, okay? I killed Obee and the ram. I even smashed the headlight on Anna's van, but that's all I did. I swear!"

"Why?" Deke persisted. "Why'd you go along with it?"

"She had leverage. I have a past, okay? All it would have taken was one word to her old man and my life would have been over. It was either do what she asked me to do or do some hard time. I didn't have a choice."

"What do you know about this?" Deke asked, picking up the rosewood box. "You said she stole it. Where'd she get the remains, and who do they belong to?"

Dobbs shook his head. "I don't know, man, and I don't want to know . . . but the fucking bitch is capable of anything."

Lucas had always hunted small game on Burl Petty's property. Lucas and Burl's son Asa had gone to war at the same time and served in the same platoon. Only Lucas had come home, and Asa had died in a firefight in the Mei Cong Delta. Burl seemed to take comfort from Lucas's quiet company after that, and Lucas, as a neighbor and friend, felt obliged to do whatever he could to help ease the isolation of the older man's lonely existence. It helped Lucas too, to give something back to a fallen friend by looking after his next of kin.

By that time, Carlotta was long married, had teenagers and a new business to run. She and Burl had always been at odds, and it had gotten worse after Asa's flag-draped coffin was put in the ground.

A few years back, Burl passed on, but Carlotta managed to hang on to the land, a tribute to her grudging admiration for the father she could never understand in life.

On bright autumn days, with the promise of snow in the air, Lucas would take his dog and drive the short distance to his friend's property, a mile from the south end of Mirror Lake. It was Lucas's way of honoring the memory of a friend, of feeling the presence of his spirit as he walked the game trails through shin-high weeds, Obee forging ahead to flush birds from the brush.

It was a fine day in spring, not autumn, and a lot had changed since the last time he visited the old place. Deke had returned from Tucson in the interim, one of the walking wounded. The Ridge-Walker had begun haunting the ridge, and shortly thereafter Obee had been killed. The Evil that had taken Maddy away and killed Matthew and little Delia had showed its ugly face again and carried off two more innocents.

And now Carlotta was gone too—killed, the rumor said, though no one seemed to know why. The world was spinning out of control, and Lucas was worried. He could feel the darkness pressing in, and he was afraid of where it all would end. Deke was looking for trouble, and Lucas knew he'd just made it worse by telling him the one truth Maddy had wanted kept secret. They hadn't had words since he was a kid, and it didn't sit well with him that he'd lost his temper with him. He shouldn't have told him about Harlan. He should have known he wouldn't accept it.

"I really screwed things up, Maddy," he said as he got out of the truck. He'd left the pup at the house because he was too young to keep up, too spirited to stay out of trouble, and Lucas was too distracted to keep an eye on him.

There would be plenty of time for him to come along when he got a little older. "Deke needs a connection, something that matters to him. I thought for a while it might be Anna, but that's not lookin' so good either."

Lucas left the truck and walked, moving away from the dirt road that separated his own property from Burl's. It was sad, the state the place was in. The house was in bad shape by the time Carlotta got it, and in the years since, it had deteriorated even further. The peaked roof had buckled in the center—little left now but rotting wood and torn tar paper. The porch where he and his friend had once enjoyed a cold brew while watching the sun set lay buried beneath a pile of debris.

Strangely, several paths cut through the weeds, too wide to be game trails, one leading straight up to the hillside. The new green of spring was just starting, and the dry winter weeds, more fragile than new grass, had broken under the tires of a vehicle, leaving its path clearly marked. Sunlight filtered through the clouds and struck something metallic, nearly concealed by the ruined weeds. Dropping into a crouch, Lucas reached down, plucking the cellular phone out of the grass. He hit the power button, and amazingly, the screen lit up, displaying the name and number.

"Carlotta's cell," Lucas said. "Now what's it doin' way out here?" Something told him it had significance, so he pocketed it and walked back to the truck. He opened the door and got in, but as he turned the key in the ignition, an SUV pulled in beside him. He knew the woman who got out. Everyone did.

"Hey, Lucas. Boy, this is a stroke of luck. I'm having some car trouble—the engine light keeps coming on, and I don't want to push it—can you give me a lift? With everything going on around here lately, I don't feel too easy about calling a tow truck, then waitin' here all alone."

"Sure thing, Ginny. Climb in." He laid Carlotta's phone on the seat between them, turning the key in the switch.

"Did you drop your cell?" she asked with a smile. "Looks like it's got some mud on it."

"Oh, no," Lucas said. "It's not mine. In fact, I need to talk to Harlan about it. I found it back there, at the old Petty place. I think it's Carlotta's."

"Carlotta's." A cold smile. "No kidding? How do you suppose it got way out here?"

The shadows lengthened as the afternoon wore on. Anna typed the most recent events onto the software's page.

Carlotta's car was found on a mountainside. She was inside. It appears to have been a murder. No suspects yet. Too many questions. Zero answers. Who wanted her dead, and why? Is this somehow connected to all the rest of it, the Call murders, the Millers, the disappearance of two women? I don't know, and I'm not leaving Nazareth until I find out.

She saved her notes, and the instant messaging program's message box appeared in the lower right corner of the monitor screen. "Felix" popped up in full-blown rant.

FELIX: Anna? Where the HELL have you been? I've been trying to reach you for two days! Do you have any idea how worried I've been?

Anna considered not answering, but she just couldn't bring herself to hurt Jay. He'd been by her side every step of the way, he'd advised, and he'd coached, and at times he'd bullied her into being the best journalist she could possibly be. He'd even brought her chicken soup when she'd come down with a virus last year.

FELIX: Anna?

ANNA: I'm here.

FELIX: Alive, and in one piece? Are you sure it's you? What's my mother's maiden name?

ANNA: It's Malkovich, now for Christ's sake, will you stop with the third degree, already? Yes. It's really me, and I'm okay. Sorry, I haven't touched base. I've been—busy.

FELIX: There's a reporter out of Santa Fe who's covering this story. He's hinting that the murders are connected. I REALLY don't like the sounds of this, Anna. I want you to get out of there.

Someone rang the bell.

ANNA: Listen, Jay, someone's at the door. I have to go. We'll pick this up tomorrow.

She signed out, closed the notebook's shell, and walked to the kitchen. The way her luck was running, it would be Francine with an early eviction notice.

Harlan stood on the landing. He looked up when she opened the door. "Anna, you mind if I come in?"

Anna pushed the door wider, stepping back.

He entered, closing the door. "We dusted Carlotta's car for prints as soon as it arrived at the impound lot, and the results just came back. You mentioned that you drove Carlotta home the night before she was killed. We found two sets of prints. One belonged to Carlotta, the other to Anna Maria Martinez. No rap sheet, but she does have quite a history as a D.C. crime reporter, and quite a following." He threw down a folder, and articles and photos spilled out, all of it connected directly to her. Her stories, her head shot. "Maybe it's about god-damned time you tell me who you really are."

Anna faced him squarely. No way would she give an inch. "Why should I explain? It looks to me like you already know."

His blue eyes snapped with anger. "Because I'd like to hear it from you."

Anna dug in her bag and pulled out her wallet, flashing her driver's license and press pass.

He took a long look, then handed them back to her. "All this time you've been lying to me, playing me for a damn fool."

"This isn't about you, Harlan, and I didn't feel like I had much choice," she said. "I had a better chance of getting you to cooperate, of obtaining information, by remaining unconnected. If I'd come here and announced that Juan Martinez was my father, that I suspected he'd been murdered before he had a chance to recant that confession, or go to trial, you would have shown me the door, and that would have been that. This was the only way I stood a chance of getting to the truth."

"Well, you got your cooperation, and your truth. Juan Martinez took the coward's way out. He hanged himself while I was at the crime scene."

"I don't know that," Anna snapped, "and neither do you! Put yourself in his position for five seconds. Your child is in danger. You're the only one who knows where she is. Would you choose to leave this world before you knew that she was safe?"

"I'm not exactly the best one to answer that question."

Anna saw the conflict in his expression, the regret in his eyes. "I think you're the only one who can answer it. If Deke were in trouble, would you turn your back and allow him to die without even trying to save him? Could you?"

"I've got no fond feelings for the press, Anna. So do me a favor and stay the hell out of my way. Put your nose where it doesn't belong for the sake of a story and you'll find yourself in more hot water than you can handle." He turned and stalked out without answering her questions, but she suspected he'd gotten the point.

Harlan's footfalls faded, and the apartment settled into silence once again. She hadn't realized that just speaking Deke's name would have the power to bring it all back. The conflict, the fury, the pain.

It was over, and she knew it was for the best. So why did she feel so empty? So restless? So out of control?

"You might as well face it," she said. "You made a huge mistake getting involved with him in the first place. An ex-narc who's been out on a ledge for months. Talk about a bad risk." She shook her head, laughing at her own lack of judgment. "Was it worth it, Anna? Was it really worth it?"

Like Harlan before her, she refused to answer, infuriated by the realization that given the same set of circumstances, she would have done it all over again.

Yes, something spoke deep inside. A voice so quiet, yet she still heard. As crazy as it seemed, he'd been worth it, even if it hadn't been destined to last.

The best thing she could hope for was to get what she came here for, and then to leave Nazareth and all of its problems behind. Getting back to the District was the best cure for what ailed her. Back to the hectic pace of life in the nation's capital, the high-rolling political movers and shakers, back to the grind. Eventually, the clear azure skies, the breathtaking high desert light, the clean air, would be a distant memory. "You're making it sound so easy," she said to herself. But she knew there were a few things that would stay with her longer, a few of the people here she would never forget. Lucas, Carlotta, Harlan, Sandy, and Deke.

As if on cue, the phone rang. She glanced at the caller ID screen. Lucas's number. "Sandoval," she said.

"Anna . . . oh God, Anna. I'm in trouble."

"Lucas?" Anna said, the fine hair on the backs of her arms standing erect. "Lucas?"

He didn't respond. A short pause, and it came again, sounding very much like the phone call she'd intercepted at Deke's apartment a couple of days ago. "Oh God, Anna help me."

"Lucas, what's wrong?" She couldn't help herself. It was instinctive to ask, even though she knew it had been scripted. A recording.

Just like the call she'd answered at the apartment days before, intended for Deke. Like the one he'd gotten the morning of the murders, the one he swore was his mother's voice.

Anna's recall of the second call was vivid. The woman's voice sounded stressed—cracking at one point, as if she'd been under a tremendous emotional strain.

The Miller woman had gone missing—just like Maddy Call—but was it possible that the same person who'd taken Maddy away had recorded her voice and kept the recording for twelve years? Then decided to replay the crime and the aftermath all over again?

As a working reporter, Anna had seen it all, and yes, given the intricacies of the human mind and the countless ways to warp it, it was possible. Jeffrey Dahmer had attempted to make zombies of his victims by drilling holes in their skulls and injecting acid into their brains. Anything was possible.

And now they had Lucas. Anna suddenly felt sick. She picked up the phone and dialed Lucas's number, but no one picked up, so she called Deke. On the fourth ring, it went to voice mail. "Deke, it's Anna. If you get this message call my cell. I just got a call from your uncle. Something's wrong. I'm on my way out there now."

She hung up and, grabbing her keys, ran from the apartment.

Chapter Seventeen

Harlan was conferring with Whitlow when the door opened and Wheeler Dobbs got a kick from behind that propelled him into the door. He was limping badly, caught his shoulder on the door frame on the way in, and sprawled on his face beside Whitlow's chair. "Keep him away from me," Dobbs begged. "He tried to kill me."

Harlan glanced up over his reading glasses to see the hard-bitten, broad-shouldered ex-narc who also happened to be his own flesh and blood standing in the doorway. "Damn it, Deke, what the hell is this?" Somehow, his voice had lost its hatred when he addressed him. Jesus, he was getting used to the idea. But could Deke adjust to it? Or would he always hate the sight of him?

Deke stalked in, picking the slighter man up by the scruff of his shirt and slamming him into a vacant chair. With an ease that was weirdly gratifying, he got in Dobbs's face. "You want to keep the rest of those toes? You tell him what you told me."

"I've got witnesses," Dobbs said, his respiration picking up speed with his panic. He was between a rock and a really tough place, and he knew it. "He shot me, Sheriff. Blew a hole through my foot."

Harlan pushed back in his chair, the leather creaking. "Is that so?"

Dobbs was sweating profusely, and he looked about to faint. Deke pulled his piece and jammed it under Dobbs's right eye. Whitlow was half out of his chair and reaching for his sidearm when Harlan motioned for him to sit back down.

"You want to live, asshole? You tell him what you told me."

"Call, you'd better have a damn good reason for this."

"Talk! Now!" He cocked the hammer, and Harlan clenched his jaws. As it was, Deke was in a lot of trouble. If he spilled the man's blood in this office, he'd have no recourse except to charge him. Somewhere inside he heard Maddy's whisper. *Trust him. He's a good man.*

Dobbs, getting that Harlan wasn't immediately putting an end to it, started to quiver. "All right! All right! I'll tell him! Just let me go! Please, God, just let me go." Deke held him fast, and the man started to babble. "I shot Lucas, and I killed his livestock and his dog. Everything that happened—it was me. All of it."

"No shit?" It was Whitlow, sitting straighter in his chair, watching and listening intently but not bothering to interfere. At Harlan's warning glare he closed his mouth, waiting.

Harlan noted the nervous darting of Dobbs's glance. He wouldn't, or couldn't, look at him directly. There was something to this, something big. "I thought you and Lucas were friends," he said. "Why would you want to hurt him?"

"It wasn't my idea. She pressured me into it."

"She?" Harlan sat up.

A jab of the Colt's barrel prodded him into taking the leap. "Ginny."

Harlan sat stock still, for an instant unable to breathe. "Ginny. My Ginny?"

Dobbs groaned. "We were—close. I'd gotten into some trouble a few years back. She found out, and she threatened me. She said she wanted Lucas gone. I didn't have a choice."

Deke eased the hammer down and put the revolver away. His gaze met Harlan's for just a second. "There's more to it. Step outside."

Harlan got up. "Deputy, if Swift-Water doesn't press charges I will. Escort Mr. Dobbs to the clinic and get that foot taken care of, but he's not to be left alone. If Doc releases him, put him in the holding tank. I'm not through with him yet." He followed a few steps behind Deke, who walked to his car and took out a wooden box, which he put in Harlan's hands.

"It came in this morning's mail. Somebody's idea of a sick joke. The box is one of Rosa Metcalf's. It originated from Dobbs's art gallery."

Harlan opened the box and stared at the contents for several moments. He had a catch in his chest, a hitch in his ribs that hurt with every breath. But it wasn't the grisly contents that caused it. It was the gold band on one bony finger. Maddy's wedding ring. He recognized it, and he knew that Deke must have too. There was no need to say anything—not until they were sure. "You think Dobbs did this?"

"Gauging from his reaction, not a chance. He screamed like a six-year-old girl, then lost his lunch all over."

Harlan's head was reeling. Jesus Christ. Ginny. Was it possible? Could he have been that blind?

"Where is she, Harlan? Where's Ginny now?"

Harlan shook his head to clear it. "She was here earlier. I ran into her outside Coyote Moon. I told her to expect the paperwork—I wanted her to hear it from me. I thought I owed her that much—"

Deke grabbed the older man's arm. He could see that he was reeling from shock, but he needed Harlan to focus. "Did she say anything?"

"She mentioned Anna," he said, and Deke could see the haze evaporate. "She seemed to think we had somethin' goin', and for once I didn't try to defend myself."

Deke let him go, heading for his car.

"Wait a minute, son," Harlan said. "Where are you headed?"

"I've gotta find Anna before she does."

Deke turned the key in the ignition and slammed the floor shift into first. The car fishtailed on the dry pavement, sending up a cloud of rubber-scented smoke. Before Harlan could reach the pickup, he was already out of sight.

At first glance, everything seemed normal at Lucas's place. His battered Chevy truck was parked outside; the sheep dotted the pasture, creamy beige dots against the vivid green. A thin curl of smoke rose from the chimney. The door was closed. Anna got out of the van, her boots striking a hollow sound as she mounted the steps and crossed the porch. She knocked. "Lucas? It's Anna."

No answer.

She tried the knob. It turned easily, and the door swung open with a light push. "Lucas?"

Through the living room and into the bedroom. There was no sign of Lucas, and no sign of a struggle. No clue that anything unusual had happened here.

She left the house, laying her hand on the hood of the truck in passing. Warm. It had been driven recently.

Deke's car was gone from its usual spot. She glanced at the apartment, then headed to Lucas's studio. She opened the door and walked in. Oppressive silence hit her, a huge, dark wall. The lights were off, the shadows deep. "Lucas? Lucas, it's me, Anna."

There was an odd dragging sound, like something heavy being borne inch by inch over concrete. Standing by the workbench where Lucas did his creating, Anna closed her fingers over a sweep gouge. With a four-inch grooved steel blade, it didn't make an ideal weapon, but it was better than nothing. With the handle in a fierce grip, she made her way toward the sound. *Drag, pause. Drag, pause, drag.*

Issuing from the shadowy recesses of Lucas's office at the rear of the building, the sound made Anna's skin crawl. This time, she didn't call out, just made her way toward the noise, slowly, carefully. Each step taking her closer, she steeled herself, laying a hand on the wood panel, edging it open. A dim shaft of light from the workshop fell over the desk and floor. Something moved just beyond it. She heard the *drag, pause,* then a soft groan.

Anna fumbled for the light switch, and the shadows vanished before a flood of fluorescent light. *Lucas.* Sprawled on his stomach, he inched forward, then fell flat, fighting for another breath, leaving a bloody trail in his fight to make it to the wall.

Anna gasped, dropping the gouge, then, kneeling

beside him, she helped him struggle up and lean against the wall. "Dear God, what happened?"

He shook his head, fighting for breath. Blood seeped from the small dark hole high on his left breast, soaking his shirtfront. From the wound's location it was a good guess that the bullet had entered his lung. Turning, Anna grabbed the phone off the desk and dialed. "Just hang on. I'll get help."

"I don't think so." A manicured hand took the receiver and jammed it back on the cradle.

Anna glanced up. Her eyes narrowed. Ginny Rudy, Harlan's wife. "He needs a doctor. If he doesn't get help soon, he could die."

"That is the general idea." She motioned with a small-caliber pistol for Anna to rise. "On your feet."

Anna stared at the older woman. "I'm not leaving him."

Ginny shrugged. "You will, unless you want me to finish him off right now. Come with me and at least he has a chance. If you insist on being bullheaded about it, he'll have none." Her hard expression shifted slightly, her mouth softening into a smile. From ice queen to small-town icon, the friendly sheriff's wife. Known by everyone, yet truly known by no one. Anna was amazed.

"It's your choice," she said with a shrug.

But it was no choice. Anna stood. "What will it take for you to let me make that call?"

"He means that much to you?"

"He's all Deke has."

"Ah, yes. Deke. Your pasts are more than a little intertwined. It plays out like a bad movie. The mystery of Maddy Call's disappearance, the identity of the killer—and let's not forget Senor Martinez. What really happened in that jail cell that night? I can help you figure it out, bring an insider's point of view. No? And then, there's Carlotta—" She clucked her tongue at Anna's reticence. "You're not very curious, for a journalist."

Lucas groaned. He was blue around the lips, and a small red trickle oozed from the corner of his mouth. Anna felt sick. He was running out of time.

"He has a much better chance of survival with you gone." Ginny's free hand closed around Anna's arm, just above the elbow.

"Let me have a word with him first. Please."

Ginny shrugged. "Make it fast. I don't have all day."

Anna knelt near enough to Lucas that she could meet his gaze. "Don't go," he said. "Not with—her."

"I'll be okay," Anna assured him. "You just hang on. Someone will come before long. I'm sure of it." She gave his hand a squeeze, her fingers closing over the handle of the gouge before she rose. Then, as she turned to face Ginny, she slipped it into her pocket. With a last glance back, Anna preceded the woman from the building and into the sunlight.

"We'll take the truck. You drive. That way you're less likely to get any foolish notions about jumping out and taking off." She kept the muzzle of the handgun jammed against Anna's ribs while she opened the passenger door and indicated that Anna slide across the seat and under the wheel.

"Am I supposed to guess where we're going?" Anna asked as she turned the key in the ignition.

"To a little place I know. You'll see. Drive along the lakeshore. You can see Lucas's tire tracks in the grass. Follow them."

Anna glanced at Ginny. Her mind was still reeling from the shock of the day's revelations, and she was trying to associate the grisly crimes with the woman seated beside her. Everything about Ginny screamed class, from the Martha Stewart hairstyle to the tips of her black iguana leather boots. As psychotic killers went, she was totally atypical. "You killed Maddy Call?" Anna said, allowing just enough disbelief to creep into her voice. "Then where is she?"

"Almost under their noses," she said, never taking her gaze from Anna's face or relaxing the hand that gripped the weapon. "You know, you remind me a little of her. You've got the same fire. I think it's what attracts Harlan. He looks at you and he's reminded of Maddy."

"You're wrong about that," Anna insisted. "No one could ever measure up to her, as far as your husband is concerned. He still loves her."

"Ouch! So the sex-kitten has claws!"

"Is that what this is about? You think there's something going on between me and Harlan?"

Ginny laughed, ruefully. "Oh, there's something between you, all right. Only it's a who, not a what. Why'd you come here, Anna? If you'd stayed away, none of this would have happened. Without you in the picture, Deke would have taken care of this situation by now. He was drinking heavily and carrying that cannon around. It was easy enough to see where it was headed."

"If you think suicide's an answer, then you're sicker than I imagined."

Ginny just shrugged and smiled a secret smile. "I'm sure once you're gone, he'll be despondent again. He's not that far from that ledge. All he needs is a little prod, and I'm certain he'll be more than happy to jump."

"You said you had answers. Why don't you start with the Call murders?"

Another shrug, and she started to talk, and Anna had

the clear impression that it was a relief for her to tell someone. "I never intended to kill the little girl. She walked in after I'd finished Matt. I saw her standing in the doorway. She was in her nightclothes and had her thumb in her mouth. When I put the pillow over her face, she barely even struggled."

"Why kill Matthew when it was Maddy you hated?"

"Because Harlan worshipped the ground Matthew Call walked on. He never would see that he was holding him back. I really believed that if not for Matt Call, Harlan would have left it all behind and went to work for my father. He wasn't the primary reason, though. It was Maddy—it was always Maddy."

"You thought Harlan was going to leave you for her."

"I'd been hearing about Matt knocking Deke around for a while, but it was getting worse, and I knew that Harlan saw it too. It was eating at him, the concern, the indecision. All she had to do was tell him Deke was his son. I knew that if I didn't do something, it would all be over, and she'd win."

Anna shook her head in disbelief. "Two birds with one stone. In taking out Maddy, you decided to rid yourself of Matthew too."

"You'd be amazed at how easy it was to take him out—a big guy like him? I know, I was. I hit him from behind, and his skull cracked like an egg. The rest was gravy. Then, after the little girl, I went outside to wait for Maddy. She never knew what hit her . . . and by the time she figured out what was happening, it was too late."

"Why did you take her away from the house? Why not just kill her there?"

"And let Harlan turn her into a martyr? You've got to be kidding." A bitter laugh. "Oh, no, I wanted him to wonder if she was ever coming back to him, just like I wondered if he'd come home when she was spreading her legs for him. She suffered for it. I made sure of it. Then, after she was gone, it was his turn." The hard bright light left her green eyes, which were opaque and empty without it. "Turn left by that cottonwood, and park beside my SUV."

Anna's throat tightened. They were somewhere back of nowhere, miles from the blacktop road. A location so remote that even someone searching for them would have difficulty locating them. An old foundation with remnants of charred wood scattered through it sat fifty yards from where she stood. "Where are we?" At Ginny's insistence, Anna opened the door and got out.

"Carlotta grew up here. The house was little more than a shack when it was standing. Her daughter, Francine, and I were friends. I came out here with her a few times. It's an interesting place with a lot of secrets." She motioned that Anna should precede her across the open area choked with weeds and shin-deep scrub grass, to a weathered wooden door framed into the hillside. "Go on, open it."

Anna pushed on the wooden panel, and a rush of cold air issued out, reeking with age and heavy with decay. "Oh my God. What is this place?"

"It's a cave," Ginny said. "Carlotta's old man added some timbers and closed it off. He used it as a root cellar. Walk in." A nudge from the barrel of her handgun. "Move. We're running out of time."

Anna stepped inside. Dust motes danced in the shaft of sunlight filtering into the cave. Lying to the far left, close to the rock wall, was a pile of debris that appeared to have once been human. Shredded rags among black, leathery-looking skin and protruding bones, and a few matted locks of hair as dark as Anna's own, as dark as Deke's.

Anna felt sick. All this time she'd left Deke and Lucas to wonder what had become of Maddy—and Harlan too—and she'd been so close. Deke had insisted that she would never have left her family of her own free will, and he'd been right. She'd been brought to this place by force; she'd had no choice in the matter.

"There's more," Ginny said, walking to the tarp, pulling it off.

A second body, this one in good condition. Another dark-haired woman, her skin a dusky, lifeless blue-gray. Bruises and abrasions covered her face and hands. The missing woman, Corrie Miller. "The cool temperature slows decomposition."

Anna turned away, sickened. "Why? For Christ's sake! Why?"

Ginny's face changed from the attractive mask she always wore to something dark and hard and malevolent. "Because for me it wasn't over. Because it never will be over. As long as Maddy exists in Harlan's memory, she'll continue to haunt me." Her tone changed, losing its fervency. "If I could bring her back to life, I'd kill her all over again. She couldn't suffer enough to satisfy me."

"So you re-created the crime," Anna said, "to satisfy the psychotic need for revenge, even if the recipient of your sick game was totally unconnected to Harlan—innocent. Jesus. You really are a piece of work. You killed Corrie Miller because she was luckless enough to move into the house where you killed the Calls. Because it would get to Deke, and to Harlan." She shook her head in sick disbelief. "But Corrie Miller fought you. She's got defensive wounds on her hands."

Ginny lifted a hand to touch the half-healed cut on her forehead. "She took me by surprise. She'd found a rock, and when I came in to finish her off, she struck me. Scalp wounds are the worst. They bleed profusely. I took care of her but went out of here in a hurry. When I came back the next day, Carlotta was here. She'd seen the blood trail on the rocks and followed it here. If she'd just stayed away, it wouldn't have had to happen."

"You mentioned my father. You said you had all the answers." It was the final remaining mystery. Anna had to ask.

"I was there that night, and I overheard his conversation with Carlotta," she replied in perfect Spanish. "He was asking after his daughter, fearful that something bad would befall her if he didn't return to her. He'd already signed the confession by mistake. Poor man thought they were trying to help him—that if he cooperated, he'd be released. He was desperate to find you. I waited a little while and then announced that Carlotta had sent me to break the news that you'd been killed shortly after he left you. He was so overwrought he hanged himself a few minutes later. I suppose he couldn't live with the guilt. So now you know, and the last mystery's solved." She motioned with the muzzle of the semiautomatic. "Turn around."

Anna went through the motions, pretending to cooperate while slipping her hand into her jacket pocket. Her fingers closed over the handle of the gouge. Turned half away, she waited until Ginny stepped close, then she spun, throwing her weight into an upward thrust of her weapon. She aimed low for the soft tissue of the other woman's upper abdomen, but Ginny saw it coming and blocked the blow with her forearm. The grooved blade sank into her forearm. Ginny cried out,

knocking the weapon aside, then striking out at Anna
with the pistol.

"Little bitch!"

The unforgiving steel connected with Anna's temple
and the dusky atmosphere of the cave imploded in a
million shooting fragments of light. Then there was
nothing.

Anna's apartment was unlocked, the notebook computer on the table. A can of soda sat beside it. He
picked up the can. Still cold. She'd been there recently.
Nothing was missing that he could determine, aside from
her keys and handbag. The phone was on the table
too, the portable handset with Caller ID screen. He took
two seconds to bring up the last few incoming calls.

4/21 2:31 P.M. registered on the display. Swift-Water,
Lucas A.

Deke took out his cell phone, hit speed dial as he left
the apartment, and impatiently counted the rings. After
what seemed like an eternity, the machine kicked on.
"This is Lucas, and I'm not available to take your call.
Leave a message after the beep and I'll get back to you
when I get in."

"Lucas? It's Deke. I'm looking for Anna. If she shows
up, I need you to keep her there. Don't let her leave.
I'll explain when I get there."

Then, as a precaution, he dialed the office. Busy.
Deke frowned. It shouldn't ring busy. The old man had
every service going, including call waiting. If the phone
was in use, it would signal the second call and he would
pick up. He hadn't.

The same tension that had uncoiled in his guts
the night Angel died gripped him as he climbed into the

car and headed toward Lucas's, a relentless gnawing unease he couldn't shake. Something was wrong. He could feel it.

He shifted into fourth gear as he reached the outskirts of town and hit the straightaway. The speedometer edged nearer to ninety. A few minutes later, he was jamming it down into third as he closed in on Lucas's drive.

Deke parked the car and hit the ground running. The busy signal meant that he headed to the office first. The door stood ajar, the lights on. Deke palmed the Colt, scanning the interior with a 180 sweep. "Lucas?"

Silence. Then a sound of movement, and something crashed to the floor.

Deke followed the sound, easing the door open, the barrel of the Python preceding him in. The desk phone was lying on the floor beside Lucas. Somehow, he'd managed to hook the wire and pull it down. Grabbing his cellular, Deke knelt beside him. He was breathing, but barely. It helped that he was sitting against the wall and not lying flat.

"911 dispatch. What's your emergency, please?"

"This is Deke Call, I need a Life Flight chopper ASAP. Lucas Swift-Water's been shot."

"Where has he been shot, sir?"

"Upper left chest cavity, looks like it involves the lung."

"I can't take that kind of order from a civilian, sir. Is there an officer on the scene?"

"Just get the damned bird to the Swift-Water Ranch! 355 Echo Canyon Road, South." Deke yelled into the phone.

Lucas's lids lifted. His breathing was so shallow and quick. The injured lung was filling with blood. If he didn't get help soon, he could go into respiratory arrest.

On his knees, Deke grasped Lucas's hand and held it in both of his. "Just hang on, *Shi-Da*. Help's comin'."

Tires crunched on gravel outside. It took Harlan a full minute to find them. "Chopper's on its way. ETA two minutes or less." Harlan crouched just behind Deke's left shoulder. "Hey, old man."

Lucas's eyes flickered. "Who you—callin' old?" A shallow breath. "Anna—Ginny's got her. I think she's— takin' her—to the Petty place. You—gotta—stop her."

"I'll take care of it," Deke promised, his vow nearly drowned out by the noise of the helicopter blades.

Harlan was on his feet and at the door, directing the attendants to Lucas. He was put on the stretcher and hustled out, and in a few seconds, he was on his way to the trauma unit at County Memorial.

As the bird lifted off, Deke moved toward his car at a trot. "Deke," Harlan said, grabbing his arm. "Son, you need to let me handle this."

Deke looked down at the strong, tanned fingers resting possessively on his sleeve and had to resist the urge to hit him. "Let you handle it? You gonna save Anna from the crazy bitch you married? Just like you saved Mama? Stay out of my way, Harlan."

Those fingers tightened. "I'm still the law in this county, and like you say—she's *my* problem. I'll be damned if I'll let her kill you too. She's taken too much away from me already."

Deke shrugged him off, giving the older man a cutting dark glance and no satisfaction. But Harlan was dogged, and he wouldn't let it go. "You need my truck, and you need me. I'm the one she wants! I'm the one she wants."

* * *

Anna's cheekbone thumped in perfect unison with her heartbeat. Her head felt larger than it should have been, and her tongue was furred as if she'd tied on one hell of a drunk. Recall was vague, fuzzy around the edges. She remembered the odd smell, the cool darkness, but in what context? Then something moved in her peripheral vision, and fuzziness shifted to sharp focus. Her hands were tied behind her, tightly, cutting off her circulation. They felt dead—icy useless lumps at the end of her wrists. She strained against the leather strap, but it refused to budge.

"Welcome back, Anna."

Anna's voice was raspy, and the woman had to bend close to hear her. "Fuck you."

Ginny chuckled. "I'll say one thing, you're a perfect match for Maddy Call's bastard son. No refinement required."

"If you're what passes for refined, I'd rather be trailer trash. Refresh my memory. How many murders have you committed? How do you sleep at night?"

A shrug. "If I lose any sleep, it isn't over that. I grew up on a ranch, four brothers and me. Killing a man, shooting a steer. There really isn't much difference."

"If you brought that warmth and spirit to the bedroom, it's no wonder Harlan turned to Maddy Call." The comment earned Anna a kick, but it was worth it to see that she wasn't impervious to everything. Harlan was her soft spot, her Achilles heel. She'd had everything money could buy, but she'd never had him wholeheartedly. There was always something held back, a part of him he couldn't or wouldn't give.

"He loved *me!*" she cried, voice grown suddenly shrill.

"But she gave him something you couldn't," Anna persisted. "A love that was selfless. In fact, she loved him enough to give him up, even when she was carrying his child. She sent him away, sent him back to you."

"You think she was a saint? Oh please! She married Matthew Call because he was powerful and because she felt the need to rub Harlan's nose in it."

"What will Harlan think of you when he finds out?" Anna said. "And he will—no matter what you do."

"He loved me!" She sucked in air, forcing herself to calm. "No more talk. It ends with you." When she came close, Anna spat in her face. Ginny wiped her face on her sleeve, then aimed the muzzle of the pistol at Anna's head. "Good-bye, Anna."

Anna couldn't look away. She saw the woman's finger tighten slowly over the trigger, then a car door slammed outside. "Anna!" Deke's voice.

Anna nearly panicked. "In here! Deke, she's got a gun!"

The rough old panel opened slowly. Deke's broad-shouldered form was silhouetted against the golden afternoon light. He stepped inside, the Colt in his waistband. "Move away from her," he said, and Anna wondered how he could be so unruffled when facing down a woman with a loaded pistol. The small-caliber semiautomatic could pump out several shots at lightning speed and could prove just as deadly as his revolver if the bullet hit something vital. Either he didn't think she'd fire or he just didn't care.

"You gonna kill her, you'll have to kill me first," he said, his voice low and rough.

"Don't think I won't enjoy it," she said. She kept the pistol trained on the broad target of his chest as he knelt beside Anna. "You should have stayed gone."

Her finger tightened on the trigger, but the voice from the doorway stopped her cold. "Put it down, Ginny. Put the gun down—it's over."

Ginny Rudy shook her head, and for the first time tears welled up in her eyes, spilling over her lashes, streaming down her cheeks. "It'll never be over, Harlan. Don't you think I know that. There will always be somebody younger, or prettier—someone else to catch your eye."

Harlan walked in and slowly approached her, his right hand extended, palm up, fingers reaching. "The gun, Ginny. Please."

"You really think it's that easy?"

Deke had cut the ties at Anna's wrists and helped her to sit up when his attention was drawn to the confrontation unfolding. Ginny Rudy hadn't moved, but something in her voice had changed, going from soft and sad to hard and icy cold.

He let Anna go and started to move—but not fast enough.

Harlan took another step toward her, and before Deke could do more than cry out a warning, Ginny brought the gun up and fired. One, two, three rounds pumped into the man's torso at almost point-blank range.

Anna screamed, but Deke had already lunged, catching Harlan as he dropped to his knees. The Colt was out and in his hand, his finger on the trigger. He itched to do it. He ached to drop her where she stood, for all the loss, the grief, the pain. She saw the desire in his eyes and smiled, then put the pistol's muzzle under her own chin and emptied the clip.

Anna scrambled to help Deke. "Is he still—"

"Yeah, he's alive." A quick glance at the cave's pitiful contents. "Let's get him out of here," he said, but he knew that he'd be back.

Chapter Eighteen

Deke sat on the bumper of Harlan's truck two weeks later and watched the forensics team carry Maddy's remains from the root cellar. Just a body bag box full of dried bones and scraps of cloth. She'd been such a big part of his life, of all their lives, that he couldn't help thinking there should have been something more substantial remaining from the end of her life. The official reports would confirm her identity—Deke had provided a DNA sample, and so had Lucas—yet no one needed a piece of paper to tell them what they already knew.

Ginny Rudy had confronted Maddy as she returned to the house that night, just before eleven. She told her that Deke had been hurt and that Matthew had sent her to take her to him. Their daughter, she'd said, was safe at the sheriff's office. Maddy went with her willingly, yet as she got out of the car, Ginny knocked her out with a single blow to the head. When she'd awakened it had been to her worst nightmare. Darkness and torture. She'd even recorded the script with Maddy's voice calling out to Deke. And finally, she'd killed her. She'd given Anna all the details.

The forensic team finished up, but as they packed up the van, Sergeant French stopped by the truck to pay his respects. He leaned on the passenger door for a few seconds, allowing the man in the passenger seat to collect himself and to wipe the moisture from his tanned cheeks.

French cleared his throat. "Sheriff, glad to see you lookin' so fit. I'm supposed to convey Captain Joseph's regards. He says he's guessin' you'll be takin' some time off to recuperate, and he's hopin' for an afternoon at the lake."

"You tell him that sounds good," Harlan said. "And I'll take him up on it. Whitlow can handle things for a while. He's a good man. Lots of promise."

Not knowing what else to say, French offered his hand.

Harlan clasped it briefly, nodding to the man, watching him walk away. Deke left his station near the front bumper, stopping at the open window. He still hadn't cleaned up his act, Harlan thought. His hair was long and getting longer, and his jaw was shadowed dark with a two-day's growth of beard. But damned if he wasn't getting used to it.

Maddy's son, clean through, but his too.

"They wrapped it up, and they won't be comin' back. You sure you want to be here for this?" Deke's black eyes met Harlan's, but the animosity that had been there previously was curiously wearing away. They were able to tolerate one another, even if they didn't talk a great deal. Maybe it would get better with time, and maybe it would always be like this. If that turned out to be the case, then, Harlan decided, it would be enough.

"I'm good. You go on, do what you need to do." He watched as Deke opened a metal box on the back of the truck and took out two paper cylinders and a roll of wire. He set the charges inside the mouth of the cave and unrolled the spool of wire to a safe distance, then hooked up the detonator.

Down on one knee on the ground, he paused for several seconds. For a moment, Harlan thought maybe he was saying a silent prayer, then he heard the words, "Good-bye, Mama." A bare whisper of sound before he pushed the plunger down and detonated the double charge.

There was a loud boom that reverberated through the ground. Dust and rock blew out and up, and when the air cleared, the cave had vanished into the loose rock of the hillside. Deke picked up the wire and the detonator and replaced them in the truck bed, then he climbed behind the wheel and they left the scene of so much sorrow behind for the final time.

As far as the Call-Miller cases, it was almost over. Wheeler Dobbs was in jail, facing charges connected with the shooting and destruction of property at Lucas's. There would be no trial for Ginny and there were only the last loose ends to be tied up.

Whitlow was waiting at the house when Deke dropped Harlan off with a few uniformed men, borrowed from the state boys. As Deke took his car and drove off, Whitlow turned his hat in his hands. The man was nervous, and it showed. "Sheriff, they're ready to begin. We'll be as gentle as possible."

"Gentle, hell," Harlan said. "I expect you to give it everything you've got. You make it clear to 'em. You're to take the place apart. There's nothing in there I give a damn about. But I need to know if it's there."

Whitlow nodded. "You comin' in, Sheriff?"

"No," Harlan said. "I do believe I'll sit right here on the deck and watch the sun go down."

For a long while, the sounds of their search filtered out from the house. Harlan could trace their progress from room to room by the occasional crash–bang. The entire process took over an hour, then finally, Whitlow reappeared. The look on his face boded trouble. Harlan faced it down calmly. He'd been through the worst that could happen, lost the woman he'd loved to the one he'd chosen, and he was staring down the rest of his life and wondering what to do with it. Nothing else could faze him.

"What is it, son?"

"I think we may have found it, Sheriff."

"Where?"

"The master bedroom, sir. Between the mattress and box spring."

"Handle it carefully, will you, Deputy? It gets sent to the lab, first thing. Thank the men for me, will you? And close the door on the way out."

Whitlow and the officers left. Alone, Harlan let the news sink in that he'd been sleeping over the crowbar that had killed his friend for twelve impossible years. It was one last slap in the face, one last kick to the dying marriage he'd tried to maintain for so long it had hurt. He thought about it for a long time, then finally he shook his head at the insanity of life. He'd been puzzling over the future for days, since his release from the hospital. He asked himself a hundred times over what he was going to do, where to start this next phase of his life, and at last, he knew. His first act as a free man would be to piss on Ginny's grave.

* * *

Anna was waiting when Deke got back. Her bags were packed and in the van, and she was ready to go. She'd gotten what she came here for, she'd said her good-byes to Harlan, and there was no logical reason left to remain. Lucas was more difficult, and he'd expressed his hopes that she would change her mind and stay. "We could use a good reporter around here. Not as much crime as D.C., but enough to keep you busy. And it sure would brighten things up around here to have you visit now and then."

"My life is back there," Anna had said.

"I don't know," he'd replied. "Deke's here."

Yes, but strangely, she needed more than that. More from him. She'd kissed Lucas's cheek and said farewell, then waited by the van for Deke to show.

He'd had a lot on his mind, it was true, but he'd given no indication that this might be long term or lasting, or anything other than the best sex she'd ever—he'd ever—had. And as sophisticated as she might consider herself, she was discovering that she had a slightly conventional side too. Not that she would admit it to him, or to anyone for that matter.

She was still waiting impatiently by the van when he pulled in and got out of his car. He was wearing a leather vest, jeans worn through at the knee, and the funky fedora hat. "Hey, baby," he said, saluting the corner of her lips with a slightly distracted kiss. "Goin' somewhere?"

"Yes, I'm going somewhere. I'm driving back tonight. I wanted to stop by and say thanks for all you've done."

"Well, come on in. You can spare a few, right? For old times' sake?"

He took her hand and led her to the stairs, while she

huffed halfheartedly behind him. "C'mon, darlin'. Shit, it's early. You've got plenty of time," he assured her. "Besides, I've got something to show you."

"I'd planned on being out of the state by sundown, and as it is I'm off schedule." As he drew her through the door, he turned, pulling her into his arms and kissing her until she forgot her objections. "Okay. So maybe I can spare twenty minutes, or so, without being too far off."

"I was hopin' you'd see things my way," he said. "Walk this way, baby—it's in the bedroom." He led her inside. The room was filled with blood red roses. Three vases on either side of the bed and one on the trunk at the foot. They were scattered across the dresser, their long stems overlapping—which brought her to the bed. The covers were turned back, and petals had been scattered over the pristine sheets. "Who said old Deke don't know nothin' about romance?"

"I'm confused," Anna said. "You get that I'm leaving town?"

"I get that your *plannin'* to, but plans can always change." He put up a finger. "Hang in. There's more." Reaching up, he hooked his thumbs under the shoulders of the leather vest, shrugging out of it, letting it fall.

Anna stared, open-mouthed. She couldn't stop herself. On his upper left pectoral was a heart, encircled by thorns, the single word *Anna* etched boldly on it. A ribbon waved beneath it, proclaiming, "Baby, we got nothin' to lose."

"Oh dear God, what have you done?"

"The chains that bind," he said, bringing her against him again. "If you leave now, I'll be screwed. How many Annas are there out there do you s'pose who'd put up with a tattooed, burned-out narc like me? C'mon,

Anna," he said softly, persuasively. "Stay awhile. Just till we figure out where this is goin'. You're my anchor, darlin'. You keep me sane."

Anna sighed, running a finger lightly over the new ink. It *was* romantic, in an unorthodox, wild, rebellious Deke Call kind of way. "I'll have to call Jay, but if I beg, he might agree to extend my leave a few more weeks."

"Or a month or three. He likes you a lot, I hear."

"Did it hurt a lot?"

"It was excruciating, but not half as unbearable as the thought of you bein' gone. C'mere, baby, let me show you just how much I love you."

As he tumbled Anna onto the bed and their clothing miraculously found its way onto the floor, she thought that she had to be hearing things. He couldn't have said it.

Could he?

About the Author

S.K. McClafferty is the author of thirteen books in three subgenres. Her interests include painting, photography, and amateur ghost-hunting. New Orleans, Louisiana, is home away from home.

Discover the Thrill of Romance With
Kat Martin

Desert Heat   0-8217-7381-X   **$6.99**US/**$9.99**CAN

For Ph.D candidate Patience Sinclair, leaving the ivy-covered campus of Boston University for the wide, open spaces of Texas means a chance to stop looking over her shoulder at every turn. Traveling incognito with the Triple C Rodeo will help her finish her dissertation on the American West while hiding in plain sight. But she can't hide from Dallas Kingman. The champion rider makes it clear that he's watching her...and he likes what he sees.

Midnight Sun   0-8217-7380-1   **$6.99**US/**$9.99**CAN

Call Hawkins just wants to be left alone and leave the past where it belongs. The bleak beauty of Dead Horse Creek is a perfect place to get away from the world...a place where nothing exists to remind him of everything he's lost. His isolation is complete—until Charity Sinclair arrives from New York City. Stunningly beautiful and stubbornly independent, she's shamefully ignorant of the untamed wilderness...and the very real dangers she'll face if Call doesn't teach her a thing or two.

Hot Rain   0-8217-6935-9   **$6.99**US/**$8.99**CAN

Allie Parker is in the wrong place—at the worst possible time...Her only ally is mysterious Jake Dawson, who warns her that she must play the role of his reluctant bedmate...if she wants to stay alive. Now, as Allie places her trust—and herself—in the hands of a total stranger, she wonders if this desperate gamble will be her last...

The Secret   0-8217-6798-4   **$6.99**US/**$8.99**CAN

Kat Rollins moved to Montana looking to change her life, not find another man like Chance McLain, with a sexy smile of empty heart. Chance can't ignore the desire he feels for her—or the suspicion that somebody wants her to leave Lost Peak...

The Dream   0-8217-6568-X   **$6.99**US/**$8.99**CAN

Genny Austin is convinced that her nightmares are visions of another life she lived long ago. Jack Brennan is having nightmares, too, but his are real. In the shadows of dreams lurks a terrible truth, and only by unlocking the past will Genny be free to love at last...

Available Wherever Books Are Sold!

Visit our website at **www.kensingtonbooks.com**.